This Ladybird Book belongs to:

Natiba   McCuchin

_____

_____

_____

This Ladybird retelling
by
Nicola Baxter

Acknowledgment
The publishers would like to thank John Dillow
for the cover illustration.

Ladybird books are widely available, but in case of
difficulty may be ordered by post or telephone from:

Ladybird Books – Cash Sales Department
Littlegate Road Paignton Devon TQ3 3BE
Telephone 01803 554761

A catalogue record for this book is available
from the British Library

Published by Ladybird Books Ltd Loughborough Leicestershire UK
Ladybird Books Inc Auburn Maine 04210 USA

FAVOURITE TALES

Cinderella

illustrated
by
JON DAVIS

based on the story by Charles Perrault

Once upon a time there was a young girl called Cinderella.

She lived with her father and two stepsisters. While her stepsisters spent their time buying pretty new clothes and going to parties, Cinderella wore old, ragged clothes and had to do all the hard work in the house.

The two sisters were selfish, unkind girls, which showed in their faces. Even wearing their fine clothes, they never looked as sweet and pretty as Cinderella.

One day a royal messenger came to announce that there was to be a grand ball at the King's palace.

The ball was in honour of the Prince, the King's only son.

Cinderella's sisters were both excited. The Prince was very handsome, and he had not yet found a bride.

When the evening of the ball arrived, Cinderella had to help her sisters get ready.

"Fetch my gloves!" cried one sister.

"Where are my jewels?" shrieked the other.

They didn't think for a minute that Cinderella might like to go to the ball!

When her sisters had driven off in their fine carriage, Cinderella sat all by herself and cried bitterly.

"Why are you crying, my dear?" said a voice. Cinderella looked up and was amazed to see her fairy godmother smiling down at her.

"I wish *I* could go to the ball and meet the Prince," Cinderella said, wiping away her tears.

"Then you shall!" laughed her fairy godmother. "But you must do exactly as I say."

"Oh, I *will*," promised Cinderella.

"Then go into the garden and fetch the biggest pumpkin you can find," said the fairy.

So Cinderella found an enormous pumpkin and brought it to her fairy godmother. With a wave of her magic wand, the fairy changed the pumpkin into a wonderful golden coach.

"Now bring me six white mice from the kitchen," the godmother said. Cinderella did as she was told.

Waving her wand again, the fairy godmother changed the mice into six gleaming white horses to pull the coach! Cinderella rubbed her eyes in amazement.

Then Cinderella looked down at her old ragged clothes. "Oh dear!" she sighed. "How can I go to the ball in this old dress?"

For the third time, her godmother waved her magic wand. In a trice, Cinderella was wearing a lovely white ballgown trimmed with blue silk ribbons. There were jewels in her hair, and on her feet were dainty glass dancing slippers.

"Now off you go!" said her fairy godmother, smiling. "Just remember one thing – the magic only lasts until midnight!"

So Cinderella went off to the ball in her sparkling golden coach.

In the royal palace, everyone was enchanted by the beautiful girl in the white and blue dress. "Who *is* she?" they whispered.

The Prince thought Cinderella was
the loveliest girl he had ever seen.

"May I have the honour of this
dance?" he asked, bowing low.

All the other girls were jealous of the
mysterious stranger.

Cinderella danced with the Prince all evening. She forgot her fairy godmother's warning until… *dong… dong… dong…* the clock began to strike midnight… *dong… dong… dong…*

Cinderella ran from the ballroom without a word… *dong… dong… dong…*

In her hurry, she lost one of her glass slippers… *dong… dong… dong.* The Prince ran out just as the lovely girl slipped out of sight.

"I don't even know her name," he sighed.

When Cinderella's sisters arrived home from the ball, they could talk of nothing but the beautiful girl who had danced with the Prince all evening.

"You can't imagine how annoying it was!" they cried. "After the wretched girl left in such a hurry, he wouldn't dance at all!"

Cinderella hardly heard their complaining. Her head and her heart were whirling with memories of the handsome Prince who had held her in his arms.

Meanwhile, the Prince was determined to find the mysterious beauty who had stolen his heart. The glass slipper was the only clue he had.

"The girl whose foot will fit this slipper shall be my wife," he said.

So the Prince set out to search the kingdom for his bride. A royal messenger carried the slipper on a silk cushion.

Every girl in the land wanted to try on the slipper. But although many tried, the slipper was always too small and too dainty.

At last the Prince came to Cinderella's house.

Each ugly sister in turn tried to squeeze her foot into the elegant slipper, but it was no use. Their feet were far too big and clumsy.

"Do you have any other daughters?"
the Prince asked Cinderella's father.

"One more," he replied.

"Oh no," cried the sisters. "She is
much too busy in the kitchen!" But
the Prince insisted that *all* the sisters
must try the slipper.

Cinderella hung her head in shame. She did not want the Prince to see her in her old clothes. But she sat down and tried on the dainty slipper. Of course, it fitted her perfectly!

The Prince looked at Cinderella's sweet face and recognised the girl he had danced with. "It *is* you," he whispered. "Please be my bride, and we shall never be parted again."

How happy Cinderella was! Her fairy
godmother appeared and, waving her
magic wand, dressed Cinderella
in a gown fit for a princess.

Then the Prince led
Cinderella home
to the royal palace.

Cinderella and her Prince were married at the most magnificent wedding that anyone could remember. Kings and queens from many lands came to meet the new Princess and wish her well.

Even Cinderella's sisters had to agree that she was the loveliest bride they had ever seen.

And Cinderella and her Prince lived happily ever after.

Dennis Wheatley

Churchill's Storyteller

For Ian Dow, late of the British Secret Service and my great uncle.
Also, to his beloved wife, Mavis, with fond regards always.

The islands have seen it and fear;
the ends of the earth tremble.
They approach and come forward;
each helps the other
and says to his brother, 'Be Strong!'

Helper of Israel
Isaiah 41:5

DENNIS WHEATLEY

CHURCHILL'S STORYTELLER

by

Craig Cabell

Foreword by Frederick Forsyth

SPELLMOUNT
Staplehurst

Permission to quote extensively from the published and previously
unpublished works of Dennis Wheatley in *Dennis Wheatley:
Churchill's Storyteller* has been granted by the Dennis Wheatley
Estate without exception. Copyright © Dennis Wheatley

British Library Cataloguing in Publication Data:
A catalogue record for this book is available
from the British Library

Copyright © Craig Cabell 2006

ISBN 1-86227-242-5

First published in the UK in 2006 by
Spellmount Limited
The Village Centre
Staplehurst
Kent TN12 0BJ

Tel: 01580 893730
Fax: 01580 893731
E-mail: enquiries@spellmount.com
Website: www.spellmount.com

1 3 5 7 9 8 6 4 2

The right of Craig Cabell to be identified
as the author of this work has been asserted by him
in accordance with the Copyright, Designs
and Patents Act 1988

Printed in Great Britain by
Oaklands Book Services
Stonehouse, Gloucestershire GL10 3RQ

Contents

Author's Note

'Perhaps I am only imagining things. But if I set down all that is happening here – or rather, that which I believe to be happening – when I look at what I have written again next day, I shall at least know that I haven't dreamed the whole horrible business overnight.'
The Haunting of Toby Jugg

In writing this book, I have studied in excess of 1,000,000 words written by Dennis Wheatley concerning his life and work during the Second World War: his war papers (those written before and during his time in uniform), his autobiographical writings (all now sadly out of print), his letters, interviews and, of course, the words of some of the men who knew him best. All of this material makes a fascinating study of one of the most popular – but today sadly underestimated – men of the 20th century.

To put into this book every nuance, perception and detail of every paper and the methods behind the philosophies and decisions made would be impossible. To get something near that would be to publish twelve volumes as thick as this one; and that set of books would not have added any more to contemporary opinion of Dennis Wheatley than this single volume.

Dennis Wheatley's work for Britain's war effort is now a point of historical interest. Appreciating the backdrop of the Second World War, we can understand how Wheatley employed his literary talents in order to help overthrow the Nazis.

It is also interesting to note that despite his long and distinguished career as a novelist, he was actually a member of all three disciplines of the Armed Forces. Today, as indeed during his lifetime, he is proof that a degree of perception, imagination and enthusiasm will make a difference despite what the odds may throw against you. Invalided out of the Great War and, by his own admission, terrible at spelling, he achieved respect from senior officers of all three Services and worldwide popularity (in over thirty countries) as a novelist, selling over 50,000,000 copies of his books.

This book is a tribute to his genius and unfailing duty to his country.

'The decline in the faiths has led to major changes in outlook and conduct by many million people – to a repudiation by the young of the authority and (possible) wisdom of their elders, a seeking for some mental stimulant that will replace accepted religions, and a breaking down of prohibitions that, through the ages, have protected society for its own good.'
Statement
The Devil and All His Works
Dennis Wheatley

During his lifetime, Dennis Wheatley was a diverse and important writer. His occult novels are still legendary, his adventure stories still respected. However, his time writing papers for Churchill's War Cabinet is almost forgotten.

This book exclusively deals with Wheatley's years working for the Joint Planning Staff of the War Cabinet and the work he did there. Throughout, I have quoted from many of Wheatley's war papers, to introduce the important work he did to a contemporary audience. The reader may observe that there are some grammatical errors, which indeed are in Wheatley's original documents.

I have not made corrections to Wheatley's typescripts in any way. Many of the papers were written whilst burning the midnight oil or, at great pace, due to short deadlines. I include any 'mistakes' the reader may pick up on, as proof of the speed and lack of proofing time Wheatley had when presenting his ideas to the War Cabinet. The papers were not written for posterity, or as major works of literature, but were written solely so that members of the War Cabinet could react immediately to the many ideas and instructions outlined, and make a physical difference to Great Britain's war effort. I feel that this is a very important point, because nowadays – in the new millennium – the difficulties faced by the British people during the Second World War seem forgotten or simply taken for granted; rarely are they appreciated, let alone understood. One of the important aims of this book is to highlight the level of terror the British people experienced during the Second World War and why Dennis Wheatley was so passionate and committed to his task.

I have written this book for two good reasons: one, so that Dennis Wheatley's contribution to the war effort is introduced to a new generation, and two, that the ingenuity, courage and imagination of our forefathers should be fully appreciated in the new millennium. The undermining of the latter was broached by Field Marshal Montgomery in his memoirs (Collins, 1958): 'The creation of the Welfare State in Britain after the Second World War led too many to think that social security and individual prosperity were the only things worth while.'

Daily life is deemed to be easier nowadays and the British people more laid-back as a consequence. So let us remember a different time, when the civilian was in mortal danger and he/she chose to face that danger head-on, with both courage and determination.

Craig Cabell
London, October 2005

Acknowledgements

I would like to thank the following establishments for their assistance: RAF Insworth, Imperial War Museum, Cabinet War Rooms, Eltham Library, Hornsey Library, Ealing Library, Bedfordshire Library, East Sussex County Library, Chief Console's Library, Whitehall Library, RAF Club, Cavalry Club, Random House Archive and Library (incorporating Hutchinson), Windsor Castle and the National Archives. I would also like to thank the people of the British Legion who have provided another valid reason for publishing this tribute to Wheatley's war work.

I would also like to thank the following people who assisted me – in ways both large and small – with the writing of this book: Dominic Wheatley, Frederick Forsyth, Christopher Lee, Richard Humphreys, Ian Sayer, Andrew Chrysostomou, John Lewes, Tracey Allen, James Herbert, Samantha Georgina (for the biblical quote), David Bush (for uncovering some interesting facts), Mavis and Ian Dow (for their fascinating stories and insights) and Crispin Jackson for his enthusiasm and support of my work.

I would also like to thank some dear friends with whom I have discussed various aspects of this book over lunch and good wine (i.e. in typical Wheatley fashion): Group Captain Jim Spurrell, Peregrine Solly, Henry Wilson, Louise Cowlin, David Barlow, Graham Thomas, Chris Underwood, Alan Hunter, Eamon Exley, Mark Ottowell; and over one of our now famous breakfast meetings, my dear 'not so much of the old' friend Tony Mulliken. I would also like to thank Jamie Wilson at Spellmount for the opportunity of putting this book out within the criteria I chose, and for appreciating the significance and good cause.

I would also like to thank Anita, Samantha (again!), Nathan, Shirley, Colin, Tom, Alice, Berny, Dave, Ray and Linda, for their unceasing enthusiasm. Also two old soldiers who made a difference in their own way: my great uncles Alf and Bill (one who lost his legs at Normandy and the other who fought tirelessly in Burma).

I would also like to thank my dear friends at Louis Latour, Berry

Brothers and Rudd, Davy's of London, Penfolds, Rosemount Estates, Brown Brothers, Waterloo Wine Co. (including Waipara West), for keeping me supplied with some excellent wines whilst I wrote and proofed this book, not just for me personally, but the various MOD charity wine tastings (NSPCC, British Heart Foundation, Macmillan Nurses, Amigos – the latter a charity for Venezuelan children with cancer) they have supported over the past five years. I'm sure Dennis Wheatley would have been impressed by the quality of the produce, not least the generosity of your donations and advice.

Finally, my thanks to the great Dennis Wheatley himself, a man I hold in the highest regard for both his fact and fiction. His obituary in *The Times* simply described him as: sailor, soldier, airman and author. Quite true, but this book explains his influence more fully and the debt we still owe him today.

List of Abbreviations

(A list of some of the abbreviations used in this book follows for ease of reference.)

AOC	Air Officer Commanding
ARP	Air Raid Patrol
CAS	Chief of Air Staff
CIGS	Chief of Imperial General Staff
CNS	Chief of Naval Staff
COSSAC	Chief of Staff to Supreme Allied Commander
DDSD	Deputy Director of Staff Duties
DMI	Director of Military Intelligence
DMO	Director of Military Operations
DNI	Director of Naval Intelligence
DPR	Director of Public Relations
EPS	Executive Planning Staff
FO	Foreign Office
FOPS	Future Operations Planning Staff
FUSAG	First US Army Group (fake)
GOC	General Officer Commanding
GSO1	General Staff Officer, Class 1
GSO2	General Staff Officer, Class 2
ISSB	Inter-Services Security Board
JIC	Joint Intelligence Committee
JPS	Joint Planning Staff
LCS	London Controlling Section
MEW	Ministry of Economic Warfare
MI1	Military Intelligence (Research)
MI5	Military Intelligence (Security Service)
MI6	Military Intelligence (Secret Intelligence Service)
MI9	Military Intelligence (War Office branch responsible for escape and evasion of POWs)

OKW	Oberkommando der Wehrmacht
PAIFORCE	Persia and Iraq Force
PMG	Postmaster General
PWE	Political Warfare Executive
RAFVR	Royal Air Force Volunteer Reserve
SHAEF	Supreme Headquarters Allied Expeditionary Force
SIS	Secret Intelligence Service
SOE	Special Operations Executive
STRATS	Strategical Planning Staff
VCAS	Vice-Chief of Air Staff
VCIGS	Vice-Chief of Imperial General Staff

A Multi-talented Man

A Foreword by Frederick Forsyth

When I was growing up, there was no television and the 'wireless' was more or less reserved for the evening news. Otherwise one read.

Among those authors I devoured was Dennis Wheatley. I was intrigued by his Napoleonic War hero Brook and fascinated by Wheatley's other forte, his weird novels about the occult, the astral plane visited by the Duc de Richleau.

But I never thought to meet the great man, nor to learn that he had made an even more fascinating contribution through the ingenuity of his mind to the Planning Staff in the Second World War.

But meet him I did, as a young and impressively naïve author myself, just after publication of *The Day of the Jackal*.

Authorship even then was still a very low-profile affair. Hardly anyone knew what authors looked like. The grin-and-shake-and-sign promotion tours had yet to be invented. (One wonders what Wheatley's response would have been if anything so utterly vulgar had been proposed!) A new book crept out onto the market with a glass of dry sherry in the publisher's office for most, and a discreet lunch for the big investments.

Having become one of these, to my own and everyone else's considerable surprise, it was at a lunch that I met the then elderly and legendary Dennis Wheatley. I recall that he was gentle, wry and immensely kind. Only now do I learn via Craig Cabell's book what an extraordinary role he had played thirty years before I met him.

Frederick Forsyth
Hertfordshire, October 2005

Part One

Old Soldiers Never Die

Macbeth: If we should fail?
Lady Macbeth: We fail.
But screw your courage to the sticking place,
And we'll not fail.

The Tragedy of Macbeth
William Shakespeare

I

A Life Stranger than Fiction

Dennis Wheatley was one of the 20th century's most popular and pro-lific novelists. For over forty years he remained loyal to one publisher – Hutchinson – and published approximately seventy books with them in over thirty countries. He sold an estimated 50,000,000 copies. However, what is largely overlooked today is Wheatley's tri-service career. As a young boy he was a cadet aboard HMS *Worcester*, and during the Great War he fought for the British Army on the Western Front. During the Second World War – which this book almost exclusively deals with – he worked for Winston Churchill's War Cabinet as a member of the RAFVR.

Today, it is only Wheatley's occult novels that remain in the public memory. Books such as *The Devil Rides Out* (1934), *The Haunting of Toby Jugg* (1949) and *To the Devil – A Daughter* (1953) are classics in the horror genre, but although Wheatley's fiction was strange and bizarre, his per-sonal life was far more fantastic.

Aside from his tri-service contributions, Wheatley had encounters with occultists. In his occult non-fiction *The Devil and all His Works* (1971), he documented the dangerous interviews he conducted in the 1930s with – as he put it – 'Men of Power'. These infamous occultists – such as Aleister Crowley and the Reverend Montague Summers – would lead him to an absolute conviction that there was more to the Black Arts than any writer of fiction could suggest.

Wheatley confessed to a minor liaison with the Devil (in his anthology *Gunmen, Gallants and Ghosts* 1943/revised 1963[1]), as a young officer during

1

the First World War; one he believed could have had major consequences for him in the after-life:

> … while convalescing, I played a lot of vingt-et-un. After one ten-hour session, having become bored from drawing few cards worth betting upon … I called on the Devil to give me luck. I drew two aces, doubled the table, drew another ace, split three times … Everyone paid me sixteen times his original stake.
>
> That shook the other chaps at the table, but it shook me infinitely more, as, sooner or later, that sort of 'luck' has to be paid for.

Wheatley was well aware that both Good and Evil were tangible forces in the world. He had seen the reality of it – by man's own doing – in the trenches during the Great War[2] and then through his talks with those 'Men of Power'.

However, it did surprise him that in 1938, in a conversation about the occult with one of his oldest friends – a man who had spent most of his life in MI5 – he was told that the government took the occult very seriously; as a threat to national security.[3] Wheatley's friend asked him: 'Does "The Shadow" convey anything to you?' Wheatley replied that it didn't. His friend made a wry grimace and said: 'Believe me Dennis, I would rather be up against a combination of the most dangerous German and Russian agents I have ever known, than up against "The Brothers of the Shadow."'

So, approximately a year before the Second World War started, a government department – namely MI5 – was interested in the people who supported the Black Arts. But why? The answer can be found in the text of Wheatley's 1953 novel *To the Devil – A Daughter*, where writer Molly Fountain talks about a friend of hers in government employ before the war who:

> [was] responsible for keeping his eye on the Fascists. Actually he is responsible for keeping his chief informed about all groups that may be engaged in subversive activities. That, of course, covers every type of secret society, including circles that practise Black Magic.

It must be understood, it was not because of Wheatley's interest in the occult that he was eventually made an honorary member of Churchill's Joint Planning Staff (JPS) of the War Cabinet. It is of course well documented that Hitler dabbled in the Black Arts himself (and indeed Wheatley wrote some good fiction about the Nazis doing so, such as *They Used Dark Forces*, 1964). But Wheatley's induction into the War Cabinet was just another bizarre incident in his life, nothing to do with the occult, as he clearly stated in *Gunmen, Gallants and Ghosts*:

... how futile it is to make plans based on information received by occult means. Hitler employed the best astrologers and soothsayers that could be found in the Nazi Empire, and never made a move without consulting them. Churchill, on the other hand, had no dealings with such people. All War Cabinet decisions were based upon reasoned assessments submitted by our Chiefs of Staff. Yet the British – for a year, alone – held the whole might of Germany at bay.

The true reason why Dennis Wheatley joined the War Cabinet is much more down to earth than avid readers of his occult novels would like to admit: he was a storyteller. And like some of today's best storytellers, Wheatley had a way of writing plausible fiction based upon fact (a skill novelist Frederick Forsyth refers to as 'Faction'). Now if that 'Faction' was leaked to the Nazis as a Top Secret document, then they could be deceived into making some very useful mistakes.[4] But before he was put into uniform, Wheatley made some valid and ingenious suggestions – essays – that they would read and digest. He didn't set out to join the War Cabinet, he was never that presumptuous; however, they would want him to join them.

This book explains how, during the Second World War, Dennis Wheatley put his novels to one side and dedicated his time to writing deception plans for the War Cabinet. It details what those papers were, why they were written and the overall reaction to them. Indeed, Wheatley's peers were so impressed with his work, they eventually put him into uniform, giving him a job in the London Controlling Section (LCS), where he worked on many strategies including that of Monty's double.

This book presents an overview of every aspect of Wheatley's work during the Second World War. He wrote much about it himself, in no fewer than six non-fiction works, now all out of print. Interestingly, Wheatley used many obscure scenarios and incidents appertaining to his secret work during the Second World War in his fiction. The book you hold in your hands is the first to bring all these aspects together. It is a broad but detailed account of Wheatley's work during the Second World War, including some additional – and previously unpublished – material, plus supporting analysis, historical detail, and critique of Wheatley's early papers. It offers an insight into the workings of Churchill's secret war rooms and, as importantly, the details of how one of Britain's best loved novelists showed the Nazis that the pen was indeed mightier than the sword.

Notes

1. References to *Gunmen, Gallants and Ghosts* are to the revised 1963 Arrow edition.
2. For further details of Wheatley's time in the trenches during the Great War, see the second part of his autobiography, *The Time Has Come. The Memoirs of Dennis Wheatley, 1914–1919, Officer and Temporary Gentleman* (Hutchinson, 1978).
3. This was detailed by Wheatley in both *Stranger Than Fiction* (Hutchinson, 1959) and *Gunmen, Gallants and Ghosts* (Arrow, 1963). Shortly before the war, MI5 did explore occult (extreme) societies.
4. In his very first war paper, 'Resistance to Invasion', Wheatley suggested that the Nazis should be fed false information.

II

Wheatley's War

'During the first weeks of the war my failure to find any suitable war employment greatly depressed me.'
Gunmen, Gallants and Ghosts

The summer of 1939 was a pleasant time for anyone not directly concerned with the mounting war effort.

In July Dennis Wheatley wanted to take a holiday in Ireland. This was not his usual choice of location, but he knew war with Germany was inevitable and he had no wish to be caught up in the initial hostilities.

However, his family did not want to lose their holiday in the Mediterranean sun and persuaded him to drive down through France for a well earned break in the south. It wasn't much of a decision for Wheatley to make – even though his wife (Joan), stepdaughter (Diana) and eldest stepson (Bill) – were highly persuasive companions. Wheatley loved the sunshine and good food and wine of the Mediterranean, and his initial protest was only a cursory note of caution. They simply convinced him to follow his heart.

So the Wheatleys took their holiday, relaxing on a sun-drenched beach for six weeks, attempting to forget the strong possibility of war. But it was during those six weeks that Hitler's revolutionary pact with Stalin was announced. Wheatley learned nothing of this, even though he had instructed a friend of his – who worked in Whitehall, London – to inform him of any developments.[1]

Wheatley received no correspondence at all, so he slowly made his way back through France, eating well, sampling the best wines (up to the early 1930s he had owned his own distinguished wine company[2]).

Towards the end of August, the family made a stop at Amiens, as he stated in the third part of his autobiography *The Time Has Come. The Memoirs of Dennis Wheatley, 1919–1977, Drink and Ink*:

> On the way back, we did not head for Paris but drove to Amiens, as I wanted
> to see again the little house I had built in 1917 against a wall of the garden

of a ruined Château. The Hôtel du Rhin at which we used to stay when on twenty-four hour leave to Amiens seemed very small compared to how I remembered it …

Wheatley then made a tour of the Western Front, over which he had fought as a young artillery officer, but there was little left of it. The Wheatleys then returned home on 31 August. Ironically, weeks later, Wheatley received a letter that had been sent on to him from Cavalaire (where he had stayed in the South of France). The correspondence had missed him by a day and was from his friend in Whitehall; it said: 'Uncle has taken a turn for the worse and, if you wish to see him before the end, you should return home at once.'[3]

Wheatley breathed a sigh of relief as the note went on to explain that Hitler was to invade Poland on 25 August. Had Wheatley known about this, he would have certainly completed his holiday a week early, but for no reason, because Hitler postponed his invasion (for a week), giving Wheatley ample time to conclude his holiday, as he mentioned in *Stranger than Fiction*:

In view of [the delay] it was lucky that the letter missed me; as we still got back to No. 8, St. John's Wood Park before the stampede, yet had our last happy week in France before the curtain of war came down.

The Wheatleys were very fortunate to have such a wonderful holiday in Europe so close to the outbreak of war and not be affected. However, they would not shirk their duty once war was declared.

At 11 o'clock on the morning of Sunday 3 September 1939, Wheatley heard the Prime Minister Neville Chamberlain make his famous broadcast. The family was at home and were joined by Wheatley's other two stepsons, Jack and Colin.

The broadcast was followed by the first scream of air raid sirens but nothing happened. It was a false alarm.

It was also at this juncture that Wheatley went down to his well-stocked cellar and brought up a magnum of Louis Roederer 1928, his favourite cuvée of that vintage and drank to a speedy victory.

Obviously, like most people, Wheatley expected there to be an immediate blitz on London. He had, of course, prepared for the inevitability of war before his holiday. It was his belief that the first air raids on the capital would concentrate on the docks and marshalling yards. Once they were damaged, supplies of food and other essentials would be in short supply. To counter this, Wheatley took in a large stock of food, enough to keep his household of seven (he had three maids) provisioned for a month.

He believed that after such time, Hitler would find it too costly in aircraft to keep up heavy raids, so the food situation would get straightened out and Britain would strike back.

He also had another concern – his house. Nearly one hundred years old, it probably wouldn't stand a near miss from a bomb. So Wheatley made two escape tunnels from it. He also reinforced the servants' sitting room in the semi-basement into a make-do air raid shelter. He did this by supporting the ceiling with three stacks of empty champagne cases and reinforcing its outer wall with sandbags laid in cement.[4]

On 4 September (the day Winston Churchill entered the Admiralty as First Sea Lord), Wheatley decided to make more preparations for war. His first port of call was Benson & Hedges. He bought a stock of Hoyo de Monterreys cigars. Being such a splendid host, the cigars were mainly for the enjoyment of his friends whilst visiting.

After Benson & Hedges, he went on to Justerini's in Pall Mall, drank a bottle of champagne with his friends Eddie Tatham and Stanley Brown and purchased the maximum amount of wines and liqueurs from them.

As already mentioned, Wheatley was once in the wine trade. In 1886 Wheatley's grandfather – also Dennis Wheatley – secured a building lease from the Westminster Estate and erected a block of shops and flats on the east side of South Audley Street (between the Grosvenor chapel and Mount Street). He then merged the wine, spirit and mineral water connection he had built up in three provisions shops that he owned in the district and housed it in the corner shop of the block, opposite the chapel. The business flourished and he retired at the age of 40. Wheatley's father inherited the wine merchants and, as his only son, Dennis was groomed to follow the family business.

He had no problem with this, so by the age of 16 it was decided that Wheatley would spend a year in Germany, a year in France and a year in both Spain and Portugal, learning about the wine trade.

In 1913 he spent a very happy year in Germany, returning home in December. It was arranged that he should go out to Rheims in August 1914 but war stood in the way. In September that year, Wheatley received his first commission in the 2nd/1st City of London R.F.A(T). He then went to France – to the Western Front.[5]

He did eventually take over the family business (in the 1920s), selling up in the early 30s – during the depression – to become a novelist.

His love of wine and food is clearly displayed in his books (including some non-fiction – see bibliography at the back of this book) and, as we will see, was used to good effect when building relationships within the War Cabinet.

After procuring his wine, Wheatley then visited his publishers, Hutchinson, and tried to persuade them to reprint all his books whilst there was still plenty of paper to hand. They explained to him that they had a large stock of paper and didn't think it necessary to reprint his books so immediately. Wheatley was disappointed by their reaction, as he would later state:

'That was a pity, as the royalties [the books] would have brought me later in the war, when I had gone into uniform and could write no new books, would have been more than welcome.'[6]

He returned home and contemplated his next move. His mind went back to the previous evening and a surprise visit from his good friend Joe Links.[7] Wheatley was astonished to see Links in the uniform of a flight lieutenant.

Links explained to Wheatley that in 1938, believing war was inevitable, he had joined the Auxiliary Air Force and was now in charge of a flight of balloons in Hampstead, north-west London. Links would end the war as a wing commander, with an OBE.

So on that Monday evening, Wheatley felt slightly ashamed that he wasn't in uniform himself. However, he was 42 by the time war broke out, unfortunately beyond the age at which ex-officers of the old war would normally be re-commissioned.[8]

However, he had no doubt about what his part in the war would be. He was a writer and believed he could best serve his country in the field of propaganda. He was confident that he would do so because he had already been officially engaged on such work since the spring, when Sir John Anderson – who had recently announced the issue of his air raid shelters – formed a panel of voluntary celebrity speakers to awaken the country to the danger it faced. They were supported by local MPs, mayors, trade union officials, fire chiefs and even matrons of hospitals. They addressed meetings in all the principal towns, urging that everyone should prepare for war by joining groups such as the territorials, ARP or, at least, take a course in first aid. Within four months they had secured two million volunteers.

Sadly, and for some unknown reason, as soon as war was declared, the group was disbanded. Before Wheatley learned of this, on 4 September, the formation of the Ministry of Information was announced, so he instantly offered his services. He received no reply. He repeated his offer to two civil servants whom the press reported were selecting the personnel for the ministry. To Wheatley's surprise and dismay, he still did not receive the courtesy of a reply. It seemed that all the preparations for war he had made, for both his family and the general public, had fallen way short of their true potential. And he felt very bitter about that.

Notes

1. See *Stranger Than Fiction* (Hutchinson, 1959).
2. This part of Wheatley's life is well documented in the third part of his autobiography, *The Time Has Come. The Memoirs of Dennis Wheatley, 1919–1977, Drink and Ink* (Hutchinson, 1979).
3. See *Stranger Than Fiction*, op. cit.
4. See *Gunmen, Gallants and Ghosts* (Arrow, 1963).
5. See *Stranger Than Fiction*, op. cit.
6. Wheatley was much disappointed by this and would mention the fact in *Stranger Than Fiction, Gunmen, Gallants and Ghosts* and *The Deception Planners. My Secret War* (Hutchinson, 1980)
7. Joe Links would later co-write the 'Murder Files' series with Wheatley.
8. See *The Deception Planners*, op. cit.

III

That's Entertainment

'On September 4th, 1939, I offered my services free for the duration of the war to the announced, but yet unformed, Ministry of Information. As my work had already been translated into nineteen languages and I was over forty, to use such talents as I have been blessed with on propaganda seemed the best way in which I could serve my country.'
Gunmen, Gallants and Ghosts

Less than a week after the outbreak of the Second World War, Wheatley's wife Joan, and stepdaughter Diana, had found employment in MI5. His eldest stepson, William Younger, was already in MI5 and his second step-son, Jack, was a regular in the Coldstream Guards.

Wheatley certainly felt like the poor relation as the only wartime employment he could find was as a group controller of Air Raid Wardens; not very taxing for a man who had been an officer during the Great War. However, an old friend of his in MI5 raised his spirits by telling him:

Don't take it too badly that the Ministry of Information has ignored your offers of service. Out of nearly a thousand people that they have taken on, fewer than thirty are professional journalists and writers, so it's a hopeless mess. One might just as well send a battleship to sea with only thirty trained seamen in her and the rest landlubbers, then order them to seek out and destroy the enemy. It would break your heart to be mixed up with such a crew. Sooner or later some job will come along in which you will be able to make much better use of your abilities. In the mean-time, hundreds of thousands of people will be in camps or spending long periods of duty in ARP centres. Their only way of passing the time will be to read and it's up to chaps like you to help entertain them.[1]

Wheatley soon took this advice to heart, writing a 186,000-word novel (the longest book he had written at the time) entitled *The Scarlet Imposter* – featuring his popular character Gregory Sallust – in little over a month.

This novel saw a wave of creativity overcome Wheatley, something that hadn't happened to him since the writing of his earliest books (his second book *Such Power is Dangerous* was written flat out in seventeen days before the publication of his first novel *The Forbidden Territory*[2]). Before mid-1941, Wheatley would write three more Sallust novels, *Faked Passport*, *The Black Baroness*, and *V for Vengeance*, but before writing these novels, he tried his hand at short stories. The first appeared in the *Evening Standard* under the title *Special Leave*. This story was part of a series – by various contributors – who had to use the black-out as a background to their story. *Love Trap* was another short story Wheatley wrote during this period; the last was *The Born Actor* written in late April 1940, just before Churchill succeeded Chamberlain and all sorts of new emergency measures were brought in, with Wheatley finally writing papers for the JPS.

Once Wheatley had started his official war writing he would have no time for short stories. However, the three Sallust novels (mentioned above) would be written late at night overlapping his work for the War Cabinet. This proved that he did take his duty as a novelist – an entertainer – very seriously, despite the importance of his work to support the war effort.

Before we concentrate our attention upon Wheatley's papers for the JPS, let us take a moment to look at the writing of his short story *Love Trap*. This is necessary as it explains an awful lot about Wheatley's generosity to friends, his status in life and consequently, shows that he didn't have to change his lifestyle much in order to 'settle in' with his colleagues in the War Cabinet. *Love Trap* was written because Wheatley attended a cocktail party to which he was not invited.[3]

During the early months of the war, a fellow writer by the name of Ursula Bloom would persuade him to sell war savings certificates with her. They spent one such afternoon at Harrods very successfully, and afterwards Wheatley was invited back to Ursula's flat for 'a throat saving drink'. Half an hour later it transpired that she and her husband were due at a cocktail party at the Ritz. Wheatley made his apologies, thanked Ursula for the drink and made to leave. However, he was told that the party had been put on for advertising purposes and he should go with them. Wheatley had no wish to be a gate crasher but was eventually persuaded to attend.

At the party Ursula introduced Wheatley to Miss Jennifer Mattingly, editor of *Woman's Own*. It transpired that Mattingly was a fan of Wheatley's work and on the spot asked him to write a short story for her magazine. To his credit, Wheatley told her that love stories were not his thing, but she was so insistent he did not have the heart to refuse.

Although the story would eventually appear in *Woman's Own*, Wheatley hated it, stating that love stories should only be written by the people who have a genius for them. That may be so, but Wheatley's ability to interact and successfully converse with a diverse range of people was a great asset to him when he eventually joined the War Cabinet; not least because so much was discussed and so many friendships – contacts – were forged over a hearty lunch.

Despite the writing of his short stories and novels, Wheatley kept abreast with every new development in the war, not just through news bulletins and daily papers, but also through his friends (most of whom had respectable jobs in the government services). Indeed this information would be used in his Sallust novels at the time but as he later admitted, anyone who would accumulate all of that factual information 'could hardly help getting ideas of the way in which the war might develop'.

Eventually two things happened, one, on 10 May 1940, Hitler launched his blitzkrieg against Holland, Belgium and France and advanced to the channel ports (posing a direct threat to Britain), and two, towards the end of the month Wheatley's wife – a driver for MI5 – was driving Captain Hubert Stringer of the War Office and he said to her: 'I've been given the job of thinking up ideas for resistance to invasion ... but apart from routine stuff ... I don't seem to be able to think of much we can do.'

Joan replied: 'Why don't you ask my husband? His speciality is original ideas, and he would simply jump at the chance of trying to make himself useful.'[4]

Captain Stringer agreed and Joan returned home to tell Wheatley the good news.

Notes

1. See *Gunmen, Gallants and Ghosts* (Arrow, 1963).
2. This was confirmed by Wheatley in his Dedication in a signed presentation copy of *The Forbidden Territory*. The book forms part of the first Dennis Wheatley box set which features Wheatley's first four thrillers, each signed 'Xmas 1936'.
3. The anecdote is related in Wheatley's Introduction to the story in *Gunmen, Gallants and Ghosts*, op. cit.
4. See *Stranger Than Fiction*.

Part Two

The War Papers of Dennis Wheatley

'After the war, when the documents of the German General Staff were seized and examined, it emerged that in Operation "Sea Lion" – their plan for the invasion of Britain – they had intended to do exactly as I had forecast.'
The Time Has Come: The Memoirs of Dennis Wheatley, 1919–1977, Drink and Ink

Dennis Wheatley's Civilian War Papers

For clarity and quick reference, the papers Dennis Wheatley wrote for the Joint Planning Staff before being put into uniform were:

1.'Resistance to Invasion' (written 27–28 May 1940)
2.'The Invasion and Conquest of Britain' (written 20–22 June 1940)
3.'Further Measures for Resistance to Invasion' (written 26–27 June 1940)
4.'Village Defence' (written 6–7 July 1940)
5.'A Supplement to Village Defence' (unpublished, written 8–14 July 1940)
6.'Village Defence' (2nd Draft) (unpublished, written 8–14 July 1940)
7.'A New Gibraltar' (written 15–17 July 1940) (referred to as No. 7 paper by Wheatley, even though the previous two papers were supplementary thoughts to paper 4)
8.'Measures for Maintaining the Independence of Turkey' (written 27–29 July 1940)
9.'Aerial Warfare' (written 20–25 September 1940)
10.'The People Want to Know' (written mid-October 1940)
11.'By Devious Paths to Victory' (written October 1940)
12.'The Winter' (written at some time in October/November 1940)
13.'After the Battle' (written November 1940)
14. 'The Nature and Principles of Total War' (first draft of 'Total War' released in December 1940)
15.'The Key to Victory' (written March 1941)
16.'The People Want to Know' (No. 2) (written April 1941)
17.'The Sword of Gideon' (written Spring 1941)
18.'Atlantic Life-Line' (written Spring 1941)
19.'While the Cat's Away' (written 12–15 July 1941)
20.'Total War' (completed end August 1941)

Note: Wheatley wrote other papers connected to the war effort but not specifically for the War Cabinet. These were:

1.'Fifth Column Fools of Hitler' (1939/40) (unpublished paper)
2.'The Great Danger' (1939/40) (unpublished speech concerning life after the war and the danger of Bolshevism)

3.'Britons Never Shall Be Slaves' (1940) (unpublished paper countering the 'call the war off' movement)
4.'Some Suggestions Regarding Propaganda' (1940) (unpublished)
5.'Time and the Blitzkrieg' (1940/41) (unpublished paper concerning the disruption to public transport caused by the bombing)
6.'The Truth Will Out' (Spring 1941) (written for *Life* magazine concerning pro-German articles)
7.'Fifth Columnists' (Spring/Summer 1941) (unpublished radio broadcast for the BBC)
8.'The Opening of the Battle of the Century' (unpublished paper dated 8 June 1944)

IV

Resistance to Invasion

' … I should never have had the impertinence to write this paper if I had
not been asked for ideas by an officer at present engaged in looking for
ideas in connection with this subject.'
'Resistance to Invasion'

Wheatley was delighted to write down some ideas for Captain Stringer
and instantly set about his task. He worked throughout the night with
a passion. By dawn he had been writing flat out for fourteen hours and
had written, re-written and corrected a paper of nearly seven thousand
words[1]. Next day it was typed and handed by his wife to Captain Stringer.
Two nights later, Stringer went to Wheatley's house for drinks.
He said:

> Well, I've read your paper and passed it on … To me it seems full of
> good ideas, but the trouble is that the machinery creaks so. Our people
> on the other side of the water are in a bad way [although Wheatley
> wasn't told, at that time Dunkirk was being evacuated]. And the
> Nazis must know that in this country there are not yet sufficient fully
> trained and equipped divisions to put up a really serious resistance. If
> they achieve a decisive victory in Belgium they may decide to take big
> chances and follow up almost at once, ignoring casualties and trusting
> to overwhelming our defences by the sheer weight of numbers they
> can throw against our shores with everything that will float. Many
> of the things you suggest should be done immediately, but it may be
> weeks before they reach people high enough up to give the orders.[2]

However, by this time, Wheatley was quite fired up by his midnight oil
writings and the urgency of the matter. He said: 'I have a few friends in the
Service Ministries who might be able to push things along. May I send them
copies of my paper, or would you regard that as short-circuiting you?'

'Good gracious, no,' came Stringer's reply. 'Go to it and good luck to you.'

Wheatley's friends were Admiral Sir Edward Evans (this was a passing friendship), Colonel Charles Balfour-Davey (Operations Section of the War Office) and Wing Commander Sir Louis Greig (Personal Assistant to the Secretary of State for Air). The results were exciting.[3]

Admiral Evans replied by a cordial letter in which he said that he had read the paper with great interest and thought parts of it would prove of value. Colonel Balfour-Davey rang up and said: 'Dennis, I am on duty tonight at the War House. Come along any time after 11 o'clock and we'll talk about your paper.'[4]

One can well imagine the thrill Wheatley got from that midnight visit to the heart of Whitehall, even more so when Balfour-Davey told him: 'I can't express any opinion on the naval and air matters, but on the military side you have certainly produced a number of ideas that have never occurred to us. And one thing I can promise you. Your paper shall reach the Vice Chief of the Imperial General Staff.'

In his book *Stranger than Fiction*, Wheatley summed up his feelings on leaving the War Office that night: 'I knew this charming and highly intelligent soldier far too well to suppose that he was making fun of me, yet, as I made my way home through the dark, deserted streets, I could hardly believe that I had heard him aright.'

It was only now that Wheatley believed that he had made a tangible contribution to the war effort; but there was still much to do. But what of his other friend, Sir Louis Greig?

Greig telephoned Wheatley three weeks later and asked him to lunch at the Dorchester. His other guests were a Mr Renny and an RAF wing commander. The latter was, in due course, to become Air Marshal Sir Lawrence Darvall. A heady lunch indeed, but Wheatley was quite at home in this environment and wanted to take full advantage of the opportunities that might present themselves.

Wheatley knew he had taken Captain Hubert Stringer's initial idea and worked it into an extremely thought-provoking paper. But how did he do it, especially as he wrote it from scratch during the course of one night?

Wheatley's first paper 'Resistance to Invasion', instantly grabbed the attention of his 'superiors' by the humble way in which he opened it (see below). The paper was written on the night of 27 May 1940, seventeen days after Churchill became Prime Minister and a day before the retreat from Dunkirk was started (which concluded on 3 June). To some, the fall of France seemed to herald the final triumph of Germany, but the British were not prepared to surrender to the Nazis; they would resist invasion:

General

1. I should never have had the impertinence to write this paper if I had not been asked for ideas by an officer at present engaged in looking for ideas in

connection with this subject. Many suggestions put forward here may seem farcical, but if there is one good one among them the paper will have been more than worth doing. I shall write it as though I were a General Staff officer although my military knowledge is limited to four-and-a-half years as an artillery officer in the last war. I apologize beforehand for appearing to lay down the law upon matters about which I know little or nothing.

All good writers know their audience and Wheatley definitely knew his on this occasion, playing down his own war experiences during the Great War – but importantly mentioning them – as his modesty would create a good impression. Indeed, the 'most humble' approach he adopted in this opening was the perfect voice. He could easily have written statements in anger – he had been so depressed at not having his experiences of the Great War acknowledged before; but professionalism won the day and he adopted his best storytelling manner in order to win over his audience and make them see the merit in his suggestions, hence: 'I shall write it as though I were a General Staff officer'. Possibly this statement could have been construed as presumptuous, but he followed it up with the mention of his military knowledge being 'limited' to those four-and-a-half years as an 'artillery officer' in the previous war. So perfect balance and brevity for complete impact. Wheatley truly was on home territory here, which is why it only took him one attempt (this very paper) to convince very influential people within the War Cabinet that he would indeed be a useful tool in the ever mounting war effort.

But let us not underestimate Wheatley's perceptions, as the second general point in his paper clearly demonstrated:

> 2. It is postulated that a German invasion is to take place by fleets of innumerable fast motor-boats holding from 20 to 40 men each. Such craft are of shallow draft so would pass over minefields, but their range is limited, so presumably the threatened area would be confined to the coast from Cromer in the North to Beachy Head in the South.

Today this would not be in doubt. That particular length of Norfolk coast line was especially susceptible during the Second World War but, at the time, it wasn't something largely appreciated, especially by civilians. Indeed, the army did test a lot of ammunition off the coast near Cromer from the 1930s but even so, the presence by the army was to conduct tests and improve the efficiency of British explosives.

So Wheatley really caught the attention of his peers with the opening of 'Resistance to Invasion'; but his thought-processes would delve deeper, i.e. he was more than an ideas man, he was a tactician. Points 3, 4 and 5 in his paper showed how the Norfolk coast could be split into zones:

3. The defence would presumably consist of three zones:
    (1) The open sea,
    (2) Coastal waters and the shore to a depth of five miles inland,
    (3) The land from five to twenty-five miles inland.

4. Zone 1 would be a purely naval sphere, and Zone 3 a purely military sphere, so I do not propose to attempt dealing with these except in as far as Zone 3 impinges on Zone 2. It is with Zone 2 that this paper is mainly concerned.

5. Should Zone 1 be pierced, the success or failure of the Military Forces in Zone 3 will depend almost entirely upon the delaying tactics employed in Zone 2. Time will be the essential factor and – to give time to our main Forces to deploy to the best advantage – skilful, original, and imaginative Shore Resistance is of paramount importance.

Did this mean civilian? Damn right it did and Wheatley's thoughts were greeted with open arms by the government:

6. For the purpose of constructing new Shore Defences local civilian labour should be employed where necessary, natural resources should be utilized wherever possible and use made of waste products which can be acquired speedily in great quantities and at no cost to the nation.

Each short paragraph was built upon basic common sense but always left the reader – a top military officer or civil servant – with an intriguing question in order to follow through to the next paragraph, such as, 'no cost to the nation'.

Points 7 and 8 would complete his general comments for 'Resistance to Invasion', explaining the 'no cost' factor, but it would also criticise the government. At the same time, Wheatley would remind his audience that he was in the last war and vital lessons could be learnt from that conflict. The result was both sobering and intriguing:

7. For this work one trained engineer will be worth fifty ordinary men. The task to be undertaken is immense. The time in which to do it is terrifyingly short. *Every engineer and engineering student between the ages of seventeen and sixty-five should instantly be conscripted.*
8. I criticize most forcefully the Government's mobilization policy in the present war. They appear to have followed the line that they will not call men up until they can be equipped. This is utterly wrong.
    At the outbreak of the last war we had far less equipment than we had at the outbreak of this one, yet within five weeks a million volunteers had been enrolled. My own unit was embodied in September 1914 but we did not get

guns or horses until nearly a year later; yet in those months of waiting an immense amount of good work was done. The men were drilled round a wooden gun, taught Signalling, harness fitting on dummies, horse manage-ment, map reading, etc. Discipline was instilled into them and the best were picked out as N.C.O.s. Since hutments were not available we lived in billets or under canvas.

The same plan should have been followed in this war, but it is not too late to start at once and the season of the year Is wIth us. A further mIllIon men should be called up and set to work under engineers on coast defence. This will at least provide the necessary labour and get men into some sort of disciplined order, even if they have to wear armlets instead of uniforms.

Simple but effective, and indeed, something that the Home Guard would later busy themselves with. Did Wheatley's comments in this paper develop the idea of the formation of the Home Guard? Probably not, but it may have supported the concept.

However, the important thing about Wheatley's paper was that it didn't preach military manoeuvres and logistics to its audience but it did provide a mechanism to get civilians battle-fit before conscription. Perhaps some of the theories came from his own frustrations at not having any official war duties for so long. He had been left to stew for a while, then suddenly he was allowed to burst his ideas and opinions upon the top men – the ones who could make a difference. And Wheatley could converse with – and inspire – them.

Obviously, many of Wheatley's thoughts had been keeping a few mili-tary minds awake at night, but it was his ability to win his audience over that mattered. He wanted a general to bark, 'Sound man, that Wheatley, can't we give him something a little more taxing to do?'

In order to get that compliment though, he had to back up his 'Resistance to Invasion' with a lot more detail. He called the second part of his paper 'Particular', which clearly showed what resistance was needed and how it could be implemented. This was a nice touch from the writer, as all he had to do was brain-storm ideas and obviously he would hit upon an idea that hadn't been previously considered (as Captain Hubert Stringer had told him). He started 'Particular' with some good common sense:

Zone 1. In addition to the Royal Navy and Royal Air Force there will presum-ably be patrols of small craft under naval orders keeping watch in the outer sea to give warning of the enemy's approach, by wireless, rockets, etc.
Zone 2. The sole but all-important function of all obstacles and Forces in Zone 2 is to delay-delay-delay the enemy in his attempts to get a secure foothold on land, so as to give ample time for G.H.Q. to get a clear picture of the situation and to find out which, out of perhaps a hundred simultaneous attempts to land at different points, are feints and which are really dangerous

threats. The main Forces in Zone 3 would then not be dispersed unnecessarily but be able to strike with maximum effect at any strong enemy force which has made a landing and hurl it back into the sea. Zone 2 must be divided into three sub-zones: (A) Coastal Waters. (B) The Shore. (C) To five miles inland.

Obviously good old common sense has an unlimited budget and Wheatley's comments – throughout most of his civilian war papers – discuss the maximum defence tricks of a Fortress-Utopian Great Britain. But it was this boldness, based upon sound reasoning, that won over his audience. He went on to give details of the three sub-zones:

Sub-Zone A. Coastal Waters
The threatened coast-line from Cromer to Beachy Head (exclusive of estuaries and small bays) measures, according to *The Times Atlas*, approximately 270 miles.
   The estuaries are as follows:

The Nore to Landguard Point	4 miles across
Sales Point to Colne Point	5 miles across
Foulness Point to Holywell Point	1 mile across
Shoeburyness to Sheerness	6 miles across
Shell Ness to Whitstable	4 miles across
Pegwell Bay	5 miles across

There are also the narrow mouths of the rivers Butley and Deben, the inlets of the sea on the Essex coast south of the River Crouch, and the considerable indent at Rye Harbour.

Booms and Gunboats
All these would presumably be defended by several lines of booms with mines attached, submarine nets, etc. In the rear of the booms, in the estuaries of the rivers Orwell, Blackwater, Crouch, Thames, Medway, and Swale, would be gunboats which together with the land fortifications should render these estuaries impregnable. This would shorten our line of coast to be defended to some 230 miles. Small bays would make the actual distance considerably longer but this can be offset by portions of the coast, such as much of Thanet, which are defended by unscaleable cliffs.

Although Wheatley pored over maps when writing his papers, it is also clear that he had a good knowledge of the British countryside, which hung flesh on the bones of his observations. However, behind every great man there is an equally great woman, as Wheatley went on to explain:

Fishing Nets
A first line of coastal water defence suggested by my wife is fishing-nets. Hundreds of miles of these are available and the men to lay them. If laid about two miles out they would foul the propellers of light motor-craft while not interfering with the operations of the Royal Navy. Light one-pound mines, if available, might be attached to them by floats, in the same way as heavy mines are attached to wire submarine nets. This 230-mile barrier of fishing-nets should prove a useful obstacle for throwing the raiding motor-craft into confusion.

So the fishing nets idea came from Wheatley's wife, Joan, an extremely resourceful lady. One can picture the Wheatleys sitting down after dinner and thrashing out ideas for the protection of Great Britain against the Nazi jackboot. Perhaps they would share a bottle of champagne before Wheatley retired to his study and wrote his papers throughout the night. All he wanted to be was an ideas man. He knew he didn't have the power to implement his paper, transforming it into policy and orders, no, his job was solely to give pause for thought. It is important to enforce this point because Wheatley was content with this job. He was a writer of fiction, a man who could employ his imagination in a logical but creative way. He continued to write:

Fire and Light
Such motor-craft would be extremely vulnerable to our guns in daylight so presumably the invasion will be attempted at night. Therefore, our most important ally will be Fire. Every possible means must be utilized to make the scene as bright as day once the attack on our shores is attempted. This can be accomplished by several means:

Floating Flares
1. The R.A.F. will naturally play its part in bombing and machine-gunning the enemy but it should also drop large quantities of floating flares such as are often attached to life-buoys.

Fire-Ships
2. The old-fashioned fire-ship should be reintroduced. Fair-sized ships should be anchored a mile and a half out, just behind the net barrier, filled with crude oil and connected to the shore by electric wires so that they can be ignited and will burn for several hours.

Spread Flaming Oil
3. A further development of this is a different type of oil filled ship which will blow up when detonated from the shore so that the flaming oil will spread over the water and ignite the enemy craft.

Wheatley's reference to fire-ships (and indeed his earlier reminiscences about his experiences during the Great War) clearly show his willingness to learn and implement effective strategies and methods from history. General Patton would also look at how famous ancient warriors tackled the terrain he was to do battle on. A lot can be gained from one's predecessors' mistakes as well as their victories. However, Winston Churchill didn't agree, as he wrote in his study of Marlborough: 'Every great operation of war is unique. What is wanted is a profound appreciation of the actual event. There is no surer road to disaster than to imitate the plans of bygone heroes and fit them to novel situations.'

Wheatley (later, as we will see) would praise Churchill highly. Politically they were very similar, but strategically they were very different. However, in war, many different but equally valid perceptions are needed; this is how one keeps ahead of the enemy.

Shore Beacons

4. Searchlights are of little use, as they can so easily be shot out by raiding planes, as our own R.A.F. frequently proved in Norway. Therefore, the old-fashioned beacon should be reintroduced; not for the purpose of giving warning but for giving several hours' steady light. If the civilians are not evacuated from the coastal area they should be called in to build these huge bonfires. If they are evacuated, newly joined militiamen could be used. The beacons could be built of any inflammable refuse available in local towns or villages or, if necessary, woods must be cut down; but they must be very big. A thousand beacons would give us one every 400 yards along our 230 miles of threatened coast. If these bonfires were made big enough they would be very difficult to put out even if partially scattered by shell-fire.

Explosive Boats

For defence nearer inshore at least 2,000 rowing-boats should be acquired. These should be filled with high explosive [H.E.] and anchored half a mile to a mile out. As the enemy craft come inshore the rowing-boats would be detonated by shore-defence parties, causing great confusion among the invaders. A rowing-boat would hold as much H.E. as about eight twelve-inch shells, so the blast of each would be terrific and devastate anything within a quarter of a mile.

Wire in Water

In the shallow waters along every particularly vulnerable stretch of coast barbed-wire entanglements will naturally be set up. Great quantities of wire will be needed but all property now belongs to the Government. It could be made obligatory for anyone who has barbed wire round fields to surrender it and turn it in for the purpose.

Wheatley paints a bleak picture of Fortress Great Britain. Its coastlines scarred by barbed wire, fire and explosives of many types. But one must bear in mind that the threat of invasion was a very real one when this paper was written. The public was scared, the authorities gravely concerned (even beautiful Victorian piers were being destroyed so they couldn't be used by invading Nazis). What Wheatley was suggesting would be hazardous to the local communities as well as to the enemy, but people were fighting for survival and extreme measures had to be implemented. Wheatley continued with his ideas on shore defence:

Sub-Zone B. The Shore

Delay Tactics

The sole function of the Forces in Zone 2 being to delay the enemy, every conceivable method must be utilized to make our beaches difficult and dangerous to cross. There is no time, and probably not the material available, to erect proper wire entanglements of sufficient depth along the whole length of them, but an immense amount could be done if the Government would face the really pressing and vital danger of invasion and issue a call to the nation.

The last couple of lines really highlight Wheatley's true feelings. He personally thought the Government could be doing more to halt the 'pending Nazi invasion'. He was deeply concerned, hence the tone and intensity of his thoughts.

Old Iron, etc.

Reception depots could be established at Town Halls and A.R.P. posts for every sort of junk which might help to provide an ugly obstacle. These articles would then be taken to the coast in lorry-loads. Old iron dumps all over the country should be cleared for this purpose and the public could provide an immense amount of material at no cost to the Treasury.

Broken Glass and Nails

I have never heard of broken glass being used as a military obstacle, and it would be ineffective if scattered loose upon a beach; but set in two-inch-thick concrete on sheets of three-ply or cardboard it would cut even military boots to pieces. The Government might issue sand and cement for the manufacture of these squares to all schools, and within a week the schoolchildren of Britain would turn in an immense quantity. There is a broken-glass dump in every town and village.

An appeal might also be issued for pieces of board with nails driven through them about two inches apart. These broken squares and nail-scattered boards could then be lightly covered with sand or pebbles on the beaches or placed through the whole length of gaps leading up through the Kent cliffs and in woodland paths leading inland from the shore.

Obstacle Belt as Substitute for Wire
Such methods may sound like Comic Opera, but the civilian population are very eager to help in this great emergency and after the military had marked out the belt to be covered I should like to see the civil population made responsible for filling it as their contribution to the defence of the country. Civil engineers could oversee the work and it would save much valuable time of R.E. units. My point is that a barrier at least 100 yards in depth should be established just above the water-line along the whole length of the 230 miles of threatened coast. Naturally, tanks would cross any such barrier without great difficulty, but even after they had passed it would still prove a most formidable obstacle for enemy infantry to cross in uncertain light under fire and would certainly cause *delay*, the great factor at which we are aiming.

Is it impossible nowadays to include the public in resistance against invasion? Look at the fall of Iraq in 2003. Even with the dictator in allied hands the people fought for their own country.

Keep Field Batteries in Reserve
Coast defence batteries will naturally play their part but all mobile artillery should be reserved for operating with the main Forces in Zone 3 against troop concentrations which have already effected a landing. To place field batteries within five miles of the coast is to risk their capture by surprise attack should the Shore Resistance fail to function properly in any sector.

Use Anti-Tank Weapons
For Shore Resistance every anti-tank gun and anti-tank rifle that can be spared should be mounted on the coast without delay. These weapons appear to have failed in their purpose except against light tanks, but they should serve perfectly to sink armoured motor-boats.

Block-Houses
The old Martello Towers should be brought into use again, also any isolated buildings along the coast should at once be converted into block-houses with sandbags and reinforced concrete. These will be very vulnerable against artillery, but the enemy motor-boats will presumably only carry light guns so the block-houses should give fair resistance (except against direct hits by bombs) and serve as rallying points.

Again Wheatley uses the resources of war already to hand (learning from history again?) – Martello Towers. He would straight away employ a similar idea at the outset of his next sub-section:

Sub-Zone C. To Five Miles Inland

Pillboxes

There are also on the East Coast a number of mushroom pillboxes erected in the last war. A machine-gun team should be allocated to each of these and many more should be built at once in Zone 3.

Wheatley's perception on pillboxes was not just noted, it was implemented. Soon afterwards, pillboxes became more numerous along the coastline of Great Britain.

Tiger Pits

Civilians or newly joined militiamen should be sent to dig lines of pits in front of all pillboxes (tiger traps with stakes in them and pointed iron railings commandeered from all coast towns to prevent the pillboxes being rushed).

Fire Trenches

In Zone 2 and 3 shallow trenches should also be dug in front of machine-gun posts and gun positions. These trenches should then be filled with canisters of crude oil or paraffin mixed with smoke-bombs which can be ignited on the approach of a superior enemy. Fire is being made great use of by the Germans and we should use it too. Such fire trenches would serve the double purpose of making a serious barrier for the enemy to cross and enabling our own units to retreat to a new position, unmolested, under cover of the flames and smoke when the material in the trenches is detonated.

Booby Traps

Land mines and booby traps should be employed on a vast scale. Every little fishing village that has a jetty offers a good point for a mine under a loose board. All houses in Zone 2, except those being used for defensive purposes, should have a booby trap laid in them.

Evacuation

Finally, with regard to Zone 2, which stretches for five miles inland, the whole civilian population which is not being actively employed under Government orders should be evacuated (a) to give the military a free hand with booby traps, land mines, etc., without endangering life (b) because refugees jam roads and hamper military operations at a time of crisis. No unnecessary person should be allowed to remain in Zone 2 in any circumstances, and the sooner it is evacuated the better.

Wheatley paints a countryside deadly and deserted, and surely as dangerous to the locals as the Nazis once the threat had gone away; and not least of all to the wildlife!

Wheatley's Great Britain is a country desperate for survival, which, in May 1940, it wasn't. It was resourceful and determined but not desperate – yet. So was Wheatley clearly showing his own paranoia? Yes, in a way, but there was no shame in that, just a desperation to help his country at all costs.

Zone 3. From Five To Twenty-Five Miles Inland

This area is a purely military sphere where the main Forces would meet any enemy concentrations which have succeeded in forcing a landing. This also should be evacuated as far as possible. Villages definitely so, to prevent cross-currents of refugees in an emergency, and if people must be left in towns they should be under orders with appointed places where they could be marshalled at the first alarm and marched out by side-roads or across country on routes laid down beforehand to an area where they will not obstruct military operations.

Land Mines

Land mines will also be used in this area, and it is suggested that it would be better to arrange these with a number of trip-wires so that the enemy set them off themselves. This avoids the possibility of Fifth Column sabotage which might occur if one relied upon wires laid a mile or so to the rear for the purpose of exploding them.

Anti-Tank Measures

General Fuller suggests in an article in Saturday's *Evening Standard* that the Germans may have (like the Russians) an amphibian tank which can be launched from motor-craft some distance from the shore and come up on land. In any case, it is hardly likely that the Germans would attempt an invasion without bringing over tanks by some means or other, so as many methods as possible of defeating these vehicles should be employed.

The idea of an amphibian tank being used in the 1940s was something akin to the work of H G Wells (i.e. a science fiction writer). Now such things are commonplace; which just goes to show – albeit in a simplistic way – how far warfare has come in sixty years.

Cone Shelters as Strong-Points

I would suggest that A.R.P. shelters are made use of. I do not mean the two-section type which has been issued to the public, but the strong, cone-shaped variety which is being used for A.R.P. posts, sentries, etc. All these could be replaced by sandbag shelters and removed to the threatened area to be erected on crossroads, with their openings facing to landward and a slit cut in the back to give traversing room for an anti-tank rifle or small gun. These shelters would resist anything but a direct hit from a bomb or heavy shell. There is space enough inside for two men and they could be moved into position very quickly.

Tree Traps

It is customary to fell trees across roads as an obstacle, but this is useless in the face of tanks – as was proved by the rapid advance of the Germans through the Ardennes. A much better method would be to select the biggest trees at roadsides and saw these three-quarters of the way through, then insert a dynamite cartridge and lay some form of trip-wire across the road so that the advance of the first tank would detonate the cartridge and bring the tree crashing down across the road. It might not catch the first tank but it would probably fall upon the second, thereby creating a much better obstacle to the others and, moreover, accounting for an enemy armoured vehicle. Wherever possible a whole line of trees should be partially sawn through and dynamite cartridges inserted in them so that the whole line of trees falls across the road, thereby creating a blockage for perhaps 100 yards or more and possibly destroying several armoured vehicles.

Tank Barriers

The barriers which are being erected on main roads are, in my opinion, virtually useless, as a medium tank can either push them down or go over them. The best tank obstacle is a very deep ditch, and I suggest that a section of every main road which leads inland (particularly where it runs along an embankment or through a marsh) should either be blown up or be dug out to a depth of at least twenty feet and a width of from thirty to forty feet. These gaps could have temporary wooden bridges thrown across them which could easily be blown up in the face of an advancing enemy. In the bottom of these pits oil-drums, etc., should be placed, together with smoke-drums, in the same manner as the fire trenches mentioned above. Flames and smoke from these would make it impossible for the enemy to bridge the gap rapidly and as they would not be able to see through the smoke-screen any defences which lay ahead of them this would necessitate their making a considerable detour off the road before advancing further.

It took time for Great Britain to build up her armoury and one can speculate about how many of Wheatley's extreme (?) ideas would have been implemented had the Nazis invaded the British Isles during 1940/1. However, one thing that is clear from Wheatley's paper is his faith in the general public. This is not naivety, because people did want to come together and fight the common foe. One wonders if that type of community spirit would exist in Britain today …

Tank Attack from the Rear

The Finnish Campaign showed us that tanks are much more vulnerable from the rear, and this apparently is borne out by officers returning from Flanders.

The Finnish method was to sling a netful of Mills bombs under the tank from behind. I suggest, therefore, that small detachments of troops should be stationed in concealed dug-outs by the roadside and ordered to remain there until the first batch of enemy tanks has passed, so that they could then come out and attack the enemy tanks from the rear.

Fire Woods
All woods in Zone 2 and 3 should have dumps of highly inflammable material in them so that the woods can be set on fire if necessary in the face of an advancing enemy.

Anti-Seaplane Measures
The Norfolk Broads, the wide basin of the River Alde, and all estuaries which extend several miles inland should be provided with anti-aircraft floats and covered by shore artillery to prevent landings by German troops in seaplanes.

Cover Aerodromes with Artillery
The ground defences of aerodromes, as has been proved, are almost useless to prevent troops landing, since the enemy bombers plaster these defences and render them ineffective before the troop-carrying planes arrive. A better way to defend aerodromes would be to have one or two more batteries of artillery covering them from a distance of about 2,000 yards. When the aerodrome ground defences have been knocked out the batteries would then come into action and shell the enemy troop-carriers as they land.

Withdrawal of Transport and Supplies
All cars, vans, motor-bicycles, carts, horses, and bicycles not in use by the military should be withdrawn to twenty-five miles from the coast; also all livestock and considerable stores of food or munitions.

Petrol Stations
Every petrol station in Zone 2 and 3 should be mined so that it can be blown up on the approach of the enemy. Or possibly an even more effective method would be to pour water into any remaining supply of petrol, as I understand that it is difficult – if not impossible – to separate the two liquids, and if the enemy use the captured petrol it would then have the effect of choking their carburettors.

I believe the best option for Wheatley's petrol scenario would be to wait until the enemy actually reached the station then blow it up. No petrol, no vehicles, maximum death toll of enemy. Surely, that is the best way to 'delay-delay-delay', as Wheatley would put it.

Civilian Liaison Officers

When touring the country last year to speak for the National Service Campaign I found that the Mayors varied greatly. Some were willing and efficient organizers, some were willing but stupid and almost lacking in education, a few were definitely Communists or Pacifists and refused to sit on the platforms with their local M.P.s and myself. To get the best out of these people they need very careful and tactful handling. Many officers doubtless possess these qualities, but I believe it would be better if civilian liaison officers were appointed to each military H.Q. in the coastal areas, if only for the fact that they could save Military Commanders an immense waste of time.

Such liaison officers could be extremely helpful in explaining the requirements of the military to Mayors, etc., and acting as buffers to prevent friction. They could also explain requirements to the inhabitants of towns and villages by public speaking. I suggest, therefore, that if this suggestion is adopted, the men selected should be as far as possible people already known to the public through the Press from their activities in civil life – well-known broadcasters, authors, journalists, etc.

I find the last paragraph extremely interesting. I can't help but feel that Wheatley was lining himself up for a public speaking job, because as the papers progress, there appears to be an increasing amount of flag-flying-patriotic speak. Obviously, Churchill was guilty of that (it is something evocative of the time), even Laurence Olivier gave rousing – embarrassing? – rhetoric to soldiers leaving portside to war. But in retrospect, Wheatley, Olivier and other entertainers – even Winston Churchill – saw it as their duty to raise peoples spirits, make them proud to be British, and my god, it worked. We can look back at some of Dennis Wheatley's writings (more explicit examples of British bravado to come) and cringe, but we must remember, the threat of the Nazis was a very real danger during the Second World War. People didn't know if they would see tomorrow and, if they did, what sort of tomorrow would it be for them and their children?

The overblown bravado raised the public above their fears and inspired them to make a difference. So Wheatley was right, people like him (and Olivier et al), could take the lead as civilian liaison officers and make a difference. Other people could too, as Wheatley mentioned in his paper:

Such men as Herbert Sutcliffe, Howard Spring, Plum Warner, Ralph Strauss, Sir Harry Brittain, Eric Gillet, George Grimaldi (organizer of Ideal Homes), A. G. Macdonell, Commander A. B. Campbell, Leslie Charteris, Peter Cheyney, Charles Cochran, Louis Golding, Leon M. Lion, Roland Pertwee, Cecil Roberts, Evelyn Waugh, Captain A. M. Webster, Valentine Williams, and Arthur Wimperis. All of these are brilliant speakers; they are mostly ex-officers of the last war who would work easily with the military; most of them have names already known to a large section of the public and many of them are professional writers capable of drafting concise publicity material or instructions for swift issue; many of them are also leaders of national thought with first-class brains who might produce good original ideas either for furthering defence or for dealing with emergencies.

In a discussion on this point it was suggested that the natural source from which these should be drawn was the Ministry of Information, but I feel that this would be a grave error. No man can serve two masters adequately, and the sole function of these civilian liaison officers would be to facilitate the work of the military with the civilian population. Therefore, they should be under the orders of the War Office – and the War Office only. If they were appointed by any other Government office it would have the effect of appointing political commissars to the Fighting Services and probably lead the military to regard them with distrust – which is the very last thing we want. On the other hand, to give them any military rank might minimize their effectiveness with the civilian authorities; but to protect them from the enemy in case of an invasion they might be given the same status as parashots, without uniform but with a military armlet and possibly a forage cap.

I know most of the above-mentioned people personally and could easily get in touch with them and with many more. If the suggestion proved acceptable I should be willing to be set about recruiting such a body immediately.

Here, Wheatley declared his hand. He was still actively looking for an important job to support the war effort and, didn't realise that with this very paper, he was indeed starting it.

Function of Parashot Troops
Obviously parashots should not be called on to assist in coast defence but left to look after their own business. When the alarm is given it can be assumed that half of them will be off duty and asleep. Each man should be notified of the post to which he is to go and it should be the nearest to his own home. They would then guard, or assist in guarding, strategic points until the enemy advanced to them and only then join in the general fray. It is unreasonable to ask these men, when they are armed only with a rifle, to attack parachute troops with sub-machine guns. If Bren guns cannot be furnished to them they should at least be supplied with six Mills bombs apiece.

Concealing Identity of Localities from Parachutists
On returning along the Great West Road, from Newbury, on Sunday night I noticed that although most of the signposts had been removed many other notice-boards, etc., still remained, which would have given an enemy parachutist plenty of evidence as to the locality in which he had landed.

The worst offenders are village post-offices, police stations, railway stations and such places as golf clubs; so could not these have their names temporarily blacked out?

Another give-away of the identity of small villages are the signboards of the inns, as by now the Germans will doubtless know that we are removing our signposts and so will inform their parachutists about the inns in the immediate area where they hope to drop troops on the lines of: "If you enter a village with an inn called The Spreadeagle it will be Midhurst" – and so on. Ordinary names like the Horse and Groom would not be very helpful, but the more unusual signboards should certainly be taken down, and this applies especially to inns on the open road, as these are very easily identified by a map if the parachutist has a list of inns for the ten square miles somewhere in which he expects to land.

This note applies particularly to the threatened area on the East Coast where all possible evidence of identity should be eliminated.

The last section is very interesting. Not only a very important idea, which could be immediately instigated by the government, but how Wheatley showcases his enquiring mind: 'On returning along the Great West Road … '

Counter Air-Attack Measures: Artillery
Field artillery should not be used in batteries, as a battery represents a sizeable object for any enemy attack by bombs or machine-gunning from the air. Batteries should be broken up into individual one-gun units covering a front of 600 to 800 yards, so that their commander can still keep control of them, but they would present smaller and more numerous objectives for the enemy which would, therefore, be more difficult to knock out.

Counter Air-Attack Measures: Infantry
The German Air Force is certain to bomb all roads leading to the coast very heavily, to prevent troops coming up. Zone 3 has no great depth. Therefore, all troops of the main Forces should revert to foot-slogging. Let the men march into action and their casualties will be far less, because they will be able to scatter more easily each time an enemy aircraft comes over than they would be able to do were they in a long line of mechanized vehicles.

Communications: Semaphore System
We must anticipate sabotage by Fifth Columnists of telephone and telegraph wires. Germany also has a greater number of broadcasting stations than we have, so wireless communications may be jammed. Therefore, the pre-telegraph semaphore system which carried news across country very swiftly should be re-established throughout the whole of Britain. Old maps of 1870/1880 will show the positions of these old semaphore stations, and semaphores which can be lit for signalling at night should immediately be re-erected upon them.

The British Trojan Horse

The Germans have taken nearly all their best ideas for this war from us, and have simply developed them to a much greater extent. It is quite time that we took a leaf out of their book. I suggest that at least four secret Forces of Regular Troops should be established upon the East Coast. These could be stationed (1) in barges on the Norfolk Boards, (2) in barges on the River Orwell, (3) in barges on the Essex creeks, and (4) at Margate, in the big caves under the town. Their job would be to remain under cover during the first stages of invasion but, of course, in touch with Home Defence Command by specially laid triplicated cables. At the right moment General Headquarters would order them out of their hiding-places to attack the enemy in the rear.

A further development of this is that Northern Command and Southern Command should immediately prepare troopships to be held in readiness at Hull and Southampton respectively. These could also be ordered to sail at the right moment and land troops behind the Germans wherever they had secured a strong foothold on the coast.

Armoured Trains

These will prove invaluable. There is an abundance of steel plating in our shipping yards and at least seventy-five armoured trains should be created immediately. One of these should be stationed at each of the twenty-five junctions forming the first line of lateral communications down the threatened coast. Two should be stationed at each of the ten junctions further inland forming our second line of lateral communications. And three armoured trains should be stationed at King's Lynn, Ely, Cambridge, Bishop's Stortford, Maidstone, Tunbridge Wells, and Lewes, which would be the bases for our main line of resistance.

It is obvious (throughout this paper) that Wheatley was meticulously studying maps and this in itself gives extra authority to his suppositions, especially when he mentions the towns (at the end of the previous paragraph).

Railway Junctions

It is certain that the Germans will endeavour to bomb all railway junctions. These trains should, therefore, never be stationed actually in the yard but on a siding about a quarter of a mile outside it. Also, wherever practicable, a short new line (even half a mile long would make all the difference) should be laid by-passing the actual junction, so that trains can be switched from one line to another without actually passing through the main station.

Camouflage

This note has nothing to do with East Coast Defence, but it might be passed to the Ministry of Supply. All Army vehicles are now camouflaged but they still remain fairly easily visible through field-glasses from a good distance, owing to their straight lines. This applies particularly to the square shields of field-guns. When there has been time to camouflage them with branches this does not matter, but in a losing battle there is not always time to cut branches for the purpose – or there may be no foliage readily available in the immediate area of protection but with a wavy outline along their foresides instead of a straight line square, as this would make them much less easily visible.

Secret Headquarters

I gather that in recent operations Fifth Columnists constantly informed the enemy of the location of General Lord Gort's headquarters, so that wherever he moved he and his staff were subjected to constant and deliberate bombing attacks. In an endeavour to circumvent the same thing happening in the event of an invasion, it is suggested that Divisional Headquarters, etc., should be located for the time being in places of which no secret at all is made, but that one or more secret headquarters should be prepared for each in country-houses a few miles away. Immediately the alarm of invasion was given, these headquarters' staffs would move to their secretly prepared battle headquarters, which would probably give them immunity from deliberate bombing attack for at least the first vital hours of the attempted invasion.'

Wheatley was concerned by the actions of Fifth Columnists, something the government was terrified of. So his ideas on how to trick or contain them were always taken very seriously.

Invasion by Glider

It has been brought to my attention that in addition to motor-boats the enemy may use strings of gliders each containing six or eight men. If these are sent over in quantity they present a far more difficult problem than a landing of troops from great numbers of fast motor-boats, as no one can tell where the gliders may land and so where to erect defences against them.

Apparently, the theory is that enemy planes will tow four to six gliders across the North Sea and release them just before reaching our anti-aircraft coast defences. At first sight the only form of defence which one can see against this form of attack – apart from fighter aircraft – is balloon barrages. The question is, will the men in the gliders be equipped with oxygen apparatus? If they are, we are up against it, because their towing planes would probably release them at a greater height than that to which we can put up our balloon barrage, thereby nullifying its usefulness.

To counter this to some extent the balloon barrage should not be erected on the coast but withdrawn inland some sixty miles, as in that distance the gliders would necessarily have to come down much lower and the balloon barrage stand a much better chance of catching them.

In my view it is, therefore, essential that an entirely new disposition of balloons should be made immediately. All balloons should be withdrawn from West and Central London, from the coast and from the whole of middle and northern England. If these places are bombed, it can't be helped. The thing is that every balloon we have should be established on the line – King's Lynn, Cambridge, East London, Tunbridge Wells and Hastings.

Undermine Enemy Morale

I would suggest that we should not try to conceal what we cannot keep secret. Let us tell the Germans that they are going to get Hell if they try to invade England. Now is the time that the Ministry of Information should drop a really useful pamphlet, particularly over German troop areas. It might run on the following lines:

Come to England this summer for your holiday and sample the fun we have prepared for you. Try bathing in our barbed-wire bathing enclosures. Try rowing in our boats which will blow up as you touch the tiller. Try running up our beaches covered in broken glass. Try picnicking in our lovely woods along the coast and get a two-inch nail through your foot. Try jumping into our ditches and get burnt alive. Come by air and meet our new death ray (this sort of lie is good tactics at a time like this). Every Nazi visitor guaranteed death or an ugly wound. England is Hell – it's going to be just the same for you in either.

A death ray akin to the Martians in *War of the Worlds*?

If we can get the enemy scared before he starts we have already half won the battle.

Urgency

Speed is essential and even if a certain amount of red tape has to be cut junior officers should shoulder grave responsibilities. Even if Hitler's new thrust towards Paris is not a feint, he may also attempt an invasion of England with the intention of preventing as many of our troops as possible being sent to France; but an immense amount of work could be done to strengthen our shore defences if we act promptly, and it may be that we have only a fortnight or less to work in.

Some could say, after reading this last paragraph, that Wheatley was a worrier. If we remember how he made escape routes from his house and reinforced the roof of the servants' quarters, we may even think him foolish. But he wasn't. Far from it. Because even with hindsight we do not see clearly. Much was going on during the war years, and as Wheatley found out more – understood more of the intricate detail – his fears, his nervous energy, would make more of a tangible difference to the Joint Planning Staff of the War Cabinet. Yes, he did go a little over-the-top in certain areas of his first paper, but if the British Isles was invaded, how many of Wheatley's ideas would have been put to good use ... ?

With 'Resistance to Invasion', Wheatley had made a very promising start, but where would his writing talents take him next?

Notes

1. See *Stranger Than Fiction* (Hutchinson, 1959).
2. This conversation was documented by Wheatley in *Stranger Than Fiction*, op. cit.
3. Wheatley listed his friends and colleagues within the Services in *The Deception Planners. My Secret War* (Hutchinson, 1980), and also in *Stranger Than Fiction*, op. cit.
4. See *Stranger Than Fiction*.

V

The Invasion and Conquest of Britain

'After the fall of France, it was painfully evident that our immediate concern must be Home Defence, and that some time must elapse before we could have the necessary resources from an offensive on any considerable scale.'
The Memoirs of Lord Ismay

On 20 June 1940 Wheatley had an important meeting. Sir Louis Greig asked him to lunch at the Dorchester. There he was introduced to Wing Commander Lawrence Darvall[1] and Mr J S L Renny, the latter a Czech armaments manufacturer operating in Britain.[2]

They talked about the war: the role Italy would now play (having ten days previously joined the Nazis and jeopardising the British position in the Mediterranean), and the plight of France, having three days since surrendered.[3]

It was a significant time. Churchill had only been prime minister for five weeks and armaments were being produced slowly. All of this made the Dorchester lunchers anxious. The Nazis had control of the ports in France and all agreed that Hitler's next step was to cross the Channel and attempt to take Britain; and she wasn't ready to counter that. Wheatley knew this, hence the desperation in the tone of his paper 'Resistance to Invasion', but he had to go one step further now.

Darvall told Wheatley that his paper was excellent, although certain parts of it were impracticable. But that didn't matter, it was about using the resources that were to hand; it wasn't about building a Maginot Line around London!

Darvall gave Wheatley another project. He wanted him to write a second paper. This time, Wheatley had to put himself on the other side – to write as though he was part of the Nazi High Command. The Paper would be entitled 'The Invasion and Conquest of Britain'.

Wheatley didn't rush home and start writing straight away. First, he went to Geographia in Fleet Street and bought two maps of the British

Isles, one a physical map, the other showing density of population. He then went home and hung them up in his library along with a map of Western Europe. Over the next forty-eight-hour period (with only two short breaks), Wheatley smoked over two hundred cigarettes and drank three magnums of champagne. The final result was a paper 15,000 words in length. Wheatley then had it typed and sent off to Darvall c/o 'Mr Rance's room at the Office of Works'. Wheatley would later find that this peculiar address was just a cover for the Joint Planning Staff's rooms at the Ministry of Defence. Also, he didn't know that his new friend – Darvall – was a strategic planner in that select team. The government wheels were turning slowly and Wheatley was being mentioned – favourably – by extremely important and influential people.

It would be fair to say that Wheatley was not over-confident in his task. In fact, he was quite concerned about sounding foolish. Obviously, the people he was writing for knew more about the intricacies of war and the resources at hand than he. Because of that, Wheatley started his paper with the following note:

> I have done my best to tackle this vast – and for me – entirely new problem in the limited time at my disposal. To get a complete picture I have frequently been compelled to state the obvious. Some points in this paper may be laughable to experts but it has been got out without any technical assistance and I can only hope that certain things raised in it may be worth consideration. DW 24th June 1940.

Unfortunately, this book – or in fact a second volume of equal length – could not contain every word of Wheatley's war papers. I have had to edit (with the odd exception – 'Resistance to Invasion'), as I see fit. That editing deletes much repetition or information that a modern reader would find either confusing, irrelevant or uninteresting. What follows is an edited version of Wheatley's paper 'The Invasion and Conquest of Britain'. It was written between 20th June and 22nd June 1940 (three months before British Spitfires and Hurricanes crushed the Luftwaffe during The Battle of Britain), and starts with a second note from Wheatley (first note detailed above):

> The first four paragraphs are, I feel convinced, the honest convictions of not only the Nazis but the Prussian-ruling caste. DW.

Please note, I have not edited any of the first four paragraphs.

GENERAL

Britain is the Enemy. France by comparison is an honourable foe. She is like a neighbour who has an old-standing quarrel about the situation of the party fence which separates her back-yard from ours; but she did not menace our livelihood. Political dissensions, a falling birthrate, and soft living made her weak and decadent. Realizing this she would have been willing to forget the past and live in peace with us; but this Britain would never do.

France entered the present war only reluctantly; she was dragged in as Britain's unwilling partner to serve as a first zone of defence while the British Empire rallied its resources. To prevent the devastation of their own country and the horrors of war touching their own people it has been the traditional policy of the British to fight their wars on other people's soil. This is in keeping with the cunning and self-interest which lie deep-rooted in the British character; but Britain will not escape this time.

It is British hypocrisy, duplicity, and greed which have consistently barred the path of German advancement and will continue to do so as long as the British Empire remains intact and Britain retains her mastery of the seas; but the day of reckoning is at hand. We have had to wait and work and deny ourselves much for twenty years, but at last we have this subtle, dangerous, and inveterate foe where we want her. She must be smashed once and for all. There is no room in the world for a great and prosperous Germany and a still powerful Britain. Therefore Britain must be beaten to her knees and broken so utterly that no possible combination of circumstances could ever enable her to rise again.

No humanitarian considerations must be allowed to deflect us from our purpose. It was the British blockade a quarter of a century ago which slowly starved German women and children to death and the iniquitous peace terms inspired by the British wish to cripple Germany for all time which inflicted a decade of ruin and misery upon the German people. We must be utterly ruthless with this unscrupulous enemy and use every means which imagination can suggest to crush all thought of resistance in the British people – even after their Government has sued for and obtained peace. Not until British women lick the boots of German soldiers on their order while British men look on can we be certain that we have achieved our final objective and that Britain will never menace us again. If there are no British men left to witness this act of degradation so much the better. The future of Germany will be all the more secure.

Wheatley really got into the mind of the Nazi. Since the end of the Great War, Germany was a brutally smashed and beaten foe, but a secret, almost silent civil war was taking place. For some, the Great War was not over. They (proud, but furious German men) didn't know the meaning of defeat, as Konrad Heiden wrote in his 1944 masterpiece *The Fuehrer*: 'The German army fights on in Germany. Every period has its methods … Two armies are fighting one another, almost unseen by the public; they are building up secret arsenals.'

Since the end of the Great War and up to the outbreak of the Second World War, the German army went through a metamorphosis, and a new breed of soldier was formed. He was strictly trained, given an ideology and told to kill for the Fatherland. Germany was on the rise again and nothing could stop her.

This hadn't gone unnoticed by the British. Indeed, while on holiday in Germany in the late 1930s, Jock Lewes (co-founder of the SAS – along with David Stirling), saw the might of the growing German army and came home with only one thing in mind: to form a squad of soldiers who were as well-trained as themselves. He knew Great Britain had to counter the rising threat from Germany.

The British newspapers – throughout the 1930s – reported this threat and Wheatley would have kept abreast of current affairs such as this.

As in his first paper, Wheatley started his second with sound reasoning, winning over his audience before hitting them with a dreadful thought:

Poison Gas and Bacteria
I advocate the use of poison gas and bacteriological warfare if our troops can be adequately protected from the latter; but this is a matter for the chemical section and the final decision in both cases lies with the Fuehrer.

The threat of chemical weapons is not a new one. Although a paranoia of the new millennium, the presence of chemical and biological warfare has been around since the Great War (mustard gas a good example). Indeed, the aim of Operation Big Ben during the Second World War was to knock out as many V1 and V2 rocket bases as possible, because it was believed by certain people that the nose cones (of the V2s and, if the war continued, V3s) were to be filled with bacteriological agents and would cause the devastation of Britain. So a special type of Spitfire (Mark IX and XVI with clipped wings) was produced to swoop down and destroy the bases in what was one of the most dangerous operations of the Second World War.

Although Wheatley was writing from a Nazi viewpoint, he hadn't lost track of his audience and indeed, his next major heading in the paper would give much pause for thought, as it simply highlighted the Nazis' ruthlessness:

Bombing
At present bombing should be confined to military objectives, because it is of greater assistance to our forces than the destruction of a number of civilians and a certain amount of property. Moreover, the bombing of civil populations tends to stiffen the resistance of an undefeated people. However, refugees

should be bombed as occasion offers, as this serves to spread further panic and block roads.

At any time when we have a surplus of bombing planes there are two types of raid which could be profitably undertaken:

(a) Against public schools and other advanced educational establishments, because these contain Britain's officer class of tomorrow.

(b) When a high wind is blowing, with the Molotov bread-basket type of incendiary bomb against open towns, as this would start fires difficult to put out and place a great strain on the enemy's morale and fire-fighting units, who would have to call in troops to their assistance; also it will tend to jam hospitals.

The Blockade of Britain

Now that we are in possession of the coast of France this becomes a practical proposition. The approaches to Britain are through the 310-mile stretch of water between Southern Norway and Scotland, the 270-mile stretch of water between Brittany and South Ireland and the 15-mile-wide stretch of water between Northern Ireland and the promontory of Kintyre, in Scotland.

It is obvious that Wheatley was poring over his maps whilst writing The Blockade of Britain paragraph, but this gave his voice a little more authority. Although the papers he had written so far were nothing short of a cornucopia of ideas, they were based upon familiarity with one's own country and a broad knowledge of current affairs, written by a sound, analytical mind. If Wheatley had any critics among the authorities, they must have been coming round to his way of thinking by now. However, it appears from the various source material we have, that Wheatley didn't have any critics. The officers and politicians who read his papers took the Nazi threat seriously. Indeed, they had to find solutions to many problems and Wheatley was helping sort the wheat from the chaff. His role was never underplayed. In fact, quite the reverse, as time would show.

Ireland

The effectiveness of such a blockade would be greatly strengthened by a German invasion of Ireland, which is perfectly feasible by air and would give us both air and submarine bases on the South Coast of Ireland, which has numerous good natural landing-grounds and harbours. Against our superior weapons, improved methods of warfare and our support from the very strong Fifth Column elements there, Irish resistance would be almost negligible.

Bases in South Ireland would enable us to render the waters between South Ireland and Brittany extremely hazardous for British shipping. And again, South Ireland is only some seventy miles distant from the North Channel between Ulster and Scotland, so this move would greatly increase our effectiveness there.

I remain uncomfortable with Wheatley's observations on Ireland's inability to defend itself. I acknowledge that they have endured many successful invasions over the centuries but they have always shown great resilience and strength (also, the Nazis didn't have the resources at that stage of the war to invade Ireland; or the power to back up any strategy based from there). Let us not forget, Wheatley considered taking a holiday in Ireland just before the war. Was this because he hadn't really been there and consequently didn't know too much about the people? Interesting that his observations only come down to one paragraph. Much shorter for Iceland though (which obviously he knew even less about):

Iceland
There remains the 310-mile stretch of water between Southern Norway and Scotland. An invasion of Iceland by air would strengthen us to some extent in this area, but not sufficiently to close the gap effectively.

I think Wheatley overestimated the magnitude of the Luftwaffe throughout his civilian war papers, but this would have become evident to him after The Battle of Britain.

Time Factor
By these means there is little doubt that we could inflict very heavy losses on British shipping and considerably reduce the supply of arms reaching Britain from the United States. In time we could also seriously affect Britain's food supply; but time is a factor which works both ways.

    Britain's anti-submarine devices have reached a very high pitch of efficiency, so even by intensive building it is doubtful if we could do more than maintain a fleet of fifty submarines permanently at sea, and the morale of the crews is apt to deteriorate under the strain of constant losses in the submarine service. Fifty submarines are quite inadequate to blockade 600 miles of water when perpetually harassed by a determined enemy, and mine-laying aircraft would meet with constant opposition entailing considerable wastage without effecting a complete blockade. Britain's almost total command of the seas makes the value of such a policy extremely dubious and it could be considered only as an adjunct to a long-term plan.

Long-term Policies
Having conquered Western Europe we now have the choice as to whether we should attempt to put Britain out of the war at once or utilize our forces for expansion in other directions. In the latter case there are three lines open to us:

    (a) A move south-east into the Balkans with a view to consolidating the whole of Europe, exclusive of Britain and Russia, into a German-led federation.

(b) To send armies into Africa via Italy and Spain with a view to founding an African empire.

(c) To drive east into Russia with a view to seizing the Ukraine and the Crimea and establishing a Protectorate over Asiatic Russia.

The first – whatever the attitude of the Balkan countries – would almost certainly result in war with Turkey supported by Anglo-French Near Eastern Armies.

The second would prove an extremely costly operation owing to the fact that the British Fleet is still dominant in the Mediterranean, and we could not maintain any considerable army in the field by air-borne supplies and reinforcements alone.

The third would involve us in a war with Russia, which should obviously be avoided until the war with Britain has been brought to a victorious conclusion.

Any of the above policies would involve us in a long campaign and it should be remembered that although Britain is only half-armed at the moment every week that passes sees her grow stronger.

Hitler never followed Wheatley's advice when it came to the invasion of Russia. Stalingrad would be a mistake on a Napoleonic scale.

Wheatley's last paragraph (above) is interesting inasmuch as it is positive. Although he knew that the mounting British war effort was painfully slow, he also knew that the more time Britain had, the stronger she would become.

Food

In the meantime there is the coming winter to be faced. With our conquests of Poland, Norway, Denmark, Holland, Belgium and France we should easily be able to maintain ourselves indefinitely once these countries are fully pacified, and their agriculture and industries put on a proper footing once again; but great dislocation has been caused in them by the effects of war and sabotage, so before we can hope to have them producing on a peace-time basis many months must pass.

In addition to her own people Germany now has to feed her conquered millions. If she fails to do this with a ration at least sufficient to maintain life there will be widespread revolts among the subject peoples. The prospects of the harvests are poor and great quantities of crops have been ruined by the war. The strain on the Gestapo is already great. It would be so highly dangerous to risk mass riots that it is vital to Germany to secure supplies before the winter.

This can be done only by breaking the British blockade. The blockade can be broken only by the conquest of Britain, which will force the British Navy to retire on bases in Canada and South Africa which are several thousand miles distant. There are others which they could use for temporary purposes, but none in which they could rely upon adequate and continuous supplies of munitions.

I had my reservations about this hypothesis. However in his diaries Field Marshal Lord Alanbrooke made the following entry on 30 May 1940[4] (whilst struggling to help save France): ' … rather nerve wracking as the Germans are continually flying round and being shot at, and after seeing the ease with which a few bombs can sink a destroyer, it is an unpleasant feeling.'

If an invasion had happened, the Royal Navy would have had to retreat a safe distance and form part of a larger (combined air and ground assault) repatriation operation, so eventually yes, I agree with Wheatley, Canada and South Africa.

> Since, even with the capture of Southern Ireland and Iceland, the blockade of Britain could not be made fully effective, and the longer Britain remains unconquered the stronger she will become, it is quite clear that no time must be wasted and no other major campaign initiated until the British Isles have been brought under German domination and British ports denied to the British Navy should the British Empire decide to continue the war.
>
> No amount of bombing is likely to achieve this objective, so the only course is an invasion of Britain.

> ### The Invasion of Britain
> In the past the British Admiralty has declared that while it does not guarantee to prevent the landing of an enemy-invading force it does guarantee that it could cut such a force off from its bases, and that it does not believe that any such force could possibly be landed which would be strong enough to conquer Britain, lacking a line of communication for reinforcements and supplies.
>
> This statement was, however, made before the German conquest of France, which in my view has altered the whole strategic situation.

It also changed the whole strategy for the British government. After France fell it was abundantly clear that the gateway to Britain was then firmly open. The British suddenly didn't have as much time as they originally thought. Also, the strength of the Nazis had been witnessed first hand in France, as Alanbrooke mentioned in his diaries on 23 May 1940: 'It is a fortnight since the German advance started and the success they have achieved is nothing short of phenomenal. There is no doubt that they are most wonderful soldiers.'[5]

In his memoirs (William Heinemann Ltd, 1960), Lord Ismay wrote: ' … Churchill was determined that we would not fall into a completely defensive habit of mind, and on the very day on which the evacuation from Dunkirk was completed, he gave instructions that raiding forces of "say, one thousand up to ten thousand" men should be organized as quickly as possible in order to harry the Germans all along the coasts of the countries which they had conquered.'[6]

So a balance between offensive and defensive had to be achieved at all costs.

Wheatley's paper continues:

> Judging by statements in the British Press, the British anticipate a landing by a force or forces of perhaps 50,000 men. They are fully aware that such a force might cause them grievous damage, dislocation, and trouble before it could be mastered, but they have little doubt of their ability to cope with such an invasion.
>
> Had the French resistance proved stronger it might have proved a most excellent diversion to land such a force, knowing that it would be sacrificed but that it would serve to create great havoc in Britain and cause her to retain there arms and men which would otherwise have been dispatched to the Western Front.
>
> But this is no question of a diversion; it is the conquest of Britain, and it will be undertaken by a picked force of 600,000 men for the purpose of securing a foothold in the country during a five-days' operation, to be followed up by a further 1,000,000 men by a line of communications which I am confident can be established ...

Wheatley then went on to explain how the invasion could be accomplished.

> No sacrifice of men and material should be considered too costly in the achieving of our objective. The loss of the entire Italian Navy and all that remains of the German Navy must be accepted. With every shipbuilding yard from Norway to the Pyrenees in our hands, and those of Italy and Britain in addition, we could in three years build a new Axis Navy which would be more powerful than the United States Fleet together with what remains of the British Fleet and any ships which America and the British Dominions are capable of building in that period. This also applies to the Mercantile Marine. We must anticipate the loss of some 5,000 aircraft but this will still leave us a margin of air superiority in Europe, and with the factories of all the conquered countries – including Britain – in our possession we can produce further quantities of planes at a greater rate than America and the British Dominions.
>
> In three years, therefore, we shall be able to proceed with confidence to the conquest of the Western Hemisphere ...

Under the sub-heading 'The Invasion of Britain', Wheatley produced some interesting ideas, progressing into a Nazi utopian world of invincible armed forces and the promise of domination of all Western countries (not far short of what Nazi propaganda promised the German people). It is clear that Wheatley overestimated the might of the Luftwaffe, however it can be argued that he was writing of a worst case scenario.

Wheatley went on to discuss the methods of invasion, which were similar in design to those he described in 'Resistance to Invasion'. But he did provide more depth and detail about how the invasion could be implemented; which worked well in juxtaposition to his previous paper:

German Agents and Fifth Column

These groups merge into each other and so can be taken together. There are already a considerable number of these men established in Great Britain. Many of them are British citizens or naturalized Britons who are above suspicion. For eight months of the war Sir John Anderson left them almost at liberty; he even failed to reintroduce the death penalty for spies caught redhanded. If Sir John Anderson continues in office we have most excellent reasons for hoping that a considerable proportion of our agents and sympathizers in Britain will remain unmolested until the invasion takes place. However, in view of events in Holland and Belgium, Sir John Anderson was at last forced by public opinion to take action and at last his active and intensely worried Intelligence Officers were allowed to have a somewhat freer hand; so in recent weeks a certain percentage of our more obvious friends in Britain have been put in comfortable concentration-camps. In view of this their numbers must be increased again by every possible means at our disposal.

During the Second Cold War (the terrorist threat of the new millennium), the Western world is again concerned about the terrorist attack from the Enemy Within. There is nothing shocking in Wheatley's comments above, except the fact that they were made over sixty years ago. Nothing changes.

Refugees

In the past, refugees have offered us a good field for this and they do so more than ever today. Germans, Austrians, and Belgians are regarded with considerable suspicion; Czech, Poles, Norwegians, Danes, and Dutch somewhat less so; while the French are still granted the full liberties of British subjects.

Taking the Poles as a serious case, these men were fearless when working for our Royal Air Force, some were even crack Spitfire pilots. And because they originated from an occupied country, they fought with their hearts firmly on their sleeves. They fought for their loved ones back home; so they fought vehemently. But, amidst this, there were some Poles – not part of our services – who fought for Hitler. And that is where the paranoia was strong. Each individual has his/her own political view, and the British couldn't disguise the fact that there could be Polish people who longed for a Nazi victory. Nothing could be taken for granted during the Second World War; and the Nazis were keen to manipulate that.

Owing to the French collapse we have here an especially promising source for reinforcing our Fifth Column. Great numbers of French troops and civilians are finding their way into Britain by one means and another. As the British Intelligence Service have been forced to work for years on a mere pittance they are hopelessly under-staffed in experienced officers, so it is utterly impossible for them to cope with the full influx of refugees. Great numbers of the French who have escaped are proclaiming their adherence to General de Gaulle, and among these it should be possible to introduce a considerable number of Fifth Columnists.

French Wounded
Further, large bodies of French troops were brought off from Dunkirk, and owing to the anomalous situation of the French Navy there are many French sailors now in British ports. Certain of these who are members of the Croix de Feu or Communists should be approached and brought over to us wherever possible by pro-German French agents acting in concert with our own secret agents. In the case of certain French officers in Britain pressure might be exercised by the fact that their wives and families are now prisoners in France.

I find the above paragraph extremely perceptive as it clearly illustrates the depth and intricacy of 'smaller' problems the British government faced during the Second World War. No government could successfully deal with all of them. Wheatley highlighted some, but many had to be ignored in favour of greater priorities. This in itself shows how much the British government left to chance at that time.

Gestapo in the Americas to Sail
Where time permits all Gestapo agents in North and South America and Africa who possess either faked or genuine British, British Dominion, American or South American passports should be ordered to sail for Britain at the earliest possible moment. Many of them will not get into the country, but many will.

It is a fact that many Nazi 'war criminals' fled to South America after the Second World War with the help of the Organisation der Ehemaligen SS-Angehorigen (ODESSA). It was not something Wheatley would have known about whilst writing his paper (the work of Simon Wiesenthal was still a long way away). But there is a connection to proved fact stemming from his idea. Again, very perceptive.

Stowaways
The Navy examination of all shipping reaching Britain is now so strict that it is unlikely that we could get a large number of Germans into British ports concealed in cargo ships ... a number who have not British or neutral passports

might succeed in getting in as stowaways, particularly if they can succeed in bribing the captains of neutral vessels bringing supplies to Britain to give their assistance.

Submarines
On the more desolate parts of the coast of Scotland it should be possible to land a number of disguised troops from submarines.

Parachutists
Owing to new regulations and increased police activities it is not now possible for Germans to maintain themselves for any great length of time in Britain without proper papers; but if they carry an iron ration they might succeed in maintaining themselves uncaptured for two or three days. Therefore just before the invasion their numbers could be considerably implemented. In addition to further coast-landings by submarine 2,000 of our parachute troops should be used for this purpose, disguised in civilian clothes, British police and Navy, Army, and Air Force uniforms. They should be dropped by night in the most sparsely populated areas of Great Britain.

… Fifth Columnists would be rounded up, stopped at the ports or killed or captured while attempting to land … but we should easily be able to establish a force of 6,000 Fifth Columnists in Britain if we include those already there who are still at liberty.

Duties of Agents and Fifth Columnists
These divide themselves into three classifications:
(a) Duties of Gestapo agents already in the country or who can reach Britain by apparently legitimate means before the invasion.
(b) Duties of such helpers as they can acquire by blackmail or other means when the invasion starts.
(c) Duties of secret agents and Fifth Column troops brought over in secret just before the invasion, when the invasion is under way.

Information
Gestapo agents must secure as much information as possible, particularly about concentrations of troops, new defence measures, the location of military headquarters and the leaders of British public opinion outside the established Government and the Services …

Tunnels
In certain areas which have been wired since the beginning of the war the military may not be as vigilant as they were, and where long stretches of wire are concerned it might be possible for our agents to tunnel a way under these and, meeting our advancing troops, guide them through the tunnel. All that

is really required is a shallow ditch which would not be too conspicuous but would enable our troops just to wriggle underneath the wire.

Reservoirs
These are very vulnerable points in a highly populated country like Britain. If bacteriological warfare is decided upon they will naturally receive special attention, but in any event Fifth Columnists should examine them with a view to finding their weakest spots so that when the invasion takes place main exits can be dynamited and the population deprived to a larger extent of its drinking water …

The first part of the above paragraph is probably more in-tune with the paranoia of the new millennium than the Second World War. When Coalition forces attacked Iraq in March 2003, the British started frantically buying bottled water in fear of reservoir contamination. Wheatley's thoughts weren't just sound, they were also ahead of their time. Indeed, as we have seen throughout this second paper, Wheatley had detailed the threat of chemical and biological warfare along with the possibility of terrorist attacks on water supplies; which does suggest that human susceptibility to terrorist attack hasn't changed over the past sixty years!

Blackmail
Lastly, agents must further endeavour to reinforce the Fifth Column by securing such helpers as they can. They should write anonymous letters to any foreign refugees whom they know to be in Britain with the simple statement that the names of the refugee's relatives who are still in Poland, Czechoslovakia, Norway, Denmark, Belgium, Holland, or France have been listed and that these will be shot unless the refugee complies with the instructions that he will receive.

Instructions can then be issued anonymously to these people twenty-four hours before the invasion, but the instructions should be of such a nature that they can readily be complied with.

Loyalty apart, such people would hesitate – however much they loved their threatened relatives – if they were told to collect a bomb in a parcel from a certain cloakroom and throw it through the window of an office in Whitehall; but if they are given tasks which entail little risk to themselves, great numbers of them will comply. The instructions should end with the paragraph: 'Remember that you are under observation. We shall know if you have carried out your orders or not. If you fail to do so your relatives will be shot.'

Many thousands of refugees will ignore these instructions and turn them over to the police, but thousands of others, through fear for themselves and their relatives abroad, will do as they are ordered if they see any reasonable chance of getting away with it.

The duties that such helpers should be ordered to perform are as follows:

1. The cutting of telegraph wires, telephone and electric cables which may run near their own back gardens.
2. The spreading of rumours to create panic.
3. The jamming of roads by taking their cars to a given spot and faking a breakdown by putting the engines out of action.
4. The starting of fires by setting fire to their own houses or quarters, thus providing additional trouble for the fire-fighting squads.
5. The spreading of mental distress to hamper coherent thought among the key men in the British defence system and others in responsible posts, by telephoning them or leaving a scribbled not by hand informing them that their wife, daughter, or son has just been killed in an air-raid.

The above points show many similarities with the threat of the new millennium, which in its own way vindicates Wheatley's (and General Patton's) view that one can always learn from history – the above points can be used today with regard to terrorist threat in the UK.

The next two main headings – beginning with 'Duties of Agents and Parachute Troops' – are less general than the ideas presented in the first part of this paper. They concern possible Nazis plans.

DUTIES OF AGENTS AND PARACHUTE TROOPS

The duties of agents and Fifth Column troops brought over in secret just before the invasion will, when the invasion is under way, be as follows:

Invasion
To facilitate the landings of further troops by parachute, troop-carrier, or water-borne means and pass to them immediately all available information about defences, troop concentrations, military headquarters, etc.

False Orders
Among the first parachute troops to be landed there will be a certain number dressed as British officers. These will assist in sabotaging the defence by issuing false orders and false instructions.

Key Points
Where it has been observed that key points in the neighbourhood of antici-pated landings are lightly guarded these should be seized, but this, of course, applies only to small objectives. It may, however, be possible to pre-vent certain small bridges being blown up and to capture telephone centres in small towns and ill-guarded hilltops from which our advancing troops can be signalled by flag or heliograph.

Railways

During the nights the invasion is in progress chairs should be fixed on railway lines for the purpose of derailing trains and switch-points sabotaged wherever possible. In lonely districts railways can be blocked where they pass through cuttings by inserting a dynamite cartridge in the cliff face and bringing down a fall of rock or cliff.

This is not as far fetched as it seems. Home made explosives, like home made biological weapons, could/can be made from items purchased in hardware stores and chemists; indeed mustard gas can easily be made by mixing two common 'widely available' substances.

Power Stations and Munition Works

These will be too heavily guarded for there to be much hope of damaging them except in cases where sabotage has been previously arranged, but bombs can be left in their immediate neighbourhood during the hours of darkness.

River Locks

Harbour locks and the big locks on the Clyde and Caledonian Canals will also probably be sufficiently heavily guarded to prevent interference, but the smaller locks on canals and rivers throughout the country may not be sufficiently guarded. If the locks on the Thames could be opened and jammed the upper reaches of the river would become a dry bed with only a trickle of water in it, which would facilitate the passage of our troops when they fight over this country. This applies also to numerous other rivers and canals ...

Gas Mains

Fifth Columnists in towns will ascertain the position of gas mains and, disguised as workmen repairing the streets, will open up the roads and smash the mains so that as much gas as possible is released, which will be ignited and cause a serious explosion either by accident or if a single inflammatory bomb falls in that area.

Assassination

Cabinet Ministers are guarded, so they form difficult objectives, but risks must be taken and attempts must be made on their lives where possible. Many of them could easily be shot when going into their homes by a Fifth Columnist who has secured a rifle and fitted a telescopic sight to it, if he could place himself in one of the upper windows or on the roof of a house opposite the Minister's residence.

There are also many key men in the British defence system who are entirely unguarded, and lists should be made of these so that as many as possible of them can be assassinated.

Fifth Columnists dressed as soldiers will post themselves upon roads as though they were doing sentry duty; they will wait until a car passes containing a General or Staff Officer and call upon him to halt. Immediately the car pulls up they will shoot the officer and, having selected a position where they have ready cover, will dive into it.

It is of the first importance that as many of the directing brains of the British defence as possible should be put out of action, and this policy will be pursued after the conquest to prevent any leaders of public thought forming an unauthorized government or even leading local riots. Every officer above captain's rank in the Army, above lieutenant's rank in the Navy and above flight-lieutenant's rank in the Air Force will be shot. We shall also shoot all officers under that rank who have earned a decoration for gallantry, all members of the House of Peers and of the House of Commons (past and present) not on our special list, all big industrialists, all prominent editors and journalists, the leading K.C.s, all militant churchmen, all well-known writers, all local magistrates and all well-known sportsmen.

This policy has been carried out in Poland and is being carried out in Holland with excellent effect. Such leaders of national or local opinion are quietly arrested and disposed of, since the policing of Europe now entails such heavy duties that it is sounder to deal with them in this way than to put them in concentration-camps where they require guards and food.

Parachute and Glider Troops

Our advance elements will consist of fully armed parachute and glider-landed troops. Parachute troops will be used for the East Coast landings and glider troops for the West Coast landings. A certain percentage of both will be dressed in captured British uniforms.

If parachutists or glider troops land in the neighbourhood of towns they will be quickly sighted and will suffer unnecessarily heavy casualties. These troops will therefore land in the most sparsely populated areas of England where they will have a much better chance of reaching the arms containers which are dropped with them and of forming into squads of ten or twenty unmolested, than they would otherwise have. Their duties are as follows:

Landing-Grounds

By the night before the invasion the Fifth Columnists will have concentrated as far as possible in certain specified areas. By the means referred to above we should have at least 6,000 throughout the country. One thousand will concentrate in the area of the North Yorkshire Moors, south-west of Whitby; 1,000 will concentrate in the Forest of Bowland east of the town of Lancaster; 1,000 will concentrate round Cheltenham, north-east of the Mouth of the Severn; 1,000 will concentrate in the New Forest; 500 will concentrate in East Kent and 500 will remain in London.

Fifth Columnists will contact parachutists on landing and direct them to the nearest stretches of level ground which are suitable for the landing of aircraft. Race-courses, greyhound tracks, cricket, football and hockey grounds, certain golf courses and innumerable stretches of meadow ground in England are all suitable for this purpose.

Communications
Parachute and glider troops will also destroy communications round the area in which further landings by troop-carriers are to be carried out.

Bridges and Ferries
Bridges and ferries should be seized wherever possible and held until reinforcements arrive.

Block-Houses
Any private houses which command road or railway junctions should be seized at once and converted into block-houses, as once well-armed troops are in possession of such cover they can hold it for many hours. It is, in fact, almost impossible to dislodge them if they have machine-guns without bringing up artillery.

There should be ample time for parachutists to do this in view of the instructions issued to local defence volunteers. They have been told that instead of making a determined attack on parachutists with such weapons as they may have, while the parachutists are still groggy from their landing and have had no time to get the heavy arms which are dropped in containers with them or to gather in groups where they could fight off a numerous enemy, the local defence volunteers are to run and find a policeman or some soldiers or get on the nearest telephone – which may be a couple of miles away across the moorland.

Too much reliance, however, must not be placed on this, as the ordinary British citizen is very ill-disciplined and has a habit of ignoring instructions in a crisis. Elderly gentlemen with shot-guns may quite possibly use them and even yokels with pitch-forks may rush upon an unfortunate parachutist if they see him lying on the ground and believe that he is still stunned from his fall. Therefore, parachutists and glider troops should instantly shoot anyone who comes in sight – men or women – to prevent such catastrophe or the spreading of the alarm that they have landed.

MEANS OF INVASION

Troop-carrying Planes
These will land on the grounds held for them by the parachute and glider troops. When advancing into enemy country it has proved an excellent device to capture a few women and make them advance in front of the troops as cover, at the point of an automatic pistol.

However, time may be lost in capturing women so each troop-carrying plane will carry two men disguised as women. These will march in front of their unit as though captured, but they will wear only the outer garments of women and wear their uniforms underneath, where they will also carry their automatics and a good supply of hand-grenades. Country-women's clothes will be most suitable. They will wear wigs and their comrades will carry their steel helmets and other equipment.

Seaplanes

Seaplanes are not best suited to this operation, on account of their vulnerability; but every means must be used to get troops over, so these will descend in suitable specified areas on the coast.

Troopships

We still have that considerable percentage of the German Mercantile Fleet which was either in or managed to reach German harbours soon after the war broke out. Our losses of transports in the Norwegian campaign have been more than offset by the shipping captured in conquered ports on the west coast of Europe.

The *Bremen,* the *Europa,* and certain other large liners will be used merely as decoys which, escorted by any vessels of the Reserve German Fleet and damaged vessels that can be made seaworthy, will draw off as many units of the British Navy as possible.

There will be no difficulty in organizing numerous convoys of medium-sized merchant ships which will carry a large number of troops for one of our main landings. Certain of these vessels are already converted with collapsible sides, cranes, drawbridges, etc., for the speedy unloading of tanks and guns upon suitable beaches.

The medium-sized ships required will be brought by night along the coast, down from Norway or up from France, and concentrated in the harbours of Denmark and Germany.

The above papragraph clearly shows the depth of Wheatley's knowledge and the extent of his research (through news-bulletins and his contacts within the Services). When these research tools are properly used – along with Wheatley's keen imagination and methodical mind – quality perceptions are made. This is typical of what the War Cabinet loved most about his war papers.

Ferries

In the coastal waters of North Germany and Denmark we have some fifty large railway ferries. Each of these are capable of transporting eight heavy tanks or twenty light tanks, but owing to the North Sea swell these ferries are not suitable for invasion purposes in that area. They will, therefore, be towed night by night along the coast down to the French ports of Le Havre and Cherbourg.

Barges
We can also muster at least 500 of our large Rhine barges, each capable of transporting 150 men. These also will be towed by ocean-going tugs down to the Cherbourg-Le Havre area a few to each of the small harbours along that coast.

Motor-boats and Small Craft
Owing to our conquest of Western Europe we now posses a vast armada of small craft, which are lying in every port from Trondjheim to Biarritz. These are to be mustered on the Channel coast, north from Boulogne and south from Rotterdam, in every harbour available.

Naval Vessels
A redistribution of these will take place so that they can provide all the cover of which they are capable to the various invading forces. Every naval vessel, except those old ships which are to sail with the decoy convoys of large liners, will have its complement doubled by the addition of troops, all of whom will be selected from good swimmers, given special equipment and provided with rubber rafts.

PREPARATORY OPERATION

Italian Navy
We shall require the total support of the Italian Navy and its morale will be strengthened by a number of German officers, N.C.O.s, gunners, and technicians being posted to each ship. It will be under the direction of the German Naval Command.

The straits of Gibraltar are only eight miles wide, heavily mined, and guarded by a considerably superior British Fleet; but it is imperative that the Straits should be forced and the Italian Navy break out of the Mediterranean.

They will be preceded by as many armed merchantmen and every type of small craft as possible to provide the maximum number of objectives to draw the fire of the Gibraltar batteries and the British Fleet; also to force minefields by the sacrifice of small cargo ships before the battle fleet attempts to pass at full speed through the Narrows.

For this operation we shall have the advantage in the air from the fact that we can send bomber and fighter squadrons from bases in the South of France (or possibly even Spain, if we can come to a suitable arrangement with General Franco): whereas the main British air strength is now based in Great Britain, well over 1,000 miles away.

Captured French Planes

In the battle of France and during the conquest of the Low Countries we have captured over 1,000 Dutch, Belgian, French, and British planes which are still fit for service. These will be brought as far south as possible and used to cover the break-through of the Italian Fleet, thereby leaving the Axis Air Force entirely untouched.

The Italian Fleet consists of:

6 Battleships
7 Heavy Cruisers
14 Light Cruisers
51 Destroyers
70 Torpedo-boats
72 Motor-boats and (allowing for recent losses) about
90 Submarines

When the advance elements have drawn the enemy's fire and exploded as many mines as possible the Italian Fleet will go through the Straits at full speed, covered by an air force of 1,000 planes manned by German pilots. No Italian ship will stop to fight and it will be a running battle, the sole objective of which is to get as many Italian ships through the Straits, unsunk, as possible.

We must reckon 50 per cent casualties in battleships, cruisers, destroyers, and torpedo-boats, but only 33 per cent casualties in submarines, as many of these should be able to get through under water unobserved.

Immediately the surviving portion of the Italian Fleet is through the Straits it will scatter, in order to disperse the pursuing British Fleet as much as possible.

On the following night the battleships (three of four) that survive the ordeal, 2 cruisers, 25 destroyers, and 35 torpedo-boats will turn in and head for the nearest French ports.

If necessary, the battleships will head for Bordeaux, but on the following nights they will work their way as far north as possible, towards Calais.

The 2 cruisers, 25 destroyers, and 35 torpedo-boats will head for Brest and later a certain number of them will work their way up to St. Malo, Cherbourg, and Le Havre.

Italian Cruisers

As Italy has 21 cruisers, some 10 or 12 should get through. Two of these are required to sail with the southern flotilla from Brittany but these dispositions will still leave us 9 or 10 Italian cruisers at our disposal.

Having broken through and scattered in the Atlantic they will rendezvous at two previously selected points in the open ocean, forming two squadrons of four or five ships apiece.

The Italian cruisers are lightly armed but they have the recompense of great speed, so these two squadrons should be able to elude the British for some time. Squadrons of this strength and speed would require a considerable enemy naval force to render them important. If left at large they would be capable of seriously damaging Britain's communications with America. Therefore, however reluctant the British may be to do so, there is good reason to hope that the British Mediterranean Fleet, now considerably reduced and crippled by our 1,000 aircraft during the forcing of the Straits, will have to be sent in pursuit of them.

Disguised Parachutists

The bombing of Britain will now cease, since a few days' extra production of munitions cannot make any material difference and we must conserve our Air Force for the main operation. This ominous silence is well calculated to cause a growing fear among the British people of terrible things to come.

Instead of bombing, however, a certain number of troop-carriers, flying very high, will drop disguised parachutists; 4,000 picked men and women all of whom speak English really fluently. They will be dressed in civilian clothes but carry automatics and an iron ration to support them for three days. They will be dropped at night in specially selected areas which are very sparsely populated. Fifty per cent may become casualties, but 2,000 should manage to establish themselves in the country.

Fifth Column

During these nights a further 4,000 Fifth Columnists will be landed upon desolate stretches of the Scottish coast, from submarines and fast motor-boats. Fifty per cent may become casualties but 2,000 of them should manage to get clear and make their way south into England.

We already have 1,000 agents and Fifth Columnists established in Britain and a further 1,000 will be going in during the period under review, on faked passports or genuine British, American, and Dominion passports and as stowaways or sailors in neutral ships. These operations will therefore provide us with 6,000 Fifth Columnists in Britain before the invasion.

I believe Wheatley was right to continue to remind the War Cabinet of the potential force of Fifth Columnists. Indeed, the threat of such terrorist activity to Great Britain during the Second World War is something that hasn't truly been written about in much detail by contemporary writers.

Dual-purpose Booby Bombs

On the first night of the invasion the balance of the captured Air Force which operated in the break-through from the Mediterranean will be sent over Britain at a maximum height so as to ensure as few casualties as possible. These aircraft will carry special cargo.

Many thousands of a new type of bomb must be manufactured. They should be inflammatory bombs with a delayed-action fuse, small in size, light in weight, and capable of being inserted in various types of cardboard disguised containers.

For the purpose of containers all sorts of articles in everyday use should be copied. A good one would be the standard English gas mask box, in a variety of covers, such as is carried by the bulk of civilians. Ordinary brown-paper parcels of small size, already addressed and stamped for the post, 100 boxes of cigarettes of well-known English brands, boxes of chocolates and tins of toffee could be used. Anything which a person seeing in the street might be liable to pick up.

Each bomb will have a twelve-hour delayed-action fuse so that if it is not picked up it will go off, and a certain number of these which have alighted on roof-tops may cause fires, or at least an alarm of fire – which will serve the dual purpose of making the fire squads rush from place to place on a number of semi-false alarms and lull the British public into a false sense of security because they would believe that an air-raid with inflammable time-bombs had taken place but that the effect of these was so comparatively negligible that they were a thing to laugh at.

At the same time, on this first morning of the invasion – when they know nothing of this new trick – thousands of people will pick up parcels, boxes of cigarettes, gas-masks, etc., which it appears that somebody has dropped, and in each case when one is opened a spring will set off the mechanism causing it to flame up in their faces, blinding and scorching them.

This dual-purpose bomb would lose much of its effect if it were scattered too thickly in any one locality, so they must be spread as far as possible over every town and city in Britain.

A total of 250 aircraft carrying 1,000 of these dual-purpose bombs apiece could distribute a quarter of a million of these booby traps, which in the early hours of the first day of the invasion would tend to cause considerable trouble and dismay among the whole population.

The British Navy

We must expect a strong and clever resistance from the powerful and ably officered British Navy and it would be a mistake to expect it to fall into all the traps we shall set for it, but if we set enough of them it must fall into some of them.

Our general policy must be to have so many ships at sea from the south coast of Norway to the western end of the English Channel that the British Navy will have so many objectives offered to it that it will not know which to attack first or be able to gather from which direction the main thrusts are coming, so that in vast area of sea there will be every hope of actually landing a good proportion of our forces on the British coast.

After that we must rely for our first successes upon the activities of Fifth Columnists and parachute troops to create confusion …

General Strategy

The possibility of a successful invasion is in direct ratio to the number of planes which we can send in support of the invading force. Therefore the main attack must be delivered within the limits of range of our shortest-range fighter aircraft.

The further from our bases the landings are attempted the more vulnerable our flotillas will be to the British Navy in their passage across the sea.

Many of the small craft at our disposal are not capable of covering any great distance and other vessels would take too long in doing so. Therefore, again, our main attack must be launched within the limits of these craft.

Lastly, if the British could bring off 335,000 troops from Dunkirk in a hastily mustered armada, in spite of continuous attack by our aircraft, there is no reason at all why we should not transport 335,000 troops to the coasts of Britain by night in spite of continuous attack from a portion of the British Navy, when we are in a position to launch an armada of at least six times that size in small craft by collecting every available ship, motor-boat, and other suitable vessel from every port between Norway and the Pyrenees ...

Wheatley then went on to give a breakdown of the volume of each of the three forces Germany had at its disposal (land, sea and air). It is not deemed necessary to include that breakdown in this book (which will not furnish the reader with any additional perception). However, it is necessary to include Wheatley's note which followed that information, describing his source material. This is interesting, as it throws further light on Wheatley's circle of friends (outside the British Government):

Note

I hope that the first Axis Air Force is overestimated here, but I have little confidence that this is so and, in any case, for the operation concerned it is not proposed to use a single Reserve German or Italian plane.

The thousand gliders is far higher than my own original figure, but Dr R. G. Treviranus, the ex-Vice President of the Czechoslovakian Republic, who is extremely well versed in German affairs, tells me that 10,000 must be considered as the minimum figure.

The German submarine fleet was heavily crippled in the early months of the war but there has apparently been very little German submarine activity for many months past now. Presumably their remaining submarines were withdrawn to port in order that the veteran submarine officers and crews could train others. Is it unreasonable to suppose that Germany has been building ten small submarines per month since the outbreak of the war, suitable for use in the English Channel? If not, these ninety new ships together with ships on the stocks at the outbreak of the war and the balance of her pre-war submarine fleet would give us our 120.

Dr. Treviranus raised the question of railway ferries in a long conversation which I had with him and Mr. J. L. S. Renny on Thursday last. The doctor

states that for years past the Germans have been practising the embarkation of tanks on to these and disembarking them upon every type of coast, so that they now have the operation timed to a split second. Obviously, these ferries would be extremely vulnerable to naval attack but if Germans can create sufficient confusion in the seas between Northern Scotland and Land's End and they were guarded by a force of 2 cruisers, 20 destroyers and 25 torpedo-boats, using smoke screens, it seems at least possible that they might be able to beach a considerable percentage of them on the South Coast if they have only to make a crossing of about 80 miles.
D.W.

Wheatley then went on to detail a five-day invasion plan of Britain with landing plans and operational details, giving specifics of total numbers of men allocated to various locations around Britain and how they were to operate when on British soil to achieve total control. Again, I have chosen to leave out these specifics. To me, they are too speculative and far too long, giving us very little more by way of thought-provoking analysis on Wheatley's part.

COMMUNICATIONS AND REINFORCEMENTS

It will be noted that of our first-line aircraft we still have:

Troop Carriers	Fighters	Dive-bombers	Heavy Bombers
621	1,333	1,333	711

We are therefore in a position to reinforce our Northern, Midland, and Southern Armies by air, if necessary.

The British Navy

But it must be borne in mind that the immense naval superiority of the British Fleet will now play its part. The Axis Fleet will virtually have been wiped out and great concentrations of the remaining enemy naval forces will endeavour to cut us off and blockade the Straits of Dover.

The British Army and Air Force

By the sixth day we shall have established 325,681 troops in England in three main forces with a considerable number of tanks, a certain amount of light artillery and, in the South, a certain number of heavy guns. We shall have inflicted great damage upon the British fighting forces and shall have seriously disrupted the communications throughout the whole country, but at the beginning of the operations Britain will have approximately 1,500,000 men under arms actually in the island, and we must pay them and their supporting Air Force the compliment of believing that they will put up a most stubborn and determined resistance.

Even with our superior arms and equipment, considerable sabotage carried out by Fifth Columnists, false broadcasts delivered in English from a wireless station purporting to be the B.B.C. and air-raids of a strength and ferocity never before known in the history of man – and consequently a state of frightful confusion throughout the whole country – the actual conquest of Britain by the forces concerned would still present a most hazardous proposition. In my view it is extremely doubtful if we could succeed in subduing the whole country with a force of 300,000 men which can be maintained only by supplies, munitions, and reinforcements from the air.

For this reason the East Kent coast to a depth of at least twenty-five miles from Dover is absolutely vital to us.

Big Guns

On the sixth night of the invasion, therefore, our fifty remaining ships which have been mounted with a single big gun, landing-gear, a supply of shells, etc., should discharge their cargoes in East Kent. Such similar ships as remain unsunk that night, after the Thames Estuary operation, will also land their cargoes on the East coast of Kent in the neighbourhood of the Deal beaches.

On the French side of the Channel we shall already have established 200 big guns which will render the Channel untenable to enemy shipping during the daytime up to thirteen miles from the French coast, over a width of ten miles. With the establishment of sixty or more big guns on the Kent coast we can render the Channel untenable for enemy shipping up to thirteen miles from that coast during daylight and perhaps for a breadth of five miles.

Line of Communications

We still have over 90 submarines, 1,333 fighters, 1,333 dive-bombers and 711 heavy bombers at our disposal. These submarines and aircraft will now have the advantage of bases on both sides of the Narrows, and with this formidable force we should be able to render a belt of at least five miles wide in the Channel, between Calais and Dover, almost immune from the enemy; so that we can bring over day by day all the reinforcements we shall require, together with munitions and supplies, by means of the many medium-sized ships and small craft which survive our operations, to complete the conquest of Britain.

CONCLUSION

The operation will unquestionably be very costly, since of the 607,978 men brought over in the first five days we must reckon to lose 282,000; but this expenditure of troops is perfectly justified if they gain their objectives.

We shall have lost 5,397 aircraft out of 9,200, but it should be remembered that we have not yet drawn one single plane of any kind from our Reserves

– which stand, with captured planes, at over 10,000. So the Axis will still have an Air Force after this operation considerably greater than anything which the United States, together with the British Dominions and French Colonies, could bring against it for many months. In the meantime we shall naturally continue to build and to train pilots so that we shall have a good lead in the war with the United States which will inevitably follow.

The Axis will have lost its entire Navy, but that can be remedied now that every port in Western Europe and the dockyards of Britain will also be at our disposal. It may be another four years before we shall have acquired sufficient sea power to sweep the British and Americans from the seas of the world, but with all Europe for our building yard they could not possibly hope to keep pace with our naval production.

It may cost another quarter of a million casualties and a further 3,000 air-craft totally to subdue Britain, but the conquest of Britain means the conquest of the world; so half a million casualties, with 8,000 planes and the remnants of the two Navies, are but a small price to pay for this undertaking.

Nazi utopia for a conclusion to this paper, but the final two paragraphs do highlight the huge threat American forces would pose if the Nazis had invaded Britain (and that is probably why it never happened). Also, the Nazis didn't have the air or land forces to invade Britain and keep the country under tight control and fight off allied liberation.

An invasion of Britain would have been foolish, because as Hitler would have his legs slapped by the Russians at Stalingrad, he would most defi-nitely have had them slapped again by allied forces (in Britain).

'The word "Stalingrad" will remain emblazoned in the annals of Russian military history for all time. It was the Russians' greatest victory since the destruction of Napoleon's Grande Armée in the terrible retreat from Moscow one hundred and thirty years earlier.'
From the introduction to *The Red Verdun*
Gunmen, Gallants and Ghosts

Back in 1940, the War Office was convinced that Hitler would try and invade Britain. They also believed that the invasion would come from the east coast. Wheatley had mentioned this in his first paper but explored other alternative routes in his second. However, another major concern of Wheatley's – and a strong theme throughout his first two papers – was the use of Fifth Columnists. Wheatley knew that before the war many German refugees had sought asy-lum from the Nazis, but he couldn't be sure how many of them would rise up against Britain if invaded, or how many were planted in Britain with the sole intention of terrorist activity (unfortunately, nor could the government).

In his 1958 work *Stranger Than Fiction*, Wheatley admitted that his 'fears may now seem greatly exaggerated but … it appeared utterly beyond the capacity of M.I.5 working night and day, to check up on all these people'. Don't forget, Wheatley's wife Joan was a driver for MI5, she had inside knowledge. However, possibly – in retrospect – a little bit of knowledge was a dangerous thing.

Notes

1. Later Air Marshal Sir Lawrence Darvall, who would subsequently write the Introduction to Wheatley's *Stranger Than Fiction* (Hutchinson, 1959). Wheatley held Darvall in high esteem, not least for introducing the sub-machine gun into Britain from Italy (shortly before Italy joined forces with the Nazis), then acquiring further guns from the United States (against the wishes of his superiors).
2. It was largely due to Renny that clover-leaf barbed wire was introduced into Britain.
3. Wheatley would have been more in tune with French thinking than German, not only because of his holiday in France that ended days before the outbreak of war, but also because of his ongoing relationship with and perception of France, dating back to his time fighting there in the Great War. And, of course, there was his time in the wine trade. All of this would inspire him to write in his 1942 *V is for Vengeance*: 'As always, in French cafés of every class, politics was the principal subject of conversation. In the course of the afternoon Gregory heard a dozen apparently heated, but actually quite good-tempered, disputes between various groups of men who were either pro-British in sympathy, or wanted the whole war over and were in favour of a new deal under the Nazis.' In short, Wheatley must have felt that, on the whole, France had been totally crushed by the Nazis and therefore could not be seen as a functional ally. This would ostensibly lead to his nervousness – manifest in his papers – on hearing that the Germans had taken French ports (i.e. there was no further resistance between them and us than the Channel).
4. *War Diaries 1939–1945 Field Marshal Lord Alanbrooke*, edited by Alex Danchev and Daniel Todman (Weidenfeld & Nicolson, 2001).
5. Ibid.
6. *The Memoirs of Lord Ismay.*

VI

Style and the British Empire

'An old fort. There are dozens of them dotted along the East Coast of England, and the South Coast too. They were built when Napoleon threatened to invade England with the army of Boulogne in 1802.'
Black August
Dennis Wheatley

I would like to take some time to explain a little bit about Wheatley's ideology and style with reference to his novels. This will give the reader a clearer picture of where the energy, enthusiasm and imagination of Wheatley's war papers came from.

Dennis Wheatley wrote his first novel *The Forbidden Territory* in 1932, creating the character of the Duc de Richleau, who would play a large part in Wheatley's most famous novel *The Devil Rides Out* (1934). It is mainly because of characters such as De Richleau that Wheatley's novels are no longer in print. Most of his books are filled with counts – the nobility – and the stuffy prose of the 'well off'. This has alienated certain readers today who demand a more gritty – liberal – style.

Wheatley frequently met Lords, politicians, royalty and high ranking officers throughout his life. He wrote about the circles he lived and worked in (not unlike Agatha Christie in that respect). But although Wheatley's work was incredibly popular for nearly fifty years (1932–1980), and remained with the same publisher during that time (Hutchinson), his books have sadly lost popularity and can only really be found on the collector's market today, where they command high prices.

Actor Christopher Lee (who played De Richleau in the Hammer movie version of *The Devil Rides Out*) knew Wheatley personally, and explains the demise of Wheatley's popularity as the decay of society, where traditional standards are lost: 'In a way, it's a very good thing that he is not alive to see what has happened today – in my opinion, the virtual breakdown of discipline in this country and in many others.'[1] Men no longer retire to the smoking room, dinner is no longer a family meal at table with an expensive cuvée. People – readers – are alienated from the world Wheatley created in his novels because time has moved on. Wheatley did write for his day. His Second World War novels are crammed with research appertaining to the war effort, for example as he wrote in *'V' is for Vengence* (1942):

> From the 8th of August onwards a large part of every news bulletin was devoted to the doings of the Luftwaffe. For a fortnight it concentrated upon Allied shipping and the nearest British ports. Dover harbour was reported as blocked with wrecks, and all the Thanet towns in ruins. Then the Germans carried their raids much further inland, attacking all the air bases in south and south-eastern England, and penetrating as far as London.

Indeed, books like *'V' is for Vengeance* and *The Man Who Missed the War* (1945)[2] owe much to the research and ideas he put into his war papers for the Joint Planning Staff, so the contemporary reader does have a problem relating to that past time.

'The British Navy had more important things to do during major war than send valuable personnel to inspect a derelict string of rafts, and Philip, realizing this, now began to feel despondent of their chances.'
The Man Who Missed the War

The intelligence in the above piece is exposed in the opening chapter of his occult novel *To the Devil – A Daughter* (1953), when describing the thriller writer Molly Fountain (one of the main characters in the book):

> Very soon she found that her war-time experiences had immensely improved her abilities as a writer. Thousands of hours spent typing staff papers had imbued her with a sense of how best to present a series of factors logically, clearly and with the utmost brevity. Moreover, in her job she had learned how the secret services really operated; so, without giving away any official secrets, she could give her stories an atmosphere of plausibility which no amount of imagination could quite achieve.

So Wheatley was both proud of and grateful to his work for the War Cabinet, as he continued to confirm in *To the Devil – A Daughter*, by even quoting his book *Stranger Than Fiction*, a book solely concerned with his war papers:

> Molly Fountain's books were … always mystery thrillers with a background of secret service. No one knew better than she that truth really was stranger than fiction; yet she never deliberately based a plot upon actual happenings to which she had been privy during the war.

Wheatley was a traditionalist and loved history, indeed he would weave it into his writings whenever possible. For example, in his book *Gunmen, Gallants and Ghosts*, he couldn't help but include some historical pieces, saying in his introduction to *When the Reds Seized the City of Gold*: 'I can only hope that most of my readers do not suffer from a positive dislike of history.' In truth, I don't think Wheatley really cared if his reader did or didn't like history, they would get it anyway.

Today, Dennis Wheatley is generally known for his occult fiction, not just *The Devil Rides Out*, but *The Haunting of Toby Jugg* (dedicated to the RAF and using a pilot as the central character), *To the Devil – A Daughter* (another book turned into a Hammer movie starring Christopher Lee). But even in his occult non-fiction, *The Devil and All His Works*, he used history as the pivotal juxtaposition for his arguments that devil worshipping is not just a thing of the past, but an Art being performed in the very suburban road you are living in. And there we have it: history influencing today. That was Wheatley's style. But unfortunately, today is now yesterday, and like any other topical writer he/she soon becomes dated, and loses relevance to a contemporary audience. The cold war novel has ceased to be, as will novels concerning 'weapons of mass destruction' in the future.

So Wheatley's stuffy style, intermixed with his topical themes, has lost him his popularity over the years. A great shame, because novels such as *Black August* (1934), which took him nine months to write, concerned a British civil war and remains to this day an excellent thriller.

Like so many good cold war novels, Dennis Wheatley's thrillers are waiting for a renaissance. Personally, I feel that that renaissance will only occur through the collector's market. An expensive education for contemporary audiences, with over seventy titles to track down and purchase in first edition alone.

'"The army," Gregory laughed. "The whole country round here is peppered with those pill-boxes; you'll find them even miles inland. They were put up in the German invasion scare of 1916."'
Black August

One can always learn from yesterday's fiction. But maybe something more: throughout this book, I discuss Wheatley's patriotism, his passion for the diminishing British Empire. He wasn't the only one. Lord Ismay came out with some wonderfully patriotic quotes in his memoirs, and there is a growing sense of patriotism in Britain in the new millennium. We see this – in an obvious sense – every time our national football team plays a major game, especially against Germany or Argentina.

'I used often to feel homesick when serving overseas, and the first sight of the white cliffs of Dover after a long absence never failed to give me a

thrill of pride and thankfulness. The greyer the skies, the more homely seemed the welcome. And when I left for abroad again, I always uttered a silent prayer that I might come back again in due season to the land of my fathers. But I never realized how precious England was to me until she was in imminent danger of violation.'
The Memoirs of Lord Ismay

Notes

1. Quote sources from Clive Barker's *A–Z of Horror*, compiled by Stephen Jones (BBC Books, 1997).

2. The central theme of *The Man Who Missed the War* was raft convoys, moved by the Gulf Stream and prevailing winds, which was one of the Joint Planning Staff war paper ideas. Also, the book was dedicated to Iris Sutherland, 'who was my invaluable secretary through the dark days of 1941–42, and who has now most generously given up her rest days from her war job to deciphering my hand-written manuscript, in order that a fair typed copy of this present book should reach my publishers and readers with a minimum delay'. The Dedication was dated VE Day 1945.

VII

Village Defence

'Perhaps there are no paving-stones in your village. All right, then. Take the headstones from the graveyard ... Those headstones are memorials to the women of Britain whose sons, husbands, and lovers died at Waterloo, at Balaclava, and at Ladysmith. They mark the resting-place of men who fought and bled to make Britain great across the Seven Seas, and a quarter of a century ago at Ypres, the Somme, and Mons. If they could rise again they would carry their headstones for you, and at this hour they are with you still in spirit to strengthen your hearts in the defence of all that they have loved.'
'Village Defence'

Wheatley's next paper ran to nearly 12,000 words and was inspired by the ideas from his last (the novelty of writing from the enemy's point of view).

The paper was titled 'Further Measures' and was presented to Darvell around 28 June 1940 (only a week after Wheatley presented the last paper). On 6 July Darvell asked Wheatley to lunch at the RAF Club in Piccadilly. Darvell made it clear to Wheatley the impact his papers were having. 'Since we last met,' Darvell said. 'You have acquired a new, small, but very exclusive public. All three of the Chiefs-of-staff have read your papers on invasion.'[1]

Wheatley was amazed, but it was made clear to him that he brought a different perspective to the military solutions being sought by the War Cabinet. The military had been taught at staff college to regard war as a matter of definite rules; but Hitler didn't abide by the rules and Wheatley knew that, as he mentioned in *Stranger Than Fiction*:

> His aircraft had machine-gunned refugees on roads as a deliberate military operation. His troops had used captive women as defence screens when advancing against opposition. His submarines had sunk defenceless liners and merchant ships and left their crews to drown. His Gestapo were not content to shoot persons whom they believed to be spies, but first tortured them.

Wheatley and Darvell discussed the abominations that would occur if Hitler successfully invaded Britain, but it didn't turn them off their lunch. In fact, Darvell let Wheatley into his confidence. He told him that he was a member of the Joint Planning Staff (JPS) of the War Cabinet. He explained that the department was formed in 1937 with one officer from each of the three forces (Navy, Army and Air Force), who worked together – for the first time – in order to co-ordinate a 'higher thinking of the three services'.[2]

In 1939 the JPS was expanded to nine officers. Two commanders RN, two majors, and two wing commanders formed the basic unit, with a more senior team consisting of a captain RN, a lieutenant colonel and a group captain. Later, this senior unit became the Strategic Planning Section and two more teams were formed. Headed by the Rt Hon. Oliver Stanley, they came under the title of Future Operations Planning Section (FOPS). The officers in this latter group formed Winston Churchill's personal staff.

The job of the JPS was to prepare draft plans for every type of operation of war, and to advise – in consultation with the Foreign Office and other ministries – on policy, future strategy, and the tasks to be given to the commanders in theatre.

In his memoirs, Field Marshal Montgomery described the Joint Planning Staff's reports as containing 'a compromise recommendation', because it consisted of the Directors of Plans from the three services. He didn't hold the JPS in very high regard and generally disagreed with their recommendations.

Perfect or flawed, Churchill's select strategists were fifteen officers in number (increasing to approximately twenty after 1942), and were totally responsible for the activities of 9,000,000 men and women in uniform.

Wheatley listened to Darvell with great interest. He was told that some of his ideas had posed some very serious questions, which were now being circulated to the Operational and Intelligence Departments in the Service Ministries for comment and further action. Furthermore, Wheatley was told that parts of his paper 'The Invasion and Conquest of Britain' had been included in a report that Churchill examined to counter a possible invasion.

Feeling quite humbled now, Wheatley asked if there was anything else he could do to assist. Darvell told him that he could write another paper. He went on to say that for some time the government had been recruiting men, especially those too old to join the armed forces, as Local Defence Volunteers. They would be brought together to police their local towns and villages from the threat of enemy parachute troops and potential terrorist attacks. The new title for these volunteers would be the Home Guard. Darvell asked Wheatley to detail in his paper how the Home Guard could be utilised for village defence. Over the next two nights (6/7 July 1940) Wheatley wrote his paper, immediately sending it to Darvell on completion:

Village Defence

Unity is Strength. The enemy is at our gates and our Prime Minister has said that every village must now be ready to defend itself. For that, the first essential is the spirit of mutual trust. There must be no continuation or any coolness between church and chapel folk, no harbouring of old grudges between landlord and tenant, no bickering between the chiefs of the different Village Emergency Services.

It Is nearly 900 years since Britain was invaded, but after these centuries of peace, while we have grown great through battles fought on foreign soil, our meadows, our farmsteads, our villages are threatened again. We can learn good lessons from ancient times when each village was a strong, self-reliant community. Let it be said of us – as it was said of Rome when Rome, then little more than a village, was attacked by the Etruscans and Horatius held the Bridge – *'None were for a party and all were for the State.'*

Arms

Arms are now pouring from our factories and reaching us from across the seas in ever-increasing numbers, but the first call on supplies is naturally for our Fighting Services, which are mobilizing thousands more men every day. After that coastal villages must have preference, so it may be a little time yet before you can get machine-guns, hand-grenades, or even modern rifles; but don't let that depress you or hold you up in your initial preparations for defence for one single moment.

We all know the fire power of modern weapons and that a single man with a Tommy-gun may quell a mob, but *you* are not going to stand about to be shot at, like a lot of nitwits, in a crowd.

When the time comes you must be under cover. The Germans should find the village silent and apparently deserted. There won't be any human beings in sight for them to aim at, and even a well-aimed brick will knock out a motor-cyclist with a machine-gun if the motor-cyclist is not looking in the direction from which the brick is thrown.

In the Spanish Civil War villagers often held up well-trained troops, and even tackled tanks, although in most cases they had only the most rudimentary arms. I refuse to believe that the men and women of Britain will be less courageous in the defence of their homes than the men and women of Spain. No one expects you to hurl back the spearhead of a German armoured division, but you can delay it. Skilful planning, quick action and resolution can often offset superior arms; and remember, in any German invasion we shall have an enormous superiority in numbers.

Obviously, Wheatley had outlined some ways to protect local towns and villages from invasion in his first paper; he now had to tailor some of those ideas to meet the criteria of this new one.

Village Meetings

Hand-printed notices should be posted up at once at the village post-office, the church, the village hall, the police station, and the school, convening a meeting for the following day at the most suitable place (the time and place to have been decided in consultation between the Chief of the Local Defence Force, the Chief A.R.P. Warden, the Chief of the local Fire-fighting Unit and the vicar).

In cases where schools have not been evacuated the schoolmaster should instruct the children to warn their parents. The village policeman, the village nurse, and the scout troop will warn the occupants of outlying farms in the village area. It should be made quite clear that in this national emergency it is obligatory upon every man, woman, and child over ten years of age to attend.

Crusade

The notices should also bear an announcement that the vicar will hold a short half-hour service before the meeting for those who wish to attend.

The service should open with a cheerful hymn – perhaps 'All Things Bright and Beautiful'. The vicar should then give a short address from the pulpit. He might even take as his unorthodox text the title of the hymn and point out how God has blessed our own land more than any other in the beauties of the countryside, which we and our forefathers have enjoyed in peace for so many centuries. He should then speak of the Nazi regime and all it stands for: the suppression of free thought, the enslavement of peoples, turning them from human beings into machines, and the denial of their right to worship God in their own fashion. He should remind his listeners that Hitler is a professed atheist, and that he has persecuted not only the Jews but also the Catholics and the Protestants, casting into prison the clergy who refuse to place him before their God – just as the pagan Emperors cast St. Peter and St. Paul into prison. He should show that Christianity is just as much threatened today by the Mohammedans when they thundered at the gates of Budapest and by the Moors when they swept up out of Africa across Spain. He should end on the note that for the salvation of Christendom we are once more fighting a crusade. It is not England alone that we defend; but we, the followers of Christ, are now waging war in very fact against the forces of Evil. When England was last invaded the Bishops and the priests led out the people under the banner of the Cross; and so today the Church must once more become militant and lead the people in defence of their homes and spiritual freedom.

The service should end with 'Land of Hope and Glory', after which the vicar, carrying the Cross before him, should lead his congregation to the meeting.

Heavy words indeed. Quite interesting that Wheatley should use a capital letter for the word 'Evil', but by the start of the Second World War he knew much about the Black Art, having researched and written *The Devil Rides Out*, in 1934. But 'Evil' is an overused word nowadays, especially when we discuss anything that appals us personally, such as the small boy who stamps on an ant in the back garden. There are levels of the evil act, as Frederick Forsyth correctly wrote in his novel *The Odessa File*, when an old Jew recollects his plight under Nazi Germany: 'I bear no hatred nor bitterness towards the German people, for they are a good people. Peoples are not evil; only individuals are evil.'

Election of Leaders

At present there is a chaotic muddle between the various local Services – in many cases the Local Defence Force has come off worst in this, as the most virile and patriotic inhabitants of the area joined the A.R.P. or Fire-fighting Service many months ago and their old chiefs now refuse to release them for any other duties. This is all wrong and there must be a new deal which will enable the village to become a coherent and easily functioning unit. All hatchets must be buried for the common cause, and with a spirit of absolute goodwill each service must, if necessary, release its members for new duties so that the very best can be got out of each individual in the task to which he is best suited.

At the village meeting three people – but not more – should speak, stating these facts, and one of the three should definitely be a woman. They should then ask the assembly to suggest names for a Committee of Defence.

This Committee should not be a large one, otherwise nothing will get done, and each person on it should have some definite responsibility so that it is modelled upon the War Council, which is the inner body of the Cabinet. Five people are sufficient and they should represent (a) Labour (b) First Aid (c) Communications, (d) Supplies and (e) Defence.

No rule can be laid down about age, but at least one – and preferably two people – on the Committee should be under thirty-five. Don't elect the vicar or the lady of the manor unless you have real confidence in them as active, go-ahead people. Class and wealth must play no part in this issue and the Committee must be elected solely on the grounds that the people appointed are popular and the best qualified for the job that they have to do. Various names should be put up for each seat on the Committee and the members elected by a secret ballot carried out on the spot with a slip of paper.

This election by ballot will enable communities to get rid of their Chief A.R.P. warden if he has proved slack and inefficient, or the Chief of their Local Defence Force if they consider him too old or too woolly to make a really good fighting leader. The election should be carried out at the meeting and concluded there, so that no time is given for lobbying or for pressure to be brought to bear by local big-wigs who want to be in the limelight, and that when the meeting closes the job is done and the people disperse with the feeling that they have appointed the men and women best-suited for the job. And the Defence Committee, having been elected, should immediately go into session with full powers from both the Government and their neighbours to act and order for the benefit of all concerned.

LABOUR

The principal qualification for the Labour chief should be popularity. He or she will be the only Committee member who will have no command, except a small staff, but the Labour chief's function is to supply the other four Committee members with the right people for the right jobs.

Allocation
Roughly speaking, the Labour chief should allocate:
    (a) All youths and men between the ages of sixteen and forty-five to Defence.
    (b) All men over forty-five and a considerable number of the women to Supplies.
    (c) The local scout troop, all boys between the ages of ten and sixteen, and a few women who have horses, if available, to Communications.
    (d) All other women to First Aid.
    (e) Invalids and cripples under either Supplies or First Aid, according to their capabilities.

Overlapping
Naturally, at first, there will be considerable overlapping, as people who have already volunteered for one Service may be found more suitable for another, but the Labour chief will have the final ruling in this. The Services concerned must show good will and realize that a large amount of reorganization and allocation to new duties may be necessary if the best is to be got out of each individual for the common support.

Census
The Labour chief should act on the general allocation given above without delay, but naturally he will exercise common sense in the allocation of certain specialists, such as doctor, blacksmith, garage man, etc. Having got matters going, he will take the earliest opportunity, with the assistance of the Parish Council, to get out a complete census of all the inhabitants in the village area so that he can see that not a single pair of hands remains idle.

Working Parties
To assist the Supply chief it may sometimes be necessary to call on the Defence chief to lend his men for unloading supplies which may come from the Government, or for other work, so the Labour chief should compile lists of people suitable to be called on for a special job outside their sphere when required.

Strangers

The Labour chief should take special pains to prove beyond doubt the identity of any strangers who may be residing in the village. If they resent inquiries – which they have no right to do in such a time of national emergency – the village policeman must be called in, since they may be Fifth Columnists. If the inquiries do not prove absolutely satisfactory, and the policeman cannot obtain an internment order, he must be made responsible for any such strangers and given a squad of children to watch them. There is no law against watching anybody in this country, and he will thus be placed in possession of their movements every time they leave their residence. It may even be possible to give the police powers to place suspicious persons under temporary arrest at a time of crisis.

FIRST AID

Children

Children (boys under ten and girls under fourteen) come under the First Aid chief. If they have not already been evacuated, they should be evacuated at the first alarm, in charge of the curate and the schoolmistress. If it is uncertain as to whether or not the neighbouring villages are in the hands of the enemy, the children should be taken to any caves, disused quarries, or woods in the neighbourhood to afford them as much shelter as possible.

A.R.P

A.R.P. is *not* active defence. Therefore it is a woman's job, and women wardens should be called on to give instructions to other women to fill the ranks of A.R.P. where gaps have been left by men required for Defence, Supply, and Communications.

Nursing

Naturally, women who have done a course of First Aid will come into this category, unless they are required for other work at which they are experts. Such women should duplicate the duties of A.R.P. and First Aid.

Casualty Station

If a Casualty Station has not already been chosen one should be selected at once, and the stronger the building the better. The thick walls of the church will certainly resist blast from any but heavy bombs, and anything but systematic pounding from light artillery, which is all that the Germans will be able to bring over in aircraft. Moreover, its pews make ready-made beds, and a number of these in the best-protected portion of the building should be furnished with spare mattresses, Lilos, and cushions. Nearby windows should be boarded up if boards are available, as a good stout board will take the pep out of machine-gun bullets, fired from low-flying enemy aircraft. If wood is too scarce, the windows should at least be covered with sacking to prevent flying glass.

Churches have been used from time to time immemorial for this work of mercy, and there is no reason whatever why they should not be so used again today. If the church is selected as the Casualty Station, and it has a lych gate, this should be removed to facilitate the entrance of stretcher-bearer parties.

If the church is not considered suitable, the village school is usually a stout building, so this provides a possible alternative; and churches should certainly not be selected where they are on private estates some distance from the village. It is essential that casualty clearing stations should be in fairly central positions.

Staff
The local doctor is the obvious choice for the chief of First Aid, and on his staff would be the village nurse, any other professional nurses residing in the area, the midwife, and the village curate.

Stretcher-Bearers
Stretcher-bearer parties should be formed from strongly built farm girls, as two of these are quite capable of carrying a wounded man, and all men except specialists are required for Defence.

COMMUNICATIONS

The village scoutmaster, schoolmaster, or vicar would prove a likely candidate for Communications chief, as such a man will be in touch with the boys who will be working under him.

Headquarters
He should make his headquarters the village post-office, and, if possible, he should be somebody who knows Morse so that he can send a message over the telegraph in an emergency if the village postmistress is not available.

The Defence force will not concentrate in one strong-point but will occupy a number of strong-points according to its size. The Communications chief will, therefore, have to make arrangements for the central redoubt to be kept in touch with all its posts and with the world beyond the village through the post-office or by other means.

Post-office
The post-office should be held as one of the strong-points, and it is most important that when its capture becomes imminent all apparatus and Morse transmitters should be completely destroyed.

Field Telephones
Quite a number of scout troops and amateur electricians have field telephone sets or, if the village is a large one and it has a wireless shop, the means are to hand of making portable field telephones. By every means in his power

the Communications chief should endeavour to secure such sets and with them run wires:
   (a) From the post-office to the central redoubt.
   (b) From the central redoubt to all strong-points.
   (c) To the villages on either side of him if wire permits.

Flag Signalling
He should also select boys who have learnt Morse and semaphore in scout troops, and post them in places where messages can be relayed from one part of the village area to another. If such boys are not available, a class must be formed for instruction at once and semaphore signalling is a thing which is very easy to pick up.

Runners, Cyclists, Horsewomen
In addition, he will select certain boys as runners to carry messages by hand in the event of all other communications with neighbouring villages and the latter will prove particularly useful as they can ride across country by the shortest routes.

Liaison with Military
Gamekeepers who know the country should be placed in touch with the nearest military force. They can then be sent off to give information about the strength and position of advancing enemy forces and lead out troops to the scene of action by the quickest cross-country route.

Hand Trolleys
If a railway runs near the village any hand trolleys that are available should be retained, as these can move at considerable speed and a messenger can be sent on them down the line to the next station if communications are cut.

Bush Telegraph
In addition to the aforementioned means of signalling, a system of bush telegraph should be devised to carry a few very urgent orders. Toy drums or trumpets will serve for this.

Look-outs
The Communications chief should arrange to have sentries posted by night and day to keep a look-out. The church tower is one obvious place, but look-outs should also be posted in woods or fields, concealed a mile or so away, on each road leading to the village, to give information at once when they hear gunfire or see any signs of an enemy approach.

Patrol Wire
Communications chiefs can assist both the civil and military authorities in their area by using some of their boys to patrol telegraph wires, military field

telephones, and electric cables in the district and report any breaks through sabotage or other enemy action. Obviously this would not be possible with a full-scale battle in progress, but if enemy parachutists land in the neighbourhood they may, before they are mopped up, manage to sever certain communications, and a swift report as to where the damage has been done will prove of great use in enabling the authorities to get the break mended speedily.

Telegraph Poles

In addition to maintaining communications for their own Defence force, Communications chiefs will be responsible for sabotaging communications when the capture of the village becomes imminent.

Telegraph poles on either side of the village can be partially cut through in advance and secured firmly with supports, so that in an emergency the supporters can be knocked away and the wires brought down.

Electricity

If the village has a sub-power-station this should also be a strong-point and measures taken to ensure the destruction of the apparatus before capture, otherwise the enemy may use it for operating his wireless-sets or charging his batteries.

Crossroads

Signposts have been removed but enemy agents and Fifth Columnists may lightly bury tins or boxes giving an identification of locality or directions to enemy parachutists. Therefore the ditches and hedges near crossroads should be searched daily.

Signs

Communications chiefs should inspect their area for any hoardings, advertisements or other signs which give away the identification of their locality. Village clubs and golf clubs often have the name of their village upon them, while house agents' boards generally give the name of the nearest town. The signs on public-houses are also liable to give the enemy information as to the point at which he has arrived; particularly if their names are unusual. All these, including the name of the village on the post-office, police station, and railway-station lamps and seats should be either removed or blanked out.

Boats

If the village is on a river the majority of the small boats in the neighbourhood should be concealed in barns under gathered crops, and arrangements should be made for the rest to be destroyed on the approach of the enemy.

Whoever takes on communications should have two or three good people on the staff to whom he can delegate special duties, such as training boys in signalling, supervising look-outs, inspecting crossroads, etc.

SUPPLIES

This is a most important post, and it should be given to someone – a man or woman – who is a really good organizer. The Government will render all the help that is possible, but time is now a vital factor and village communities must do every mortal thing they can to provide for their own requirements in everything except modern arms and ammunition, the production of which is being pushed forward with all possible speed.

Staff

There are so many things which a Supply chief will have to attend to that apart from specialists, such as ex-soldiers, the doctor, the scoutmaster, etc. – who will naturally be posted to other sections – he should be given the brains of the community to work under him. His lieutenants will be:

(a) Treasurer
(b) President of the Women's Institute
(c) The local builder or estate carpenter
(d) The village blacksmith
(e) The village garage proprietor
(f) A good cattle-man
(g) The local Stationmaster or carrier

Treasurer

Pending the arrival of Government supplies the community must purchase certain items, such as cement, petrol, paraffin, building materials, disinfectants, etc., which cannot be manufactured locally. Further, certain men – such as blacksmiths, builders' labourers, etc – will have to go on a whole-time job and they must be paid a full-time wage so that they can keep going like other people.

We all know that the calls upon the nation's generosity have been heavy, but now is the time when national needs must give way to local needs. Charity begins at home, and it is incumbent upon every single person in the village to give lavishly according to their means, so that in the coming days, every hour of which is precious, work may not be held up but can be financed at once from a local defence fund.

The money should, however, only be used to pay wages where this is essential and to buy such materials from the local builder and others as these people cannot possibly afford to give.

Stores

The Supply chief will appoint a number of people to comb the whole district for materials, and they should all be patriotic, persuasive beggars … items should be collected into a common store and issued as required. If the village school is not being used as the First Aid post, that would make an excellent quartermaster's store, otherwise the village hall might serve.

All firearms, picks, shovels, carpenters' tools, and other returnable objects should be listed, with the names of their owners and the person to whom they are issued …

The paper continued along these same lines for some time, occasionally reiterating certain points raised in 'Resistance to Invasion'. Then, Wheatley decides to talk more directly about death:

Gravestones

Perhaps there are no paving-stones in your village. All right, then. Take the headstones from the graveyard for your redoubt. These are just the right shape and will serve even better because they are larger. This is not sacrilege. Those headstones are memorials to the women of Britain whose sons, husbands, and lovers died at Waterloo, at Balaclava, and at Ladysmith. They mark the resting-place of men who fought and bled to make Britain great across the seven seas, and a quarter of a century ago at Ypres, the Somme, and Mons. If they could rise again they would carry their headstone for you, and at this hour they are with you still in spirit to strengthen your hearts in the defence of all that they have loved.

I don't think any paragraph could be more typical of Dennis Wheatley than the one just read. Wheatley fought at the Somme, and the vision of someone rising from the grave to carry their own headstone is in line with the more macabre offerings in his fiction. Then there is that undercurrent of pride in the old British Empire. But that is fine, because he basically speaks sacrilege and has to explain himself, to win over his audience again.

Kill Your Man

When you see the enemy do not have compassion on him if he happens to be a young, fair-faced boy. Don't say to yourself, 'Well, after all, he's not so different from my own son except that he wears a different uniform, and in any case it's a dirty trick to shoot him while he is not looking.'

Remember that if that young German had a little more brains and guts he would be in the Nazi Air Force, then switch your mind back to the women and children of France and Belgium who were mercilessly massacred by machine-gunning from the air. If he had the chance, that German would do the same thing to your wife and children, and should they become refugees he *will* do it at the first opportunity if you let him live.

Wounded Germans are especially dangerous. As they are well armed you want their weapons and ammunition, but a wounded German will kill you if he can when you go out into the open to take his automatic rifle or pistol from him.

Therefore, whenever you get the chance, don't hesitate, but shoot to kill. *That is your duty.* And you owe it to your friends and your country.

GENERAL

On looking through this paper you may say: 'But how can we do all this when there are so many things – all of which are urgent – to be done?' Away with that thought instantly! Many hands make light work. Get busy and you will amaze yourselves at the progress you will make even in a few evenings or a week-end. These are the things to be done:

1. Call a meeting at once, forget all old quarrels and jealousies and elect your leaders.
2. Never mind what war work people have been doing up till now. A.R.P. and fire-fighting must give way to active Defence. Each service must support the Labour chief by willingly accepting his decisions.
3. Make your appeal for money and supplies at the initial meeting so that no time is lost. Everybody can contribute something – even the children will contribute their toy soldiers willingly if they know that they are to be melted down into bullets.
4. Select the site of your redoubt, strong-points, and road barriers. Even a hamlet of twenty people can make one road barrier and a redoubt into which to retire. A village with 100 inhabitants can make two road barriers, two strong-points and a redoubt, as road barriers constitute only a first line of defence and out of 100 adults one should be able to raise twenty-five fighting men – six for each of the strong-points and twelve for the redoubt. Larger villages can do better, according to their size. A village of 500 inhabitants should be able to man a road barrier on each of its three, four or five roads and rough Boundary Defence between them; and the defenders should be numerous enough to hold five or six strong-points and the redoubt when they retire.
5. Remember that road barriers must not be erected until the military give the order, otherwise you will block the movements of our own troops. Outer barriers of carts, old cars filled with earth, etc., should be assembled on the roadside in advance so that they can be drawn across at a few moments' notice by the defenders. Inner barriers in the village street itself can be made while the Defence is in progress by women throwing oil, manure, and broken glass on to the roads.
6. At the first alarm being given the Defence force should hurry to the Defence Boundary, while the women bury the food, man the casualty station and see to the evacuation of the children and the cattle.
7. Do not waste powder and shot upon tanks or attack them unless you find yourself very close to one. The military will take care of the tanks further

along the road, but tanks must be supported by enemy motor-cyclists and infantry and it is these that really are your pigeon. If one of your marksmen can spot an enemy cyclist as he comes round the bend of the road, the whole column will probably halt for a few moments while the enemy motor-cyclists take cover, as they have no means of knowing if they are up against you or a strong force of British troops, and every moment that you can delay the enemy is of value.

8. Delay – delay – delay. That is your function. Don't retire to your strong-points until you have sustained a few casualties; and when you do get to your strong-points, hold them as long as you possibly can. Don't fire from your redoubt at all until you have something really worth firing at. Then let the enemy have it good and strong.

9. Above all, don't rely upon support from neighbouring villages or attempt to give it to them. Even trying to keep in touch with them is a waste of valuable men once the action is on, and you have given the alarm to the nearest villages in your neighbourhood. If a village Defence force attempts to cross country it will only be cut to pieces by machine-gunning from the air, whereas by sitting tight in its strong-points and redoubt it can hamper the enemy enormously. For support, each village must rely upon regular troops, which will come to its assistance wherever possible; but it must be absolutely self-dependent, and there must be no question of retiring from it as, quite apart from any question of heroics, its defenders will not only serve their country better but stand more chance of coming through alive.

10. If you have a flagstaff in the village, get a Union Jack and nail it to the mast. Every one of us is in the front line now, and what would your life be worth to you under the jackboot of the Nazis? A new and great adventure has come into the lives of us all, and it is in that spirit that we should forget our personal worries and the perils that may lie before us. For these summer weeks we shall be together in a new sense. Out of these days will blossom undying friendship and as great a chance to cover ourselves with glory as ever Drake's men had against the Spanish foe.

Roll up, then. Not an hour's delay. Heat up the forge. Get out the guns. Collect the spades. Let's hear the hammers ring on wood and nails. You *can* turn your village into a fortress *without* waiting for the Royal Engineers to help you or for supplies from the Government. Remember that we are the champions of Light facing the creeping tide of Darkness which threatens to engulf the world. Every man and woman must rise in answer to the call; so that in a thousand years the valour of our generation shall still be told and hearts shall quicken to hear the tale of how Britain stood alone – but triumphant.

Again, Wheatley talks of the powers of 'Light' and 'Darkness'. Note the capital letters and the religious connotations. Wheatley's mind was naturally drawn to the threat of 'evil' in the world. It isn't something I want to overplay in this book, but one cannot ignore the fact that the author had more than a flirtation with men of Power. And by Power I mean occultists. This is well documented in Wheatley's non-fiction of the occult *The Devil and All His Works* (Hutchinson, 1971). Since at least the Great War, Wheatley was aware of the powers of the occult and how dangerous they were. He always kept his distance, but – to this day – his most memorable works are those which include the occult (especially in his fiction). Indeed *They Used Dark Forces* (Hutchinson, 1964) mixes the Nazis and the occult quite chillingly.

Notes

1. This conversation was documented by Wheatley in *Stranger Than Fiction* (Hutchinson, 1959).
2. As detailed by Wheatley in *Stranger Than Fiction*, op. cit.

VIII

Inspiration and A New Gibraltar

'That afternoon a submarine had suddenly popped up and ordered them to take to the boats; the captain had refused, upon which the British submarine began to shell them and put a shot into their bows. Fortunately an Italian aircraft came on the scene so the submarine was compelled to submerge and the Frenchmen got away … '
'A New Gibraltar'

Wheatley saw writing as his major contribution to the war effort. Even if a small percentage of his thoughts and opinions were incorporated into the reports and orders of the War Cabinet, he would deem his civilian war papers valid documents, and rightly so.

Since 'Resistance to Invasion', he had copied all his papers to friends in various parts of the government[1], not just the War Cabinet[2]. He felt comfortable with this idea because he had not been given any intelligence to assist him. The papers were therefore unclassified and, ostensibly, anyone could read them.

He received much praise in return, as Colonel Balfour-Davey's letter dated 18 June confirms:

> I thought you would like to know that your paper on 'Resistance to Invasion' has been a great success. On further consideration, I gave it first to the Home Defence people. The chap who read it described it as extraordinarily interesting. They have sent it to G.H.Q. Home Forces, and a copy has gone to the Director of Home Defence here.

On 17 July Wheatley received an official letter of thanks from the Deputy Director of Military Operations, who added that he would be glad to have any other ideas on the subject.

This feedback must explain why Wheatley worked so hard on his papers. Often he would write throughout the night, producing approximately 15,000 words over a two-day period and delivering the final product to the JPS the following day. He knew he had something valid to contribute, but his other spur – as we have already analysed – was his (and the British public's) fear of enemy invasion.[3] Wheatley believed that the threat of invasion was on Britain as soon as the Germans had successfully invaded France and taken control of the ports.

So there were many things working in juxtaposition, and Wheatley more than had his spur. It was only a week after 'Village Defence' that he penned his next paper. This was at Darvall's wishes again (14 or 15 July 1940). The Prime Minister had demanded that his Chiefs of Staff come up with a plan to hit back at the Nazis after Dunkirk (obviously Wheatley knew nothing of this but Darvall's request would be enough incentive to write such a paper). Wheatley went home, pinned up a map of Europe on his library shelves and stared at it for literally hours until an idea came. It was late in the evening when the idea of 'A New Gibraltar' struck him. The paper was written between 15 and 17 July 1940:

A New Gibraltar

The Still Small Village

'The Navy is magnificent! The Air Force is performing miracles. On the few occasions that it has had a chance to get at the enemy the Army has put up a splendid show.' That is the sort of thing everybody is saying, but sooner or later in every group that discusses the war somebody pipes up a little hesitantly, 'Still, it would be nice if we could take the offensive sometimes for a change.'

Part of the Army's problem was neatly explained by Field Marshal Lord Carver in his excellent book *Britain's Army in the 20th Century* (Macmillan, 1998):

[by April 1940] the army had become involved in the first of those strategic mismanagements and tactical failures which were to dog its path and tarnish its reputation in the first three years of the war, the campaign in Norway. This originated in the British and French desire to deprive Germany of iron ore from the mines in northern Sweden ...

It took time to give the Army direction, let alone give them the equipment they needed. However, in his memoirs, Field Marshal Montgomery blamed 'Whitehall' for the mess the Army was in at the outset of the Second World War: ' ... the appointment of Gort to command the B.E.F. was a mistake. I have never departed from that view, and am still of the same opinion.' However, he went on to say: 'The first point to understand is that the campaign in France and Flanders in 1940 was lost in Whitehall in the years before it ever began, and this cannot be stated too clearly or too often.' Montgomery was disgusted that two major appointments were made at the time of war being declared (Gort, BEF; Ironside, CIGS). They were faced with an almost impossible task, so straight away the task was uphill for the British Army.

Wheatley's paper continued:

> If there is a serving officer among the crowd he patiently explains that we must wait until our new armies are fully equipped and that it is impossible to launch an offensive until we have more planes. While to any suggestion that for once we should move a jump ahead of Hitler and occupy a neutral position, the reply is that we can't do that because we should give umbrage to the Americans. Nevertheless when the group disperses the uninitiated go away with the feeling that the hesitant voice was right. We have been at war for close on a year and our command of the seas remains unimpaired, so it really is quite time that somebody thought of doing something that would take our enemies by surprise instead of letting them make the running the whole time.

Of the papers Wheatley had now written, 'A New Gibraltar' is the most direct. It's not a brainstorm of ideas on paper, the natural progression of one initial thought. It's novel, fascinating and deeply intriguing. It was for these more direct, methodical ideas that Wheatley was later inducted into the JPS.

The Facts
There is no concealing the actual facts:
1. We allowed Poland to be overrun without attempting to bomb the Ruhr – which might have drawn off some of the German Air Force from Poland and enable her to prolong her resistance, thereby inflicting a greater number of casualties on the enemy.
2. For eight months we pursued a policy of sloth while the French sat in their dugouts taking it for granted that the Siegfried Line was impregnable, instead of testing it out by a number of attacks in force, thereby giving Hitler time to build his new heavy tanks and get his reserve divisions into good trim.
3. We deliberately threw a challenge to Hitler by mining the waters off the coast of Norway without having prepared an expeditionary force to go to the support of the Norwegians at once if he invaded the country. In consequence, our forces arrived a whole week later than they should have done, during which Hitler was pumping the place full of his airborne troops, so that by the time we got there he was so well established in the country that we could not gain a foothold and were ignominiously driven out with considerable loss of valuable war material.
4. We knew that the Dutch were poorly armed and that they would find it impossible to hold North Holland for very long if Hitler launched a *Blitzkrieg* against

them; yet we made no attempt to evacuate as many of their troops as possible and land them in South Holland and the region of Antwerp to support the Belgians.

5. Through no fault of our own the British Expeditionary Force was cut off in Flanders, and, however brilliant the evacuation from Dunkirk, the fact remains that we lost the entire equipment of our nine first-line divisions and were chased out of the country.

6. Finally, through no fault of our General Staff, we were compelled to evacuate our remaining troops from France, once more sustaining enormous losses of material, much of which had never been utilized in action.

Now, in the eleventh month of the war, Hitler lords it from Eastern Poland to the Channel ports and from the Arctic Ocean to the Pyrenees. So far, apart from certain brilliant Naval and Air Force actions which have not materially altered the main course of events, the war for us has been one long series of defeats and disasters.

What Now?

At the moment we appear to be waiting to see what Hitler will do next. Will he invade Ireland or Britain, or just blockade us while he tidies up the Balkans and establishes himself as the Emperor of North Africa?

In the meantime our friends in the Balkans have been stunned by the huge success of the German arms. Rumania has thrown our guarantee overboard as a worthless scrap of paper; Greece must be wondering of what value our guarantee is to her; our good friend Turkey sits looking on uneasily, speculating as to whether she has backed the wrong horse after all. Egypt submits to air-raids rather than declare war in Italy, as she would have done without hesitation had offensive action been taken against her a few months ago. The Japanese threaten us in the Far East and are kept in check only through having weakened themselves so greatly in their attempt to swallow China and the fear that open hostilities with us would bring the United States in against them; while America is wondering if Britain can possibly hang out, and if instead of sending arms to us it would not be wiser to reserve them so that she can get her own defence programme going more rapidly.

There is no doubt about it that British prestige is in a very bad way, and the only thing which will restore it is some entirely unexpected lightning blow against the enemy which will at least temporarily give us back the initiative and sway world opinion once more to the belief that there is a real chance, after all, of Britain emerging victorious.

In my view there is only one way to do this. It is by carrying the war into the enemy's country.

The Impossible

On the face of it this may sound impossible. Time was when sea power gave one the immense advantage that an invading force could be landed at any time and almost at any place upon an enemy coast; but this is no longer so today. To accomplish such an operation successfully the mastery of the air is also necessary, and this we do not possess. Any attempt to land troops on Germany's coast would be to court certain disaster. To land them in Norway, Denmark, Holland, Belgium or France would only be slightly less hazardous.

Moreover, no sane person could consider a landing upon a western coast of Europe until we are in a position to dispatch and support a full-scale expeditionary force equipped with a sufficient quantity of tanks and guns to wage a major campaign; otherwise our enemy would bring superior forces against us and the operation could only end in another appalling and fatal disaster.

Any attempt to invade Italy would be almost equally hazardous at the present time since, even if we had an initial success owing to the poor morale of the Italians, the weight of numbers they can afford to throw against any invading force which we could afford to send would almost certainly turn the scale in their favour and, even if the Italian Army broke, Hitler would send a million Germans hurrying down the Peninsula to turn us out.

There remain the Italian Colonies, but they are removed from the main theatre of war both geographically and in the public mind. To achieve any noteworthy success in Libya or Abyssinia considerable forces, which could ill be spared, would have to be sent. The great areas of the country to be conquered would also necessitate a campaign of many weeks – perhaps many months – but an even more important factor against any major operation of this kind is that the public regard these places as sideshows, where the odds are in favour of Britain anyhow, so even a big advance of these fronts would have little power to influence world opinion.

It seems that the dream objective which we require in this dark hour of the war should have the following qualifications:

(a) It should be one at which we can strike swiftly, so as to get results within the next few weeks.

(b) It should be one which we can tackle with a comparatively small number of troops so that we do not have materially to weaken our Home Forces or our Forces in the Near East.

(c) It should be one which is sufficiently far removed from the enemy air bases to make it possible for our Fleet Air Arm to prevent serious interference with our operations by enemy aerial attack.

(d) It should be one where in the event of failure we need not risk the loss of any more of our precious stocks of the most modern war material – that is to say, a place which can be taken without the use of tanks and mechanized forces.

(e) It should be one where, once our Force is established, it can live on the land except for munitions, thereby halving the difficulty of keeping it supplied.

(f) It should be one where in the event of reverses our Force should be able to hold out without difficulty owing to the nature of the country.

(g) It should be one that will immediately restore our prestige through having carried the war into the enemy's territory.

(h) Above all, it should be one in which, once established, it will be impossible for the enemy to bring any portion of his main Armies against us.

The questions are, therefore, WHERE can such an objective be found? HOW can it be captured? And WHY – quite apart from any question of gaining a temporary renewal of our prestige – we should be justified in maintaining a force there for the duration of the war?

WHERE

Almost in vain the eye roves over the map for some such place, and it seems an almost insoluble problem until the eye suddenly lights upon Sardinia.

With due deference I would maintain that Sardinia *possesses all the above qualifications.*

Sardinia

Area 9,299 square miles.

Population 972,153.

Capital and principal port, Cagliari; population 111,187.

Maximum breadth 80 miles.

Only industrial exports – zinc, lead, silver, salt, and antimony.

Main occupation the production of *wine, olive-oil, tobacco, wheat, and cattle.*

As will be clear, Wheatley's strategy concerning Sardinia did hold water, perhaps more so than the decision that was finally made …

Principal Towns

Sassari: Ten miles inland from the north coast.

Alghero: a port at the northern end of the west coast.

Iglesias: seven miles inland from the centre of the west coast.

The only ports, apart from Cagliari and Alghero, are small places – Terranova, on the north-east coast, which is the nearest point to Italy; Porto Torres, on the north coast, which serves Sassari; Bosa, near the middle of the west coast, which serves Iglesias; and Arbatax, in the centre of the east coast. All these are linked by railway, but none of the other coastal villages has a railway service.

Country

Sardinia has a rugged and indented coast and is mountainous in the interior, but its fertile stretches are well cultivated. The principal of these are the valley of the Campidano, which runs from Caligari north-westward right across the island to Oristano, and the lowlands of the north-western peninsula north and west of Sassari.

The average population of the country can be termed 'thin rural', as it runs to approximately one hundred to the square mile. But the town of Cagliari contains over one-tenth of the total population, so outside it the average is about ninety to the square mile. For comparison, the populations of the following countries per square mile are: Albania 84, Eire 112, Spain 120, Greece 124, Yugoslavia 140. A further comparison is that the interior of the country is populated at about the same rate as the interior of Devonshire and Cornwall. The population is, however, by no means evenly distributed, as the mountainous districts of the north-east, middle-east, and south-east form one of the most sparsely populated areas in Europe and may be compared to the north-west of Scotland.

This great slab of enemy territory nearly ten thousand square miles in extent, an island averaging 140 miles in length and 70 miles across, possesses no industries that are vital to Italy's war effort. It is, therefore, reasonable to assume that it is comparatively lightly garrisoned.

Distance from Italy

Its northern port, Terranova, is 150 miles from the nearest Italian port of Civitavecchia. Its capital, Cagliari, in the south, is 210 miles from the small port of Trapani, the nearest point of Sicily. Cagliari is also 270 miles from Italy's naval base at Naples, and 230 miles from Italy's nearest air base. The island is, therefore, very satisfactorily set apart from its Motherland, being even further from Italy, at its nearest point, than Norfolk is from Holland. So here, surely, is a case in which our mastery of the seas should prove a deciding factor.

It seems, therefore, that if secrecy and imagination were employed we could capture Sardinia with a comparatively small force and maintain it there against anything that the Italians could send against it.

Owing to the wildness of a great portion of the country it is just the sort of place from which an invader, once established there, would be very difficult to turn out; yet, owing to its fertile valleys and the normal occupation of its inhabitants with agriculture, such an invading force should be able to make itself practically self-supporting through raids into, or the capture of, the Lowlands.

I have no idea of the strength of the Italian forces at present stationed in Sardinia, but Intelligence should be able to give reasonably good information about this, and once the garrison is overcome our Navy and Air Force could render it difficult – if not impossible – for Italy to send reinforcements or another invading force for its recapture.

In view of the fact that there is nothing vital to Italy in the country, and little trade with the mainland except in agricultural produce, zinc, and lead, it is highly possible that not more than two or three divisions are stationed there, and it is hardly likely that these would be highly mechanized or Italy's best troops. If this is so, although one should not underrate one's enemy, it is not unreasonable to assume that a total force of 25,000 British, given naval and air support and the initial advantage of surprise, would be sufficient to capture the island.

HOW

Once more my apologies for writing of such matters without any technical knowledge, but I will proceed to state how I would set about the job.

Mixed Force

(a) I would employ a mixed force so as to make it an Empire operation.
(b) I would select Ghurkas, Guides, Highland regiments, Australians, and other troops that are used to fighting over rough country.
(c) I would put away from me all thoughts of mechanized warfare and make them flying columns, well armed but carrying the absolute minimum of equipment.

Levelling Up

In my view, tanks and Bren-gun carriers with motorized transport would greatly add to the difficulty of the landing; also, when landed, they tend to confine an advance to roads and need to be supplied with petrol.

The Italians may have a number of tanks and motorized columns in Sardinia, but it should be possible to deal with these fairly early in the operation with anti-tank guns and, once they have been eliminated, the Navy and Air Force should be able to render it impossible for the Italians to land any more armoured vehicles, which would at once level up the arms employed by the contending forces.

Big Guns

The same remarks apply to heavy guns. It is doubtful if the Italians retain many heavy batteries in Sardinia, except in their fixed shore defences. In any case, up-country, big guns are more bother than they are worth during a war of movement in which they have no target to fire at except vast stretches of woodland and mountains in which a comparatively small enemy force lies concealed. We should not, therefore, need to take heavy batteries, so once more could eliminate the difficulty of supplying these with their weighty ammunition; and outside the range of the coastal defence batteries our landing-parties could be supported up to ten miles inland by the heavy guns of our fleet.

Supplies

By these means we could reduce the maintenance of our invading forces to the comparatively easy problem of keeping them supplied with anti-tank ammunition and small arms ammunition, and, in fact, reverting to the type of warfare which was waged half a century ago, except for the fact that our men would be armed with anti-tank guns, Bren guns, and plenty of Mills bombs.

Aerial Attack

Aerial attack is the greatest danger which any landing-force has to fear at the present day, but the actual landings would be made at night and by surprise. Since no mechanized forces would be concerned, it should be possible to accomplish the landings so swiftly that the beaches would be clear by the time enemy aircraft appeared upon the scene and, for a few hours after that at least, our Fleet Air Arm should be able to give our landing-parties protection. Once these have disappeared into the woods and mountains of an island over nine thousand square miles in extent, what are the enemy bombers going to aim at? It should not, therefore, even be necessary for our force to be equipped with anti-aircraft guns, since the enemy should find the problem of locating them like looking for a needle in a haystack. If during an operation in open country they are attacked by low-flying aircraft they can utilize their Bren guns, and each time they undertake an operation against a town our own aircraft can be informed by wireless beforehand so that they can afford our troops special protection at that time and place. In this campaign it is we who should, at last, reap the inestimable advantage of the attacker, and it will be the unfortunate enemy's job to puzzle his wits as to the direction in which we intend to strike next.

Transport

For transport I would suggest the employment of mules and donkeys, which are easily obtainable in Palestine and Egypt. The landing-forces should carry nothing at all with them which would confine their operations to roads. They would take only light artillery, and anti-tank guns should easily be converted so that their parts could be carried on mule back like mountain batteries. The only requirements at all of the landing-forces would therefore be a plentiful supply of iron rations and a plentiful supply of munitions. Sardinia is a well-watered country, as its mountains feed innumerable small rivers. Information should be obtained whether a large proportion of these are dry during this season of the year, but in view of the agricultural activity in the country this seems unlikely.

Forces Required

I would suggest five separate forces, as follows:
1. A brigade of Gurkhas and Guides with two mountain batteries.
2. Brigade of English infantry with two mountain batteries and the Scots Greys with their horses.
3. A Highland brigade with two mountain batteries.
4. An Australian brigade with two mountain batteries.
5. 2,000 to 3,000 French sailors and Army officers who have decided to fight on with Britain.

The number of guns might have to be increased, but this depends upon our information as to the forces which the Italians have garrisoning the island.

In order to preserve the utmost secrecy our forces should be assembled and sail separately.

Operations

Force No. 1 (the Gurkhas and Guides) coming from India would debouch into the Mediterranean at Port Said.

Forces Nos 2 and 3 (the English and Highland brigades) would come from Britain, but they should sail in separate convoys from different ports and be kept several hundred miles apart until nearing the end of their voyage. The Scots Greys – who are, I believe, stationed in Palestine – would also sail separately.

Force No. 4 (the Australian brigade) would sail from Haifa.

Force No. 5 (French sailors) would sail from Alexandria.

Exclusive of the French and the Scots Greys, each of the four main forces would consist of about five thousand men, so it should be possible to send each of them with their mule transport in ten medium-sized ships, so that each force will appear to Italian air observation only as a normal convoy; and medium-sized ships would be able to get closer in to the beaches.

Force No. 1 would land in the early hours of the morning on the low beaches at the north-west of the island about the mouth of the River Coghina.

Force No. 2 would land on the low beaches of the coast which faces north to the east of Cape Mannu, in the centre of the western side of the island. It would be better still if they could land actually in the Gulf of Oristano, but it is almost certain that the Italians will have shore batteries mounted on the two horns of this huge lagoon at Cape Saint Marco and Cape Frasca, thereby rendering the penetration of the Gulf hazardous or impossible.

Force No. 3 would land on the low beaches to the north of the village of Sarroch, in the south of the island, just out of range of the land batteries protecting Cagliari.

Force No. 4 would land on the low beaches a few miles east of Quarto, which is west of Cagliari and just out of range of the land batteries protecting Cagliari.

Force No. 5 is intended to play the same part as the German troops concealed in barges played in the taking of Norwegian ports, but a new twist can be given to this trick owing to the recent change in the international situation.

Trojan Horse

In Egypt and Palestine there are now considerable numbers of French soldiers and sailors who have declared their determination to fight on with

Britain. The most trustworthy of these should be approached and asked if they are prepared to partake in an enterprise which will entail considerable risk but which, if successful, will revenge the Italian rape of Nice.

It should not be difficult to muster 2,000 or 3,000 of these men and put them on a large liner (French, if possible) at Alexandria. In the liner there would be concealed a considerable number of machine-guns, automatic rifles, hand-grenades, and a good store of explosives. In a large ship there are many places in which such items can be concealed, where they will escape detection except on a really rigorous examination, and all that is required is that these munitions should not be discovered for a matter of a few hours.

The ship would sail under British escort until within some thirty miles of Cagliari and arrangements would then be made for it to appear seriously damaged as though by an act of war. The forepart of the ship could be cleared and its bulkheads closed, then, if this is not too dangerous, the accompanying escort could put a small shell into it just below the water-line so that the forepart of the ship filled with water and it gets an obvious dip at the bows, although remaining seaworthy.

The escort would then leave the liner and in the late afternoon, hoisting the French flag, she would proceed towards Cagliari.

As soon as she is sighted by the Italians and the Sardinian port authorities come on board the terrible tale would be told by the infuriated captain. He and his 3,000 passengers and crew are all loyal Frenchmen who are determined to stand by the Pétain Government. They were disarmed by the British and received permission to return to France. They hoped soon to find their wives and children in their desolated land and had accomplished the major portion of their voyage successfully when they were sabotaged and almost sunk by the filthy British.

That afternoon a submarine had suddenly popped up and ordered them to take to the boats; the captain had refused, upon which the British submarine began to shell them and put a shot into their bows. Fortunately an Italian aircraft came on the scene so the submarine was compelled to submerge and the Frenchmen got away; but if it had not been for that they might now all be dead, and without even the chance of firing a shot, since they have not so much as an old pistol amongst them.

With her forehold full of water the ship is no longer in a condition to proceed on her voyage in case a storm blows up, so the only thing she can do is to limp into Cagliari for repairs. As his ship is crippled it should be possible for the captain to persuade the Italians to let him take his ship right into the harbour, but even if they are suspicious and make him anchor in the roadstead our purpose could still be achieved.

The captain would fraternize to the utmost of his power with any Italians who come on board and he would ask permission for his passengers to be allowed ashore the next morning, as most of them have been stationed in the

Near East without leave for the last eleven months and, having saved quite a lot of their pay, have plenty of money which they would like to spend in the town while the ship is being repaired.

This is pure bluff with the object of establishing good relations, and to make the Italians think that if there is anything phoney about this considerable number of Frenchmen they do not intend to try any tricks until *after* they have succeeded in getting ashore on the following day.

In no case should any of the liner's passengers be allowed to speak to the Italian port authorities. Only the captain and his most trusted officers could be allowed to do this, as a very necessary protection against the possibility of there being a Quisling on board who might attempt to tip the Italians off as to what is intended.

At midnight the French would overpower any guard which is placed on the ship and, if machine-guns are trained on it from the quay, destroy these by hurling Mills bombs at them. If the ship has to lie out in the roads the French would come ashore in their boats after having over-powered the guards on board.

Objectives (The French Force)

The objective of the French force would be to blow up the shore batteries protecting Cagliari.

These batteries will be trained to cover the sea approach to the port and the harbour. Therefore, it is almost certain that they will not be able to bring their main armaments to bear upon any force which has actually landed and is climbing the hills in the dark towards them.

With their Bren guns the French should be able to overcome the Italian sentries and force the outer defences of the forts, which would enable them to scale the emplacements and place large boxes of dynamite under the muzzles of the big guns, as was done by the German parachutists at Liège, in Belgium.

They would also endeavour to secure certain strong-points in the town. The railway station – which is of considerable size – lies right on the harbour and this should be seized if possible. There is also the building of the port authorities and a smaller station, which are situated on the eastern wharf.

The French would then endeavour to hang on to these places until the arrival of reinforcements.

Air Force

Our bombers would be timed to arrive over Cagliari at 12:15, as fifteen minutes' start should be suffient for the French. Our aircraft would then proceed to bomb the Carlo barracks and military district which, fortunately, is situated right at the back of the town nearly a mile from the shore and so well away from the scene of French operations.

Army

Our four landing-forces would begin to disembark as soon after this as is considered expedient, and the business of disembarkation should be well under way before dawn. Their objectives would be:

Force No. 1 (Indian brigade). To advance up the valley of the Coghina River to the village of Oschini, which lies about thirty miles inland, where they can cut the railway connecting the port of Terranova with the rest of the island. They would then advance south-west along the line of the railway to the village of Chilivani, a further fifteen miles. At this junction four railways meet. If it can be seized the whole of the northern sector of the island, including the important and populous district of Sassari, will be cut off from the south.

Force No. 2 (English brigade and Scots Greys) would advance across the Low Country on the west coast of Riola, and thence south-east to the village of Simaais, which lies on the River Tisso. The main north to south railway of the island crosses the river here by a viaduct and there is no other railway connecting the two halves of the island; so this, having been seized or destroyed, will cut the island in two.

While the infantry brigade attack the town of Oristano – which is only five miles west of Simaais – the Scots Greys would advance through the valley of the Campidano, which is broad, fertile, and several miles in breadth, towards Cagliari.

Forces 3 and 4 would converge from the west and the east along the coast to support the French and capture Cagliari.

Fleet Air Arm

As soon as dawn breaks, our aircraft would bomb the Sardinian air bases to prevent their local Air Force getting into the air.

Navy

If the French succeed in capturing or sabotaging the Cagliari land-batteries, the British Fleet could then move in to bombard Italian strong-points or troop concentrations as required.

Naval Operations

If the French do not succeed in accounting for the land-batteries the ships of the British Fleet should be kept out of range and the batteries will have to be isolated and starved out by our invading troops.

In my view, not a single ship of the Fleet should ever be jeopardized except in a purely naval action, or as may be required by such operations as the present. To have risked any portion of our supremacy at sea by sending capital ships into Trondhjeim with the Germans in possession of the land-batteries would, to my mind, have been the most criminal folly.

A touch of Lord Nelson in the line, 'In my view, not a single ship of the Fleet should ever be jeopardized … ' Even at the Battle of Trafalgar, outnumbered by the combined fleets of the French and Spanish, Lord Nelson failed to lose any of his vessels; well in fact, he refused to allow any ship to be lost! So there is something historically British about Wheatley's perception.

Minefields

As rapidly as possible after the attack has been launched the Navy would lay minefields outside the Sardinian ports to prevent the Italians rushing reinforcements by sea from the mainland during the following nights, when they might escape observation for a few hours by our naval and air patrols.

Supplies

The Italians may attempt to reinforce their garrisons by air but, as their nearest bases on the mainland would be over a hundred and fifty miles away, once we have seized the Sardinian airfields the R.A.F. would have as good a chance of intercepting and destroying their planes as it has of preventing German troop-carriers, sailing from Holland or Belgium, landing in England.

Our own invading forces, with their mule transports, should be able to be self-supporting for at least a week. During that time the cavalry, particularly in the Campidano region, should by their forays have succeeded in securing considerable quantities of cattle, forage, and foodstuffs.

As our forces would be so lightly equipped there should not be great difficulty in supplying them with their requirements in ammunition and further iron rations by parachute containers dropped at night from the air. Where forces are still in touch with their original landing-beaches ships could also be run in at night if necessary; or supplies could be slung overboard in large numbers of small barrels which, on a rising tide, would be carried up on to the beaches, and these could be collected in daylight by scattered groups who would afford only small targets for enemy aircraft.

Civil Population

There remains the problem of the civil population, which is getting on for one million strong. Most of the younger men are almost certainly already mobilized in Italy's conscript armies, but the subjugation of such a large civil population still presents a special problem.

Islanders of any kind are nearly always very insular in their mentality, and I should think it improbable that the Sardinians are an exception to this rule – in fact if they are anything like their neighbours, the Corsicans, they have very little time for their overlords on the mainland at all.

If you ask a Corsican if he is not proud that his country produced Napoleon he will shrug his shoulders, spit and reply: 'Napoleon? What did he ever do for Corsica? He sacrificed the interests of Corsica to become Emperor of the French.'

The only historical figure that the Corsicans have any time for at all is their local patriot, Paroli, who, financed by Britain, governed an independent Corsica for a few years in Nelson's day, while the great Admiral used the ports of the island to revictual and supply his ships during his operations against the French.

Sardinia has also been the plaything of many masters during its long history, so no strong allegiance to any particular country is ingrained in its people. Up to 1720 the island belonged to Austria, but it then became part of the Dominions of the Duke of Savoy and it was not until 1860, when the Duke became King of Italy, (only eighty years ago), that Sardinia entered the Italian federation.

Proclamation

I believe that with skilful propaganda the Sardinians could very soon be brought to welcome our occupation. The measure to secure this would be a proclamation, to be issued on the first day of our invasion, saying that we had come to rescue Sardinia from the tyranny of the Fascists; that all food and items commandeered would be paid for: that only troops under arms and members of the Fascist Party would be regarded as prisoners-of-war and the remainder of the inhabitants would be allowed to go about their normal business. We would offer to buy their crops and other exports so that the business of the island could continue uninterrupted. And, lastly, we would offer to re-establish the ancient kingdom as a self-governing Republic with an invitation for them to re-elect new mayors and their own Parliament on a free franchise to enact their own future laws.

Cagliari

Cagliari, having a population, in 1936, of 111,187, is a considerable town and for comparison I give the population of the following: Oxford 80,540, York 84,831 ...

But Cagliari contains more than one-ninth of the entire population of the island; so if we can win the town over, half the battle is won, because the people in the country districts will be even more insular and anti-Fascist.

Broadcasts

On the morning of the invasion every British broadcasting station should be turned on to talk to the Sardinians in their own language, varying the wave-length used every five minutes and broadcasting the same message of peace and goodwill the whole time.

Broadcasting from Warship

As our main broadcasting stations are a considerable distance from Sardinia, has the possibility ever been considered of fitting up a transmitting station of considerable power in a ship? If so, this could be used off the Sardinian coast even more effectively, as it would be nearer to Sardinia than the Italian stations.

Leaflets

A number of leaflets could be dropped by aircraft over as many towns and villages in Sardinia as possible, but particularly over Cagliari, and these leaflets would bear a simple statement on the lines given above together with a request that people should keep in their houses until the fighting is over, so as to avoid the overcrowding of hospitals and the killing of civilians which the British are most anxious to avoid.

Such leaflets would obviously have to be printed in considerable numbers some time before the invasion is carried out. Therefore it is absolutely essential that they should address the Sardinians as 'You' and that no mention of Sardinia should be made, so that it may appear to the printers and handlers that these might apply to Libya, Abyssinia or any other Italian possession; otherwise the secret that an invasion of Sardinia is contemplated might leak out and the whole plan be ruined by the Italians reinforcing the garrison before we get there.

Holding On

Should the attack upon Cagliari prove a failure, or the Italian resistance prove stronger than we anticipate, our forces will have the great advantage that in every area where they are operating they can easily retreat into the mountains, from which they would be very difficult to dislodge.

Force No. 1 could base itself on Mount Limbara, in the north centre of the island, and still continue to render the railway from Terranova unusable by the enemy.

Force 2 could retire into Mount Urtigu district, in the centre of the west coast.

Force 3 could retire into Mount Caravius district, in the extreme south of the island.

Force 4 could retire to the Mount Serpeddi district, in the south-east of the island.

The last two forces could continue to harry the Cagliari neighbourhood from their strongholds in the hills and, even if these retirements prove necessary, it should be borne in mind that the venture will have by no means been a failure, *because we shall have gained the kudos of having carried the war to the enemy's soil.*

Should I be told that I have greatly underestimated the numbers of the Italian garrisons in Sardinia, I would reply: 'Very good, then; send 50,000 men. It would be well worth it.'

WHEN

Speed

Should this suggestion of an invasion of Sardinia be feasible, in the light of knowledge that I do not possess, and seriously considered, it should be carried out at the earliest possible moment.

The numbers of troops required are not large and their equipment is not complicated, so it should be possible to dispatch them in a very short time.

An Indian brigade could be ordered to sail tomorrow and be on their way while other preparations are going ahead; or, if this will take too long, a brigade of New Zealanders could be sent from Egypt instead.

The reconstruction of anti-tank guns so that they will be transportable in parts on mule back, and the manufacture of sufficient mule packs, if these are not already available, could surely be accomplished in a fortnight, and the greater the speed with which these preparations are carried out the less likelihood there would be of any leakage about them.

Secrecy

The utmost secrecy should be maintained. All captains, both of warships and transports, should sail under sealed orders, not to be opened until they are within a few hours' steaming of Sardinia. All preparations could be put in hand without disclosing the object for which they are intended. Since some would be made in England, some in Palestine and some in Egypt, their scale would be so comparatively small that undue comment upon them could easily be avoided.

As far as I can see, there is no reason whatsoever why anybody outside the Chiefs of Staff Committee and the War Cabinet should be told anything about this plan, and even the principal officers concerned in the operation need know nothing of it until a few hours before they are due to go into action.

Everything depends on secrecy.

If we are going to invade Sardinia we should do it soon, otherwise Hitler, with Mussolini's consent, will forestall us by using it as a halfway-house for his contemplated descent on Africa.

WHY

Apart from the fully sufficient reasons which are given above, why we should invade Sardinia there are these others:

(a) If Hitler had our sea power and the other forces at our disposal he certainly would. Why, therefore, should we show less initiative?

(b) The ancient kingdom of Sardinia became a domain of the Princes of Piedmont in 1720. The Princes of Piedmont are of the House of Savoy and the present rulers of Italy. To rob them of Sardinia would be to strike a blow right at the heart of the reigning Italian house. It would be like wresting the principality of Wales from the Crown of England.

(c) No one would suggest that Gibraltar is no longer of use to us, but the Rock has already lost much of its potency, and looking ahead it is obvious that its days are numbered.

The area of Gibraltar is so small that, apart from the racecourse, I doubt if there is any place on which land-planes can land. Therefore it presents a fixed target to enemy bombers.

As the potency of aircraft grows, as it obviously must, until we include aerial battleships carrying 100 men and heavily armoured among our air fleets in the not so very distant future Gibraltar will become more and more untenable.

If we are to maintain our power in the Western Mediterranean we must have some much larger base where we can maintain a powerful air fleet and room enough to spread it out so that it cannot easily be destroyed by the enemy

Sardinia is the price that Italy must pay for entering the war against us. Let us take it, hold it and keep it.

We can give the Sardinians self-government in their home affairs on the same lines that we gave self-government to Egypt, but in exchange they must allow us complete and permanent control of certain harbours and such military zones as we require for our naval and air bases.

With Sardinia in our hands – a new Gibraltar nearly ten thousand square miles in extent – Britain can remain supreme and dominant in the Western Mediterranean for centuries to come.

Wheatley probably went a little over the top with his last line, but he did favour an invasion of Sardinia over that of Corsica. Indeed, he would return to the idea of the invasion of Sardinia in his papers, and although history books dictate that it never happened, allied forces did come close to invading the island. 'Operation Brimstone' was a very real possibility up to the Casablanca Conference (January 1943), where it was decided that the ultimate objective was to take Italy out of the war, as Wheatley wrote in *Stranger Than Fiction*:

General Eisenhower's army was firmly established in Algeria, and General Montgomery's successes had brought the Eighth Army to Tripolitania. It remained only to close the gap and it was already agreed that the allies' next step should be to launch an invasion across the Central Mediterranean against the 'soft underbelly of the Axis'. The only question which hung in the balance was, should the first step be against Sicily or Sardinia?

In his memoirs, Field Marshal Montgomery wrote of the campaign in Italy:

... the next task... was to knock Italy out of the war... we were to capture Sicily but there was no plan for operations beyond. There should have been a master plan which embraced the capture of Sicily and the use of the island as a spring-board for getting quickly across to Italy, and exploiting success.

If the campaign in Italy was instigated between 3 September 1943 to 31 December 1943 (as Montgomery wrote in his memoirs), why hadn't much notice been give to Wheatley's 'A New Gibraltar' paper? Or indeed, any of his other papers that broached the subject and suggested a course of action. Basically, it does come down to (as Wheatley states above) the positioning of allied forces moving on towards Italy at the time of the Casablanca talks. Although there was some confusion as to what to do after taking Sicily, the act of taking the island was deemed to be the logical option by the Chiefs of Staff and not even Montgomery would argue with that.

Darvall wrote in his Introduction to *Stranger Than Fiction* in 1959:

> And what of Wheatley's pet scheme for seizing the great island of Sardinia? Later, when it was a choice of going into Sardinia or Sicily, the question was hotly debated. Accordingly to Field Marshal Viscount Alanbrooke, it was his victory over the Joint Planning Staff and his colleagues that led to Sicily being chosen. Yet the long slog up the leg of Italy need never have taken place. From Sardinia a relatively quick entry into Austria, South Germany, and Hungary might have been possible.

So what of Alanbrooke? The answer can be found in his *War Diaries*:

> I have the most vivid recollection of that exhaustive evening! ... suddenly the Joint Planning Staff reappeared on the scene with a strong preference for Sardinia and expressing most serious doubts about our ability to take on the Sicilian operation! They had carried with them Mountbatten who never had any very decided opinions of his own. ... I had three hours of hammer and tongs battle to keep the team together and to stop it from wavering.

Alanbrooke had agreed with the American Chiefs of Staff to take Sicily and was not prepared to go back on his word. He explained this by stating:

> I told them (the JPS) that such a step would irrevocably shake their confidence (American CoS) in our judgement. What is more, I told them frankly that I disagreed with them entirely and adhered to our original decision to invade Sicily and would not go back on it.

But why not? Alanbrooke explained:

> ... it was an example of one of those occasions, which occurred frequently, when it was a matter of utmost difficulty to adhere to one's plans and not be shaken in one's decisions.

Wheatley's papers were ingenious and unique and won him many fans in high places. Darvall wrote in his Introduction: 'Reading these papers, no one can say that uninstructed imagination, vision and ability to write attractively are not a great asset if they can be properly harnessed.'

Notes

1. These friends were people such as Sir Walter Womersley (Minister of Pensions), and Sir Walter Monkton (Chief Censor). Wheatley detailed these recipients in *Stranger Than Fiction* (Hutchinson, 1959).

2. Wheatley greatly increased his circle of prestigious friends when he was serving in the War Cabinet. As he said in *The Time Has Come. The Memoirs of Dennis Wheatley, 1897–1914, The Young Man Said* (Hutchinson, 1977). 'In the Second World War I had the exceptional good fortune to be specially commissioned in order that I might become a member of the Joint Planning Staff. Three years in the offices of the War Cabinet brought me into intimate contact with some of the finest brains in the three Services. This enabled me when already middle-aged to form a new circle of personal friends, many of whom later became admirals, generals and air-marshals, and, several, commanders-in-chief.'

3. Also, Wheatley's watchword was 'Never put off until tomorrow what you can do today'. See *The Time Has Come … The Young Man Said*, op. cit.

IX

A Royal Handshake

'I wrote twenty papers, amounting to half a million words, on such diverse problems as 'Village Defence', 'How to Keep Turkey Neutral' and 'Strategy in the Mediterranean' at the request of members of the Joint Planning Staff of the War Cabinet. Extraordinary to relate, these papers were read even by His Majesty the King, who did me the honour to send me his commendation upon them.'
A Few Words From the Author
Gunmen, Gallants and Ghosts

Although Wheatley requested (in 'A New Gibraltar') that there should be some secrecy surrounding the plans he proposed concerning the invasion of Sardinia, the paper, along with all his others, was circulated further than the Chiefs of Staff of the War Cabinet. Wheatley's contribution was taken very seriously, so much so, that King George VI was sent copies. Wheatley was told this by Sir Louis Greig (for many years Equerry to the king whilst he was Duke of York).

Greig told Wheatley that he was one of the king's favourite authors, and that His Majesty insisted on being kept informed on every aspect of the war, so Greig showed the king a copy of Wheatley's first paper. The king was so impressed that he demanded to see copies of any further paper written by Wheatley.

Greig went on to say that the previous night a meeting of the Directors of Plans had been called to discuss Wheatley's paper on Sardinia, and that as the JPS had only Darvall's copy on which to brief them, he had asked Louis Greig to help them by borrowing His Majesty's copy. Sir Louis had telephoned the palace and the king had promptly sent his copy along.

The king was so security conscious that he addressed the envelope containing the paper in his own hand, marking it 'Personal and Urgent'. Greig then presented the envelope to Wheatley who wrote of the incident[1]: 'It was … typical of Louis Greig's kindly thoughtfulness that he should have kept the envelope and sent for me to give it to me. I now have it framed, as my most treasured souvenir of the war.'

Indeed, Wheatley's activities during the Second World War were indeed stranger than fiction, and his papers were highly thought of, as Darvall wrote in his special Introduction to *Stranger Than Fiction*: 'These papers are the prelude to his appointment to the Joint Planning Staff and are the reason why such a relatively obscure figure should have been called to such an exalted task.'

Darvall is not putting Wheatley down with these words. What he simply meant was, Wheatley was an author not a politician, or a civil servant, no one would have considered asking for his assistance if it was not for his dear wife Joan and a chance conversation she had. Darvall went on to say in his Introduction:

> It is a great credit to his keenness that he seized the slender opportunity offered to him, and to his knowledge and industry, so that in a short time his papers became "best sellers" in that very, very restricted circle, the Chiefs of Staffs, in the middle of our greatest war – and His Majesty King George VI, who read them all with the greatest interest.

Obviously with such a distinguished supporter as the king, it must have been a mere formality to put Wheatley into uniform at the Joint Planning Staff; however that didn't happen immediately.

After writing his paper 'Aerial Warfare' (20–25 September 1940), Wheatley wrote 'This Winter' (October 1940). This paper – sadly no copy survives – included the suggestion of a new medal for outstanding civilian bravery. Although Wheatley never claimed to have suggested the introduction of the George Cross and George Medal, he knew the king read all of his papers, so quite possibly, he put the idea into the king's mind.

Note

1. See *Stranger Than Fiction* (Hutchinson, 1959).

X

The Independence of Turkey

'Fortunately, the God who looks after England while the rest of us play cricket decreed the Sino-Japanese War, and for the past three years these powerful little yellow islanders have been fritting away their strength by endeavouring to gobble up China.'
'The Independence of Turkey'

During the last week of July 1940, Wheatley had lunch with Darvall. He was told that one of the biggest problems facing the JPS was the Nazis' possible invasion of Turkey en route to Russia.

Darvall told Wheatley that the Turks were our good friends but it would be almost impossible to get military assistance to them. So what else could we do to help?

Wheatley was thus given the spur for his next paper, which he would call 'Measures For Maintaining the Independence of Turkey'. This would be Wheatley trying his hand at more of a political paper. He wrote it between 27 and 29 July 1940 and a little daunted by the task, started on home territory, using his own experience and love of history; after posing himself an essay question:

The problem is, in the event of a threat of invasion from Russia, how can Turkey be prevented from seeking the protection of Germany?

In October 1937 I published a book called *Red Eagle*, the story of the Russian Revolution and of Marshal Voroshilov. For this book I had forty-six accounts of Voroshilov's activities, all written by people who knew him intimately at various stages of his career, translated from the Russian specially for me. I also had accounts of the lives of Stalin, Lenin, Voroshilov, Tukachevsky, Blucher and Budenny translated from the Russian, French, and German. In addition, I interviewed a considerable number of people, all experts on Russia, but having the most diverse political outlooks and ranging from H.I.H. Prince Dimitri to an ex-Bolshevik Commissar who joined the Party as early as 1903 and had known all the principal figures in the Russian Revolution personally.

In consequence, I gained a certain amount of information about Russia and the following were the conclusions that I formed.

The Russian Revolution was ghastly beyond belief. There is no internal upheaval in all history which can compare with it for the sum total of human misery brought about. Among the population of one-sixth of the world's entire land-surface, murder, rape, torture, arson, pillage, every kind of violence, cholera, typhus, and death from starvation were daily events for more than three years.

These years of Revolution and Civil War devastated the country from end to end. When the Reds at last succeeded in suppressing the Whites so much blood had been spilled that Russia was utterly exhausted. Her whole social structure was in ruins; added to which the Bolsheviks had not a friend in the world who would assist them with loans or trade or technical experts to help them bring order out of chaos.

After their defeat in their Polish Campaign of 1920 they abandoned all idea of trying to carry Communism across Europe by fire and sword. The only thing they could do was to crawl back into their own kennel, lick their wounds, clean it up as best they could and keep themselves free of further quarrels. The one thing they needed was peace – peace internal and external; not five years of peace, but fifty; a solid half-century of peace during which they could exploit the vast resources of their enormous territories – in the same way that the Americans exploited the United States in the 'sixties and 'seventies of the last century – so that in time they might become as rich as the United States and as independent. From 1920 on they realized that they had everything to lose by risking further wars. The only thing they had to fear was an attack while they were still devoting their energies to the construction of the new Russia. In consequence, the whole Russian strategy, directed by Marshal Voroshilov, has since been based upon the defensive; in the belief that Russia might be called upon to resist aggression herself but would never become an aggressor.

Voroshilov has laid it down in his military writings that *'owing to the tremendous development of air-fleets in the Western European countries, questions of frontier and* definitions of front and rear, *in the countries engaged, will no longer have their former significance.'* In consequence, when he reorganized the defence of Russia he withdrew the military heart of Russia right back to the edge of Asia. The old munitions plants of Moscow, Leningrad, and Kiev have been scrapped and vast new ones built with aerodromes for the main Russian air-fleet over a big area in the north, which has its centre just east of the Urals. It is there that Russia's fighting strength is concentrated today.

The effect of this strategic change is that, while the main Russian forces can strike with equal ease at Central European or South-Western Asia, if desired, it would not be practicable to send large fleets of planes under war conditions against Britain, France or Italy, because the distance of these countries from the new Russian bases is too great; *but* this also cuts the other way. Even Germany is too distant from the Urals to send air-fleets over 1,700 miles of enemy territory, so she could not possibly destroy the Russian bases.

It is clear from Voroshilov's military works that he is counting upon a great belt of Russian territory, including the cities of Leningrad, Smolensk, Minsk, and Kiev, being rendered untenable. He is doing everything in his power to strengthen the moral resistance of the civilian population in this belt but he will fight back from the Urals, destroying the enemy armies as they advance into Russia, and it would be practically impossible for any European nation to dislodge him.

The above paragraphs upon Voroshilov's strategy are a verbatim quotation from the book that I published in 1937 and I have no reason whatever to alter that opinion today. Twenty years ago Russia was in ruins and the standard of life in Russia at the present time is probably still no better than it was in Tsarist days, but that does not affect the fact that colossal undertakings have been carried through for the reconstruction of the country. To mention but a few – the opening up of the Arctic, the development of a huge internal commercial air-service, the vast engineering works which now carry electric power over thousands of square miles of territory, and the linking of Russia's four seas – the White sea, the Baltic Sea, and the Caspian Sea – by the greatest canal system ever conceived and carried out by man.

These are achievements of which the people's commissars may well be proud, but they have yet to pay a dividend by lifting the whole scale of living of the Russian people, for which purpose they were originally designed. Another war with a major Power or another revolution would rob Russia of the benefits for which her people have made such enormous sacrifices. Therefore I maintain that Russia still needs a further twenty-five years of peace, internal and external, in order that she may reap the benefits of her labours.

Since the suppression of the Tukachevsky conspiracy there can be little doubt that Stalin and his supporters are the complete masters of Russia and that they have little to fear from a disruption of their programme coming from within. But how do they stand about the possibility of its being sabotaged from without?

After the World War Germany also was left exhausted and disorganized but, owing to the fact that she was far in advance of Russia before the World War opened, and that her cities were not destroyed, she was able to recover much more quickly. With the coming to power of the National Socialist Party Germany began to grow strong again. By 1935 it was obvious to every thinking man that in a few more years she would once more constitute a threat to the peace of Europe; and such people began to ask themselves what form that threat would take.

In his *Berlin Diary 1934–1941*, American reporter William Shirer[1], confirmed this fact, writing: 'Somehow I feel that, despite our work as reporters, there is little understanding of the Third Reich, what it is, what it is up to, where it is going, either at home or elsewhere abroad. It is a complex picture. Certainly the British and French do not understand Hitler's Germany. Perhaps, as the Nazis say, the Western democracies have become sick, decadent, and have reached that stage of decline which [Oswald] Spengler predicted.'

But where did all this come from (National Socialism – Nazis)? In *The Fuehrer*, Konrad Heiden's quote sums it all up (when he described Adolf Hitler): 'He is a mirror of our time, for his strange personality, with its contradictions of pathos and unbridled passion, revolt and submission, greatness and depression, is the extreme type of modern man; technically, highly developed; and socially, profoundly unsatisfied.'[2]

Germany had been shattered and depressed since the end of the Great War. National Socialism and Adolf Hitler, was the resulting cancer.

Wheatley continued:

> Would Germany endeavour to revenge herself for the defeat by entering into another death-struggle with the Western Powers, or would she march east into Poland, Czechoslovakia, and the Ukraine? Nobody knew for certain, but the Nazi leaders made it abundantly clear, by the Anti-Comintern Pact and practically every speech they made, that they considered Bolshevism as their implacable enemy.
>
> Stalin had no reason whatever to love Britain, France and Italy, but he had no reason to fear an attack from any of them. In any case, they were too far removed from Russia's frontiers to cause him a moment's worry. Japan might give him a certain amount of trouble, but only in the Far East, and every other nation was either too weak or too remote to constitute a serious menace, with one exception of Germany.
>
> Hitler had written in *Mein Kampf* that Germany should turn her eyes east-wards, to the great cornlands and oil-wells of the Ukraine and the Caucasus. Hitler had gained power, and with every week he was growing stronger. Right up to the summer of 1939 Stalin must have regarded Germany as the one and only enemy really to be feared. Germany alone was in a position to nullify his twenty years of peaceful reconstruction and bring his whole régime crashing about his ears at any time that she chose to launch her land, sea, and air forces against him.
>
> In August 1939 the Russo-German Pact was signed, but in all essentials Russia's situation is exactly the same as it was this time last year. If we do not think of this year or next year, but regard the matter in terms of long-scale policy, the Russo-German Pact has altered nothing.
>
> Why did Stalin make it? Many people have argued that if he had come in with the Allies this would have enabled him to put his enemy, Germany, out of business for another twenty years as he would have had the benefit of the Allies' help; but this argument does not hold water.

France had her Maginot Line to protect her, Britain had the seas; Russia had only Poland and the puppet states of Lithuania, Latvia, and Estonia between her and the enemy. It is almost certain that if Stalin had come in with the Allies this war would have taken the same course as the 1914 War (the Great War). Germany would have overrun Poland and invaded Russia through the Baltic States and probably through Finland as well, while France and Britain sat looking on and, as was proved in the case of Poland, quite unable to help him. He would have had to face the whole might of the Nazi war machine – and he wasn't playing!

It was so much simpler to leave the Allies to pull the chestnuts out of the fire for him, and if they looked like winning he could always come in later and administer the *coup-de-grace* to Germany. On the other hand if the Germans won, and he had kept out, he would still have his full military strength unimpaired to resist German aggression.

It is my belief that the last thing that Stalin wanted was another World War but as he had no means of stopping it he sat down at once to consider how its outcome might affect him, and he was faced with two problems.

1.   If Germany wins, what happens then? She will be glutted with power, victory, and the looted wealth of other nations. Hitler will be the master of Europe with almost limitless resources in the way of munition-plants, shipyards and enslaved peoples to cultivate crops for him. He may take a breathing-space of a year or so to reorganize, but he will consider himself another Alexander the Great and he will not for long be content with what he has got. He will start talking about oppressed minorities and the next thing that will happen is a demand that I should hand over the territories in which lie my great cornfields, the coal in the Don Basin, and my oil-wells.

2.   If Germany loses the war, what happens then? For a time they will be in a muddle again and I shan't have to worry myself, but history has shown that every muddle – even our own Revolution – sorts itself out in time. Unless the Allies proceed to the extreme step of emasculating all male Germans – which I don't believe they have the sense to do – however badly Germany is cut up geographically, the German race will still be there; and, given another twenty years, the German people will be solidified with a single will and purpose once more. The Nazi Party may only be history but another Kaiser Wilhelm II or Adolf Hitler will arise and this virile, unsuppressable people will be clamouring for *lebensraum* again. Will Germany have a third crack at Britain and France? No, I don't think so. Once bitten, twice shy. Twice bitten, and the game quite obviously is not worth the candle. In that case, then, in twenty years' time Germany will definitely march East and Britain and France will not help Russia, because Russia did not help them.

Something I find personally quite interesting about the last paragraph is Wheatley's comments on a Germany 'given another twenty years.' Somebody who witnessed that Germany was a young Reuters reporter,

Frederick Forsyth. The Germany he observed would inspire his second novel *The Odessa File*. Forsyth told me about the German mentality he witnessed in the early 1960s: 'At the start of the Cold War, the German generation that had taken part in the Second World War kind of blanked out what had happened, and it stayed blanked out for roughly 20 years. Obviously, today we have Holocaust memorials all over Germany, so there is now a complete admission by the German people for what happened, but that wasn't always so. In the mid 60s – when I was there – for young West German children growing up, it was an unspeakable subject … In German school books, the whole of the Second World War was about five lines. Some war to be covered so superficially. No mention of the camps, like Auschwitz, Treblinka, Ravensbrück, Balzac, Bergen-Belsen.'

However, there has been a strong, albeit covert, Nazi presence in Germany since the Second World War and into the new millennium.

In consequence, I suggest that Stalin came to the conclusion that it was 'heads I win, and tails you lose': whichever side emerged victorious from the new World War Germany would attack Russia either in about 1944 or 1960, and he proceeded to play his cards accordingly.

By the Russo-German Pact he had undertaken to supply Germany with certain war supplies; but that didn't bother him, because he meant to see to it that they would not receive enough to make any material difference to the outcome of the struggle, and in return the Germans had given him a more or less free hand with the Baltic States. Any lingering vestige of authority possessed by the ally-subsidized League of Nations had flickered out with the declaration of war, and Germany had her hands full. It was his job to make his particular world 'safe for democracy' while the others were at each other's throats.

Hitler mopped up the Poles for him in the most satisfactory manner, and at no cost to himself in men, money or munitions he acquired half Poland, advancing his frontier an average of 250 miles on a front of about 500 miles.

He then turned his attention to the 'little fellows' – Lithuania, Latvia, and Estonia – advancing his frontiers to the sea on a front of a further three hundred odd miles – once again without any expenditure of men, money or munitions.

So far, so good. By taking control of the forts, harbours, and air-bases in the territories of his small neighbours he had deprived any future German state of utilizing these nearest and most obvious jumping-off places for an attack on Russia. Moreover, they all had very considerable German elements among their population, who would have acted the part of Fifth Column and made them particularly susceptible for use against him had he been unwise enough to leave these states their independence. Germany now had only one possible jumping-off place against him left in the West: namely, Finland.

Finland was very strongly anti-Bolshevik and almost equally strongly pro German. It was only with the help of the Germans that Finland had managed to gain her independence by throwing the Bolsheviks out of the country in 1919, and the Finnish border was only eighteen miles from Leningrad. Worse, the border had been immensely strongly fortified by the Finns, so it would be no easy business to launch a sudden invasion of Finland in an emergency.

What was to prevent the Germans and the Finns making a secret agreement at some future date? Choosing their own time, the Finns might pick a quarrel with Russia and the Mannerheim Line would be quite strong enough to resist any attack that Russia could launch against it until Germany could land a considerable expeditionary force in the Finnish ports to reinforce it. Then the enemy would stage a great offensive, take Leningrad and strike south-east direct at Moscow.

People laughed at the Moscow broadcasts in which the Russians declared that the Finns were threatening them. On the face of it, the suggestion that a nation of 4 million people can threaten one of 180 millions is laughable: but when we get down to the real root of the matter it is not laughable at all. The Kremlin obviously could not announce the fact, but what they really meant was that at some future date four million Finns, *backed by eighty million Germans*, might constitute a threat to Russia, and of such a combination they had every reason to be very frightened indeed.

The English papers printed a lot of blather to the effect that Stalin had at last come out in his true colours and shown himself for the brigand that he was. They said that all his talk about preserving peace because it is the workers who suffer most in any war was mere eye-wash, that he didn't give a damn about the workers and had revived all the old Imperialistic aims of the Tsars.

That, in my view, was nonsense. Stalin may be a thug but he is *not* an Imperialist. He would still prefer to have peace if he could get what he wants without war, but in the case of Finland he could not get it, and so he went to war.

Moreover, he went to war when he did because he could not afford to wait any longer. November is the classic time for launching an attack on Finland. Earlier in the year the ice has not formed on the lakes and marshes in sufficient thickness to carry guns and transport, while after January the snow is too deep for major operations to be possible. If he had waited and continued only to threaten through those precious winter months of December and January he would have lost his chance for another year. In that time the whole world situation might have altered – in fact, it has altered – and Germany's position is so much stronger now that, had Stalin deferred his attack on the Finns until November the 30th, 1940, Hitler might have told him that either he must call it off or German aid would be sent to the Finns, and it is doubtful if Stalin would have dared to proceed with an attack on the

111

Karelian Isthmus if he thought that Hitler would support the Finns with even a single army corps, which he could now perfectly well spare.

Stalin *had* to go into Finland in the winter of 1939 or he might have lost his chance of doing so for good.

The fighting proved a costly operation for Russia, but even the price that Stalin had to pay for breaking the Finns was fully justified because he succeeded in locking that last vulnerable north-western gate.

After this, things doubtless looked pretty good to Stalin as he had succeeded in placing a wide belt of territory, which was fully under his control but not populated by Russians, between himself and Germany. On surveying the new map which showed that belt extending from the Finnish lakes to the Rumanian frontier Voroshilov must have rubbed his hands with glee, since it was such an enormous improvement on and development of the strategy which he had laid down for Russia years before. In those days he had decided that he would have to abandon Leningrad, Smolensk, Minsk, and Kiev and a belt of territory two or three hundred miles wide to be ravaged by the enemy. *Now* there would no longer be any need for this; the Finnish, Estonian, Latvian, Lithuanian, and Polish belt would be sacrificed and ravaged instead.

If Stalin had *wanted* to fight anybody he now had a first-class opportunity to do so. He could have attacked Norway and Sweden with a view to securing ports on the Atlantic, or he could have gone down and fought the Rumanians to get back Russia's old province of Bessarabia. But he did nothing of the kind.

By her passive connivance in his take-over of half Poland, the Baltic States, and the Finnish territories Germany had shown that she was in no position to resist his aggression outside her own sphere for the time being and, although she might have had to advance her programme by going into southern Norway and Sweden if he had moved, there is no reason whatever to suppose that she would have gone to war with him if he had attacked those countries in the North. In spite of high feeling in the Allied countries over his wanton aggression against Finland, the Allied Governments had made it quite clear that they did not wish to go to war with him unless they absolutely had to, so it is virtually certain that they would have brought pressure on King Carol to surrender Bessarabia to him had he threatened to move in that direction; but he did not take advantage of either situation. For the time being he was safe and he was quite content to remain so although neither Germany nor the Allies were in a position seriously to interfere with him if he cared to go adventuring.

The next act was the collapse of France, and this automatically called for fresh action on Stalin's part. France and Britain had established a large army in the Near East which, with Turkey as their Ally, was to be used to carry out their guarantee to Rumania if Hitler threatened that country. Hungary was still a neutral but she played the part of a buffer state and although she was

In no position to resist German aggression it was considered that by the time the Germans had advanced over the not very good roads in her territories to the Rumanian border the Rumanian Army would be in its battle positions with the Near Eastern Allied army moving up through Turkey and across the Black Sea to its support. Stalin had reckoned that the Allies would hold Rumania for him, but now the situation was altogether different.

With France out of the ring the Syrian forces are immobilized and the Turks are taking a rather different view of things. Now that Italy has thrown her weight into the scale with Germany can Turkey afford to defy the Axis Powers with only the British Near Eastern army to reinforce her? By Italy's entry into the war Hungary is rendered entirely helpless. She needs only the promise from Hitler of the return of her lost province of Transylvania to go in on the side of the Axis and attack Rumania while German and Italian forces are rushed to her assistance. The Turks may refuse to move or even to permit the British to march through Turkey. The balance of naval power in the Mediterranean has been entirely upset by the entry of Italy into the war and the defection of the French Fleet which may even go over to the Axis. Stalin sees that even before matters have clarified Hitler may launch another blitzkrieg with the help of Hungary and Italy, and Rumania will be overrun before the Turks have decided on their new policy or the British have been able to assist Rumania in any way.

As a shrewd man Stalin has always seen the possibility of some such situation arising, so he already has troops massed on his Rumanian border; he does not hesitate, but sends a twelve-hour ultimatum. The Rumanians give way and the Russians walk in, taking not only their old province of Bessarabia but the Bukovina and other territories as well. *As long as it looked as though Rumania would be able to maintain her independence Stalin refrained from action, but directly she was threatened by Germany he acted* and the Russian chastity belt now extends unbroken from the Baltic to the Black Sea.

This brings us up to date, and the sole reason for this long preamble, which is taken almost entirely from *Red Eagle* and Chapters X and XI of my last thriller *Faked Passports*, published in May of this year, is to show my assessment of the Russian policy and *that Stalin's actions have been absolutely consistent throughout.*

Chapters X and XI of *Faked Passports* are entitled 'Grand Strategy' and ironically 'Faked Passports'. During the war, Wheatley decided that he didn't want to write too many works of fiction because sensitive 'intelligence', knowledge and ideas (sourced from his war papers and conversations with government employees), could filter into his fiction and inadvertently leak to the enemy. As we have noted, his war novels did include some of the ideas used in his war papers. With *Faked Passports*, the ideas came before the paper (unlike the ideas used – as we have previously explored – in *'V' is for Vengeance* and *The Man Who Missed the War*).

113

The two chapters in *Faked Passports* concern Wheatley's gentleman spy Gregory Sallust, and a conversation he (the fictional character) has with real-life Nazi, Goering. They discuss Germany's war-time strategy in a similar way to how Wheatley outlined the Stalin/Far East ideas in this paper. Wheatley simply updated/refined those ideas for serious study for the Joint Planning Staff. In fact, what we have discovered so far in this paper is Wheatley's pro-active approach to the potential future problems with the Nazis. He quotes from two of his recent books (one fiction, one non-fiction) and speaks with some authority, almost in an academic way. This could not fail to impress the War Cabinet, for Wheatley had proved that he was a sound reasoner and his 'contributions' in juxtaposition with the strategies planned by the cabinet would be invaluable background material. Wheatley was using his published work almost as a thesis. His Sallust novels would allow him (up to *Faked Passports*) to present some of his more extravagant ideas and show more depth to his thought processes, rather than spontaneous thoughts from direct questions (from the JPS) or perceptions based upon recent news stories. By the end of July 1940, Wheatley knew what his 'job' for the war was, the same as it was before it – a writer, an ideas man, someone with the natural-born perception to inspire pause for thought, to hit upon the crux of a problem and come up with a logical solution. Now that solution may not always be the right one, but it would inspire more mature thought on the various strategies. Obviously, these would be discussed at a very high level within the War Cabinet (Chiefs of Staff and Winston Churchill himself) and the time would come when Wheatley would be called to some of the meetings himself, to thrash around his ideas and perception as a member of the Joint Planning Staff. It was mature papers such as 'The Independence of Turkey' that would inspire that decision.

> The new development is that, for all practical purposes, Hitler has now become the master of the Balkans. He and Mussolini can walk into Hungary, Yugoslavia, Rumania, and Bulgaria any day they like, and nobody is going to oppose them. In consequence our old friend, the Turk, is getting very nervous; because he knows the Russians better than we do.
>
> With Germany moving south-eastward Stalin is going to say: 'Somebody in Berlin may be looking up that old file about the Berlin-Baghdad railway and other files about Iran and a descent on India. If Hitler is contemplating that sort of thing he must come down through Turkey, so his Frontier is going to march with mine in the Caucasus; and that I will not have – it is much too near my oil-wells. The time has come when I must once again extend my chastity belt.'
>
> In consequence, Russia is now suggesting that she should give her protection to Turkey and be allowed to send her warships into the Bosphorous and the Dardanelles.

Turkey and Russia have reason to be good friends. At Genoa and other world conferences after the last Great War, Commissar Chicherin and Ismet Pasha stood together when every hand was against them; at Lucerne they even defied the mighty Curzon. Moreover, it was the Russians who made possible Kemel Attaturk's defeat of the Greeks by giving him at no charge all the guns and munitions supplied by the Allies to Baron Wrangel and captured in the Crimea; so it may almost be said that modern Turkey owes her very existence to Bolshevik Russia.

But it does not follow that the Turks are prepared to allow Russia's armed forces entry into their country. They probably feel – as the Poles felt – that once you ask a Russian in it is exceedingly difficult to persuade him to go home again, and Turkey does not like the idea of becoming a member of the Union of Soviet Socialist Republics. If Stalin becomes really pressing, therefore, what is Turkey to do?

She has an understanding with Britain, but how much is that worth now that France is out of the game? As long as Hitler keeps an army of three or four million men in the field, and Mussolini keeps another million or two under arms, Britain will need all the men she has to protect her own shores and to keep the Italians from achieving any major successes in Egypt or Kenya.

Even if Britain were prepared to do so, she could not put an army into Turkey of sufficient strength to resist Russia's millions. Even less could she effectively support the Turks against a combined attack by Germany and Russia – such as that which resulted in the partition of Poland – but this must be considered as a definite possibility if Turkey rejects Russia's demands and calls Britain to her aid.

It seems, therefore, that as Britain is now such a weak reed to lean on in the North East the Turks will shortly have to consider whether it is better to accept Russian protection or German protection as the only means of preventing their homeland, upon the reconstruction of which they have lavished such devoted toil, from being destroyed by a joint attack from both.

The modern Turkey is very different from the old Turkey. An immense amount has been done in recent years to build up the industries of the country, and Turkey now has ambitions to become a trading power of considerable importance. Russian ways are still slipshod and old fashioned. German ways are perhaps the most advanced in the world as far as commercial enterprise is concerned. Already, quite recently, Turkey has signed a very far-reaching trade agreement with Germany and she is, apparently, now considering if, of the two evils, it would not be better for her to defy Russia and open her gates to Germany as a more powerful and reliable protector who would offer her better prospects in the future.

Some people consider von Papen a fool but it does not seem to me that he is by any means a witless person. He has been up to the neck in every conspiracy for the last quarter of a century, yet he has managed to keep his head on his shoulders and is still one of Hitler's trusted envoys when nearly all of his past associates have paid the penalty for their trickery. Doubtless he is now working overtime for the Nazi in Turkey and his capabilities should not be underrated. If he succeeds in bringing Turkey over to the Germans, what happens next?

Russia will probably move again very quickly on the excuse that Turkey's Armenian territories are really the property of the Soviet Armenian Republic, but she will not *fight* Germany. The Turks will be told that they had better not oppose Russia in this, as Germany will not support them if they do, but that she will guarantee the rest of Turkey's territory. Germany will then move an army over the Bosphorous and the way will lie open to her through Kurdistan to our oil-wells at Mosul, and for an advance into Persia and to India by way of Baluchistan. It may well be Hitler's intention to fight us in Iraq, where he can bring superior forces against us with the connivance of the Turks, rather than to attempt an invasion of Britain where we should have the advantage of numbers over any forces that he could send against us.

Any such combination of events would be most gravely to our disadvantage and it seems to me that there is only one way in which we can counter this extremely serious threat. *It is by, taking for once, a really bold decision and bringing off a diplomatic coup of the first magnitude.*

The first thing is that we must make up our minds quite definitely who could be made our friends and who are clearly minded to be our foes in this titanic struggle. It is no good trying to placate Russia by sending Communist Sir Stafford Cripps there as our Ambassador and trying to placate the Japanese by closing the Burma road when we know that the interests of Russia and Japan conflict so strongly. We ought to choose one or other of these major Powers and henceforth go all out to make that Power our real friend, even if it necessitates giving open offence to the other one.

The choice should be governed by the following considerations:
1. *Which of these countries is the more likely to go to war with us whether we like it or not?*

   In my view our break with Japan, made solely to curry favour with the United States and without any reciprocal advantage of a guarantee by America of our interests in the Pacific, was one of the major blunders in our diplomatic history; but it is no good crying over spilt milk. Our refusal to renew the Anglo-Japanese treaty of alliance was felt by the Japs as the most terrible loss of face that they have ever sustained, and they have never forgiven us for it. Moreover, the situation has been aggravated by the aid we have given to China.

   The ideology of the Japanese Army Chiefs is very close to that of the Nazis. They are a most bellicose race – as they have shown most markedly in the last half-century of their history – and they are out to found an empire in the East if they possibly can. British interests and Empire strategy block their way to the achievements of this ambition more so than those of any other nation, the United States not excepted; and note that we have our hands full in the West it is generally acknowledged that Japan might declare war upon us any day.

Russia, on the other hand, has nothing whatever to gain from a war with Britain and, as I hope I have shown in the preceding pages, Stalin, having more lebensraum for his people than any other ruler in the world and the natural resources of one-sixth of the world's land surface as yet almost undeveloped, has no territorial ambitions. All he wants is to be left in peace so as to be able to raise the standard of living of his people.

2. Which of these two Powers could do us the most damage if we went to war with either?

The Japanese could cause us the gravest inconvenience in the Pacific, but for the reasons given below I believe that we could cope with this. In any case, Japan is too far away to aid Germany materially in the West, since she could not send troops and munitions while our Navy still holds the seas and she could not reinforce Germany's Air Force with her own for the bombing of Britain.

On the other hand, Russia could immediately place her armed might at Germany's disposal for operations in Europe and the Near East, a drive on India or a descent into Africa, and she could also send her very considerable Air Force to assist the Germans in an attempt to subdue Britain.

3. Which of the two would we stand the best chance of defeating if we had to fight one or the other?

Fortunately, the God who looks after England while the rest of us play cricket decreed the Sino–Japanese War, and for the past three years these powerful little yellow islanders have been frittering away their strength by endeavouring to gobble up China.

Apart from the severe strain upon Japanese man-power and military resources, this has had a most disastrous effect upon Japanese finance. The country was never rich and it is now on the verge of bankruptcy. In the event of war with Japan we could close her cotton-goods market in India and take many other measures which in a comparatively short time would kick the last flimsy supports from under her financial structure.

Moreover, the interests of the United States march with those of Britain in the Far East so there is good reason to suppose that America would at least place her Pacific fleet at our disposal. If it actually came to a Japanese invasion of New Zealand and Australia feeling among the American people would run so high at the thought of a white race being overrun by a yellow people that is virtually certain that the United States would enter the war on our side.

Therefore although the Japanese Fleet might cause us serious inconvenience in the Far East I believe that if Japan were added to our enemies we could defeat her.

On the other hand, if Russia went in with Germany I do not see that we could do very much about it. In the first place she is, for all practical purposes, self-supporting and has few external markets which we could damage. In the second place, her resources and man-power are almost inexhaustible. In the third place, she is naturally protected from any aggression by us by a huge belt of territory consisting of Western Europe and Southern Asia. About the only place where we could inflict serious damage on her is the Caucasus, where we could bomb her oil-wells from our bases in Iraq; but that would not put her out of the war.

Moreover, the United States has no quarrel with Russia and if, to counter the hostility of Russia, we were compelled to give further concession to Japan in order to secure some measure of friendliness from her, this would serve to annoy the American people and render the United States less likely to give us armed help against Germany.

In consequence, I see no way at all in which we could defeat Russia, and I think that the Government was extremely well-advised in refusing to be drawn into war with her over Finland, as if Russia once became Germany's full ally and our active enemy there could be no foreseeing any end to the war at all.

Wheatley suddenly paints a very dark picture on a world-size canvas, clearly displaying the paranoia of the British people at the turn of the 1940s, a side rarely seen, let alone written and understood, from a purely civilian point of view.

Regardless of political blunders by the British governments through the ages, Wheatley points out where we did at least make one very good 'war-time' decision: don't declare war on Russia!

If this analysis is correct the answer is quite clear. (1) Whereas we have no ground at all at the moment for believing that Russia will enter the war against us, we have every ground for supposing that Japan might do so at any time. (2) In the event of our having to fight either, Russia could do us infinitely more damage than could Japan. (3) And, whereas we could not defeat Russia, we could defeat Japan.

It therefore seems abundantly obvious that we should keep friendly with the Russians even though we may give considerable offence to the Japanese.

It is *not* suggested that we could induce Russian to enter the war actively on our side to the extent of launching her army and air force against Germany; *in fact, as one must take a long view of possible developments in Europe after the war there are very good reasons for regarding a Russian invasion of Germany, by way of Poland, as extremely undesirable,* however gratifying it might be at the present moment. But it is suggested that if we are prepared to pull some of Russia's chestnuts out of the fire for her she would take an altogether different view, cease giving any aid to Germany and be of very material assistance to us by giving us limited but most useful help for a specific purpose.

That specific purpose would be to prevent Germany moving East and so establishing herself in the Black Sea and on Russia's southern Asiatic border, *and to prevent this without it being necessary for Russia to force her protection on Turkey.*

The first step is a proposal to Turkey that she should open the Dardanelles and the Bosphorous to the British and Russian fleets.

It is, of course, fully appreciated that Turkey has already refused to open these narrows to either of us separately but this becomes an entirely different proposition if it was suggested that she should open them *to BOTH the Russians and the British at the same time, and that neither would be allowed to occupy the straits with more than a specified tonnage in warships at any period.*

The Turks would, of course, retain their land batteries and their own fleet, so in effect they would still control their own waters because *they would hold the balance of power.* Any act of aggression by one of the visiting fleets against Turkey would, under this proposed agreement, be considered an act of war upon the other visiting fleet, which would immediately render full assistance to the Turks, and in this way Turkey might reasonably consider herself safe from aggression by either.

The limitation of the tonnage of the visiting fleets would be restricted to Turkey's territorial waters so that Russia could pass her Black Sea fleet into the Mediterranean squadrons through the Black Sea if she so desired.

If this arrangement could once be brought about, Britain and Russia might then jointly guarantee Turkey from invasion *by sea* by Germany; as an Anglo–Russo–Turkish fleet would be able to safeguard Turkey's south coast from an Italo–German invasion from Rhodes and Greece.

This would leave only Turkey in Europe and the Straits to be defended, but the Bosphorous is only twenty miles in length and the Hellespont about fifty; so with Anglo–Russo–Turkish naval forces in the Sea of Marmara and Anglo–Russian air support, Turkey would have only a land front of about seventy miles to hold. As the Turks can put 800,000 men in the field and the zone under discussion is already heavily fortified, they should be able to resist anything which can be brought against them on so short a front without having to receive one Russian or British soldier on Turkish soil.

But if Russia is going to accept the responsibility that she might be drawn into war as our ally in the defence of Turkey, even if it would only involve action by her fleet, she must be given some inducement. Again, if Russia is to play a purely passive part and not even fire a shell against the Germans, but occupy the Dardenelles with us solely so that Turkey may retain the balance of power in her own waters, Russia would certainly require some *quid pro quo* for allowing us entry to the Black Sea. It is here that I propose a very revolutionary measure.

Because Hitler has had a great spectacular success people are now far too apt to think that he holds *all* the cards, and that the only thing left for us to do is to sit tight and die in defence of our island fortress. But that is not really the case at all. Hitler's power is still confined to Europe, whereas ours is far more broadly and more strongly based owing to our strategic strongholds scattered all over the world. We have enormous assets if we only care to use them.

My feeling is that now Goering lunches in Oslo, Goebbels has tea in Warsaw, and Hitler dines in Paris it really is quite time that we scrapped a lot of our old ideas. We are always accused by foreigners of being greedy land-grabbers who seize everything we can get and hang on to it without any thought for the interests of other countries at all. Now is the time to show a different spirit.

By this I do not suggest for one second that a single Union Jack should be hauled down in any part of the world, or our future interests jeopardized in any particular place, but I do think it would be a gesture which would pay us over and over again if, for once, we let a few other people share in our abundance while taking very good care to see that we were not in any way weakening ourselves.

Now, what have we got in our rich store-cupboard that we could give to Russia which would please her mightily?

Russia's main purpose, as I hope I have shown, is to seize every opportunity to strengthen herself against aggression by Germany, whether the attack, which she feels quite certain she will have to face, comes in the near future or in another twenty years' time. Her secondary purpose is to strengthen herself against Japan, and I believe that we could aid her enormously in the latter objective.

I propose that our inducement to Russia to help us to protect Turkey should be an offer to Russia of facilities for her fleet at Singapore.

Japan is just as much a threat to Russia in the East as she is to Britain. At present in the event of a future Russo–Japanese war Russia's naval operations, in the face of Japan's more powerful battle fleet, must be confined to the waters west of Japan centring on Vladivostock. But if Russia had dockyards, munition-depots, and other facilities at Singapore she would be twice as dangerous to Japan because she would also be able to operate in the waters to the south of her enemy.

As nobody has ever offered Russia anything I believe that the effect upon public opinion in Russia of such an offer by Britain would be simply tremendous and possibly sway the whole nation in our favour.

Next: what is Turkey to get out of this deal in which she opens once more her jealously guarded straits to two mighty foreign Powers? Certainly she gets their protection against a German invasion for the time being, but will they both be willing to go quietly away after the war? Probably not; and personally I don't see why they should. But is there any reason why Turkey should not be given something which would make her quite agreeable to accepting us as permanent guests?

In exchange for the freedom of the Dardanelles Russia might be agreeable to giving the Turkey Fleet facilities at Sevastopol and we could give Turkey facilities in our fine naval base at Alexandria.

As she is not a first-class Naval Power Turkey might not consider such facilities to be worth a great deal, although such a gesture would go down extremely well with the Turkish people.

However, we have other assets in the bag. There is the Suez Canal. Apparently, a seat on the board is prized beyond rubies – at least, Mussolini appeared to think so – and we have ten seats. Is there any reason why we should not give one to our good friends the Turks? They may not be a first-class Naval Power, but in recent years they have developed a fine merchant-fleet and are doing everything possible to promote their commerce. Their country lies so near the Canal that they must view it with considerable interest, and the gift by us of a seat on its board would almost certainly be considered by them as a really valuable asset.

The question now arises – what would Japan say to all this? She certainly will not like it, but surely it is worth running the risk of offending the Japanese if we can keep the Germans out of Turkey and not have to worry ourselves about any possibilities of an attack by the Axis Power on our oil-wells in Iraq and an advance by them towards India.

One thing is certain – that we shall not prevent Japan declaring war on us by showing further weakness. The utter failure of such a policy was shown with abundant clearness in the case of Mussolini. If, instead of pandering to him for eight solid months while he acted as a supply line for Hitler and stocked every warehouse in Italy full to the roof-tree with war materials for his own use, we had handled him firmly from the beginning and allowed him only enough imports to keep his own people from starvation it is virtually certain that he would never have dared to enter the war against us, even after the collapse of France.

Japan may fight, but she may not; and if we handle the situation really skilfully we might be able to keep her out through causing her to believe that she had no chance at all of emerging victorious from a conflict with us.

The interests of Britain, Russia, and the United States are common in the Pacific. All three of us wish to curb the growing power of the Japanese. Therefore I suggest that if it is any way possible the United States should also be brought in on this revolutionary deal.

The United States' main naval base in the Pacific is at Honolulu. To protect our common interests America might be willing to give both Britain and Russia facilities there, and in exchange the Russians might give America facilities in Vladivostock while we gave America also facilities in Singapore.

If this could be brought about all three of us would then have Japan caught in a triangle by which if she went to war with any one of us that power could threaten her sea routes simultaneously from Singapore, Vladivostock, and Honolulu, and it seems to me that while all the three Powers concerned would be very happy about such a situation Japan would then think twice – or even three times – before declaring war on any of us; and against a combination of two she would stand no chance at all.

It may be argued that Russia's Fleet in the Far East is so inferior to that of Japan that in any case she would not be able to wage a successful naval war against the Japanese single-handed. That may be so in her present situation, but with facilities in these other two bases the situation would be very different. The Russian Fleet may, or may not, be up to much but it is certainly growing in size with considerable rapidity. The Italian Fleet does not appear to be up to much, but that does not alter the fact that Britain has had to cease sending her merchant ships through the Mediterranean. With three bases in the Pacific I maintain that Russia could make things very uncomfortable for Japan indeed, as she would be able to threaten *all* Japan's sea routes even with inferior forces, and to bring about such an admirable situation I believe that Russia would go a very long way indeed to assist those who made this possible for her.

It should be remembered that I am not suggesting that anybody should surrender any strategic base to a foreign Power. In each case the facilities would be limited to a certain naval tonnage at one time, the use of dockyards by arrangement and a long-term lease on a square-mile or so of territory in which the lessee could erect repair-shops, buildings to contain supplies and munitions, and possibly establish a commercial air-base with permission to use it for a limited number of military aircraft. Each base would harbour the ships of three Powers and the present owner would retain possession of all land-batteries, thereby retaining the balance of power over its base and security from surprise attack by either one of the visiting fleets. Moreover, in this deal only strategic strongholds are involved and so any question of foreign Powers taking over populated territories where a plebiscite might be necessary is avoided.

Lastly: What would be the effect of such a deal upon the whole strategic situation?

1. We should enable Turkey to maintain her independence without accepting foreign soldiers on her soil.
2. We should prevent the Germans crossing into Asia and so might rest easy about India and our oil-wells in Iraq.
3. With Turkey secured and between the Germans and Iraq and with Russia our good, if passive, friend we should be able to withdraw a considerable portion of our Near Eastern Army from Palestine to reinforce Egypt; which is a matter of importance now that the Italians no longer have to wage war against the French on the Algerian frontier of Libya and can concentrate all their Libyan forces for a move towards the East.
4. Again, with Russia as our good, if passive, friend, we could withdraw a much larger proportion of our forces from India to reinforce Kenya and with

the assistance of Abyssinian rebellions possibly put the Italian forces in Abyssinia right out of the war.

5. With the naval squadrons of Britain, Russia, and the United States all dispersed and ready to operate from Singapore, Vladivostock, and Honolulu, and quite evidently a good understanding between these three countries, of which Japan will have no means of knowing the *full* details, there is a reasonably good prospect that she will not dare to move against us.

Obviously the entry of the United States into such an arrangement is most highly desirable, but it is by no means essential to the plan. If we can reach a good understanding with both Russia and Turkey by giving them something that they would value very highly we can still keep the Germans out of Asia – and that is what matters for the moment.

We have assets. Surely *now*, if ever, is the time to use them!

Notes

1. William L Shirer, *Berlin Diary 1934–1941*.
2. *The Fuehrer*, Konrad Heiden.

XI

Aerial Warfare

'To increase the enemy's uncertainty, a number of bombs with a time attachment might also be released from our bombers, attached to balloons … according to their setting, an hour or two after our pilots had gone home the bomb-carrying balloons would suddenly release their load … '
'Aerial Warfare'

Wheatley wrote 'Aerial Warfare', a paper – I consider – one of his best, between 20 and 25 September 1940. The blitz was two weeks old and Wheatley poured his concerns into the paper. However, he stated in *Stranger Than Fiction*:

> By the time it [the paper] reached the Planners many of my most vitriolic criticisms of the Government's handling of the situation [the blitz] had been rendered obsolete by vigorous orders from the Prime Minister …

I do feel that Wheatley was a little hard on himself with this comment, because the paper is written with a clear passion. It has sound structure, it's not just a cornucopia of ideas. In my opinion, 'Aerial Warfare' is the most direct and productive paper Wheatley wrote:

Aerial Warfare

When the history of this war comes to be written it will be said of August 1940 that the tide appeared to have turned in favour of Britain. The maximum power of the German Air Force was launched upon us and sustained a crushing defeat, while our own Air Force was able to take the initiative and with comparatively small losses inflict great damage upon the German military machine by nightly bombings. For more than thirty days in succession the enemy lost an average of forty-five planes per day definitely accounted for. It may also be reckoned that for every three aircraft actually seen to fall a further two failed to get home, were useless for further service when they limped in, or were destroyed on the ground by our bombers. At this rate the Nazis were losing 27,000 planes a year. It was therefore obvious that if this state of things continued for another few months Britain would have gained complete mastery of the air and thereby hold the golden key to the success of all future strategic operations.

But of September 1940 it will be said that while the Royal Navy continued paramount upon the seas, while the military strength of Britain remained unimpaired, and while the R.A.F. continued to perform prodigies of valour in both defence and attack, Britain, nevertheless, sustained a considerable defeat and her war effort was as seriously crippled as if she had lost a major battle.

The indiscriminate night bombing recently indulged in by the Nazis has had little effect upon us as a Power, and even the damage done to property – regarded on the scale of the World War – is, so far, comparatively negligible; but the cost to Britain in labour hours and dislocation of commerce has been utterly appalling.

In recent weeks Goering has greatly reduced the scale of his massed attacks in daylight, which played into our hands, and it must even be regarded as possible that he may stop these altogether; thus conserving his whole strength for night bombing. Should this prove the case we shall have no means of destroying the German Air Force until our own Air Force is sufficiently strong to treble its attacks on enemy air-bases and over a long period of weeks gradually reduce the German air-strength on its own soil.

This means that for many months to come Hitler will still be in a position to send over several hundred planes each night throughout the winter, and if these indiscriminate bombings cannot be checked, the results – judged by the last fortnight – may prove for us positively disastrous.

Fortunately, the damage so far sustained can be allocated at approximately 10 per cent due to enemy action and 90 per cent due to the lack of forethought and crass stupidity of our own civil authorities. It seemed to me, therefore, worth while to examine this question and, with due deference, put up a few suggestions which might possibly help to counteract the inroads at present being made upon our national life.

In considering counter-measures which might be taken these fall under three heads: (1) Military (Offensive), (2) Military (Defensive), (3) Civil Administration.

MILITARY COUNTER-MEASURES (OFFENSIVE)

Military and Non-Military Objectives

The declared policy of the Air Ministry has, so far, been that we should confine bombing attacks to enemy military objectives, and on broad lines this, obviously, is absolutely sound. It seems, however, that while the policy is clearly stated it is either not carried out in fact or certain other Government Departments do not subscribe to it.

On the one hand we are from time to time given a somewhat self-righteous statement from the Air Ministry that our bombers, owing to poor weather conditions, failed to locate their targets and so the pilots, like the good, obedient boys that they are, dutifully brought their bombs all the way back to England.

On the other hand the Ministry of Information issues photographs of shops and houses in Berlin which quite clearly have no military significance but have been destroyed in our recent air-raids, and the Press points with justifiable glee to the fact that we are at last giving the Huns some of their own medicine.

The feeling of the public upon this question is very plain. They realize the necessity of going for military objectives but, at the same time, they are delighted to think that the Germans are now compelled to suffer the same inconveniences as themselves, and in view of the slaughter among our own women and children they are not in the least concerned by the fact that our bombs may have killed a certain number of non-combatant Germans.

In fact, the man-in-the-street is stating in no uncertain terms that it is quite time that the people responsible for the conduct of the war took off their kid gloves.

Personally, I feel that the pompous gentleman in the Air Ministry should be called off, because his statement can only mean one of two things: (a) that we are so short of bombs that we dare not spare one for anything which is not a definitely specified target, or (b) that he is asking for an infuriated mob of East-Enders to come up one day and hang him from a lamp-post.

In the first case it is extremely bad propaganda to suggest that we are short of war material, should this be so; in the second, the public is far past the state where it will allow its Service chiefs to regard this war as a game of cricket. *Any* gas-works, railway station, bridge, road junction, wharf or canal in the whole length and breadth of Germany *is a military objective,* so if a pilot cannot put his bombs on the target he has been given it is sheer lunacy that he and his crew should be asked to risk their lives and an expensive plane and use up valuable petrol to take bombs hundreds of miles through the night into Central Germany and bring them all the way back again. Surely common sense demands that he should drop them on any suitable objective that he may find before passing out again over the North Sea.

If the dropping of bombs upon non-military objectives is considered at all, it should not be thought that the gain is limited merely to the destruction of German property and the killing of a certain number of Germans which may possibly include a few combatants or officials. There is another very definite gain. Each such raid gives a definite satisfaction to the bulk of our own people. The great majority of them know little of the strategic necessities and it is a real tonic to them to think that we are giving back as good as we get. Therefore, while the policy of continuing to devote our main efforts towards the destruction of military objectives should be maintained, I feel that it might be a good thing perhaps once a week to order a raid on a non-military objective. But this type of retaliation should not be carried out in the haphazard manner of the Nazi; it should be definitely planned and it will then be three times as effective.

Non-Military Objectives

The thing to aim at is not the destruction of large numbers of unfortunate German working people but the destruction of the symbols of the New Germany that Hitler has created during his years in power.

Here are just a few of the targets which might be considered:

(a) The Brown House in Munich is the spiritual home of the Nazi Party. Moreover it contains the Party records, so its destruction would be a serious blow against the enemy.

(b) Berchtesgaden may be so well protected that it would not be worth risking our airmen's lives in an attack upon it, but on a cloudy day possibly a single plane with a couple of large bombs might get through. Hitler has not scrupled to attempt the life of our King and Queen in their home, and although it is unlikely that the Fuehrer is often resident at Berchtesgaden in these days it would give enormous satisfaction to a vast number of people if it could be satisfactorily blown up.

(c) Karinhalle. The same applies to Reich Marshal Goering's palatial home.

(d) The Brandenburg Gate. It is reported that this has already been damaged – presumably by accident. How sad! Yet it is one of the things that embodies the spirit of martial Germany which has brought such misery upon the world, and therefore it would be an admirable work to lay the whole thing in ruins.

(e) The Denkmal, opposite Rudesheim. This huge statue which symbolizes the watch on the Rhine might be difficult to destroy but its isolated situation near no military objective or populated area leads one to suppose that it is probably not defended at all, so a flight of bombers might tackle it on a moonlit night without opposition and blow it to pieces.

(f) The Opera House in Berlin, which has been the scene of so many of Hitler's bombastic speeches, should certainly be singled out for attention.

(g) The Air Ministry is now perhaps the finest building in Berlin, which is a shoddy city, possessing few buildings of which she can be proud, and it quite definitely comes under the heading of military objectives.

(h) Hitler's new Chancellery would also be a good objective if it is at all practicable.

(i) The Fuehrer Schools. There are a number of these in Germany, and it should not be thought that by attacking them we should be wantonly destroying helpless children. Each contains several hundred young brutes between the ages of eighteen and twenty-four who have been picked from the whole German nation to be the leaders of the Nazi Party of tomorrow. They are coached in Gestapo methods and as fanatical in their worship of Hitlerism as the inmates of any Jesuit monastery were fanatical upon the subject of their religion in the days of the Inquisition. If we desire peace in the world, as many of these people as possible should be exterminated while the going is good and, even if they have been evacuated, the destruction of the colleges would be a good blow at the very heart of Nazidom.

(j) The German forests. Certain journalists pressed most strongly for the destruction of these by fire all through the long, hot summer and it seems that a belated attempt was made to fire them early in September. It may perhaps be too late in the year now to start large-scale fires in them but the Germans are both great believers in the use of fire as a weapon and very frightened of it, so great forest fires would have a most desirable effect upon them.

(k) The rivers. I heard a rumour that while the French were still holding the Maginot Line our Navy, with its usual zest for unusual operations which might embarrass the enemy, sent a unit to Strasbourg which tipped a considerable number of mines into the Rhine there, with the idea that they would be carried down the river and blow up any shipping or the piers of bridges that they might encounter. This sounded to me most admirable work. Is there any reason why our Air Force should not drop naval mines into the Rhine and other swift-flowing rivers? As a target the rivers present to us the enormous advantage of their great length, which means that they cannot possibly be adequately protected along their whole course. Therefore, it should not be by any means a difficult operation for our bombers to select quiet stretches and drop the mines in without serious interference.

(l) The Tannemberg Memorial.

These are the type of semi-military objectives which I suggest should be attacked by possibly one out of every twenty raiding forces sent into Germany. In spite of the strong censorship of the Press, they could not possibly conceal for long such acts as the destruction of the Brown House or the Denkmal; and here our propaganda people should play their part by having leaflets printed after a successful operation of this kind, which should run on the following lines:

Germany is wantonly and deliberately destroying the homes of our workers and killing our women and children; we have so far refrained from this inhuman method of warfare. But that the Royal Air Force can bomb anything it wishes has been proved to you by the destruction on Saturday last of Goering's home at Karinhalle (aerial photograph herewith). The war will never end until Hitler and the Nazis are removed from power so you should most seriously consider any steps which may lead to this, otherwise a time may come when we shall have to reconsider the situation and, instead of bombing statues and palaces, destroy the most highly populated centres of Germany's cities.

Hummers

The great disadvantage under which we labour at the moment in our aerial war against Germany is that their bases are so much nearer to London than ours are to Berlin. They can, therefore, render our population uneasy for ten hours per night whereas we can only render the population of their more distant cities uneasy for about three hours. The lengthening of the nights will enable us to lengthen the duration of our raids but that also applies to the enemy.

As our bombers must get out of Germany before dawn, it it not possible for our scientists to invent some mechanism which our pilots can leave behind them in the air?

I imagine that the note of a British aeroplane could easily be taken on a gramophone record and the record run off again with a sound-amplifier attachment, so that if it was floating about at, say, 10,000 feet above a city it would create the impression that an enemy plane was still droning over-head.

If this could be achieved it would greatly puzzle and disquiet the Germans. They would not be able to sound their 'All-Clear' with real conviction until possibly hours after our planes had gone home, and they would probably expend a great deal of ammunition shooting at a sound-box.

The problem is how to keep the hummer floating in the air, and I think it might possibly be done in one of two ways:

(a) A small model aeroplane which could be dropped out of our bombers with its rudder set so that it went round and round in circles for an hour or two before reaching the ground.

(b) By attaching a hummer-box to a small balloon which could be put out by our bombers on the windward side of any German city before their departure for home.

To prevent the Germans finding out about this new dodge the hummer might be blown to pieces by a small time-bomb attachment before it was due to reach the ground, but even when the enemy discovered what we were up to this would not really matter, because during the hours of darkness they would never know if it was a bomber overhead or only a hummer.

Balloon Bombs

To increase the enemy's uncertainty, a number of bombs with a time attach-ment might also be released from our bombers, attached to balloons. The bomb-carrying balloons would then drift with the hummer-carrying balloons and, according to their settings, an hour or two after our pilots had gone home the bomb-carrying balloons would suddenly release their load, which would descend, spreading consternation and dismay among the enemy, who had come to believe that in the small hours of the morning there was no longer anything except hummers overhead.

This, admittedly, means indiscrimate bombing, but here, I maintain, indis-criminate bombing is absolutely justified. Hitler started this nerve war and it is the maintenance of morale which is going to win in the end; so we have every possible right to utilize any conceivable method which we can think out to wear down the nerves of the German people.

There followed ten pages of suggestions for Defence Measures; some of which were doubtless very wild and woolly. They were mainly concerned with:

Lighting up the sky to give us a better chance of bringing down the raiders – by parachute flare shells, lights attached to balloons, etc.

Aerial Q-ships in the form of manned balloons, and aerial magnetic mines.

An inverted cable barrage flown from civil aircraft.

Possible ways of camouflaging the Thames, the Serpentine, and other landmarks which on moonlight nights gave the raiders their position over London.

The paper then continued:

CIVIL ADMINISTRATION

The effects of indiscriminate bombing are as follows:
1. Casualties to combatants and non-combatants.
2. Destruction of property.
3. Nuisance value, mainly through dislocation of the telephone system and rendering cross-London travel lengthy and difficult.
4. Loss of sleep and undermining of the health of the population.
5. Lowering of morale of the population through all amusements being closed and resulting boredom.
6. Loss of working hours, resulting in great falling-off of industrial output and general dislocation of commerce.

Casualties
About the casualties which are the direct result of enemy action there is little to be done except to evacuate badly bombed areas as far as it is possible, and this matter appears already to be in hand.

At a rough approximation the casualties have probably been in the neighbourhood of 1,000 a day since indiscriminate bombing started but, as Mr. Churchill has pointed out, less than one-fortieth of these are members of the Armed Forces; so, apart from the horror with which such senseless slaughter fills us all, the casualties sustained are nothing like as great as those suffered by our Army during the last War, and will not seriously affect our war effort even if they continue at this rate for many weeks.

Damage to Property

Damage to property is also the unavoidable result of enemy action but the military damage so far done is comparatively slight while, when surveying the vast acreage of houses, shops, and offices still untouched, it is clear that it is going to be a very long time yet before London is rendered untenable. The American correspondent of the *New York Times* put his finger on it recently when he wrote that at this rate it would take Hitler 2,000 weeks to destroy London and that he did not think it likely that Hitler had another forty years to live.

Under this head of destruction of property the question of salvage should be considered. These great heaps of debris, although still comparatively few and far between in most London districts, are a depressing sight and for that reason alone they should be tidied as soon as possible.

I do not know what the present figure of the unemployed is, but have reason to believe that it still runs into hundreds of thousands. Surely this is the very work for our great reservoir of unskilled labour? Gangs of unemployed could be set to work under the direction of builders' foremen to sort the heaps of rubble, remove to dumps all timber, iron, and usable bricks for sorting and further use and then, having tidied up the site, run a board fence along its front so that it becomes indistinguishable from a house which has been pulled down and is awaiting rebuilding.

Nuisance Value

Much greater damage done by the indiscriminate raiding, so far, has been the nuisance value caused by the disruption of the telephone system and transport services.

With regard to the telephones, it seems to me that the post-office is much to blame for not having taken precautionary measures by laying alternative lines in anticipation that some of their main cables might be damaged in air-raids.

However, it is not too late to do this, and I suggest that the Royal Engineers should be employed to lay air lines along London's lamp standards as an alternative service which will link up the Exchanges. In warfare air lines have an enormous advantage that any break in them can be very quickly located and repaired.

With regard to travel, time-bombs make circuitous routes in certain places unavoidable, but the policy of the London Passenger Transport Board seems to have been somewhat muddled and obscure.

Their underground trains continued to run, yet all their stations were closed immediately a siren sounded, so that nobody above ground could get down to the trains.

Presumably, this policy was adopted because the L.P.T.B. did not wish their stations to be choked by crowds taking shelter during air-raids. But surely this could have been avoided by police supervision to ensure that anybody taking a ticket during an air-raid was compelled to travel whether he liked it or not. This might have led to some crowding of the trains, but I doubt if they would have been more crowded than during the normal rush-hours, owing to the fact that London is now so empty.

As far as the buses were concerned, the L.P.T.B. appear to have left it to the discretion of their drivers as to whether they continued on their route or packed up and went down with their passengers into an air-raid shelter. Obviously it was the right thing to do for them to stop and take cover while an enemy plane was actually droning overhead, but large numbers of the men stopped at the siren, and this should definitely not be permitted. London's taximen set us all an admirable example by continuing to function throughout raids from the very beginning, and in my view every possible thing should be done to continue all transport services except in areas where the firing of guns demonstrates that the enemy is actually overhead and there is danger from either bombs or falling shell-splinters.

Loss of Sleep

With loss of sleep we come up against a far more serious side of the problem, and one for which the enemy is only partially responsible.

The facilities for shelter afforded by the Government to the population of London have been handled in – to say the least of it – a curious manner. Before the war there was much discussion as to whether we should be given deep shelters or above-ground shelters, the net result being that we were not given any shelter at all, except damp, draughty Andersons and a few trenches in the parks, until the war had been in progress for some ten months, at any time during which Hitler might have turned the whole of his Air Force upon us. The Home Office then started frantically building brick street-shelters, great numbers of which are not even yet completed or are still lacking their roof protection.

Possibly the decision to build above-ground shelters may have been sound, in view of the great area of London and the difficulty and expense of making proper underground shelters, but while only partially solving the problem of protection these above-ground shelters do nothing at all to alleviate the mental stress of a population that may have to sustain air-raids continuing for many hours each night.

I understand that plans are now being discussed – somewhat belatedly – to make these street-shelters more habitable by placing benches, and in some cases wire bunks, in them. This would be a great improvement but it by no means solves the problem, as is demonstrated by the fact that many thousands of people are now taking their bedding down each night on to the platforms of the Tube stations.

In any great city the obvious air-raid shelter is its underground system, and I understand that it is now proposed to close the short stretch of Tube railway between Holborn and Aldwych to convert this into a really safe air-raid dormitory; but what good is this going to do to the people living in Kensington or Baker Street?

I would therefore suggest that the Underground railway should continue to run up to and round the Inner Circle, but that all stations inside that area should be closed and the tunnels between them converted into dormitories.

This would give us the following stretches of tunnel: (a) Notting Hill Gate to Liverpool Street, (b) South Kensington to King's Cross, (c) King's Cross to Broad Street, (d) St. Paul's to Farringdon Street, and (e) Charing Cross to Baker Street. If possible the scheme should be extended to cover the Waterloo area, thereby giving us the three lines under the Thames for the large population on the south side of the river.

Allowing for double tracks, the interior lines of the Inner Circle would give us twenty-six miles of deep shelters and if the three river-tunneled, together with the Tube lines as far as the Elephant and Castle, could be included we should have some thirty-five miles, in which a very considerable portion of the population of Inner London could be accommodated for the night without moving out of their own districts.

Travellers by Underground would be brought each day to the station on the Inner Circle nearest to their offices and they would then have to go by bus or on foot for the remainder of their journey. But this would not prove a very grave inconvenience if additional bus services were put on to run only from point to point on the circumference of the closed area, and in conformity with a new A.R.P. policy all drivers were instructed that they must continue to drive their vehicles until enemy aircraft were actually overhead in their locality.

The present situation, in which the L.P.T.B turns a kindly blind eye to crowds invading its stations each night but has announced no official policy, and is given no lead by the Government, is scandalous. By such unorganized crowding we are positively asking for an epidemic of some unpleasant nature to sweep the city. But London citizens must sleep safe and sound if they are to continue with their work each day. Therefore, it is of the utmost urgency that some schemes such as I suggest should be organized at once to ensure the many thousands who live in Central London proper, uncrowded accommodation.

Interference with the liberty of the individual is always regrettable, but for the maintenance of public health it may even be necessary for a general inspection by Police and Health Officers to take place in each district in order that Health Officers may satisfy themselves as to the sanitation, etc., of the night accommodation now being used by all the inhabitants of the city. If such accommodation is not of a satisfactory nature in the poorer quarters, and it is found that great numbers of people are crowding into basements in conditions likely to foster the rapid spread of disease, it will have to be made compulsory for such people to sleep in deep shelter dormitories whether they wish to or not, as the health of the population must be maintained at all costs.

Lowering of Morale

While one appreciates that, short of closing the Underground railways of inner London, the provision of new deep air-raid shelters for so great an area of London would have been a gargantuan task, I still feel that the authorities should have prepared a certain number of deep shelters many months ago.

As the hours of darkness increase with advancing winter it is reasonable to suppose that the length of the enemy's air-raids will likewise increase. Therefore, unless we are to risk heavy casualties by bombs falling upon large assemblies, the people will have to be robbed of their cinemas, theatres, dance-halls, boxing matches, dog matches, dog racing, speedways, etc.

The maintenance of public morale is a matter of very great importance and it will certainly suffer very severely if all amusements are denied to the population and they are expected to sit gloomily night after night in small groups in cellars or shelters. Intense boredom and discomfort will certainly breed war weariness and peace talk, and once this gets a hold on the civil population it may soon affect the Fighting Services also. Therefore not only must the people be given bread, they must also be given games.

To endeavour to create an underground West End where restaurants and dance-places would continue to function would by no means solve this problem, because it would necessitate the great bulk of the population travelling to and from the West End during the black-out and while air-raids were in progress. Such an arrangement would in due course become known to the enemy and it would be inviting particularly heavy raids, purely for terrorist purposes, upon the West End each night between ten o'clock and midnight, at which time the people would be returning home in large numbers from their amusements.

My suggestion is that in each district Borough Surveyors should be consulted as to the buildings in their own localities having deep deep basements which might be strengthened and converted into places of amusement for use during the winter.

All over London there are a number of underground garages, big cellars under solidly built Town Halls, spaces under railway arches, etc. Such places are already reasonably safe and at a not unreasonable expenditure, in view of the millions which are being expended upon A.R.P., the most suitable among them could be strengthened to a degree of absolute safety by additional concrete floors above, shoring-up underneath, emergency exits, sandbagged entrances, etc.

Within a month we might have perhaps three such safe and commodious centres in each postal district and these could then be used as amusement centres for the people of their locality. Railway arches which are fairly lofty might be turned into cinemas, while Town Hall cellars, underground garages, etc., which lack height, could be used for dance-places, restaurants, and bridge or whist drives and lecture halls.

The scheme would, of course, have to be run by the Government to ensure all classes of the population benefiting from it. To avoid over-crowding, entrance tickets would have to be obtained in advance – just as in pre-war days people booked seats for a theatre. For three nights a week it could be made moderately expensive, in the same way that the first day of any exhibition is always more expensive, thus giving the wealthier classes their opportunity to avoid the poorer section of the community if they are prepared to pay for it.

In any case, whatever the arrangement about payment, *the mere fact of being able to get a few hours' carefree recreation in an absolutely safe place once a week would be an incalculable moral asset to the population during the coming winter.*

Loss of Working Hours

Here one comes to a matter where the damage that we have sustained from indiscriminate bombing in the past few weeks is really frightening, but fortunately it can soon be rectified, as the loss of working-hours resulting in a great falling-off of industrial output and general dislocation of commerce can only in a very small degree be attributed to enemy action and must be laid almost entirely at the door of the Civil Administration.

Most of us visualized an aerial attack on London as the sort of party with which Hitler threatened Chamberlain at Munich; namely, 100 planes per hour over London for twenty-four consecutive hours.

If that threat, or anything like it, had matured it was obviously the sensible thing that for the period of attack everyone who had not vital work to do should take shelter; but we all knew that no attack of that kind could be maintained for any length of time, and certainly not for weeks on end. Therefore the assumption was that after the first big attacks there might be others but they would be launched possibly only two or three times a week for a period of three or four hours, during which we might all have to stop work and take cover, but that even if we lost two nights' sleep a week and – say – one whole day, for the other six days of the week everybody would continue to do their jobs as far as raid damage permitted and even, perhaps, work an hour or two longer on all-clear days to make up the lost day in order that our war effort might not be too seriously affected.

While any such large-scale air-raid remained an unknown factor it was perfectly understandable, and even laudable, that the authorities should have issued standing orders that at the wailing of the siren we should all go to ground; but the civil authorities have put major air-raid precautions into operation where, so far, during the daytime at least, our own Air Force has rendered all but minor air-raid precautions unnecessary.

The result has been that during the past fortnight millions of hours of labour-time have been absolutely thrown away when not more than one out of every thousand persons sitting idle was in the least possible danger.

By far the worst offenders were the post-offices and banks. At the first note of the siren the personnel of these institutions from one end of London to the other slammed their doors and rushed for cover, while their customers, who, for the most part, kept their heads, stood champing with fury in the streets and even forming queues, by which they were in danger of a stray bomb, as they impatiently waited to register a letter or cash a cheque.

I particularly stress the blame attaching to the P.M.G. and the chiefs of the big banks because it is these institutions which set the standard for the whole commercial life of the capital.

If the post-offices and banks close it is not unnatural that the great majority of shops and offices should close too, because a civilian employer of labour naturally feels that if the Government and the banks demonstrate so clearly that they will not risk a hair of one of their employees' heads it is hardly right for him to expose his employees to the slightest possible danger either.

The big stores naturally followed the Government's lead, which has led to a situation which would be laughable if it were not scandalous. In the middle of the morning a little piping whistle goes and every shop assistant knocks off work, even in the basement. The lady who is just about to purchase a pound of rice or a couple of kippers is told that she may not do so until the air-raid is over, but in the majority of cases neither the lady nor the shop assistant goes to any deeper shelter; they just remain there for an hour or more, facing each other across the counter, while possibly in some remote London district an enemy reconnaissance plane is humming overhead.

This sort of thing is bad enough because it frays the nerves of the civil community and means that it has to spend on daily ploys much additional time which otherwise might be spent in resting, which would to some extent compensate for hours of discomfort at night in air-raid shelters or uncomfortable basements.

But what is infinitely worse is that this same amazing procedure has been permitted in many factories – witness the astonishing scandal exposed by the *Sunday Dispatch of September the 22nd, in which during a night in the previous week 1,500 paid workers in an aircraft factory on the outskirts of London stopped work from 8.30p.m. until 5.30 the following morning, although not a single bomb fell in that district and only for one hour was an enemy airplane overhead. No wonder that Lord Beaverbrook, who has done such marvels in reorganizing our aircraft industry, was moved to violent disapproval and urgent appeal that our output should not be sabotaged in this senseless manner.*

For the first day or two of the indiscriminate bombing it was perfectly under-standable that full precautions should be taken until the results of the attack could be judged; but surely within forty-eight hours the authorities could have seen that the effect of the bombs did not for one moment justify this incredible dislocation of industry and it should have been quite unnecessary for Lord Beverbrook to make his personal appeal many days later. I do not believe, either, that any such appeal would have been necessary if it had not been for the extraordinary attitude of the Civil Administration, which almost makes one suspect that somebody high up in it is using Hitler's indiscriminate bomb-ing as an excuse deliberately to sabotage our war effort.

Even the service ministries are not entirely immune from this suicidal policy. The War Office, for example, has a ruling that personnel in uniform may work through air-raids, but that personnel not in uniform must go to earth. It would be most interesting to know upon what grounds this strange decision was taken.

In France, both in this war and the last – just as they carry on in London today – the women drivers of the A.T.S. and other units have always carried on their work behind our battle-fronts well within the range of heavy guns. Why, therefore, should War Office clerks, male or female, be considered as more precious to us than the men and women who actually wear His Majesty's uniform?

London is unquestionably in the front line of the battle today and all its citizens must henceforth consider themselves as soldiers. The great bulk of them are willing and proud to do so. In the past week some uncoordinated effort appears to have been made to get the post-office and the factories going again, but this is not enough; there is an urgent call for a declaration by the Prime Minister of an entirely new policy, whereby the life of the nation can be freed from the shackles put upon it by a cowardly administration and be enabled to function fully once again.

A NEW A.R.P. POLICY

I wrote in an article, very early in the war, that the country which would win this war was that which could manage to maintain its normal life during the war better than its opponent, and that Britain would certainly be able to do so because no blockade could affect her to the same degree as her blockade could affect Germany.

This statement is every bit as true today, but it will not continue to be so if we allow our whole national life to be disrupted by indiscriminate bombing.

In this matter the Finns set us a magnificent example. They had practically no Air Force with which to counter the massed attacks of the huge quantities of Russian planes which were sent against them, so they were bombed day and night from November the 30th to March the 13th almost without intermission, yet they so adapted themselves to this unhappy state of affairs that even after three and a half months of bombing their war effort was not seriously impaired.

The Jim Crow system[1] of look-outs was, of course, universally adopted for all factories, big office blocks, towns, and even villages, and three air-raid warnings were given.
1. General Alert. On this, all reasonable precautions were taken and children and non-workers went to cover.
2. Planes over. On this, non-essential workers and such people as office clerks who could continue their work underground went to cover, but factories, etc., continued in full operation.

3. Planes actually spotted or first bomb. On this, everybody in the local-
ity went to ground, with the exception of the A.R.P. services and the men
needed to keep the machines running. A few of these remained in every
shop and with them there remained a member of the directing staff, purely
for morale effect, so that acute danger was shared by all classes in common,
but the *factories and essential services never ceased to run at all.*

It is a surprising but definite fact that many bombs can be aimed at a factory
which is protected only by a few Lewis guns without the enemy bomber
being able to come low enough to ensure a direct hit. Therefore, although
the experiences of these brave Finns must have been at times extremely
nerve-racking, their casualties – all considered – were amazingly few; which
more than justified their decision to carry on.

CONCLUSION

The inadequacy of proper night air-raid protection for London has already led
a portion of the population to crowd the Tube stations in such an unhealthy
and ill-disciplined manner that we are already liable to the outbreak of an
epidemic which may do us more harm than Hitler's bombs.

This state of affairs, together with the dislocation of all commerce and a
positively shocking delay in the postal services, is attributable to the Civil
Administration, who showed complete lack of initiative in taking steps to
counter the results of indiscriminate bombing.

The only national institution which showed any initiative was the Press.
Within forty-eight hours of the opening of the *Blitzkrieg*, without any lead from
the Government, the Press had determined that their service to the nation at
least must not be interrupted and forthwith, in a most praiseworthy manner,
they had their editions out within minutes of their normal time in spite of all
air-raids. So far their casualties have been no greater than those in any other
section of the community and Mr Churchill showed his personal approval
of this fine spirit by a telegram of congratulations to the *Evening Standard*,
whose News Room was bombed, for getting their edition out just the same.

If the Press could do this there is no fraction of an excuse for Government
departments and other national institutions to have taken not days but weeks
to realize the situation and issue fresh orders. Many of them have not even
yet instructed their staffs to carry on.

In consequences, at the risk of giving grave offence, I consider it my duty to
conclude upon a personal note which I am absolutely convinced expresses
the opinion of the great majority of London's citizens.

Nine-tenths of the damage done to our war effort since Hitler began
indiscriminate bombing is the direct responsibility of the Cabinet Ministers
and the high Civil Servants working under them who control our Civil
Administration.

These men have proved themselves lacking in vision, tortoise-like in adjusting themselves to new conditions, incompetent and gutless. They bring grave discredit upon their colleagues of the Fighting and Supply Ministries and are unworthy to serve under our lion-hearted Prime Minister. The man-in-the-street considers that it is a scandal which stinks to heaven that while our airmen, sailors and soldiers daily give their lives in our defence such men as these should be allowed to continue to jeopardize the health, morale, commerce and safety of the nation. Therefore the public is asking that a full inquiry should be instituted into the men responsible for this cowardly policy which has cost the nation so dear at such a vital time, and that those who have shown themselves incapable of leadership should forthwith be relieved of their responsibilities.

Even Wheatley admitted in *Stranger Than Fiction* that he had gone over the top by the end of this paper. Or, as he put it 'Dear, dear; I had got myself into a tizzie, hadn't I?'

Note

1. The definition of a Jim Crow is a sortie that patrols the home coastline in order to intercept hostile aircraft; its additional role is to spot invasions (Air Historical Branch)

XII

Winter of Discontent

After 'Aerial Warfare', Wheatley wrote a paper entitled 'The Winter' (see my comments at the end of Chapter VIII). He then wrote two papers concerning the new Europe that would develop after the war (I will deal with these papers later).

In October 1940 Darvall was promoted to Group Captain and – after training – was sent to the Far East as Air Staff Officer to Air Chief Marshal Sir Robert Brooke-Popham, who was the newly appointed Commander in Chief Far East (for both air and land forces).

Darvall did not forget Wheatley though, passing him over to his successor, Wing Commander Roland Vintras. Vintras didn't set Wheatley such intricate tasks as Darvall, but he did make use of him.

Like Darvall before him, Vintras had lunch with Wheatley many times, along with other members of the Joint Planning Staff, such as Group Captain Dickson and Wing Commander Dawson. They discussed many aspects of the war, most notably – for Wheatley – the public's unrest after enduring the blitz. The planners told Wheatley that there were certain things the public could be told and things they couldn't concerning the governments plans. However, morale had to be maintained and Wheatley was asked (some time in mid-October 1940) to write a paper dealing with these very sensitive issues. The paper ran to 11,000 words and like some of Wheatley's earlier papers was a brainstorm of ideas. What follows are some of the key points he raised:

The People Want to Know

The Home Guard. Complaints by men and junior officers that 'dug-out' generals who had served in the South African War and knew nothing of modern fighting had been appointed as Battalion and Zone commanders; the danger of subversive influences exercised by the Spanish Communist Instructors who were running an anti-tank course for them at Osterley; and a suggestion that one battalion of the Brigade of Guards should be dispersed so that its officers and N.C.O.s could be used as instructors in tactics.

War-Strain. The mental effect of delays caused by air-raids, often hours long, on people in trains and tubes going home from their daily employment could be minimized if a campaign were run to induce them all to take either needlework or books with them.

Books for the Forces. This service was being most haphazardly run on a tiny grant which was inadequate for the enormously increased numbers in uniform. Mr. Thomas Joy, then Chief Librarian of Harrods, had volunteered through me to run, in collaboration with the Chief Librarian of W.H. Smith & Son, Boots, and *The Times*, a really adequate service, at a cost which would have worked out at only a halfpenny a volume.

Headline Offensives. There were rumours that successful raids against enemy bases on the French coast had already been carried out. I asked why, if this were true, the public had not been given such heartening news, and went on to suggest various types of 'combined operation' raids. This section ended,

I do not suggest any serious dissipation of our forces. One man can make headline news if only his exploit is audacious and daring enough. How much more so, then, could a few hundred used in skilfully planned operations help to re-gild the tarnished laurels of the British Army and give our people infinitely more confidence in our military leaders when they undertake the greater operations which are yet to come.

The uniformed masses, too, were already crying out for a 'Return to the Continent'; so I got Diana to draw for me a proposed poster illustrating what the fall of France had meant to us, and why we must wait until the United States 'gave us the tools to finish the job'.

Spies. The Home Office was still handling enemy aliens, caught red-handed in subversive activities, with kid gloves. I suggested that next time Hitler scored a success, the public's mind should be taken off it by a good, old-fashioned spy trial, followed by a firing squad at dawn in the Tower of London.

Air-Raid Shelters. That 'fine old War Horse', as the Prime Minister had termed Sir John Anderson, when forced to defend him the House of Commons, had, after doing nothing about public air-raid shelters until the bombs began to fall, allowed each Borough Council to run up any old brick structures it liked. I suggested that designs should be submitted by leading architects, the best being chosen, built, and tested for resistance by R.A.F. bombing, then the most satisfactory made the standard type for the whole country. *And* that they should be equipped with wire bunks, or at least benches to sit on.

Aliens. From having done nothing about the thousands in our midst up to the summer of 1940, Sir John had suddenly gone to the other extreme and clapped the whole lot into jug. The vast majority of these unfortunate people were our friends, and I asked that speedier measures should be taken to release those against whom no evidence of Nazi or Communist sympathies could be found.

Cabinet Ministers. Some, like Mr. Bevin, Lord Woolton, and Lord Lloyd, had won the confidence of the people but others, from their acts and public pronouncements, gave the impression of being woefully incompetent and inept. I suggested that if the latter were really worthy of being restrained in their jobs, they should at least be told to keep their mouths shut, and should each be provided by the Ministry of Information with an intelligent *alter ego* who would explain away their apparent shortcomings by inspired articles in the Press and talks on the B.B.C.

London's Streets. The measures for repairing bomb damage were still tardy, primitive, and ill-organized, thus causing immense waste of time through traffic delays. I instanced one hole in the road of more than four feet in diameter at Marble Arch which had remained unrepaired for five weeks. I urged that some vigorous personality should be given control of conscripted labour and other facilities to deal competently with this irritating and depressing result of the enemy's nightly bombing

Peace Talk. In certain areas of the East End, particularly where the population was largely foreign, the horrors of the Blitz had resulted in quite widespread murmurs to the effect, 'We have nothing to lose and could not be worse off under Hitler.' To counter this, I suggested B.B.C. talks and the issue of pamphlets setting forth what had happened in Poland – Jews of both sexes slaughtered out of hand, other males sent to forced labour on starvation rations, wives and daughters given over to storm-troopers, raped to increase the Aryan race, then turned out to work in the fields.[1]

In April 1941 Wheatley expanded upon the previous paper with 'The People Want to Know (No. 2)'. In *Stranger Than Fiction,* he gave a brief outline of this paper, which built upon some of the ideas outlined above.

The winter of 1940/1 was one of discontent for the British public. Churchill had not really shown them what the might of the British forces was. We had endured heavy blitz, retreated from Normandy and seen France collapse. Something had to be done to counter this Nazi threat. And the answers were slow in coming, hence the need for the above papers.

Could Britain fall under the Nazis? What was the War Cabinet up to? Didn't they realise that the Nazis were about to pounce on us at any moment?

Britain didn't just have to prepare its Armed Forces during the Second World War, it had to protect its civilians against widespread paranoia and panic. So structured activities had to be applied, not underground leisure centres (as Wheatley had suggested), but more 'official' duties (through the Home Guard and ARP for example), so people felt that they were doing their bit to protect their country from invasion.

Note

1. The Plight of the Polish was indeed diabolical, even after the war under Russian rule.

XIII

Darvall and a New Europe

Before Darvall left the Joint Planning Staff, Wheatley gave him a bachelor dinner-party at his home. Wheatley's other guests included Captain Hubert Stringer, Sir Louis Greig, Colonel Charles Balfour-Davey, and Captain Peveril William-Powlett, RN. All of these gentlemen had read Wheatley's papers and encouraged him to write more.

The dinner party went well – with the interruption of an air-raid – and Wheatley was pleased that he could personally thank the man who had presented him with the themes and encouragement that enabled him to make a positive contribution to the war effort. However, this wasn't the end of Wheatley's and Darvall's friendship, which would continue long after the war. Indeed Darvall wrote the introduction to Wheatley's non-fiction *Stranger Than Fiction* (1959)[1], writing of Wheatley's paper 'After the Battle':

> Each time I read that paper my admiration for Dennis Wheatley's breadth of imagination, insight, reasonableness and good sense increases. To me it still seems incredible that one brain in the tumultuous conditions of 1940/1 could have produced so inspired, so sensible and so far-seeing solution.

Both men were bonded by duty and mutual respect for each other's skills, but that bond was temporarily broken during the war.

There were more changes afoot for Wheatley. In December 1940 the blitz had rendered the author's home unsafe, so he moved to Oakwood Court, Kensington, where his wife Joan was already staying with friends. Soon afterwards, the couple took a flat in Chatsworth Court, Earl's Court, and remained there until the end of the war.

Despite the personal upheaval, Wheatley still managed to lunch with the Joint Planning Staff and discuss the war, and naturally more work came his way until the time – in December 1941 – when he would be inaugurated into the Joint Planning Staff himself.

However, one of the main reasons why he was inaugurated was the work he put into two papers that dealt with the state of Europe after the war and how a Third World War could be avoided in twenty years' time. 'By Devious Paths to Victory' and 'After the Battle' outlined many scenarios and took nearly two months to write. They would be the last two papers Wheatley would write for Darvall, and probably the most impressive too.

Wheatley poured everything he could into these papers. He would build upon themes he had previously tackled, but at the same time pull all the ideas together into a logical narrative – almost a strategy. And the Joint Planning Staff loved that.

Because of the length of these papers and because they do repeat certain ideas previously detailed, I have provided only a shortened version of each in the next chapter.

Note

1. Wheatley had provided Darvall with a draft Introduction to *Stranger Than Fiction* (see photo section), but Darvall decided to write his own – a mark of the respect he had for Wheatley.

The author in September 1914

1. Dennis Wheatley cut his teeth in military life at a very young age as this study from The Great War shows.

2. At a younger age Wheatley was a navy cadet aboard HMS *Worcester*; he would eventually serve in all three of the services.

3. Squadron Leader D Y Wheatley pictured in 1944. Wheatley would hold a temporary promotion to Wing Commander whilst serving in the Joint Planning Staff.

4. Wheatley had more than a passing respect for his commanding officer, Bevan. He noted him as one of the most charming but professional of men he had ever worked with.

5. Whilst Wheatley and the deception planners worked in the depths of Whitehall, London lay under siege, first from the Luftwaffe and later from V1 and V2 rockets; but the determination was undaunted.

6. The deception planners. Bevan centre, Wheatley immediately to his left.

7. Winston Churchill shares a joke with the troops. Behind him, Montgomery gives a token grin for the cameras. Wheatley recalls that Monty acted inappropriately whilst the 'Monty Double' deception was being conducted.

8. The ever-stylish Dennis Wheatley would impress his superiors not just with his many ideas for deception plans but also his marvellous and most convivial company at lunch and dinner. His wine cellar was extensive and always at guests' disposal.

9. Wheatley and friends having a rip-roaring time at a party. His wife Joan sits beside him, his great friend Joe Links second from right. Wheatley was always an extrovert and raconteur, as this photograph clearly illustrates.

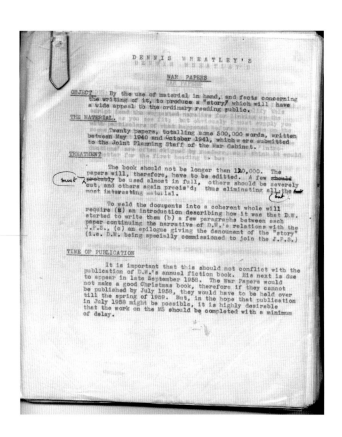

DENNIS WHEATLEY'S

WAR PAPERS

OBJECT   By the use of material in hand, and facts concerning the writing of it, to produce a "story" which will have a wide appeal to the ordinary reading public.

THE MATERIAL.

Twenty papers, totalling some 500,000 words, written between May 1940 and October 1941, which were submitted to the Joint Planning Staff of the War Cabinet.

TREATMENT

The book should not be longer than 120,000. The papers will, therefore, have to be edited. A few should be used almost in full, others should be severely cut, and others again precis'd; thus eliminating all the most interesting material.

To weld the documents into a coherent whole will require (a) an introduction describing how it was that D.W. started to write them (b) a few paragraphs between each paper continuing the narrative of D.W.'s relations with the J.P.S., (c) an epilogue giving the denoument of the "story" (i.e. D.W. being specially commissioned to join the J.P.S.)

TIME OF PUBLICATION

It is important that this should not conflict with the publication of D.W.'s annual fiction book. His next is due to appear in late September 1958. The War Papers would not make a good Christmas book, therefore if they cannot be published by July 1958, they would have to be held over till the spring of 1959. But, in the hope that publication in July 1958 might be possible, it is highly desirable that the work on the MS should be completed with a minimum of delay.

10. *Above:* The original manuscript of *Stranger Than Fiction*, hand-typed by Wheatley himself and signed on the last page (*Humphreys Collection*).

11. *Right:* The rare proof copy of Dennis Wheatley's war papers, titled '*Stranger Than Fiction*', first published in 1959.

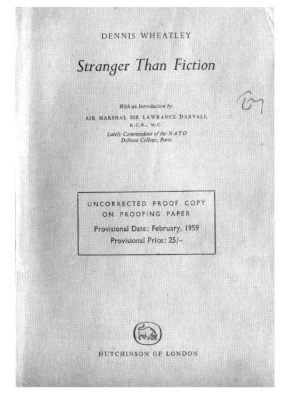

DENNIS WHEATLEY

Stranger Than Fiction

With an Introduction by
AIR MARSHAL SIR LAWRANCE DARVALL
K.C.B., M.C.
Lately Commandant of the NATO
Defence College, Paris

UNCORRECTED PROOF COPY
ON PROOFING PAPER

Provisional Date: February, 1959
Provisional Price: 25/-

HUTCHINSON OF LONDON

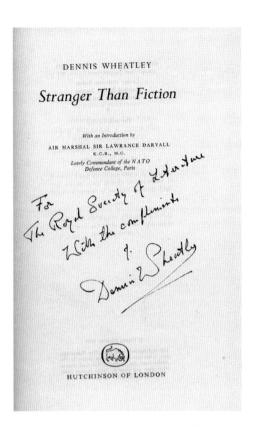

DENNIS WHEATLEY

Stranger Than Fiction

With an Introduction by
AIR MARSHAL SIR LAWRANCE DARVALL
K.C.B., M.C.
Lately Commandant of the NATO
Defence College, Paris

For The Royal Society of Literature With the compliments 9. Dennis Wheatley

HUTCHINSON OF LONDON

12. *Above:* The title page to the first edition of *Stranger Than Fiction*. This copy Wheatley has signed to the Royal Society of Literature, but it now resides in a private collection.

13. *Left:* Wheatley would use some of his deception ideas in his novels, most notably *The Man Who Missed the War* (as this paperback reprint illustrates).

14. Wheatley as a baby, pictured with his mother.

15. Wheatley always maintained he learnt a great deal during his time in the trenches of the Great War, so much so, he was full of ideas when it came to the Second World War. He was upset that he was not automatically called up for service at the outset of the Second World War, but duty finally called and his experience proved invaluable.

16. A sense of patriotism overrides this dramatic study of Squadron Leader Dennis Wheatley, and perhaps an air of concern.

17. The book-plate commissioned for Wheatley's own library, which boasted practical books on a wide range of subjects including history, and diversely, brick-laying. Wheatley's library would assist him greatly when writing both fact and fiction.

18. Wheatley was immensely proud of his commission into the Joint Planning Staff. He is seen here with his greatcoat (with the bright red lining) sporting his Squadron Leader insignia and his swagger stick that concealed a short sword.

19. Squadron Leader Dennis Wheatley sits behind his desk at the Joint Planning Staff in Whitehall, London.

20. Prolific novelist of adventure stories, and most notably, of the occult, Dennis Wheatley was one of the great writers of the 20th Century, being often overlooked. Wheatley typified the stoicism and stiff upper lip of the British citizen during that most trying time.

XIV

The Shape of Things to Come

'We found we supplemented each other. I had a ready unclouded imagination and he had the knowledge. We would go on the speculative spree together.'
The Shape of Things to Come
H G Wells

It was Winston Churchill who asked the Joint Planning Staff to craft a paper on the theme: what measures shall we take, having won the war, to prevent Germany starting a Third World War in twenty years' time? It was Darvall who said: 'Let's give this one to Wheatley.' However, they weren't prepared for the magnum-opus they eventually got:

By Devious Paths to Victory

I was asked to write a paper on 'The Shape of Things to Come' with particular reference to the possibility of Western Europe being in a state of famine and revolution by the spring of 1941.

Upon such a vast subject it would be easy to write a quarter of a million words of speculation, but that would serve no useful purpose, as nobody who is attempting to get on with the war would have time to read it. Therefore, I have tried to reduce my speculations to the barest outline. Even so, to be at all coherent, they must run to some 20,000 words, so I felt that the best thing to do was to divide the subject into two natural halves (a) BY DEVIOUS PATHS TO VICTORY, (b) AFTER THE BATTLE.

As this first portion of the paper deals almost entirely with problems of strategy, a subject in which I have had no professional training whatever, I put forward my views with great diffidence and must ask the indulgence of those serving officers who may read this paper, but it is written in the hope that as a very broad analysis of the general situation it may serve as a suitable introduction to the subject in hand.

For Western Europe to be in a state of famine and revolution by the spring of 1941 postulates the collapse of the Nazi régime, and it seems that the first thing to consider is the various ways in which such a desirable state of affairs might be brought about.

1. By the landing of a British Army on the Continent and a defeat of the German Army in the field.
2. By a British military victory in any other theatre.
3. By the collapse of Italy.
4. By some action or reaction from Russia.
5. By economic pressure though the maintenance of our naval blockade.
6 .By intensive bombing by the Royal Air Force.

A CONTINENTAL CAMPAIGN

A British landing in force on the continent might be (a) a surprise invasion, (b) a landing by invitation.

Surprise Invasion

The first might be launched (a) against the extremities of the Nazi-held territories, Norway and Denmark, or perhaps, in view of possible eventualities, against Portugal and Spain, (b) in the centre, against Holland, Belgium or France, (c) against Italy, (d) in the Balkans.

1. As it is universally admitted that defence is superior to attack, now that the Nazis have had many weeks to establish themselves in Norway and Denmark any attempt to capture either of these countries would meet with very considerable opposition. The operation might be successful but it would be more costly to us than to the enemy and a victory in either of these spheres would not necessarily have any decisive effect upon the military situation in the main portion of the Continent.

    Should Hitler go into Spain, Portugal naturally comes into view as a jumping-off ground against him, but here I feel that the lesson of Norway should be remembered. Moreover, while it is true that Wellington defeated the French in the Peninsula Campaign, it should be recalled that the Spaniards were then our Allies and by their guerilla activities proved a positive nightmare to the French; whereas, this time, presumably the Spaniards would either become active partners of the Axis or at least be passively against rather than for us.

    It seems, therefore, that any attack of the extremities would be costly, out of all proportion to the results achieved. Even if we gained an outstanding victory in any of these spheres it would not put Germany out of the war. Therefore, in my view, any landing on the extremities would be an unwise dissipation of force.

2. An invasion of Germany through Holland, Belgium or France is a very different matter and one gathers from statements appearing in the Press that it is

with such an object in mind that we are now building up an army which it is hoped will eventually comprise some 3,000,000 or 4,000,000 fully equipped men.

Obviously we shall be in no position to put such an army into the field until 1942 at the earliest, so that alone rules out this possibility for the purpose of this paper. Nevertheless, as that appears to be our eventual design, it is worth while to digress for one moment upon this subject.

Even the largest army which we could ship over to the Continent in 1942 or 1943 would still be numerically inferior to the German Army, and the German proportional effectives could be yet further increased by the utilization of Italian troops for garrison purposes in other Nazi-occupied territories, and in Germany herself, thus enabling her to put almost her entire force into one great effort to smash the British on land. The Germans also have many vassal states in which they can now draw upon the enslaved population for man-power to build defence lines behind any front that they might be called upon to establish, and even use as labour corps in the actual battle-zone. Moreover, actually to penetrate into Germany we should have to establish long lines of communication, possibly through semi-hostile country. We could not count upon any military assistance at all from the so-called friendly countries in which we might make our landing, and it would be rash even to assume that they would supply us with any great quantity of non-combatant labour. Finally, if we succeed in carrying the war on to enemy soil nothing could be so well calculated to re-animate the fighting spirit in a war-worn German nation as the invasion of Germany herself.

We should be taking on an enormously superior enemy with nearly everything in his favour except possibly a shortage of food and petrol. The campaign would most probably be long and we should almost certainly sustain hundreds of thousands of casualties. When within an ace of having won the war by our blockade, and having achieved air superiority, we should be exposing ourselves to the possibility of losing it at the eleventh hour by a crushing military defeat on the banks of the Meuse or the Rhine. Personally, therefore, I sincerely trust that the great army now being trained will *never* be called upon to undertake a campaign upon the Continent of Europe.

It is the hope of us all that our Military Commanders will re-gild the laurels of the British Army which, most regrettably, have become somewhat tarnished of late, but I shall tremble for their chance of fame should they choose Western Europe, while still Hitler-dominated, in which to attempt it, *unless by then the United States has come into the war as our ally* – and there are many other spheres in which I believe the army can be utilized much more effectively.

3. With regard to the Italian mainland, Italy's coast is so long that, unlike Germany, she is extremely vulnerable to invasion and it would be a glorious

thing to carry the war into the enemy's territory. It has, however, to be borne in mind that *wherever* we might land on the Continent of Europe it would be only a matter of days, or weeks at most, before Hitler's main forces could be brought against us. There is, I believe, from the study of a map, one point upon the Italian mainland where a lightning invasion carried out with secrecy and in considerable strength might well put Italy out of the war. If desired, I should be happy to write further upon this in another place, but it would be extraordinarily hazardous to attempt the operation which I have in mind until such time as Germany has her hands full with trouble in her occupied territories or at home and could not dispatch any considerable forces to Italy's assistance.

I feel, therefore, that no invasion of the Italian mainland could possibly be justified for some time to come…

A British Military Victory in Any Other Sphere

Repulsion of Invasion

The danger of an invasion appears temporarily to be fading owing to the splendid work which our Armed Forces has put in on Hitler's invasion bases, but the more desperate Hitler becomes the more likelihood there is of his attempting an invasion as a last gamble. With everything going to pieces all round him he might well feel that if by the sacrifice of half a million men he could conquer England he might yet save himself at the eleventh hour and, if not actually win the war at one stroke, at least break the blockade and thereby give the Axis a new lease of life.

The time we have had to prepare our resistance since the collapse of France has now given us a justifiable confidence that we can repel any invasion which Hitler might launch against us. With regard to Ireland, this is a much more debatable problem as, although the greater distance to the Irish coast must render the Nazis' transport much more vulnerable to the attentions of the Royal Navy and the Royal Air Force, the ostrich-like Free State Government has, apparently, refused to enter into any understanding which would enable us to help them to put their land defences in order. Therefore, it is reasonable to suppose that with their own very limited means they are in no condition to repel any well-equipped and ably directed force of even a few divisions which the Germans might succeed in landing in Southern Ireland.

As we should be able to cut off from its bases any German Force which landed in Southern Ireland – except by air – it does not seem to me that we have any great reason to fear such a German operation; but, be that as it may, while it would be a serious blow for Hitler to attempt an invasion of either England or Ireland and fail, it would not necessarily bring about a German collapse, because news is so strictly censored that it is doubtful if the great bulk of the German people would learn until months later that any really serious attempt at invasion had ever been made …

The Collapse of Italy

I do not believe that Hitler will ever sue for peace, but it is quite possible that Mussolini may do so. This depends upon two factors: (a) the initiative displayed by our forces in the Mediterranean and the adjacent territories, (b) the intensity and ingenuity of our propaganda.

Before Mussolini entered the war he was making an excellent thing out of it. While the shipping of nearly all the other great European powers was occupied in war services, Italy's mercantile marine was positively coining money. Mussolini was also making millions a week by acting as a contraband smuggler for Hitler. Therefore, like many other people, I did not for one minute believe that he would be fool enough to enter the war against Britain.

While I proved completely wrong on this point the fact remains that Mussolini did come in only owing to an entirely unforeseen circumstance – namely, the total collapse of France.

In spite of all his drum-beating I don't believe that he would have dared openly to declare against the Allies except for the fact that France was already as good as out, and that Hitler had convinced him that by the early autumn he would have dealt with Britain.

Hitler needed Mussolini as an active ally in order that Italy's entry into the war should pin down a large portion of the British Navy to the Mediterranean while the Germans launched their invasion against Britain. Keeping a portion of the British Navy occupied for a few months must have seemed a small price to Mussolini for a considerable share of the plunder, and it seems that the temptation proved too much for the normally shrewd and extraordinarily far-sighted Italian, but I doubt very much if he could have been persuaded into this bargain if he had not had a definite assurance that within a few months Britain, the citadel of the Empire, would have fallen to the Nazi onslaught. Italy has too many commitments outside her own borders to have any chance of waging a successful war against Britain while the very heart and controlling brain of the Empire remains unwounded and can still direct its limbs to exert pressure upon him in all his most vulnerable points.

Hitler's failure to invade and conquer Britain has committed him to nothing, but it has committed Mussolini to a first-class war in which half Britain's Navy, at least half her Army, and a good portion of her Air Force can be directed against him and, as Hitler has slipped up with his end of the axis, it seems to me that Mussolini must now be a very worried man indeed.

Italy's Military Situation

Italy's Forces in Abyssinia achieved temporary successes on the borders of Tanganyika, in the Sudan, and in overrunning Somaliland, but the fact remains that these paper victories have not got them anywhere and that they remain cut off from home with their supplies and munitions daily growing shorter. Moreover, if our secret agents and propaganda people know their business, a seething cauldron of trouble should now be brewing among the native population who would, unquestionably, cut the throat of every Italian in Abyssinia with the greatest possible delight if only given a lead to do so. I rather doubt if any Italians at all will get home from Abyssinia and I am quite sure that, before this party is through, those curious necklaces so prized by Abyssinian warriors, which consist of portions of their late enemies, will have gone down in price to six for the Maria Theresa dollar.

In Libya the Italian situation is not really much better. The Libyan Forces are still to some extent in touch with home but their line of communication is a most hazardous one, since every convoy that they are sent has to run the gauntlet of the British Navy, and it is quite out of the question to keep the considerable Libyan Army solely supplied by air. Moreover, one gathers that the native population do not regard Marshal Graziani with any favour at all. His little pastime of taking their local Sheks up in aeroplanes and pushing them out to be dashed to pieces on rocks a thousand feet below has hardly been calculated to endear to his subjects this unworthy successor of the great Roman pro-Consuls of Cyrenaica. Once again, if our secret agents and propaganda people know their business, there is going to be a great throat slitting before many months are past in Libya, and if arrangements are properly made the signal for this should be the defeat by General Wavell of Marshal Graziani's army in the Libyan Desert.

Since, unlike Germany, his territories are not protected from assault by a cordon of conquered countries, there are, I am convinced, quite a number of other things which could be done to bother Mussolini, and in this connection I would draw attention to a scheme outlined in my paper No. 7, on seizing Sardinia. This limited-liability offensive has the enormous advantage that while our risk would at the worst be a defeat by no means as serious as that we sustained in Norway our success would have such enormous repercussions throughout the whole world that it might well prove the turning point of the war.

As I resume this paper the morning's news is that General Keitel has gone to Libya with a large staff of Germans to 'advise' Marshal Graziani. This is a pretty clear indication that at the latest Brenner meeting Hitler persuaded Mussolini to go ahead in Egypt while presumably, as many other news items indicate, promising that for his part the Nazis will now make a great drive across the Black Sea to the East.

Personally, I regard the news of Keitel's new job as excellent. He and his staff can have had little, if any, practical experience in Colonial administration or desert warfare, whereas Graziani, however unpleasant a personality, has spent many years in Africa and must be considered as an expert on the problems which he now has to face. The Germans, true to type, will almost certainly be full of bluster and puffed up with pride about the European blitzkriegs in which their new technique has proved so successful. Graziani will doubtless say: 'Yes; but you can't do that sort of thing in Africa.' He will probably be overruled, or divided counsels will result in half measures, and it's a foregone conclusion that the jealousy and fundamental dislike of the Germans and Italians for each other will be gravely aggravated; which entitles us to hype more than ever that the Libyan Army will be delivered over in good time to a smashing defeat from General Wavell ...

Propaganda

... Italy – while defeats of her armies in the field are bound to have an enormous repercussion on her population, to reap the full benefit of their effect our utmost ingenuity should be utilized in the sphere of propaganda.

During the early stages of the war our propaganda was so bad that words fail to describe its rottenness. For this the Government officials who formed the Ministry of Information should yet publicly be brought to account, since their selection of staff, regarded from the realistic point of view and the fact that the country was about to wage a war for its existence, was little short of treasonable.

For the staff of the Ministry they selected 999 people, only thirty-odd of whom were trained journalists. The Admiralty might just as well have recruited the 960 non-journalistic members of the staff, added to them thirty-odd officers and men of the Royal Navy and put this strange crew on board HMS *Nelson* with instructions to take the ship to sea for the purpose of seeking out and destroying the enemy.

However, in the latter part of the last war we led the whole world in the art of propaganda; so one still hopes that we may do the same in the latter part of this war if the right people are brought in to handle this tremendously important fourth arm of modern warfare.

The Italian people are by no means shackled to the same degree as the German people. Therefore if our propaganda is skilful and intensive, together with a continuance of our blockade, a defeat in the Libyan Desert and a large-scale rising in Abyssinia, or the successful putting into operation of Paper No. 7, they might well start a nation-wide peace agitation.

I feel very strongly that Mussolini must already be conscious that he has got himself mixed up in a far more desperate business than he ever bargained for, and I have no doubt at all that he would not hesitate to double-cross his partner without the least scruple if he found himself faced with a threatening agitation to call off the war. It is, therefore, quite on the cards that he would try to make the best terms with Britain that he could while Italy still had something to offer – namely, the very fact that by getting out of the war she would free our hands to devote every punch we had to the major criminal.

In view of this, I feel that nothing should be left undone which might cause Mussolini to rat on Hitler, and it is not unreasonable to hope that this could be brought about by the early spring of 1941. Yet, although the repercussions of the Italian collapse would be tremendous in Germany, I very much doubt if they alone would be sufficient to bring about the downfall of the Nazi Government.

As a Result of Action or Reaction From Russia

In this connection there are two possibilities: (a) that Russia will attack Germany, (b) that Germany will invade Russia.

A Russian Attack on Germany

Unfortunately, I fear that there is extremely little chance of our being able to persuade Russia actually to invade Germany while the Nazi regime still functions, although there is a possibility that she might do so when Germany is bordering on collapse, and if she did so then it would be prejudicial rather than favourable to our interests.

However, should Germany make a descent on Turkey through Rumania and Bulgaria there is a definite possibility that Russia might give armed aid to the Turks and so, collaterally, to Britain.

As my views on Russo-German relations are fully set forth in my Paper 'Measures for Maintaining the Independence of Turkey' [No. 8 in the original series], I will not go further into this matter here except to express the opinion that should Germany attack Turkey we shall suffer another major diplomatic defeat, for which there can be little excuse, if we fail to get the Russians to give us full military support in defending Asia Minor, since the interests of Russia and Britain are absolutely identical in this sphere.

The recent Axis Pact with Japan bears out the probabilities forecast in Paper No. 8, which was written some considerable time ago; but I will note with regret that in the meantime we do not seem to have drawn any nearer to Russia, although it appears perfectly obvious that by doing so we should be able to counterbalance to a large extent any assistance which the Japanese may render to Axis interests in the Far East.

Few people can claim to have been more anti-Bolshevik at the time of the Russian Revolution – and for a number of years afterwards – than myself, and I do not for one moment suggest that the present rulers of Russia are either likeable or trustworthy people, but a great deal of water has flown down the Volga since Joe Stalin and 'Clim' Voroshilov together held the salient of death at Tsaritsyn for the tottering, newly born Red Government of Moscow nearly a quarter of a century ago.

There is no little truth in the saying that the day on which a Socialist buys his first top-hat he becomes a Conservative, and for many years past now Stalin and such of his fellow-commissars as he has chosen to refrain from murdering have enjoyed a very different status from the poverty-ridden, street-corner agitation, chased by the police in the days of their youth. It is only reasonable, therefore, to believe them to be quieter and saner men now, who have long since realized that if they set the world on fire they may eventually get burnt themselves.

Stalin is undeniably a big-time crook, but that does not in the least prevent him from also being a very great statesman. One has only to follow Russia's diplomatic moves throughout the last twelve months to realize that wicked 'Uncle Joe' knows to a split hair what is good and what is not good for Russia.

He does not care about anything else. Why should he? With the one exception of Turkey not a single Power has shown the least desire to extend any genuine friendliness to Russia in the last twenty-three years. Therefore, we must not be surprised that the Russians choose to play their own game quite regardless as to how it may affect any other European Power, except in so far as the rise or fall of that Power may affect themselves; and that is the crux of this whole question.

Only two Powers have ever been potentially dangerous to Russia in the last twenty years – Germany and Japan. This remains so at the present day. Therefore, while Stalin has not the least intention of pulling our chestnuts out of the fire for us, he might quite well be persuaded that it is very much in his interests to render us limited assistance to defeat his principal potential enemy in the West and cripple the power of his lesser potential enemy in the East.

When dealing with a crook it is quite unnecessary to use above-board methods, so I do not suggest that he should be called on openly to scrap the Russo–German Agreement of 1939. But one could put it up to him that we should be willing to regard with an open and favourable mind any reasonable requests which he cares to make to us, if for his part he will find it more difficult to carry out his commercial undertakings with Germany owing to internal problems of his own which the Germans could hardly be expected to understand or appreciate.

My feeling is that now, if ever, being the time to utilize some of our vast assets we could, if we cared to take a new and generous view, greatly assist in protecting Russia's interests in the Pacific (see Paper No.8. It was there suggested that we should offer Russia naval facilities at Singapore which would tremendously strengthen her hand against the Japanese).

While this was put forward as a practical suggestion I went on to the then almost impossible dream that we might even succeed in involving America in a general deal with regard to naval bases. I suggested that we should also give the United States naval facilities at Singapore, while they should give the Russians and ourselves facilities at Honolulu and the Russians should give the Americans and ourselves facilities at Vladivostock, thereby placing Japan right in the middle of an Anglo–American–Russian triangle of impregnable sea bases.

Curiously enough, the dream of involving America in some deal involving the sharing of naval bases has now become a glorious fact, although, so far, only in the Atlantic Ocean; yet the equally vital question of giving Russia something which would induce her to line up with us remains, apparently, only a dream.

However, the American deal has opened a long-sealed door to all sorts of interesting possibilities by which in the course of time those Powers that stand for peace may yet place a stranglehold upon the aggressor nations, and it is to be hoped that nothing will be left undone which might draw the vast power of the Soviets for good or ill into a policy where for their self-interest alone *they* would be willing to render us a certain limited assistance against our enemies.

Nevertheless, even supposing that Russia gave us armed assistance in the defence of Turkey which led to a German defeat in the Near East, it is unlikely that this fact alone would bring about the collapse of the Nazis.

A German Attack on Russia

While the possibilities of our persuading Russia to invade Germany in the next few months are almost non-existent there is a very real possibility that Germany may invade Russia.[1]

Hitler will certainly not wish to do so while he still has Britain unconquered in his rear. On the other hand, if the blockade continues to play its part and he finds it impossible to break out of his cage by way of the Near East, Egypt and Morocco, his only other line is a descent into the Ukraine and the Caucasus where, all ready to hand for the taking, lie those tempting supplies of badly needed grain and oil.

If Hitler does move against Russia he is asking for very big trouble. It should not be assumed that because the Finns held the Russians up the Red Army is altogether rotten. No one would wish to detract from the magnificent gallantry shown by the Finns or their individual superiority as intelligent human beings over the Soviet soldiery, but in addition the Finns had many things in their favour. They were fighting mainly behind their strongly fortified Mannerheim Line, the appalling climatic conditions afflicted the attacker infinitely more than the defender and, further, the Russians were most severely hampered by the very narrow field of the Karelian Isthmus with its bottle-neck communications, which prevented them from using their superior forces to the best advantage.

There is a possibility, therefore, that with ample area for manoeuvre and better climatic conditions the very considerable Russian Armies may make a better showing than is expected. Moreover, the German Air Force has now been considerably crippled owing to the immense wastage sustained in Nazi attacks on Britain, whereas the huge Russian Air Force, although somewhat dated, suffered little in the Finnish War and so remains, for all practical purposes, intact. Finally, in numbers the Russians are almost countless and behind their armies they have a depth of territory the thought of which may well prove a nightmare to any German general who is entrusted with the task of attacking and defeating them.

On the other hand, German organization, discipline, equipment, and military technique are so immensely superior to those of Russia that it is reasonable to assume that after severe fighting the Nazis will succeed in overrunning the Ukraine in another blitzkrieg. They may halt there of their own volition, but it is most doubtful if they will have entirely defeated the Russian Army. If the Germans press on they may be halted on the line of the Volga, or even on the line of the Urals; but wherever they halt it is virtually certain that Soviet Armies will still be in the field against them, and the essential point is that the Germans will have to occupy the territory that they conquer.

In this connection we may recall with some pleasure the fate which overtook a great German Army which conquered and occupied a considerable portion of Russia during the last war. When Lenin assumed power he had no possible means of defeating the Germans and throwing them out by force of arms, but he conquered their army with paper and sent it absolutely rotten.

After the Russian propaganda had done its work the men refused any longer to obey their officers or to do anything at all except live on the land. The state of these German units in Russia became so deplorable that in the latter part of the war the German High Command did not dare to move to the Western Front most of the incredibly badly needed eighty divisions which were stationed in Russia, because they knew that if they did these troops would contaminate the rest of the German Army, causing it to pack up and go home.

It was, in fact, these German soldiers in Russia who, straggling back by degrees to their own country, preached revolution on the home front, and the Germans themselves say that it is difficult to estimate which factor really contributed most of the collapse of Germany in 1918 – the British blockade or the Red poison brought back by the troops who had been stationed in Russia.

I feel, therefore, that should Hitler take the desperate step of invading Russia to secure supplies it is highly possible that exactly the same thing might occur again, and that in this way the collapse of the Nazi régime might be brought about.

Economic Pressure through our Naval Blockade

In this connection it seems that there are two points to consider: (a) the cage, (b) the time factor.

The Cage

For an uninformed person like myself to assess the economic state of Western Europe at the present moment is an impossibility. One can only formulate a general view based on established facts.

The first fact is that when Germany started the present war she was still very far from having recovered from the effects of the last war. One small example will show the sort of thing I mean. In 1917, when Germany became short of metals, she turned to her hidden reserves, stripped the lead from the roofs of the old houses, carried away the church bells to her foundries and collected the brass pots and pans of her housewives. To a far lesser extent this was also done in Britain, but while Britain replaced her borrowing of this nature from the national treasure after the war Germany never recovered sufficiently to replace one-tenth of her borrowings.

The food situation in Germany before the war was no secret. It was difficult to obtain more than a very small portion of butter even in the best hotels, such as the Regina Palast in Munich. Eggs were scarce and cream unobtainable. For years the diet of the German people has been on an extremely low level, even to the point where rickets has increased to a most alarming degree among her infantile population. Therefore, the German people cannot possibly have entered the war with the same physical stamina as in 1914.

It is said that Reich Marshal Goering laid in enormous stores of food, but it is difficult to believe that any accumulated reserves – however large – would be large enough to do more than provide a few ounces a day to bolster up any current ration for more than a few months when those reserves are being drawn on by 80,000,000 people.

I think, therefore, that we may accept it as a fact that by the spring of 1940, after their first winter of war, the German people were living in a far from enviable state and that there must already have been considerable concern in high quarters about the dwindling stocks of food supplies and war materials.

The blitzkrieg of April the 8th–June the 17th altered all that. Norway, Denmark, Belgium, Holland, France; in an uncheckable torrent the Nazi Storm Troopers streamed over these huge territories, gathering into their net innumerable cities, towns, villages, factories, and farmsteads, with all their wealth in material and stores.

For a little time there must have been great rejoicing among the German housewives as the rich produce of the conquered countries came in train-load after train-load to fill the German shops and markets that had been drearily half-empty for many months; and while they guzzled these good things it is greatly to be doubted if more than a very small percentage of them realized that they had already killed the geese that had laid the golden eggs.

Before the blitzkrieg Germany was at least able to import from Denmark, Holland, and other countries such goods as she was able to pay for, but that is so no more. Our blockade immediately sealed these conquered territories, with the result that the Danes and others could no longer secure the cattle-feed and corn necessary to feed their herds and flocks, so these had in a very large measure to be slaughtered.

Again, as the blitzkrieg swept through the Low Countries into France much of the fighting was carried out among the standing corn, so the 1940 harvest of these countries must have been very seriously damaged.

Italy, too, up to this time had served as Hitler's main artery for contraband of war, but upon Mussolini's stabbing the French in the back the British Mediterranean Fleet put out minefields and sealed his ports. Italy, for the size of her population, is a poor country and she produces hardly any of the commodities necessary to wage a modern war; so from the economic point of view she became, by her entry into the conflict a grave liability to Germany, instead of an asset.

Spain still maintains her non-belligerency although now that France is out of the war Hitler can draw direct upon the peninsula for such goods as the Spaniards can sell him. But three years of civil strife have left Spain in a state of ruin and destitution. She is having immense difficulty in feeding her own people and I doubt if Hitler could get much out of her even if he sent his Storm Troopers there to take anything they could lay their hands on. Again, before Italy's entry into the war Spain was at least able to act to some extent as a corridor in securing supplies of petrol, etc., from America and shipping these on to Italy, but now our blockade closes the Italian ports to Spanish shipping and our closer arrangements which might be useful to the Axis Powers are no longer shipped to Spain.

Hitler has just walked into Hungary, Rumania, and Bulgaria, but this is only an open declaration of a state of things which has existed for a long time past. Hungary, from her geographical position, has found it essential to be subservient to the Axis Powers from the very opening of the war, while Rumania also considered it wise to sit on the fence and treat all Nazi commercial demands with favourable consideration; so it is extremely doubtful if Hitler will get more in the way of raw materials and foodstuffs from the Northern Bulkans that he was already getting before the blitzkrieg broke.

The Southern Balkans, Yugoslavia, and Greece are poor countries which have little to offer. They were already short themselves long before Hitler was in a position to threaten their territories from the North. As far back as the early winter of 1939 it was already impossible to secure sugar in the British Legation in Athens. Hitler and Mussolini are not going to get very much from these countries even if they walk into them.

Sweden and Finland are within the Nazi sphere but it is doubtful if the Germans can get from them any greater quantity of goods than they were purchasing before the blitzkrieg.

There remains Russia, but I have a feeling that Stalin does not intend to help Hitler very much and if the Kremlin is skilfully handled by our diplomats there seems good reason to believe that German supplies from this quarter might be cut off altogether.

There is, of course, always the possibility that the Axis Powers may break through the iron ring of the blockade in one of the four ways listed under a previous heading but, for the moment at all events, we are entitled to believe that they will not succeed in doing this.

Therefore it seems that, although Hitler's territorial conquests are beginning to rival those of Napoleon, from an economic point of view he has done little more than enlarge his cage while taking a number of less ferocious but equally hungry animals into it.

The reference to the Napoleon causes me to add that although he in his day was also subject to a British blockade there were very definite reasons as to why he was able virtually to ignore it and to continue his conquests unaffected by it over a period of years. In the Europe of Napoleon's time a far greater acreage per head of the population was under cultivation. Wherever his armies moved, therefore, he was able to a large extent to live upon the land, bringing, it is true, poverty and distress in his train but leaving the great bulk of the territories over which he ruled comparatively little affected. Moreover, Napoleon's horses could be supplied with fodder acquired in the campaign area, whereas Hitler's tanks and planes must be fed with petrol bought over great distances and from sources where the supply is by no means unlimited. Finally, it is doubtful if Napoleon required in a year as much metal for the manufacture of arms and munitions as Hitler needs to keep his foundries going for a week.

Without any wishful thinking the Nazis are, therefore, as I see it, in as grave a situation economically this autumn as they were last and, in view of the additional millions of people for whom they are responsible, their outlook is infinitely worse, but Goering and Co. are not the people to sit down and do nothing about it.

The Time Factor

We must give it to the Nazis that they are magnificent organizers and I have no doubt at all that thousands of fat, bald-headed German business men are now busy in every city of the conquered territories, together with those of so-called unoccupied France and the Balkans, endeavouring to get the industries of these countries running at full pressure again, and also arranging for the maximum possible acreage to be ploughed and sown so as to ensure a bumper harvest next year.

Whether Europe could continue to function as a separate unit cut off from the rest of the world still remains to be seen – and I certainly hope that we shall never see it – but although the standard of life throughout the whole Continent would be appallingly low it is just possible that it might be converted into a self-supporting unit and it is perfectly obvious that Hitler's industrial and agricultural experts will endeavour to make it so.

From lack of certain raw materials, and the denial to commercial concerns of those necessary for the manufacture of armaments, it is clear that many factories and businesses must go out of operation altogether, but the conquered territories have certain natural assets and since the German scientists lead the world in the production of substitute products we can be quite certain that every possible ingenuity will be employed to get as many factories as possible going on the manufacture of some useful article or other.

This, however, will take time. Many of the factories concerned were either damaged during the blitzkrieg or sabotaged by their owners before they became refugees. An enormous amount of replacement, repair, and adjustment will be necessary before the wheels of industry can again really start to turn on anything approaching a peace-time basis in Western Europe.

Moreover, the Nazi organizers, although extremely numerous, cannot be everywhere at once and will meet with stubborn opposition from a considerable section of the working population.

Nevertheless, given time, remarkable feats for the reorganization of industry in the conquered countries will undoubtedly be accomplished, as the Nazis are competent enough and hard-working enough to repair the ravages which they themselves created sufficiently to keep the bulk of the people that they have conquered employed in one way or the other; and where there is employment of any kind, however poorly paid, there is always hope among the employees of better times to come.

On the other hand, however clever they may be as organizers and scientists, nothing that the Nazis can do will make the fields of Europe bear their crops one day earlier than nature has intended. In the meantime, terrible as it may sound to say so, we must pray for a grim and wicked winter in order that by its rigours these unhappy millions may be the more quickly brought to a state in which measures may be taken to assist them to regain their freedom.

It is probable that this winter the Germans will suffer less than they did last winter, because whoever else has to go short Hitler will see to it that his own people receive a living ration, but the months ahead are grim indeed for the legions of poor folk who are the victims of Nazi aggression.

When there is a famine in an Asiatic village an Indian or a Chinaman will sit down and philosophically starve to death, even though he knows that in villages on the other side of the mountain-chain there is food to be had for the taking; but the reaction of the European in such a situation is very different. When he has tightened his belt to the last hole, and has seen his baby die because the milk in his wife's breast has dried up, he takes the nearest weapon to hand and goes out to get food or die in the attempt; and that may well be the state of things in many parts of Western Europe this winter.

The Gestapo and the German police battalions will do their best to keep order but, numerous as they are, it is going to be impossible for them to do so over the whole vast area from Northern Norway to the Pyrenees and from Rotterdam to the shores of the Black Sea when the subject peoples have reached the state where they know that in another week or so they will die of starvation anyhow, so it doesn't very much matter any more if they die by a German bullet instead, and they feel that it would be some satisfaction at least to kill one of their oppressors before they pass out.

That there will be a great deal of garotting of solitary German sentries and murdering of Nazi officials in their beds, I do not doubt, but whether this will lead to any large-scale revolts in which over any wide locality all Germans will be killed or driven out by starving mobs it is impossible to forecast.

Should such a state of things come about there are bound to be serious repercussions in Germany, because the commandeered food supplies from the captured territories will cease to come in and, however rigid the censorship, the news that various areas of the enslaved lands are in a state of revolt is bound to leak out.

If, in turn, the food shortage then becomes acute in Germany it is a possibility that almost overnight, in one of those queer mass movements for which it is difficult to account, the whole German people may realize that the game is up. Things that have only been whispered in fear as dread possibilities may be shouted aloud and asserted as facts, a furious nation may crowd the streets stricken with the awful truth that they have been fooled again, that Hitler's conquests are slipping away from him, that their own situation is becoming ever more precarious and that the Nazis are no nearer to the conquest of Britain than the Kaiser was in November 1918.

The German High Command will naturally be well aware of the true facts. I do not think it likely now that they will act on their own initiative before the German people have realized the truth themselves, but if there are spontaneous uprisings all over Germany the chances are that the generals will then confront Hitler and either he will commit suicide or he will be deposed. We shall then have brought about our desired result, which will justify the immense sufferings which must be caused to many millions of people through our blockade.

On the other hand, I feel most strongly that we must not disregard the time factor in considering the possible effects which our blockade may have. If through the grim months of winter the Nazis can reorganize Europe to such a degree as to give the conquered peoples some hope of a better future and provide them with a living ration, barely sufficient to maintain health, perhaps, but just enough to maintain life and to prevent their breaking into open revolt, we lose the deal.

The harvest of 1941 will, in my opinion, save Hitler if he can only keep things going long enough to gather it in, and if he can harvest the crops of 1941 there is no reason why he should not harvest those of '42, '43 and '44. Therefore, we dare not count upon the economic pressure of the blockade alone to bring about the downfall of the Nazi régime.

Intensive Bombing by the R.A.F.

As I hope to have shown above, if Hitler can manage to tide over the coming winter and spring there is a reasonable possibility that he might reorganize industry and agriculture in Western Europe so as to provide a bare living for its inhabitants, although cut off from the outside world, for a number of years to come. However, one of the essentials to any such reorganization is peace in which to carry it out, and fortunately there is no question at all of giving Hitler one moment's peace as long as a free hand is left to our magnificent Air Force.

Doubtless, ways will be found to reduce the damage which Hitler's indiscriminate bombings are doing to Britain, but whatever that damage may be it is now abundantly clear that the British people are quite prepared to stand up to anything Hitler may attempt against them, and in standing up to such attacks they have one enormous advantage over their enemies.

Our admirable Food Minister, Lord Woolton, has filled us all with confidence that although we may have to go a little short of some staple commodities here and there and from time to time, according to the seasons and markets, by and large the people of Britain are not to be called upon to suffer as long as our glorious Navy holds the seas; and that matter may be left to it with every confidence.

In consequence, fed not luxuriously but on a scale which will maintain health and vitality, we shall stand up to enemy bombings very much better than the Germans, and here the infinitely improved arrangements for heating our homes which the government have made for the coming winter, as compared with last winter, also deserve full praise. Given food and warmth and a reasonable degree of protection, which the Home Office, now in other hands, seems at last anxious to provide, we need not worry overmuch. But in Germany the situation will be very different, and if our nightly bombings continue even on the scale of the last few months there is every reason to hope that the morale of the German people will suffer most severely.

Yet, one understands, by the spring we hope to do even better in this direction than the splendid havoc which we have wrought so far. Climatic conditions in the worst months of the winter may make distant night-bombing difficult, but after the turn of the year our raids should increase enormously in intensity, since our new fleets of bombers, manned by the pilots both at home and overseas who have been training for just this work, will be ready to take the air.

Therefore, while the Nazis are frantically endeavouring to reorganize industry in the Low Countries and France we shall be smashing and pounding at their industries at home, so any small gains they may make upon the roundabouts will be more than lost to them upon the swings.

In addition there are, as I pointed out in my paper on 'Aerial Warfare', certain semi-military objectives which I feel we should be well advised to go for when we have a surplus of bombers. These objectives in the main represent either the symbols of the militant spirit of the German people which has caused such havoc in Europe during the past half-century or the symbols of the New Nazi Germany which is Hitler's personal creation. The destruction of these objectives is a thing which will make news and, however heavy the censorship, it will be whispered from mouth to ear throughout the length and breadth of the land, so that wherever these tidings of destruction go they will spread a far wider defeatist spirit among non-combatants than the bombing only of purely military objectives, which one fully agrees must remain our first and main task.

Further to this, when we have the aircraft to spare we could greatly increase the effects of the shortage of food and raw materials in Germany by endeavouring to institute a *blockade within the blockade*, by bombing.

There are certain key routes into Germany by road and rail, from the conquered territories and, while the railway junctions and possibly the roads are being severely damaged already, I see no reason why, given a sufficiency of bombers, time-bombs should not be dropped each night in the vicinity of the places where each railway line or arterial road crosses the German frontier.

In the bombing of London we have seen quite recently how many bombs have to be left undealt with sometimes for days at a stretch because only a limited number of very gallant men understand the mechanism of time-bombs and these men have more urgent work elsewhere. Such important highways, for example, as the Great West Road and the Finchley Road have now been blocked for over a week, and this presumably can be only because the defusing experts are occupied in immunizing bombs which have fallen in localities where they could do much more damage.

There is no reason to suppose that the Germans possess a greater proportion of these bomb experts than ourselves and, if this is so, were we to put fifty large time-bombs down per night in the places indicated we might virtually cut Germany off from her sources of supply in the occupied territories.

With intensive bombings there is also the question of leaflet raids, and while I am not averse to any serious proportion of bomb-load being sacrificed to paper-load I do consider it most important that this means of introducing propaganda into Germany should not be neglected.

I dealt with this matter at some length in the latter part of my Paper, 'The Winter', so I will not dwell further on it here except to draw attention to a passage in it which refers to the value of handwritten propaganda.

The suggestion was that the Germans and Austrians in our concentration camps and prisoner-of-war camps should be informed that if they care to write to their relatives we will do our best to deliver their mail, providing that it satisfies the requirements of the censor. Such letters as were unsuitable would be thrown out but those which told the truth about the excellent food situation in Britain and indicated that we had not the least intention of giving up this struggle until Hitler was totally defeated would serve our purpose well. Many, of course, would be specially inspired and written with the co-operation of refugees from Nazi persecution. Then every bomber that went over Germany could take a few packets, which would not interfere at all with its bomb-load, and scatter these as nearly as possible over the cities to which they were directed. Each would, of course, be addressed to an *actual individual in Germany with a view to those that were picked up being read by the finder and either passed on one possibly posted to their destination.*

I maintain that each such handwritten piece of propaganda would be worth a thousand printed leaflets.

However, in spite of these numerous forms of aerial activity, it is, I believe, generally maintained by the military experts that bombing alone, however intense, is not sufficient to secure the defeat of a nation in arms, so – once again – we cannot count on this factor to bring about the fall of the Nazi Government.

CONCLUSION

Therefore, to sum up, it seems that although there is no likelihood of our defeating the main German Army in the field during 1941, there is reason to believe that the collapse of the Nazi régime might be brought about next spring by the combination of a certain number, though not necessarily all, of the following factors:

1. *That the Axis Power be held fast in their cage and prevented from breaking out either in the Near East, through Egypt, or down into Africa by way of Morocco.*
2. *That our naval blockade continues to be exerted with maximum pressure.*
3. *That our bombing of Germany continues with maximum vigour.*
4. *That propaganda is used with greater ingenuity and intensity in both Italy and Germany.*
5. *That we succeed in forcing Italy out of the war.*
6. *That Hitler finds himself so short of supplies that he takes the desperate step of invading Russia.*

The combination of a number of the foregoing factors is by no means improbable and the first four, together with either 5 or 6, would definitely, I consider, bring about the collapse of the Nazi régime. We should then be called on to clear up the incredible mess that the Nazis have made; so we must now pass to the second part, and main purpose, of this paper, which is to consider what we intend to do.

Note

1. Stalingrad became Hitler's humiliation by the Russians from August 1942 to February 1943.

XV

After the Battle

To conclude this part of the book, I would like to present a portion of one of Wheatley's longest papers 'After the Battle'. It was thought out in September and October 1940, and written in November of that year.

Although some of the larger ideas are quite out-of-date by today's standards, they were perfectly sound for their day.

Wheatley's longest paper 'Total War', which is probably his most comprehensive, I have not included. In its original form, it was slightly shy of 100,000 words long and was published in book form during the war (albeit in cut form).

The edited version of 'After the War' presented here showcases some of his more fascinating observations, which a contemporary audience would find of interest.

After the Battle

Dover is only three minutes' flying time from Calais
DOVER IS ONLY THREE MINUTES' FLYING TIME FROM CALAIS
DOVER IS ONLY THREE MINUTES' FLYING TIME FROM CALAIS

THAT is a cardinal fact which must be held ever present not only in the minds of every British statesman and diplomat who may have even the remotest hand in the making of the Peace but also in the forefront of the consciousness of every man, woman, and child in both the British Empire and the United States.

Whether the war is brought to a conclusion in the spring of 1941, or whether it drags on for several years, there can be no question about our final victory. Therefore, sooner or later, we shall be called upon to clear up the incredible mess that Hitler has made.

Europe will be down and out, bankrupt and starving.

It is highly probable that before the Nazis finally collapse at home we shall have gone to the assistance of various people in the conquered territories who have already thrown off the Nazi yoke but, be that as it may, all Europe will be dependent upon the British Empire and the United States to save it from chaos and anarchy and to succour its starving peoples ...

THE HOME FRONT

Before we can pass to possibilities on the Continent and what we may or may not be able to do in bringing about a settlement which will ensure a lasting peace we must consider the Home Front, by which I imply the British Isles. The two major problems which will confront us here are (a) health, (b) the maintenance of law and order.

HEALTH

It is highly probable that, weakened by under-nourishment, great multitudes of the population on the Continent may be subject to sweeping epidemics of the most dangerous nature, and very careful advance planning should be made with this possibility in view.

As long as the war continues with Britain shut off from the Continent we shall have comparatively little to fear from any such epidemic, but should we send an Expeditionary Force to support a wide-scale revolt in any of the Nazi-occupied territories, or in an endeavour to restore order in the event of a sudden unexpected collapse of the Nazi regime, the way will immediately be opened for any such epidemic which may be raging on the Continent to be carried to our shores. It is, therefore, a definite responsibility which rests upon the Government to see that great stores of disinfectants and serums are accumulated in this country and a big increase made in the number of our fever and isolation hospitals.

Healthy, well-fed people are, generally speaking, much less prone to suffer the ravages of an epidemic than the under-nourished, so it is to be hoped that our own population will be able to stand up reasonably well to any disease, such as Spanish 'Flu, which might be brought over from the Continent once relations are re-established with the mainland.

However, in resistance to disease, equally important to normal health maintained by sufficient nourishment is the question of cleanliness. Our evacuation schemes have revealed to our shame the squalor in which the very poor in many of our great cities still live. The Minister of Health would, therefore, be well advised to get out in advance a much wider scheme for public baths, etc., than is in being at present, and also to formulate with his advisors a definite health drill for the entire population.

The average citizen hates having his personal habits interfered with, but in this case it may be a matter of national necessity that every member of the population should gargle each morning and night and have a bath at least twice a week. Any such programme will certainly meet with passive resistance in some quarters and would, admittedly, prove extremely difficult to enforce. Nevertheless, an enormous amount could be done to this end by skilful propaganda designed to make the nation 'danger-of-disease-conscious', and in securing general acceptance of the fact that uncleanliness at such a time will be just as mean and unpatriotic as being a conscientious objector.

THE MAINTENANCE OF LAW AND ORDER

It is virtually certain that however undesirable a change of Government will be, in fact at such a time the nation will demand a General Election, and this will be fraught with the gravest dangers to us all.

The war has already brought about so many changes in our national life that it is quite impossible to tell what sort of Government the country might return if Peace were declared tomorrow and a General Election held next month. It is reasonable to assume that the great bulk of the country would wish Mr. Churchill to undertake a further term as Prime Minister, but it may be questioned if it would return the Party that he leads if that did not also mean such men as Mr. Ernest Bevin, Sir Archibald Sinclair, and Mr. Morrison were not to be retained in his Cabinet.

Yet, a Coalition Government cannot go on indefinitely otherwise Party Government, upon which our Constitution is based, is at an end. There must sooner or later be a parting of the ways, not necessarily between Mr. Churchill and certain of his present colleagues, but if the Government is to continue virile there must be an active and healthy Opposition.

This is no place to dwell upon Party politics, but for those of us who have a real stake in the country, either large or small, it would be well to remember that very few of the Conservative leaders who served in Mr. Chamberlain's pre-war administration are considered by the public with any favour at all, and that Mr. Churchill himself was in opposition to that administration. It is, therefore, not too much to say that if the Conservative Party depends upon its pre-war leaders to lead it again after the war it is utterly and finally damned.

On the other hand, while people of all classes regard several of the Socialist leaders with growing admiration for the vigour and drive they are displaying as their contribution to the national war effort, there is in Britain an instinctive and deep-rooted fear of any Government of the Left which might tend to alter our way of life too rapidly through excess of zeal.

To whom, then, will the bulk of the electorate turn? After such an upheaval it is a foregone conclusion that adventurous extremists will be proclaiming from every street corner policies full of wild promise which are incapable of fulfilment, and it is absolutely vital to the well-being of the nation that from the lack of a clear-cut policy and leaders in whom they have confidence in the two great Constitutional Parties the masses should not be carried off their feet and return to power a gang of irresponsible adventurers.

There are, I believe, certain ways in which this risk could be circumvented and I made some notes upon it in the first month of the war, but a detailed account of possible measures to stave off any political landslide which might place an Extremist Part in power would overburden these pages ...

AN ALLIANCE WITH AN OUTSIDE POWER

(a)With the United States
While it is very much to be hoped that the one really good thing which may emerge out of the present conflict is an Act of Union with the United States of America, this would by no means be sufficient to protect Britain from aggression in years to come.

Such a union would, I believe, ensure an Anglo-American victory in any future war...

AN ALLIANCE WITH A CONTINENTAL POWER...

(a) France
At the moment, while the bulk of the French nation stands horrified and bewildered by the fate which has overtaken it, there are two groups of Frenchmen who have definite and entirely opposed policies for their country:
1. Monsieur Laval and his associates, who would like to give full co-operation to Hitler, even to the extent of utilizing the armed forces of France against Britain, to assist in a Nazi victory.
2. General de Gaulle and his friends, who have decided to fight on with Britain and will use every possible endeavour to ensure the minimum possible co-operation of their compatriots in France, and elsewhere, with the Nazis and eventually engineer an attempt by these compatriots in France to throw off the Nazi yoke.

There is also General Weygand, who now appears to be hesitating between these two policies and, having enormous influence, could unquestionably bring over a great body of the French power to whichever side he eventually decided to support ...

A CLEAN SWEEP

Having examined so many widely varied proposals for resettling Europe upon a basis of permanent peace, and found them all impracticable or fraught with grave danger to the security of Britain, it seems that the problem is insoluble. Yet it must be borne in mind that every proposal so far examined postulates the restoration of national frontiers upon the Continent as they were before Munich, except in the cases of France and Germany. It therefore still remains to be seen if some practical way could be found out of this impasse by making a clean sweep of all pre-Munich national frontiers and giving Europe a New Order.

Our position as the dominant Power after the war would certainly enable us to do so and, although we might for a time have to bear the odium of friends as well as foes, by sweeping away the whole legacy of muddle and warring interests with which the international agreements made by the states of Europe have entangled them in the past hundred years, there is at least a possibility that we might produce a better solution than could be obtained by the most carefully designed patching-up of the old structure.

This bold policy was adopted, in the main, after Napoleon had altered nearly every frontier in Europe at the Congress of Vienna, and as a result peace was maintained in Europe for the best part of half a century …

Again, Wheatley looks at history to form opinions about the future and, by doing so, nearly pre-empts the Common Market.

The papers Wheatley wrote before being put into uniform are – today – fascinating for their perception and freeform ideas; but they were worth so much more at their original time of writing, during the blackest days of the Second World War.

Part Three

Wing Commander Dennis Wheatley

' ... having served as one of Churchill's staff officers for three years during the Second World War, I had garnered a fine little collection of stories
illustrating his brilliant gift for repartee and skilful way of extricating
himself from awkward situations. My ability to imitate his voice enabled
me to enliven many a dinner party.'
*The Time Has Come: The Memoirs of Dennis Wheatley, 1914–1919, Officer and
Temporary Gentleman*

FUTURE OPERATIONS PLANNING STAFF AND ITS SUCCESSOR

<u>Deception Section of Future Operations Planning Staff</u>
(formed December 1941)
Lieutenant-Colonel A F R Lumbley, CIE, OBE (December 1941)
Pilot Officer D Y Wheatley, RAFVR (January 1942)

<u>London Controlling Section</u>
(detached from FOPS and renamed, June 1942)
Lieutenant-Colonel (later Colonel) J H Bevan, MC Controlling Officer
(June 1942)

Flight-Lieutenant (later Squadron Leader and then Wing Commander) D Y Wheatley, RAFVR (June 1942)
Major (later Lieutenant-Colonel) Harold Peteval (August 1942)
Major (later Colonel) Ronald Wingate, CIE (September 1942); appointed Deputy Controlling Officer December 1942; appointed Controlling Officer, in succession to Colonel Bevan, September 1945
Major Neil Gordon Clark (March 1943)
Major Derrick Morley (March 1943)

Attached:
Sir Reginald Hoare (Foreign Office representative)
Professor H A de Andrade, President of the Royal Society (part-time scientific advisor)

DENNIS WHEATLEY – BRIEF SERVICE RECORD

(The following is a brief list of Wheatley's Second World War commissions as held in the Officer Service Records Department of RAF Insworth.)

Name: Dennis Yeates Wheatley

Service Number: 113781

Dates of Service: 12 December 1941–20 December 1944

Entry rank: Pilot Officer 12 December 1941

Promotions:
    Flying Officer 12 February 1942
    Flight Lieutenant 12 May 1942
    Squadron Leader August 1942
    Wing Commander July 1944

Rank on completion of duty (22 December 1944): Squadron Leader (acting Wing Commander but retained rank of Squadron Leader)

DENNIS WHEATLEY'S WAR PAPERS IN-HOUSE AT FOPS AND LCS

1. 'Basic Principles of Enemy Deception' (re-written as 'Implementation of Military Deception' by Lieutenant-Colonel Bevan)
2. 'Deception on the Highest Plane'

3. 'Cessation of Hostilities'
4. 'Deception and Attrition in the Pacific'
5. 'Deception – Return to the Continent' (written by Bevan with contributions from Wheatley)
6. 'The Art of War'
7. 'Information to the Press'

XVI

The Commission

'All of us have setbacks, but gradually we move up the ladder, acquiring wisdom as we go, and the virtues of fortitude, forbearance, generosity and gentleness. Eventually the time comes when we face the great test, by being given a position of high responsibility, and we are granted the power to influence for good or ill large communities by leadership, example or our writings.'
The Devil and All His Works

After writing his war papers, Wheatley had earned the respect and trust of members of the Joint Planning Staff, so much so that he counted them among his best friends.

In November 1941 Group Captain William 'Dickie' Dickson (who afterwards became a Marshal of the Royal Air Force and Chairman of the Chiefs of Staff Committee) asked him to lunch to meet Colonel Oliver Stanley. Dickson had just been promoted Director of Plans (Air); Stanley was the Chief of Future Operations Planning Staff (FOPS).

It didn't take long for Wheatley to work out that he was being vetted for some kind of official job, probably, he assumed, in a propaganda department. A few days later Stanley summoned Wheatley to his office and told him that he was to work under him on the Joint Planning Staff. Wheatley was both surprised and delighted.

In early 1940 there existed at the War Office a section called MI(R). This consisted of five people: Colin Gubbins (later Major-General and head of SOE), Joe Holland (later Major-General), Norman Crockatt (later Brigadier MI9), Eddie Combe (late Lieutenant-Colonel and Military Member of the Inter-Service Security Board), and Joan Bright (later on the staff of General Sir Hastings Ismay).

Unfortunately, these forceful personalities came into conflict with the policies of more staid and powerful people. In consequence MI(R) was dissolved and its more bizarre activities were taken over by a new

department named Special Operations Executive, and the Inter-Services
Security Operations Executive, and the Inter-Services Security Board
was formed to carry on certain other functions, including the construction of cover plans. But cover plans are only the defensive side of
deception plans and it was no part of the board's business to plan offensive deceptions, such as threats to the enemy unrelated to any actual
operation.

Cover planning was only incidental to ISSB's charter. Its main concern
was security, with all the problems that entails (issue and registration
of code words, the grading of documents, censorship of mail, cables,
telegrams and phone calls, visitor bans in certain districts, leakages of
information and much more).

Soon, the Twenty Committee was formed, which consisted of the senior
members of the ISSB, together with representatives of the three Directors
of Intelligence, of MI5, MI6, SOE and PWE. This 'most secret' committee
met every Wednesday afternoon to decide what items of information
should be channelled to the enemy.

This continued until November 1940, when General Sir Archibald
Wavell, C-in-C Middle East, sent a signal to CIGS asking that Lieutenant-
Colonel Dudley Clarke should be sent out to join his staff.

Wavell had been on the staff of General Lord Allenby in 1918 and he had
never forgotten how the final victory against the Turks had been achieved.
A great number of camels had been assembled and ridden into the open
desert beyond the Turkish flank, and the clouds of dust sent up by them
had led the Turks to believe that their army was about to be encircled.
When they had hastily redisposed their forces the British launched a full-
scale frontal attack, taking them entirely by surprise. This deception plan
foiled the enemy so completely that, on the morning of the breakthrough,
the German C-in-C, General Leman von Sanders, had to quit his headquarters in pyjamas to escape capture.

When Dudley Clarke reached Cairo, General Wavell reminded him of
this successful stratagem and charged him with setting up a small section
for the sole purpose of formulating and implementing plans to mislead
the enemy.

Dudley Clarke was a regular Gunner and he had already seen considerable special service in the war, an account of which he published in his
book *Seven Assignments*. He was the first officer to lead a reconnaissance
party back to set foot on the continent after the evacuation from Dunkirk,
so he was in a way the father of Commando Raids as well as Deception
Plans.

In his book *The Deception Planners – My Secret War*, Wheatley described
Clarke as 'a small man with fair hair and merry blue eyes, an excellent
raconteur and great company in a party'. Sounds a kindred spirit to
Wheatley, who added:

[he had] a strange quietness about his movements and an uncanny habit of suddenly appearing in a room without anyone having noticed him enter it. His great sense of humour must have been contributed in no small measure to many of his successes in causing pain and grief to the enemy, while his military knowledge, combined with a most fertile imagination and tireless energy, made him the perfect deception planner. His ability to seize at once on the essentials of a problem and his facility at putting his thoughts clearly and briefly on paper led more than one of his staff officers to say that his gifts amounted to near genius.

Heavy praise indeed, but all the officers who found themselves working on deception plans were the cream of the crop. In short, they had earned their position and their reputation was second to none.

Clarke's section grew into a secret army. It became known as 'A' Force, consisting of a vast and tortuous network of deception personnel and secret agents throughout the whole of the Mediterranean, the Middle East, and Africa as far south as the Cape, in addition to which, in collaboration with Brigadier Crockatt of MI9 in London, he handled all measures in his theatre for assisting our prisoners of war to escape from enemy camps.

So successful was Dudley Clarke in his deception activities that in October 1941 General Wavell sent him home to give a personal account of his work to the Chiefs of Staff. This so impressed the Chiefs that they decided to create a similar body in their own organisation to keep in touch with 'A' Force and to study the possibilities of applying organised deception in the European theatre. Such work fell into the category of future planning, rather than that of the Strategic Section of the JPS, which dealt with immediate matters, so Colonel Stanley was instructed to form a new team of three GSO1s as an addition to his FOPS.

The War Office nominated Lieutenant-Colonel A F R Lumbley, CIE, OBE, who duly reported for duty late in December 1941. The Admiralty nominated Captain Hollorhan, RN, who, after a tour of duty with ISSB, had been appointed British Naval Instructor at the Turkish Staff College; but with the proviso that, as he was already engaged on an important mission, they were reluctant to recall him until the deception set-up was really under way. The Air Ministry said bluntly that, as the RAF was fighting the war, they could not possibly spare a Group Captain for work of such problematic value. It was then that one of Wheatley's friends, probably either Group Captain Roland Vintras or Air Commodore Dickie Dickson, said 'What about Wheatley?' and it was agreed to recruit him into the service.

XVII

The Fortress

'Another group which came under my wing … and added a spice of variety to our daily round was the handful of planners who were responsible for inventing cover plans for mystifying and deceiving the enemy.'
The Memoirs of Lord Ismay

After Wheatley's interview with Stanley, he was taken through endless corridors to Dickie Dickson's office in the Air Ministry. It was here that the writer was told more about the work he was to be engaged in. He was then told that he needed to attend a compulsory three-week Intake Course at Uxbridge.

As they were talking, a siren sounded and Wheatley was told that every Saturday at 4 o'clock they tested the alarm; Wheatley had to get used to his new surroundings and security was paramount. The offices of the War Cabinet were heavily guarded. A special troop of Home Guards, armed with revolvers, was always on duty to examine passes. There were sentries furnished by the Brigade of Guards inside all the entrances and armed Royal Marines who acted as officers' servants down in the basement, added to which there was a machine-gun post covering the broad stairs up to Winston Churchill's private apartments. Yes, let us not underestimate how new all this was to Wheatley, but he soon rose to the challenge.

On 2 December Wheatley received from the Ministry Form 1020, the application for a commission in the RAFVR, and Wheatley's supporters were Dickie Dickson, Director of Plans (Air) and Sir Louis Greig, Private Assistant to the Secretary of State. Wheatley then went to Adastral House at the bottom of Kingsway, which housed the administrative staff of the Air Ministry, for his interview. A Group Captain gave one glance at the signatures, smiled at Wheatley and said, 'It doesn't seem that there's any point in my asking you any questions, you'd better ask me some.'

It then transpired that the next Intake Course for 600 new officers was already full and that there was a further waiting list of 700. But Oliver

Stanley wanted Wheatley at once, so he was pushed to the front of the queue and started at Uxbridge at the end of that week.

Wheatley declared (see *Deception Planners*) that Uxbridge was a waste of time, but he admitted that it was so different to his normal life that it 'was an interesting change'. However, things wouldn't be normal for Wheatley again until after the war.

Wheatley had been in the trenches during the Great War and a Naval cadet in his youth, so he was a natural when it came to 'square bashing' and the obligatory barrack room banter.

On 30 December 1941 the course ended and Wheatley returned to his flat at Chartsworth House in West London. The next day he reported for duty at the offices of the War Cabinet.

The block in which he was to work for the following three years lies at the extreme western end of Whitehall, and it housed many ministries. Its side facing Whitehall was the Home Office, that facing Parliament Square the Treasury – which had been bombed out of its own office on the far side of Downing Street – that facing on to King Charles Street the Operational Department of the Air Ministry, and that facing on to St James's Park the offices of the War Cabinet. But on the third and fourth floors numerous sets of rooms were occupied by various Ministers of State whose work necessitated only a small staff.

To the right of the great bronze doors opening on to St James's Park the ground and first floor rooms had been given over to Winston Churchill and his personal staff, because Downing Street was 200 years old and, having no steel girders in it, very vulnerable to air attack. Churchill lunched, dined and held meetings at No. 10, but he slept and spent much of his time in this other accommodation, which was known as 10 Downing Street Annexe. Churchill's secretaries, Martin, Peck and Rowan, worked in the ground floor rooms adjacent to his bedroom, and he also had a private map room run by Captain Pim, RNVR.

On the floor above were the offices of Churchill's personal assistant, Major Sir Desmond Morton, his ADC, Commander 'Tommy' Thompson, RN, and his scientific advisor, Professor Lindemann; there was also a mess for his staff.

Below Churchill's own rooms and extending to the north-west corner of the building, lay the fortress basement in which worked and lived the Cabinet Secretariat and the Joint Planning Staff, so night or day, he had only to phone and any aides could be with him in two minutes.

The basement consisted of a warren of narrow passages and well over one hundred rooms. It was also designed as a retreat for the War Cabinet in the event of a landing by enemy parachutists. There was an office, bedroom and small dining room for Churchill himself. There was also a bedroom for Atlee, Beaverbrook, Eden, Bevin and the other members of the War Cabinet, who used them on nights of heavy raids, and bedrooms for Sir Edward Bridges, General Ismay, Brigadier Hollis, Colonel Jacob, Brendan Bracken, Harvey Wyatt and other members of the War Cabinet office.

There was a big room in which the War Cabinet met on nights when there were air raids, a similar room for meetings of the Chiefs of Staff, accommodation for typists, a large map room staffed by twelve officers representing the three Services, and a tiny mess. This last had originally been established only to provide the map-room officers with a snack, but by the time Wheatley arrived it had become customary for members of the JPS to lunch there if they were not going out to their clubs. Being under the north-west corner of the building, it formed the segment of a circle. Behind a curtain in one corner, Royal Marine orderlies could heat soup or knock up a dish of eggs and bacon but, in the main, Wheatley and his colleagues were fed cold food (hams, tongues, biscuits and cheese – good food for the war years). The centre of the room was only large enough to take two card tables, which put together would seat six at one time. In the other corner there was a steel filing cabinet which held drinks.

This underground fortress resembled the lower deck of a battleship. It was painted white and along the ceilings of its narrow passages ran a mass of cables carrying light, heat, telephone and air-conditioning to the many rooms, most of which were like a ship's cabins. Down there was a small room that held the Atlantic telephone on which Winston Churchill talked almost daily to President Roosevelt. There was also a special telephone exchange, from which skilled Post Office engineers had laid deep underground lines to the HQs of the various commands outside London, and to Edinburgh, Glasgow, Cardiff, Birmingham, etc., so that, should every telephone exchange in London be destroyed, communications with these centres would remain unaffected. The basement was gas proof, flood proof and had a four foot thick layer of concrete inserted between it and the ground floor of the building. It held an ample supply of medical stores and was provisioned for three months. So even had German parachutists temporarily seized Central London, the fortress would have closed up like a clam and Churchill and his advisors would have been able to continue to direct the war from there.

The principal offices of the War Cabinet were on the second floor. It was there that Bridges (the Secretary of the War Cabinet), Ismay (Churchill's principal Staff Officer), Hollis (his deputy), and Jacob (responsible for communications), all had their offices. On that floor, too, was the room in which the Chiefs of Staff met every morning, and it always intrigued Wheatley that outside it in the corridor there stood a hat stand – the only one in the whole building that was not inside a room! Why it should have been placed outside Wheatley didn't know, but it always fascinated him to pass at about 11 o'clock in the morning. Only hats hung on it: that of Admiral Sir Dudley Pound, First Sea Lord and CNS, that of General Sir

Alan Brooke, CIGS, that of Air Chief Marshal Sir Charles Portal, CAS, and, a few months after Wheatley joined, there was added to them that of Lord Louis Mountbatten as Chief of Combined Operations. No other hat stand can ever have habitually carried such a weight of gold braid.

The third floor also had large spacious rooms. There the Minister without Portfolio and the FOPS had their offices.

As Director of Plans (Air), Dickie Dickson had one of the big second floor rooms on the Air Ministry side of the building. Vintras had also been transferred from the JPS, and had become Dickson's senior Staff Officer. On arriving, Wheatley reported to him. Then he took him through the maze of corridors and up to FOPS.

Wheatley was nervous about entering his new world. He was concerned that he could be out of his depth, but he took a deep breath, just like a new boy on his first day at school. It was one thing to meet men like Lawrence, Darvall and Dickson as a well established author, but quite another for Wheatley to be taken into an organisation consisting of the picked brains of the three Services and to make their acquaintance as a pilot officer RAFVR – the lowest form of commissioned life. Wheatley felt that his new colleagues would have good reason to look on him as an interloper who had been foisted them on a whim. Also, Commander Robert-Shaw was the only member of the FOPS to whom he had spoken, and it was quite possible that none of the others had ever read any of his papers, as these always went to the STRATS.

An added embarrassment for Wheatley was the fact that in his last week at Uxbridge he had contracted a heavy cold. By the time he reached the Cabinet Offices, his voice had been reduced to a croak.

However, despite his uncomfortable condition, Wheatley was soon taken under the wing of Group Captain Groom and taken into the two-roomed Deception Section next door. He was introduced to Lieutenant-Colonel Fritz Lumby. Lumby got up, limped over to Wheatley and shook his hand, he then pointed to a large desk and told the writer that it would be his.

The two men hit it off almost straight away, with Lumby telling Wheatley that he had lost a leg at Loos in 1915 but remained in the Indian Army and spent the period between the wars in India as an Intelligence Officer. Lumby was a tall, thin, dark man with an exceptionally low voice, a shy manner but a bawdy sense of humour.

In no time at all, Oliver Stanley appeared and announced that Wheatley should now read himself into the war.

XVIII

Getting Started

'I … keep invention in a noted weed
That every word doth tell my name
Showing their birth, and where they did proceed'
William Shakespeare

Lumbly handed Wheatley several stiff-backed folders. Inside, Wheatley was surprised to find minutes of recent meetings of the War Cabinet, the Defence Committee and the Chiefs of Staff.

It wasn't long before Wheatley realised that he had to spend many hours a day reading documents in order to have knowledge of every aspect of the war. Additional reading comprised: the Joint Intelligence Summary, the separate Intelligence Summaries of the three Services, the Political Warfare Summary, minutes from the Prime Minister, the Chiefs of Staff and the Directors of Plans, reports on the state of equipment of all divisions being formed, of the production of munitions, of stocks of food and petrol, statements of manpower, aircraft, tanks, shipping and landing craft available, directives to force commanders, dispatches from all C-in-Cs, draft plans under consideration by both the STRATS and FOPS, Foreign Office telegrams in and out, and numerous long papers put in from time to time independently by Cabinet Ministers, containing ideas on how the war could be better fought.

That first day, Lumby took Wheatley to the Liberal Club for lunch. However, that afternoon, a plump, fair haired, red faced Major, wearing the Glengarry and tartan trews of the Royal Scots, stood there and gave Wheatley a smart salute. Wheatley at once came to attention. The Major had brought a letter over from the War Office and, having introduced himself as Major Combe, asked Wheatley if he would lunch with him one day. Surprised but pleased, Wheatley accepted. They instantly made a date.

For Major Combe to deliver a document by hand was most unusual; but he later admitted to Wheatley that he wanted to meet him. Normally, all inter-departmental memos were sent from ministry to ministry (and even from office to office) in locked wooden boxes covered with either black, grey or red leather, and stamped with the Royal Arms. The red boxes contained the most Secret of papers and recipients carried keys according to their seniority to open them.

The next day, Wheatley lunched with Roly Vintras in the basement mess, of which he told Wheatley that he was now entitled to be a member. Whilst they were having a drink General Ismay entered. Roly introduced Wheatley, and a firm friendship was forged.

The day after, Victor Groom showed Wheatley the RAF canteen on the ground floor. It catered for all ranks and both sexes, and by that stage of the war the food there was far from appetizing, so Wheatley never lunched there again.

Wheatley and Lumby were regarded as the most Secret section in the whole building, and were not even at liberty to tell other members of the JPS what they were up to. However, for the first several weeks of Wheatley's appointment, they weren't up to anything. The only communication allowed to them was through the Inter-Service Security Board. Before the creation of their special section, the Board had handled all cover plans, now they were to act as Wheatley's and Lumby's executive.

The ISSB met every morning at the War Office, and one day, shortly after Wheatley's arrival, Lumby took him across to meet the officers who would implement the plans they might make.

The Chairman of the Board was a pleasant old gentleman – Colonel Graham. The Naval member was Commander 'Ginger' Lewis, RN, a grand chap who had brought his destroyer back to port with the whole of her front half shot away. The Air Member was Wing Commander Byron. MI5 and MI6 were represented by Lieutenant-Colonel Gilbert Lennox, a fat and jovial man whom Wheatley already knew. It was Lennox who had vouched for him – from a security point of view – with Oliver Stanley. The Home Office was represented by a Mr Buckley.

Their deputies were Major E P Combe, Lieutenant-Commander the Hon. Ewan Montagu, RNR, Flight Lieutenant Tennant and Major Cass of MI5. The secretariat consisted of Combe, who was its senior member, and Majors Brunyate, Goudie and Moffat.

For two years, Wheatley attended the daily meetings of the ISSB, and ceased to do so regularly only after his section was expanded with the inclusion of Major Neil Gordon Clark, who was duly given the job.

The first meeting Wheatley attended coincided with his lunch date with Major Combe, so after the meeting, he went off to Rules in a taxi.

Wheatley soon found that Major Combe (or 'Eddie' as he became known) had spent the whole of the Great War on the Western Front, being one of only a handful to have survived those gruelling four and a half years without becoming a casualty. He had seen over twenty Colonels come and go (killed, wounded, promoted or sacked) and was a double MC.

After the war he had retired to become a stockbroker, and for a number of years was the London representative of the great New York firm, Clark, Dodge Company. Eddie Combe was a single, wealthy man and a most generous host. At Rules a corner table for six was always kept for him and, unless he was lunching with someone else, he entertained a party there every day. His guests were from all three Services, and there can hardly have been an officer playing any part that really mattered in the 'behind-the-scenes' side of the war who did not lunch at some time or other with Eddie Combe at Rules. Wheatley did many times, and each time became an invaluable experience for him, as he networked with some of the most fascinating men. Later, when Wheatley needed the help of any of their departments, he would only have to say over the phone: 'You may remember we met a few weeks ago when lunching with Eddie Combe.'

The thing that made Eddie's lunches so special to Wheatley was the food. At that particular stage of the war good food and wine was very difficult to come by. But to start with, Wheatley and Combe always started with two or three Pimms at a table in the bar, then a so-called 'short one' well-laced with 'Chanel 5' as Eddie termed Absinthe. Old Tommy Bell, who owned the place, or his top girl, Ivy, always took the order, first letting them know what the specials were: smoked salmon or potted shrimps, then a Dover sole, jugged hare, salmon or game, and a Welsh rarebit to complete the menu. Good red or white wine washed this down and the lunchers invariably ended with port or kummel.

On their return from such a lunch engagement, Eddie – despite his portly frame – would run up the stairs to his office, Wheatley, however, would sometimes need to lie down for an hour or so to sleep it off. He didn't feel guilty about this; he had put in many hours, having worked through the night when writing his original war papers. He asked his Naval colleague, James Arbuthnott, to wake him with a solitary ring on the phone if he was needed urgently.

The teams that worked in the FOPS under Oliver Stanley consisted of three GSO1s: Captain Buzzard, RN, Lieutenant-Colonel White and Group Captain Groom; and three GSOs: Commander Robertshaw, RN, Major Mann and Wing Commander Harvey. These names are of historic interest because during December 1943 and throughout 1944, hundreds of officers worked on the preparations for the return to Europe. But it was Oliver Stanley's FOPS who drew up the original appreciation in the spring of 1942. They made a study of the beaches from northern Norway to the Pyrenees, arguing that the Normandy beaches offered the best bet.

Stanley had an unorthodox custom, which was most agreeable to his staff. Every afternoon, he would organise the men to meet in the GSO2's room for tea and cakes and a quarter of an hour's general chat. An old office messenger by the name of Baker always fetched the cakes from a nearby shop, but he also did Wheatley a greater service during the early days of Wheatley's time at the JPS. After only a few days in post, Wheatley's voice had not returned, so Baker told him to boil up equal parts of turpentine and glycerine in a tin cup, soak a big pad of cotton wool in the mixture, put it on the throat as hot as could be suffered and bandage it there all night.

Wheatley's wife, Joan, was afraid that the turps would take all the skin from his neck. But Wheatley was desperate enough to try anything, and the remedy worked like a charm. Within twenty-four hours, he was speaking normally again.

During the lean period at the start of Wheatley's time in the JPS, he took it upon himself to begin work on another war paper entitled 'The Basic Principles of Enemy Deception'.

Oddly, nobody had put down on paper the principles of the job of deception, so partly for order and discipline and partly for something to do, Wheatley continued with the work he knew best: writing original thought-provoking ideas. He opened his paper in the following way:

> 1.Enemy deception falls under three heads;
> (a) A long-term deception policy as to the manner in which we intend to bring the war to a victorious conclusion.
> (b) A number of large-scale preparations for possible future intentions in each separate theatre of war, or to induce him to believe that we have decided to open up new theatres in localities where we have no intention of attacking him.
> (c) A week-to-week review of operations in all theatres with a view to disguising or implementing cover plans to mislead the enemy with regard to raids and troops or convoy movements.

Again, Wheatley constructed a good sound base for his thoughts. The important point about his war papers was that they never fell into the realms of fantasy. They were basic, constructive ideas. Admittedly, occasionally, in some of his papers, his enthusiasm would run away with itself, but he could never be criticised for over-egging the mixture.

Even in a short space of time, Wheatley had learnt a great deal about deception. Just being around the right officers in the JPS gave him a natural instinct for the job. The many lunches he had with the staff – and of course Eddie and his cloak-and-dagger friends – would give him a further insight; then there was the normal office chit-chat. Put that altogether with the most Secret papers that filtered through to him – all that reading matter – Wheatley *was* now in a position to write for the War Cabinet. After writing some details about the formation of ISSB and deception policy of the Chiefs of Staff, Wheatley continued with the following general principles:

Wherever possible, deception plans should be tied up with forces and shipping already earmarked for dispatch from one of our bases.

Our deception plans must be logical and therefore cause German Intelligence to take *serious notice* of them, otherwise our efforts would be a waste of time.

They should be within the scope of the resources that the enemy *believed* us to possess.

They should be plans which we should *actually carry out* if we had the shipping, trained personnel and materials at our disposal.

That no measure, short of definitely hampering our genuine war activities, should be neglected which would be taken were we actually going to carry out the deception plan.

That the fullest possible information should be made available to us of all enemy reactions to the deceptive material put out.

That as few people as possible, having regard to practical necessities, should be allowed into the secret of any deception plan.

Wheatley then listed every means he could think of to provide the enemy with material evidence which would convince him that a deception plan was a genuine operation. The paper then concluded with several paragraphs on the importance of complete liaison with force commanders overseas, to ensure that their cover plans should not conflict with overall strategic deception policy, likewise with PWE and SOE for the same reason; and the value of seeking the co-operation of the Foreign Office and a list of the Chiefs of Departments, who would have to be informed of the plans in order to implement them.

Six months later, when Lieutenant-Colonel J H Bevan, MC succeeded Lumby as the head of Wheatley's section with the title of London Controlling Officer, he redrafted the major portion of Wheatley's paper, putting it into approved staff form, and retitled it 'The Implementation of Military Deception'.

XIX

The Art of Writing Deception Plans

In January 1942 Wheatley was told that although an invasion against Norway in the spring was not feasible, a deception plan to persuade the Germans that the British intended to land a force in the Stavanger area around 1 May, was required.

Both Wheatley and Lumby set to work at once, but did so with some trepidation, as for many years, these two men had been used to working with experienced secretaries, and because the work they were now doing was considered super-secret they were denied secretarial support.

When Wheatley had learned this, he became a little anxious, because although his thrillers were said to keep people up at night in every part of the civilized world, he was hopeless at spelling and knew nothing about grammar; this was in the days before computers and spellcheckers.

Wheatley had always relied upon his secretary to interpret his writing. In fact he had been so ashamed of the exercise he had written for Stanley while at Uxbridge (about persuading the enemy that the British were sending all their tanks overseas), that he couldn't bring himself to hand the final paper to him as it stood.

Fortunately, Wheatley had already met Joan Bright, formerly of MI(R) now in General Ismay's office, at one of Roly Vintras' dinners at the RAC (in her honour). Wheatley, with his wife Joan and Peter Fleming went along shortly before Wheatley was put into uniform. Having learned from Vintras that Joan was one of the very few people who knew about the work Wheatley had been brought in to do, he simply got her to type his paper for him. Obviously, Wheatley and Lumby couldn't task Joan with typing all the work emanating from their section; they had to do a lot of the preparation and drafting themselves – with two fingers.

The duo's handicap was soon found out, but no one on the JPS – including Stanley – had a private secretary. All the work had been done by typists from the pool, and the work of Wheatley and Lumby was considered too secret for a bunch of young women in the typing pool, despite the fact that these women were entrusted with the typing of plans for real operations.

This eventually worked in the duo's favour, as they were given their own private secretary, Joan Eden. She typed Wheatley's forerunner of the deception bible, then the ideas for drawing Germany reinforcements up to – most uselessly – southern Norway!

When Stanley had passed the final draft of the Norway paper, it was taken to ISSB. It was then their business to provide a codeword for the operation, and Lumby very kindly suggested that Wheatley should choose it.

This was not as easy at it first appeared. ISSB kept a register of words that had already been used, as it was essential not to re-use a codeword, and a thick book was produced for Wheatley to choose from in which the words still free were not ticked.

Wheatley selected the word 'Hardboiled', and the next day, when Stanley saw it on one of his office memos, he said, 'Who was the bloody fool who chose such a silly codeword?'

Stanley always wanted the codenames of major operations to mean something. For example, after the invasion scare that came to nothing the codename 'Cromwell' had to be changed – they chose 'Aflame'. As in the old days beacons were always made ready for lighting should Britain be invaded, the choice could not have been more stupid, for had any document so headed fallen into the hands of the enemy, he would have needed little intelligence to guess that it referred to the British plans for resistance to invasion. 'Overlord' became the title of the operational return to Europe, but Wheatley for one was shocked by the codeword for the initial landing on the Normandy beaches – 'Neptune'. The German high command was just as stupid, for they gave their plan for the invasion of Britain the codeword 'Sea Lion'. So, in short, Britain was just as bad as the Germans at encrypting their plans in a satisfactory way.

Wheatley told Stanley that he had chosen 'Hardboiled' as the codeword. He also pointed out that the whole object of a codeword was to conceal the matter concerned. Major operations should have codewords such a 'table', 'dress', 'wedding cake', from which the enemy could deduce nothing.

Stanley obviously thought Wheatley had a point as he authorised the codeword 'Hardboiled'. The next step was to now implement the paper. A more tricky exercise. And this was how they did it:

A meeting was held at the War Office by the Deputy Director of Staff Duties. It was attended by several Generals, some Brigadiers, the members of the EPS and ISSB, Stanley Lumby and Wheatley. As far as the EPS (Executive Planning Section) was concerned, they worked in their respective ministries under their own Chiefs of Staff. They were not concerned with making plans, but when an operation had been approved it was passed to them. Their business was then to report on the troops available, the shipping and supplies required, to make the operation a practical undertaking.

Stanley, having been Secretary of State for War, was always received at the War Office with considerable deference. The only open opposition offered was a certain amount of headshaking about the practicability of actually getting done some of the measures for which he asked.

This was the only meeting of its kind that Stanley attended; afterwards he would delegate the task to Wheatley and Lumby, when the reception became much more hostile. This was simply because senior officers lacked imagination and the idea of a deception plan, as distinct from a cover plan for a real operation, was a totally new gambit to them, which they truly didn't appreciate, mainly because it would mean a lot of extra work.

A deception plan would mean training men, calling up provisions and clothing from stores and briefing on an operation as if it was the real thing (but nobody would know that it wasn't, that was the point). Men would be called off their normal training practices and maps printed (only to be unused and destroyed); it was all too much of a waste of time, with no guarantee of a deception being successfully presented to the Germans. Most of the EPS believed that this new strategic deception idea was invented by a crackpot and presented no justification for wasting everybody's time. Unfortunately, Lumby had not the sufficiently forceful personality to convince them otherwise. 'Hardboiled' was eventually conducted by the Royal Marine Division in Scotland. They were furnished with equipment as though it was a real scenario but were not told otherwise. Then measures were taken to provide material evidence of preparation for an operation, which it was hoped would be reported by enemy agents in Britain; or by careless talk from troops.

Once the operation was underway, Wheatley and Lumby had little to do, save finding sanctuary for Norwegian sailors who broke away from German-supervised fishing fleets and escaped to Britain. These people would be held in South Kensington until MI5 had satisfied themselves that they were not indeed enemy agents.

It was decided that two of the Norwegians would be brought to the Cabinet Office and closely questioned about possible landing grounds for aircraft.

As it was an air matter, Wheatley was tasked with questioning the men. Victor Groom loaned Wheatley his tunic during the interview, so for a brief hour he masqueraded as a Group Captain with two splendid rows of decorations. Apart from this little matter all other measures had been taken out of Wheatley's (and Lumby's) hands by ISSB. In fact, each morning Lumby spent an hour doing *The Times* crossword puzzle. Wheatley busied himself with other trivialities. He had his great coat lined with scarlet satin (not unlike the Brigade of Guards of the German General Staff) and he had some swagger sticks made, approximately 18 inches long, wrapped in blue leather and each concealing a 15-inch blade (in case of trouble during a black out).

Wheatley was certainly beginning to feel the part, and it suddenly occurred to him that it needed a large chunk of men to implement a really telling deception plan to the enemy. Indeed, the Russians had plenty of men; so why not propose such an operation to them?

FOPS vetted Wheatley's plan and Stanley liked it, but no one seemed to have a workable military link with the Russians. The best Stanley could do was speak to Anthony Eden about it and suggested that he should put the idea into the head of the Soviet Ambassador Mr Maisky, when they next met.

During February 1942 the idea of deception plans became a popular one. Peter Fleming was called to join General Sir Archibald Wavell, who was then Commander-in-Chief India, in his own deception centre. Fleming pulled off a marvellous coup in Burma. During the retreat, he put a number of 'most secret' documents containing false information into a suitcase into the boot of a car and overturned the car down a steep embankment where the advancing Japs were certain to come upon it an hour or so later.

After the retreat he operated from General Wavell's HQ at Delhi, and on one occasion when a high-powered Anglo-American-Chinese staff conference was held there he succeeded in selling faked minutes of the decisions taken to an enemy agent for 10,000 Chinese dollars.

Despite this, Fleming did find the selling of deception to senior officers an uphill task. In a letter he wrote to Wheatley in mid-1942, he said: 'This is a one-horse show and I am the horse.'

Although no one entering the RAFVR at that stage of the war could be given a higher rank than Pilot Officer, the appointment specially created for Wheatley on the JPS had been that of a Flight Lieutenant, so he was entitled to that rank as soon as Air Ministry regulations permitted his promotion to it. In consequence, on 12 February, having served for two months, Wheatley automatically became a Flying Officer and changed one thin ring on his cuffs for a thick one (he would become a Flight Lieutenant three months later on 12 May 1942).

By March 1942 Wheatley and Lumby were still twiddling their thumbs. To break the gloom somewhat, Stanley suggested that Wheatley should write a paper concerning the situation Britain might face when the war ended. Wheatley thought this was a splendid idea and instantly produced a paper over 10,000 words long.

Part I (three quarters of the paper), dealt with the different circumstances in which an end to the hostilities might come about. Part II dealt with the probable state of Europe after the war and how a balance could be made (pre-empting the formation of the Common Market by a pooling of interests by several nations).

By way of conclusion, Wheatley's paper made the following radical observations:

1. The United States would endeavour to secure financial control of Europe as a great market for her manufactured goods.
2. The Soviet Union would endeavor to federate the European states as workers' republics on the Soviet model.
3. Most of the smaller powers would be striving to regain their independent national status.

In short, Wheatley's paper concluded that the greatest menace to Britain's continuance would come from her two most powerful allies, the USA and USSR, whose interests were divergent from hers and from each other's. Stanley was impressed by the paper and circulated it to the JPS and its associated bodies.

Whilst Wheatley had been writing the paper, he found that there was a problem with 'Hardboiled'. He was informed that certain air operations due to take place over southern Norway would conflict with the deception plan; so the implementation of it had to be postponed.

Further troubles lay ahead though. The Japanese were advancing quickly in South-east Asia and the War Cabinet feared that they might launch a seaborne invasion of Ceylon. Alternatively, they could by-pass Ceylon completely and establish themselves in Madagascar, which would give them strategically an excellent base to plan forward operations (exposing both Ceylon and India). A British Expeditionary Force had to be sent in to seize the port. Unfortunately, the Chiefs selected the Royal Marines Division of 'Hardboiled' (the only division trained in mountain warfare). Hence Operation 'Hardboiled' was shelved and Operation 'Ironclad' was born. Wheatley was invited into Room 330 at the War Office to discuss cover plans for 'Ironclad'. This was a most secret and dangerous expedition. The Eastern Mediterranean was closed to the British at the time, with Malta in a state of siege (so all reinforcements for the Middle East had to be sent round the Cape). But the Germans would not have imagined that the British intended to go into French North Africa with a single division (this was something the likes of Alistair Maclean and Frederick Forsyth would only write about in their fiction years later)!

There were many problems with the planning of the operation, which should have fallen on the shoulders of Lumby, but as he had taken the day off, the responsibility of attending the meeting and suggesting possible solutions fell to Flight Officer Wheatley.

It was time for Wheatley to feel humbled by the ranks of his peers in the meeting: five Generals, two Admirals, an Air Vice Marshal, ten Brigadiers, plus a cross section of Colonels, Captains RN and a Group Captain RAF. What concerned him more was the fact that the single ring on his two sleeves acquired more than one glance of surprise and, consequently, raised eyebrows.

The operation was discussed in full and after an hour the conversation turned to cover plans. A sticky situation ensued. General Sturges, probably of too lowly a rank to have been let into the secret that a special section of the JPS had recently been formed to deal with such matters, had very properly told a member of his staff to think one up, and he proceeded to outline it.

During all this time, Wheatley had remained silent but, seeing that the General's plan had no relation to that devised by Lumby and himself, he thought it only proper to clear his throat and interrupt the General.

'Sir,' Wheatley began, addressing the Director of Staff Duties. 'With due respect, I fear I cannot agree to this.'

There followed a moment of stunned silence, but Wheatley was not to be intimidated. He continued: 'I am here to represent the Joint Planning Staff of the War Cabinet, by whom a cover plan has already been formulated, which has received the approval of the Chiefs of Staff.' One could have heard a pin drop as Wheatley went on to tell them what they were required to do.

After some reluctance, General Sturges accepted the plan Wheatley put forward. Others found it amusing that the most junior officer of the most junior service was sent to give them their orders.

To implement the cover plan, Peter Fleming gave invaluable help by flying to Ceylon and commandeering many buildings to accommodate the division during the fortnight it was supposed to be going to spend there. General Smuts came in and commanded his security police to Durban to temporarily intern anybody suspected of being an enemy agent.

Owing to these measures and a very great deal of luck the cover plan succeeded and the expedition achieved complete surprise. When the convoy arrived early one morning off the west coast of the northern tip of Madagascar, within a day's march of Diego-Suarez, the only people to be seen for miles were a man and his girlfriend bathing.

General Sturges then threw away the splendid advantage he had been given. On finding that the man was a French officer, instead of making him a prisoner, then marching through the jungle to take the great port in the rear and by surprise, he sent him off ahead to announce that the British were on their way and request the French C-in-C to surrender.

The French General sounded the alarm, had every gun in the place manned and for several days fought like a tiger, with the result that the British suffered quite unnecessarily a considerable number of casualties before Royal Navy warships shelled the port into submission.

Meanwhile, the job of deceiving a division of troops into believing they were to be sent to Norway, in the hope that careless talk would reach the ears of enemy agents, had to be started all over again. For this purpose the 52nd Highland Division was commissioned to 'Hardboiled'.

Wheatley and Lumby were not exactly snowed under with work during the second attempt at Operation 'Hardboiled'. FOPS were writing a plan for the return to the continent (to land on the Normandy beaches and cut off the Contentin Peninsula). Also, the Norwegian government in exile asked the Prime Minister to form a plan – with the Americans – to ensure that in another twenty years the Norwegians would not be overthrown again in another world war. None of this work went to Wheatley and Lumby. On 28 March Lumby went on leave. He had left a memo in Wheatley's tray that conveyed his low spirits: 'This day has brought forth absolutely nothing – not even a lemon.' So Wheatley took radical action. He decided to ignore military deception and write a paper concerning political warfare. By 10 April, he had completed a paper which he called 'Deception on the Highest Plane'.

The paper outlined how Hitler had failed to achieve victory in the West by 1942, and had added the USA and Russia to Germany's enemies. Wheatley surmised that great numbers of Germans must have now lost faith in their Fuehrer and, recalling the miseries they had suffered after their crushing defeat in the Great War, would be dreading the terrible experiences that lay ahead. So the time was right to play upon the Germans' fears and persuade them that their one hope of escaping the worst was to make a complete reassessment of spiritual values. This, Wheatley suggested, could be done by causing them to believe that a new leader would prove their salvation.

This leader, who of course would not exist, was to be a Christ figure on lines acceptable to modern thought; no virgin birth but born of poor parents, a period of retirement from the world, demonstration of supernatural powers and, finally, revelation of his mission. He was to have been seen in places all over Germany, preaching his doctrine of peace, universal brotherhood and passive resistance to all further war activities.

Every possible means was to be used by the British political warfare people to spread rumours about him; so that in due course the Nazis would be forced to run a counter-campaign denying his existence. In such circumstances there are always queer characters who, to gain notoriety, will swear that they have actually seen such a mystical figure; so there was a good hope that within a few months he would become the talk of Germany.

When Lumby returned from leave, he was enthusiastic about Wheatley's plan. Having a German mother, he had considerable knowledge of the German people and told Wheatley that the Germans were susceptible to ideas of sentimental mysticism. Furthermore, he told Wheatley that his character should be called the 'Bote' (messenger) and be a descendent of the Emperor Barbarossa.

Stanley liked the paper and when Wheatley took it at his order to General Brook at PWE, he also agreed that it had possibilities and said he would have it examined by the German experts.

Wheatley's next job was even more unorthodox. Oliver Stanley, having read some of Wheatley's books with occult backgrounds, asked him to write a paper stating that Wheatley had killed a black cock and white hen and, having performed certain curious rites, was granted a supernatural preview of a map of the world showing the situation on all battle fronts, as published in a copy of *The Times* on the day war ended. The paper was to be called 'Cessation of Hostilities'.

Wheatley predicted the date for the collapse of Germany to be 8 November 1942. Obviously, to a contemporary audience, it seems ludicrous, but Wheatley had based the date upon two major assumptions. Firstly, the Joint Intelligence Committee believed Germany to already be in great difficulty over oil and that within another six months she might find herself desperate for that commodity. Moreover, the JIC were of the opinion that the German war effort was by then being hampered by many shortages and that a considerable proportion of the people were turning against Hitler.

Later, Wheatley learned the reason for these ill-founded beliefs. While MI5, which was responsible for home security, did an excellent job and succeeded in catching nearly every spy sent over within forty-eight hours of his arrival, MI6, which was responsible for our spies in enemy and neutral countries, was pathetic.

During the Great War, MI6 had the reputation of being one of the finest of such organisations around the world. However, by the Second World War, it had lost direction. Britain had a lack of worthy secret agents, consequently the JIC were not even aware that Hitler had started to build huge factories for the production of synthetic oil, so there was not the least likelihood of German supplies drying up; and that, far from being half-starved of supplies, the Germans were living on the fat of the land by forced buying, with almost worthless currency, of food, clothes and all sorts of things from the countries they had over-run.

Wheatley also couldn't believe that the German General Staff would allow Germany to fight on until she was utterly exhausted and would suffer again the terrible times of the early 1920s. It seemed likely that they would realise that there was no hope of victory and depose Hitler and seek a compromise with the enemy.

Stanley's comment on Wheatley's paper was: 'I think you put the German collapse a little too early. I should have given them another three months and put it at February 1943.'

Wheatley and Lumby were a maverick – and most secret – team, but they found themselves more detached from day-to-day operations when they were moved to third-floor offices to bring Stanley (FOPS) closer to his colleagues in STRATS in the basement (this excluded Wheatley and Lumby from the opportunity of FOPS' daily tea party and whatever they would learn from that gathering).

Come early May, the duo was asked to write a paper on 'Deception and Attrition in the Pacific'. The object was to draw the maximum number of Japanese forces away from the Indian Ocean. At last they had been given work of the type they had been brought in to do in the first place. They immediately proposed measures that might have some small effect. However, it was quickly found that this was all an exercise to keep them busy. Lumby became more depressed and spent even longer doing cross-word puzzles. But this was not to last. Lumby would soon be appointed GSOI to SOE in West Africa.

As Lumby was to leave Britain at the end of the month, he at once set about making his arrangements and claimed a fortnight's embarkation leave, which he was entitled to. Lieutenant Colonel Bevan was appointed his successor and Stanley was anxious that he should join the JPS at once (to have as much handover time from Lumby as possible). But GHQ Western Command, where Bevan was GSOI Intelligence, said they could not spare him until 1 June. Then SOE said it was absolutely essential that Lumby should do a fortnight's special course before sailing for West Africa, so apart from one brief visit, Wheatley would never see him again. Less than two years later Lumby was killed in an aircraft crash.

As soon as Lumby left the department, Stanley took leave. His wife was unwell and it was soon found that she was dying. So, for the last three weeks of May, Wheatley was his own boss. He had no master or even colleagues. Quite frankly, he was in his element. There was nothing like solitude to fuel the creative juices.

XX

Wheatley Continues to Make a Difference

Before Stanley left, he had asked Wheatley to write a paper that might help matters in the Far East. For this he created an imaginary task force consisting of two infantry and one armoured division and chose for its objective the Kra isthmus. Had the British actually had such a force available, by seizing a belt of territory about a hundred miles long, along the narrow neck of the isthmus, they could have cut Japanese communications between Malaya and Burma. But they could only implement the deception by putting out rumours, so it had little effect. It is interesting to note that several months later Mr Amery, who was a Cabinet Minister but not a member of the War Cabinet, put in a paper with exactly the same idea but proposing that it should be carried out as a real operation.

On 21 May a telegram came in from General Wavell. In it he again stressed the splendid work Dudley Clarke had done for him in Egypt, and the amateur but successful contribution now being made by Peter Fleming in the Far East. He reproached the Chiefs of Staff for neglecting to use the invaluable asset of strategic deception in Europe, or to support him in the Far East.

It was obvious that he knew nothing of the efforts by the JPS to help him with their paper 'Deception in the Pacific'. Wheatley also found that Clarke had not heard of 'Hardboiled', which made him feel like the lost section of the War Cabinet.

Wheatley sent the General a long telegram to put the record straight. In it he stated that there should be a meeting each week of the Controlling Officer and his staff with representatives of ISBB, PWE, SOE, MI5, SIS, MEW and the directors of plans, to co-ordinate strategic deception in all theatres. Stanley had already turned it down on the grounds that they must keep their work super-secret and, presumably for this same reason of putting an unjustified degree of security before efficiency, Wheatley's recommendation was not adopted.

On the day General Wavell's telegram came in, the Prime Minister had the bright idea that the JPS should deceive the Japanese into believing that the British were converting Madagascar into a bastion similar to that which Singapore should have proved.

To meet this suggestion Wheatley wrote another long paper in which he pointed out that, although the British had captured the great port of Diego-Suarez (which would give them command of only the northern tip of the huge island), the rest of the 2,500 miles of coastline would belong to the Vichy French and therefore be hostile to the British. Wheatley thought the idea impracticable but nevertheless went along with it.

Since 1 May Wheatley had been compiling a report on 'Hardboiled'. Despite the setbacks and the distressing lack of co-operation he had faced, there was light at the end of the tunnel.

On information from the JIC, Wheatley was able to report that, to meet the deception threat, German forces in Norway had been nearly doubled, bringing them up to a strength of 200,000 men. Also Bergen harbour had been closed to all shipping from 11pm every night (owing to shortage of food on account of the greatly increased occupying force), the Gestapo in Oslo had been greatly increased, and that three German Generals known for their ruthless methods, Daluege, Gelis and Rodeise, had been sent to take over the command of the SS troops and police.

So, all things considered, by tying up an extra 100,000 Germans who might have been sent to Russia and causing the German authorities quite a lot of unnecessary trouble, Wheatley and Lumby had made a significant difference in the formation and implementation of deception plans; and not least, the restructuring of large numbers of Nazi troops.

Towards the end of May, Wheatley received the comments from Brook's German Section on his paper 'Deception on the Highest Plane'.

Colonel Chambers (Brook's senior staff officer) said that while they were in agreement with the basic principles of the plan, it would be difficult to implement because, to start with, rumours of a new anti-Hitler leader could be plausibly put out only inside Germany and means of doing that were very limited. He went on to say that the German section of PWE did not think that a Christ-like mystic was the sort of thing the Germans would fall for, but they had adopted some of the ideas in Wheatley's paper and from 10 April had been putting out such rumours as they could in Germany about a mysterious personality who was a creation of their own. He was to be known as Z, looked a little like Bismarck when he was young, and had already established an underground organisation. Pastor Niemoller was said to be backing him, and Falkenhausen, Willi Messerschmitt and Sacht were in with him. They were buying up corner houses to be used as machine-gun posts that would dominate the main squares of cities when the time came to rise against Hitler, but one could join Z's organisation only if one spoke perfect English.

Obviously, PWE's German section had missed the whole point of

Wheatley's paper. How they thought they could spread pacifism among the German people, or do Hitler any harm, by spreading rumours about a young Iron Chancellor who had no real existence, perplexed Wheatley. As for the idea that no German should be allowed to join a subversive organisation unless he could speak his enemy's language perfectly, seemed even more ridiculous.

On 29 May Wheatley wrote another paper politely pointing these things out, but this got him nowhere. The bastardised plan also got nowhere.

By the end of May 1942 Wheatley had written ten individual papers in-house at the JPS. Obviously, the one upon which the deception bible was based, he was most proud of. But also there was the success – against the odds – of 'Hardboiled' and his own passion and enthusiasm when fighting his corner at meetings with extremely high ranking officers. Obviously, one can say that Wheatley's experiences in uniform during the Great War and his experience – and dare I say – confidence, as a writer stood him in good stead. I say this because, when one reads his early war papers (those he wrote before going into uniform, as published at the beginning of this book), there is an uncertainty in Wheatley's voice. But gain in confidence he did, which led him to the quality work he had achieved in his first six months in the War Cabinet.

On 1 June 1942 Lieutenant-Colonel John H Bevan, MC arrived in Wheatley's office. Shortly afterwards Stanley left the FOPS to become Secretary of State for the Colonies. Consequently, Bevan's section ceased to be part of the FOPS and he was appointed London Controlling Officer of the LCS, a post he held until the end of the war.

With Bevan now in control, things would gather momentum, to such an extent, the Chiefs of Staff concluded that their work had made 'an outstanding contribution to victory'.

But what work did Messrs Bevan and Wheatley embark upon, and how did it influence the outcome of the war?

XXI

War Games in the Basement

Bevan was an interesting fellow to work for. In the three years he worked in the War Cabinet, his hair went grey, he suffered bouts of insomnia (and when very bad insomnia took him, very bad tempers too), but Wheatley greatly liked the man. He found him modest and tremendous company when off duty.

Wheatley was aware that Bevan was under a great deal of strain, which is why he suffered from insomnia and consequently why he was occasionally bad tempered.

Bevan was acutely aware that if a cover plan failed to deceive the enemy, not only would the Commander-in-Chief be deprived of the element of surprise, but many thousands of lives would be lost and a whole campaigning season wasted.

Bevan had been an Infantry man during the Great War and had been on the active Intelligence lists at the beginning of the Second World War up until the evacuation of Norway, where he served.

But why did things become more intense for the JPS after Lumby left the department?

Simply, during his first five months on the staff, Wheatley had made friends with many high ranking officers through his unique position. Many had read his books, or indeed, some had read his twenty-odd war papers before he was put into uniform. Because of this, most accepted Wheatley's offer to lunch or, even to dine with him and his wife Joan in the evenings. This was unusual, because Wheatley was a junior officer and strictly it wasn't the 'done thing', but Wheatley was an exception rather than the rule. And where Lumby was shy to lunch or dine with other officers in the War Cabinet, Bevan wasn't, so together, Wheatley and Bevan forged great friendships and contacts in a short space of time that benefited their joint cause.

However, things didn't start out that way. Bevan read his way into the war, spending the first month reading and attending ISSB meetings, not dissimilar to Wheatley's introduction to the section. Then Bevan rewrote Wheatley's paper on military deception, bringing it into line with the way papers should be written by military officers (as learnt at staff college). This was done; the paper became the deception bible for both the British and the American commands.

Bevan then brought some order to the office filing system (something civil servants still find appallingly difficult to achieve even today). Joan Eden took the lead in this, and once procedure and order had been arranged, Bevan wrote his first paper, giving it the reference JB and DW/SD No. 1. It was titled 'Strategic Deception – Sweden', and outlined how to bring Sweden into the war against Germany, or at least, to give the impression that it was coming into the war against Germany.

Wheatley loved the paper but the Foreign Office – concerned at giving offence to neutrals – dismissed it. Bevan was disheartened but then decided to write some directives for his new office. None had been in place before and none of the Chiefs of Staff knew very much about deception, so passed the directives and suddenly the work really began to pick up. Wheatley was pleased to say the least, because without Bevan he wouldn't have known the military procedures that had to be in force before the work of the section would be taken seriously.

Bevan then took steps to return his section to the basement, to be closer to the STRATS and FOPS. This was a major task because the rooms available were emergency quarters for the hierarchy if there was an invasion. However, Bevan got his way and Wheatley soon found himself in more cramped basement accommodation. Lino became the substitute for pile carpet. Wheatley was appalled and instantly brought in a Persian carpet. Although disappointed that he had to leave the palatial splendour of the third floor, Wheatley realised that it was for the best. Bevan's military mind had relocated them to the hub of activity and it would become much more difficult for other sections of the JPS to ignore their existence in the basement.

This indeed was the hub of activity. One day Mr Churchill suddenly decided to attend a Directors of Plans' conference. On arriving, he looked at the clock, thought himself late and politely apologised. Then, glancing at his watch, he discovered that he had arrived dead on time. Most annoyed, he ordered steps to be taken so that this 'should never occur again'. The war rooms' clocks had been set ten minutes fast so no one would be late for a meeting!

Bevan and Wheatley then set up connections with other departments in the ministries, as the ISSB, although very useful, were sometimes a barrier between them and the other departments they needed advice from. Bevan thought this essential, but knew that if they were to do this, and ostensibly take on the implementation of their own plans, he would need to increase the staff of his section.

America joined the war and a Major Michael Bratby was posted to Bevan's section for a ten-day attachment to learn about deception plans on his way to the Imperial General Staff in Washington.

The ten days soon passed and Major Bratby moved on to the ISSB for a similar period of familiarisation.

At this time STRATS released a paper stating that British forces should sit still until thousands more Americans arrived in Britain and the air strength became superior to that of the Luftwaffe – which could not hope to be achieved until the following summer.

Churchill was appalled by this paper and wrote his own in response. He made it clear that a major offensive had to be implemented some time in 1942; the Nazis would not just sit back and wait for the Allies to get their act together before implementing their own plans.

Bevan seized on the Prime Minister's paper as an excellent opportunity to state his case. His thesis was that, while the risk of actually attempting a landing on the continent outside fighter cover might be considered too great, the JPS could deceive the enemy into believing that British forces did indeed intend to do so. If this succeeded, the enemy would have to withdraw considerable forces from Russia, to form a powerful reserve in central France and to strengthen his garrisons along the now lightly held coasts northward from the Pas de Calais and southward from Cherbourg.

This fascinating paper went to Churchill as 'JB and DW2, Deception – Return to the Continent'.

Wheatley didn't totally agree with Bevan's paper and decided to write his own ('The Art of War'), using the Americans as back-up. Wheatley concluded that in 1942 the British could not – without great risk – launch an offensive against an enemy-held territory; but with the Americans behind them, could be strong enough to take no more nonsense from the neutrals.

Spain was allowing Hitler to use her ports to shelter U-boats and helping the enemy in other ways, but was reported to be in a desperate way for food and raw materials; so, as an example, Wheatley suggested that General Franco be offered a choice. Either he should throw the Germans out, accept the Allies' protection and allow them to establish bases in Spain, in which case the United States would feed its people and send him the essentials to keep his industries going or, when it suited the British, invade Spain and take the country over.

Franco might possibly have agreed, but if not, Wheatley's plan was that the British should go into northern Spain, both from the Atlantic and the Mediterranean simultaneously, to seize swiftly the great barrier of the Pyrenees before the Germans had time to bring south sufficient forces to launch a counter-stroke.

The occupation of Spain would have been invaluable to the Allies. By dominating the Mediterranean coast they could have much more easily reinforced Malta and, in due course, have mounted an operation against French North Africa, or the south of France, or have seized Sardinia as a stepping stone to Italy.

However, if Franco didn't want to play ball, he would have to ask Hitler for help, which would result in up to twenty divisions being pulled from Russia to protect Spain.

Having written his paper, Wheatley didn't really know who to send it to first. He knew it was useless to go through the channels of STRATS and FOPS; he needed to get the paper to the Prime Minister himself.

As usual, when in doubt, Wheatley would approach an old friend, in this case Maxwell Knight of MI5, and of course, he solved Wheatley's dilemma. The Prime Minister's personal assistant was Major Sir Desmond Morton, and Maxwell Knight and Morton were old friends. Knight, having read Wheatley's paper, gave him an introduction to Sir Desmond. As a result, towards the end of July, Wheatley was suddenly invited 'upstairs' to Churchill's quarters. It was only then that he became concerned. As a civilian, Wheatley was perfectly entitled to express his views about the conduct of the war to anyone who would listen. But as a very junior staff officer all he was entitled to do was put his ideas informally up to the STRATS, whose function was not only to make plans for such operations as their masters were contemplating, but to write papers on others they considered feasible and put them forward with the opening sentence 'In anticipation of the wishes of the Chiefs of Staff...' They could, therefore, had they liked Wheatley's suggestion, have written an official paper on it which would have gone to the Directors of Plans, then the Chief of Staff and, if not thrown out by either, been submitted to the Foreign Office. However, Wheatley had the audacity to by-pass the lot.

Fortunately for Wheatley, Sir Desmond had arranged to take him to one side and explain why his plan wouldn't work. After an hour, with Wheatley feeling that he had been justifiably 'shot down in flames', a friendship had sprung up. The following week the two men lunched together. Indeed, they would do so several times, eventually Sir Desmond dining with the Wheatleys at Chartsworth Court.

Now Wheatley had the advantage of being friends with the man closest to the Prime Minister.

XXII

Churchill's Storyteller

In the second part of his autobiography (*Officer and Temporary Gentleman*), Wheatley wrote of Churchill:

> Winston Churchill's portrait, on the other hand, always affected me entirely … the magnificent broad forehead, the calm intelligent eyes, bespoke a first-class brain, competent to deal with great issues in a great way. It is not hindsight that causes me to write of him with admiration. In a non-fiction book of mine published in 1936 – when he was still in the wilderness – I described his brilliant conceptions of seizing Antwerp and the Dardanelles; and in the Second World War he unquestionably proved himself to be a better strategist than any of our generals.

Even before the Second World War, Wheatley held Churchill in high regard, and in juxtaposition to his pride of being a member of the JPS, it is not surprising that Wheatley approached his work with such sincerity and temerity. He had pushed the boundaries of military formality with his unorthodox approach to the Prime Minister's inner sanctum, but make it he did, forming a great friendship into the bargain.

Maybe it was no surprise that late one afternoon in July, Bevan was sent for by the Chiefs of Staff. He returned with tremendous news. A firm decision had been made to mount an expedition against French North Africa that autumn.

The chiefs had instructed Bevan that he was at once to set about the preparation of a cover plan, and that in no circumstances whatever was he to mention the work on which he was engaged to anyone else. Not even the ISSB or the other members of the JPS were to be told. The latter had, of course, written the plan for the operation, but they had also written numerous others for possible use and it was not until nearly a week later that they were informed that 'Torch' had been adopted.

During those few days, Bevan and Wheatley worked with intense concentration and far into the night, for they were very conscious of the great responsibility they had been given, the lack of prestige that their section had so far laboured under, and the handicap of being amateurs with only rudimentary knowledge of campaigns conducted at the highest level.

It was little more than two months since Bevan had taken over. Now he was faced not only with the task of preparing a detailed deception plan to cover Britain's greatest amphibious operation, but also with the immense labour of thinking out scores of minor pieces of information which, suitably conveyed to the enemy, would give him the false picture they wished him to accept.

By his own directive, Bevan had freed himself from the ISSB, who had previously been responsible for implementing all cover plans. This meant that he and Wheatley should have to undertake the innumerable tasks connected with implanting the plan themselves. In consequence, when Bevan sent up their proposals for deception, he also submitted his request for an increase in their section. The result could not have been more helpful. Early in August, the Chiefs took the proposed cover plan for 'Torch' and gave their approval to the general concept. They also agreed that arrangements should be made as a matter of urgency to provide Colonel Bevan with the necessary staff.

I am not convinced that Bevan achieved all this himself. I believe that Wheatley's friendship with Sir Desmond played a large part in the radical change. However, it would be typical of Wheatley to modestly hide his influence over his new friend during the odd lunch or dinner. Perhaps another reason for Wheatley's secrecy in this matter would be the unconvential way he by-passed Bevan – and everybody else – to make a connection with the Prime Minister in the first place. Wheatley had initial concerns about this, but he had set the wheels in motion by then and came out of it productively, albeit by the skin of his teeth. He had no intention of bragging about it, but he must have impressed the PM.

Wheatley had great regard for Bevan's military procedure and this won them much respect, as well as the opening of official avenues that had to be respected by higher ranking military personnel. It is true to say that Bevan and Wheatley were in one way chalk and cheese – although good friends – but the difference in personalities assisted their greater plan: to be recognised and taken seriously. Bevan was conventional (although he hadn't done anything in deception before joining the LCS), whilst Wheatley had time to understand what the War Cabinet wanted but would always adopt his own maverick way of implementing his opinions, mainly because he was not familiar with the correct procedure. The two officers would continue to assist each other in pulling off their finest work during the Second World War. The beginning of that was 'Torch'.

XXIII

'Torch'

German air reconnaissance had identified that many men and ships were being gathered into one area, so consequently it was known that a large operation was brewing. A deception had to be crafted to steer the enemy away from the real target, North Africa. Bevan and Wheatley began to draft a deception designed to accomplish this.

The intention of their paper was to convince the enemy that the operation was to target Norway, instead of North Africa.

All very simple? Well, not quite.

It was assumed that the enemy knew there was a large concentration of troops in south-east England and that the majority of that force was the Canadian Division,

The Clyde would have been the base chosen if a real landing was organised against Norway, so Wheatley and Bevan ensured that that became part of the deception plan. However, simultaneously, with the dispatch of the expedition to Norway, they had to attempt to keep the concentration of troops reinforcing Norway to a minimum, so they used the Canadian Division and other troops in the south for a cross-channel operation against the Pas de Calais, in order to force the Germans to keep a maximum number of troops in that area.

The Norway deception plan was given the name 'Solo One', while the deception plan against the Pas de Calais was called 'Passover'. These were chosen in the hope that a German Intelligence Officer might associate the anagram Solo with Oslo, and Passover with the crossing of the channel.

In order for the deceptions to work, there had to be many smaller plans crafted. Wheatley drew up a large chart to ensure that every aspect of the deception plans was covered.

This was a time of great change for Wheatley, not just because his work was now being turned into action, but his section yet again had come under reorganization. Air Commodore Bill Elliot had taken over from Dickie Dickson as Director of Plans (Air). Bevan's application for more staff (which included a GSO2 Air) had been passed and Wheatley was automatically promoted to Squadron Leader. Also, Major Harold Peterval joined the team. Early in September, Major Ronald Wingate too joined the fray. Lumby soon moved on and Wheatley found himself the oldest member of the section.

Wingate was a quick learner. He knew no more about the organisation of the modern army than Wheatley knew about the Royal Air Force, but all his life he had dealt with government hierarchies and his knowledge of politics was considerable. As far as his appreciation of protocol was concerned, he was a master. By using the right approach, he was often able to achieve results which would have been beyond the scope of anyone lacking his life-long contact with the gentry.

The basic deception plan Wheatley and Bevan had drawn up was never departed from in principle, but it did develop quite significantly. For example, 'Solo' became two separate plans. The first concerned the shipping concentration in the Clyde, the second the 52nd Highland Division's notional invasion of Norway. There were also 'Passover', 'Cavendish', 'Overthrow' and 'Kennicott', and to merge these plans successfully was difficult to say the least. Operation 'Torch' became the joint title of the deception plan.

But what were the intricacies of the operation? Why so much detail and additional planning?

It was anticipated that when Operation 'Torch' convoys sailed, they would be sighted by enemy U-boats or long-range aircraft, heading west instead of north. The enemy would smell a rat, so the cover destination had to be changed to the Azores. On arriving outside the Straits of Gibraltar, this cover would also be blown and the enemy was to be told that the convoys were on their way to invade Sardinia. This final cover destination was later changed to the east coast of Sicily, then Greece.

Meanwhile, the United States forces, which were actually to land at Casablanca, were told that they were being sent via the Cape as reinforcements for the Middle East and, to account for the fact that the ships were assault loaded, that they were to undertake operations against the Azores on the way.

If the 'Torch' forces really had been going to the Middle East, they would have been issued with tropical kit, but for North Africa in winter tropical kit was not required. And for the Middle East, all tanks and vehicles would have been painted with desert camouflage, whereas in North Africa the terrain was greenish-brown. There were indeed rings within rings and much had to be considered to make the operation plans plausible to the British soldier let alone the enemy!

What was also found – to everybody's amazement – was that after three years of war not a single division in the south of England was ready to take part in operation 'Torch'; not without borrowing men, equipment and supplies from other divisions. This would create its own problems, as the men – divisions – left behind would know that they would not see action for some time and morale would drop. Also, there was still a lot of resistance to deception plans amongst the high ranking officers controlling such divisions; they didn't want to waste time and material in training troops to carry out operations that were never going to happen. However, when 'most secret' intelligence was sent to Lord Gort and General Mason MacFarlane (the Governors of Gibraltar and Malta respectively) concerning naval problems to do with the 'Torch' deception plan, it was decided that a member of the Royal Navy should join the team to add assistance in naval matters. By the end of September Commander James Arbuthnott had joined the team, which upset Bevan slightly as he was an Army man through and through. But Bevan was conscious of morale and team spirit. He made it clear to each member of his team on joining that since they were all of a particular age and held responsible jobs in civilian life, he did not favour a strict military regime. He was keen that they worked together as a group of friends, not least because of the long hours and stress associated with their jobs.

The coming of James Arbuthnott filled the fifth desk in the cell-like office. Bevan sat at the centre below the clock; Wingate and Arbuthnott sat on his right and, facing them (on Bevan's left), Wheatley and Peteval. This crowded room was so lacking in comfort that Bevan and Wheatley named it 'the schoolroom'.

Their lives had changed dramatically since joining the basement. With staff, a constantly ringing telephone and many visitors, there was no spare time. With Operation 'Torch' live and Gibraltar being crammed to bursting with every type of store and ammunition, let alone fighters and fuel, Wheatley was faced with crafting another reason for the build-up of forces there. He started to write a new paper along the following lines: A second attempt to land at Dakar was ruled out because it would have alerted the French throughout the whole of North Africa. Sardinia was undesirable because it, or possibly Sicily (which was settled on later), was to be the cover objective for the final phase, and pointing to either prematurely might result in the Axis strengthening their forces there and thus render Allied landings in Algeria most hazardous. A breakthrough in the Mediterranean to reinforce the Middle East was not plausible, because that could only have been done without casualties by following the then normal practice of sending troop convoys round the Cape.

But the threat of a landing in Southern France, then only occupied by Vichy forces, could suit (LCS/Wheatley's) purposes for the following reasons. If Vichy reinforced her south coast with units from North Africa, this would be ideal. If the threat resulted in the Axis taking over Vichy France and sending German forces south, these were unlikely to be drawn from the Channel coast, owing to 'Passover', so they would have to withdraw troops from Russia for this purpose; which again would be ideal. And a stronger garrison in the South of France would not be near enough to North Africa to prejudice Allied landings there.

Bevan accepted Wheatley's arguments and put them in proper shape for submission to the Chiefs of Staff, who approved them. The team then began passing new information through their secret channels to the Germans to build up Wheatley's deception.

Next, the team wrote a long paper on 'Information to the Press'. It would not have been prudent to put an embargo on British newspapers and periodicals being sent to neutral countries; so British dailies were flown out regularly to Lisbon, where copies were bought by the German Embassy and sent on to Berlin. Their contents, including the advertisements, were minutely scrutinised by German Intelligence. Obviously the deception plans would be greatly assisted if the JPS could bring about the appearance in the press of articles slanted in the direction required.

The top men in Fleet Street were, within certain limits, trusted, but not with particulars of forthcoming operations and never anything to do with the deception. However, the LCS could put ideas into their minds through the Directors of Public Relations in the service ministries, whose rank was on Brigadier level.

For this purpose, Bevan's team produced several lines of thought which would support a belief that the Allied forces meant to invade Norway, others which would support a belief that, simultaneously, there was to be an attack on the Pas de Calais, and a greater number which indicated various reasons why it would be ill-advised to attempt to go into North Africa. From then on, hints were dropped by the DPRs to the military correspondents, which led them in their speculative articles on future strategy to give the enemy the picture the JPS desired.

It was during those weeks that Bevan's team came into direct contact with the Americans. General Eisenhower, until quite recently only a Divisional Commander, had arrived in England as President Roosevelt's nominee to be Commander-in-Chief 'Torch'. He had been given Norfolk House as his headquarters and a combined staff of American and British officers to carry out the detailed planning.

The main LCS contact with him was through Brigadier Mockler-Ferryman. He was a great friend of Charles Balfour Davey's, who by then had been made Commandant of our Staff College. Wheatley had met Charles before the war. He was known to his friends as 'the Moke', but, far from there being anything mulish about him, he was a most receptive, highly intelligent and very charming man.

'The Moke' had several American officers under him and he charged a Lieutenant-Colonel Goldbranson with keeping in touch with the LCS and doing everything possible to assist with their deception plans. In civilian life a shrewd Mid West railway executive, he was surprisingly both competent and cordial. He actually sailed to North Africa with 'the Moke' and for some months was in charge of the first Deception Section in Algiers.

Most people, if responsible for implementing 'Torch' cover plans, would have felt that they had quite enough on their plate, but not Bevan. He was also concerning himself with many other problems, the chief of which were how to get Washington fully into the game, the new measures which would be necessary to co-ordinate deception between Dudley Clarke and Goldbranson once the 'Torch' forces were established in North Africa, and the spheres of influence over which the various commands and the LCS should exercise direct control, for nothing had ever been laid down about that, which had caused conflict.

Early in October, Bevan decided that the best way to straighten things out was to call a conference in London. To it he invited Dudley Clarke, Peter Fleming and Lieutenant-Colonel Peter Cooke, the Washington representative of the DMI, under whom Michael Bratby (Bevan's liaison officer) was working.

The preparations for the conference were immense. For days, the LCS sweated blood getting out a vast agenda, writing long papers on the innumerable ways they might hope to deceive the enemy, upon grades of operators and spheres of influence, and arranging accommodation for visitors.

One by one, having flown thousands of miles from their respective continents, the mystery men came in. For the conference the LCS had secured the loan of the room in which the Chiefs of Staff held their meetings on nights when there was a blitz – the second largest in the basement, the biggest being that in which the War Cabinet held theirs. When the great morning came, everything and everyone was ready for the meeting round the large mahogany table at ten o'clock – everyone that is, except Wheatley.

The reason for this was a mystery to Wheatley who, normally quite punctual, overslept. He woke at 11:05hrs. His wife was away at the time, but he hadn't indulged in any late night binges while she was away, he simply overslept.

Horrified, he quickly shaved, got dressed and took a taxi to the Cabinet Offices. When he walked into the Conference room – at 11:45hrs – he decided to tell the truth about his tardiness. Standing to attention, he said to Bevan: 'I'm terribly sorry, sir. I overslept.'

Bevan stared at Wheatley for a moment, then burst out laughing. The others followed suit and an absolute roar went up. However, Wheatley saved face over the next three days by taking an active part in all debates, reaching agreements on all topics essential to the meetings. Bevan and Wheatley had heard so much about Dudley Clarke that they were most intrigued to see the 'great deceiver' in the flesh. He proved to be a small neat, fair-haired man, with merry blue eyes and a quiet chuckle, which used to make his shoulders shake slightly. He was a Gunner but had served very little of his time with the Royal Regiment, having been selected again and again for unorthodox assignments.

He had been among the first officers to land in Norway, carrying £10,000 in notes, which had been thrust upon him at the last moment. He had surveyed the route from Mombasa to Cairo as a possible means of reinforcing forces in the Middle East. He had originated the Commandos and, after Dunkirk, been the first officer to land again with a raiding party on the coast of France. It was whispered that in Spain he had slipped up and been arrested while disguised as a woman. In fact, he was a truly legendary figure. He got a great deal of fun out of intrigue of every kind. He even had the crowns on his shoulders, red Staff gorgets and medal ribbons fitted with press studs so that, by removing them, he could appear at will to be an inconspicuous subaltern; although the pilot's wings of the Royal Flying Corps on his tunic gave it away that he had served in the Great War.

Wheatley was obviously won over by this officer, having served in the Great War himself, but he also found him extremely perceptive in all areas of deception. Clarke and Wheatley soon became the best of friends, a friendship which lasted long after the Second World War. Indeed, in 1965, Clarke gave Wheatley a china figure of Marshal Marmount to add to his collection of Napoleonic soldiers.

During the week that followed the conference, the 'schoolroom' was a hive of activity. The LCS visitors had numerous contacts to make while in London, and Wheatley's little office was the only base they had in which to make their arrangements and where telephone messages would be certain to reach them. Despite the confusion, Bevan managed to get the 'Torch' cover plans completed.

The conference had been held in mid-October. The first 'Torch' convoys were due to sail and troops were now moving to concentration areas preparatory to embarkation. The mass of shipping in the Clyde was constantly increasing. With growing anxiety they listened every morning to the Home Security reports furnished by ISSB on enemy air reconnaissance over the UK. So far, Bevan's team had been lucky. For weeks past no German 'recce' aircraft had flown over the Clyde. But they felt their luck was too good to last. One glimpse of the tremendous activities now taking place up there and the Luftwaffe might be sent in force to create havoc among the closely packed shipping. But the enemy somehow remained blissfully ignorant.

At last the armada sailed. It was routed far out into the ocean but, even so, there was the risk that it might be sighted by a long-range Focke-Wulf and that the large packs of U-boats then scouring the Atlantic might be concentrated against it. Every morning at 09:00hrs, Bevan went to the Admiralty War Room, took note of the latest U-boat dispositions, brought them across to the LCS, then plotted them on a chart which they had installed for that purpose.

At the time the U-boats were mostly in the neighbourhood of the Canaries. As the convoys passed out of the range of the enemy reconnaissance aircraft, they came ever closer to the main hunting ground of the U-boats. It needed only one of these to sight the 'Torch' armada and, whatever the risk, she would break wireless silence to call up the whole U-boat fleet and send the news to Berlin. However, that never happened and the convoys arrived off the Straits of Gibraltar, still unreported.

For some reason, the Admiralty had insisted that, before entering the Mediterranean, the convoys must have a whole two days in which to regroup for the assault and pass the Straits. They did this successfully at night.

In that vast array of ships were a large number of the regular officers, non-commissioned officers and men who had been brought off from Dunkirk. There were also the newest tanks, guns and other weapons that for two years British factory personnel had been working day and night to produce. The attitude of the French in North Africa was unpredictable. The best elements of their regular Army were stationed there, and it was certain that Vichy would order them to resist British landings. If the assault failed, it could prove disastrous. British forces, driven back to the beaches, would be 2,000 miles from home; there could be no rescue operation like Dunkirk.

As the operation had been mounted in the UK, planning the cover for it had been the sole responsibility of the LCS, but, from the beginning, as far as the Mediterranean theatre was concerned, Dudley Clarke had given them the maximum possible assistance. Now that the convoys were actually moving into his territory he put over to the enemy certain last minute information which had been agreed between him and Bevan.

On the morning after the convoys passed the Straits, an immediate alert was ordered by the enemy in all Axis-held territories in the Mediterranean as far east as Crete.

This was a pivotal moment; would the enemy suddenly guess the convoy's intentions against North Africa? Had the LCS really succeeded in lulling suspicions of Vichy? Could the Germans possibly believe the last stories the LCS had put over, first that it was their intention strongly to reinforce Malta, and later that they meant to invade the South of France? Would they fall for the last-minute bogus information that the landings were to be on the heel of Italy or in Greece?

In short, the 'Torch' cover plans were a resounding success, as a captured German U-boat commander confirmed a few days later: all U-boats in that area had been ordered to concentrate hundreds of miles east of the LCS objectives.

Although the LCS had a long way to go, no one could underestimate the need for carefully planned strategic deception; Bevan, Wheatley and their team could be justly proud of themselves.

On the afternoon of 8 November, the following memo arrived, It was from the Prime Minister:

'General Ismay: for circulation to Chiefs of Staff and JPS.
The news of our first successes in North Africa is most heartening but it is over a week since I have heard anything of our plans for going into Norway. Pray let me hear more of this as a matter of urgency.
W.S.C'

This was of course a joke, because there was not one single battle-trained Division left in the UK, much less a landing craft, and there would not be for many months to come, as the Prime Minister knew only too well.

The Americans soon landed at Casablanca, led by General Patton. It was the first time they had been engaged in active warfare. They were success-ful. Air Commodore Elliot had the dubious pleasure of dealing with the flamboyant American General. One evening, a few weeks before D Day, Wheatley had a drink with Elliot just after the Air Commodore had had a conference with Patton. He told Wheatley that he had asked him for the umpteenth time how he proposed to ensure the supply of fuel to British aircraft, which was an American responsibility. To Elliot's frustration and distress, Patton laughed, clapped him on the back and said 'Don't you worry, Air Commodore. Don't you worry. Your boys shall have all the juice they need, even if I have to carry every can in on my own back.' Unfortunately, Patton had no plan to back up his bravado.

XXIV

Onwards to Casablanca

The original 'Torch' plan drawn up by the JPS envisaged three landing sites in North Africa: Oran, Algiers and Philippeville in Tunisia. But the Americans insisted that, instead of Philippeville, the third landing should be made at Casablanca, because if operations didn't lead to the conquest of North Africa, forces would have a line of retreat in Casablanca.

On New Year's Eve 1943 Wheatley and his wife gave a party at Chatsworth Court, which included a dozen generals. Bevan didn't attend (because he was on leave), but Ronald Wingate (who was temporarily made Wheatley's chief) did.

Before leaving (around 3am), Wingate took Wheatley to one side and told him that the President of the United States was soon arriving in Britain to talk to the Prime Minister. The meeting was super-secret and Wheatley should take the following day off in order to craft a cover plan to prevent anyone from getting wind of the fact or, that the PM, and the Chiefs of Staff had left Britain for the Casablanca Conference.

Wheatley did as he was asked, constructing his plan for 'Symbol' (the codename given to the Casablanca Conference) the following day and handing it to Wingate soon afterwards. Wingate was pleased with the plan, but still re-wrote it. Wheatley was content with this as he said in *The Deception Planners*: ' ... he rewrote it himself, retaining parts of it but altering and improving it immensely.'

The Casablanca Conference was the biggest think-tank of the Second World War. Not only were the President and Prime Minister there, but also Chiefs of Staff from America and Britain, Directors of Plans and many other high ranking officers from both the United States and the UK. It was imperative that the enemy did not find out about the conference. However, that would prove difficult considering it was to last ten days.

So it was decided that halfway through the conference it should be leaked that a conference was being held but, misleading information was to be circulated.

Wheatley chose Madeira (a half-way house between America and Britain). This was deemed to be impractical, so it was settled that Khartoum should be the location for the cover plan.

It was very difficult to conceal the fact that the Prime Minister and his top men had left the country, because so many people had access to their daily minutes. Wheatley suggested to Bevan (who was now back from leave) that the minutes should be forged.

All these perceptive plans nearly turned Wheatley and his team into a pumpkin because of a small act of indiscretion from the Casablanca party themselves.

When it was suggested to the fleet of dignitaries bound for Casablanca that they stop in a village pub for a drink (near the airfield), everybody quickly agreed. The entire convoy stopped. Brooke, Portal, Mountbatten and many others, smothered with gold braid and their chests full of medals, crowded into the bar. The amazed publican quickly produced his very limited stock of hard liquor, and the place was soon drunk dry. However, MI5 soon found out about this 'innocent' little stop and placed the landlord, his family and staff under house arrest. They also put his pub out-of-bounds to the public for a month and set a guard on it to prevent any of its occupants telling others about the night when a gilded throng made merry on the premises.

The 'Symbol' conference was not to be held actually in Casablanca, but at Anfa, some miles up in the hills. The village consisted of a large hotel and a number of villas. As the airfield was a considerable distance from Anfa, to reach it the distinguished visitors would have to be driven through several Arab hamlets. Codrington, the head of Cabinet Office Security, had been sent on ahead to make suitable arrangements for the reception of the Prime Minister.

From the aircraft, Churchill was taken straight to a small van, shut inside and driven to his destination. So none of the locals caught even a glimpse of him. The British concern for secrecy and strategy was always paramount. However, when the President of the United States arrived, he received a guard of honour and a cavalcade of cars, and accompanying cyclists with sub-machine guns.

Despite this indiscretion by the Americans, security was uppermost in their minds. They enclosed the whole conference area at Anfa in a great barbed wire fence and stationed half a dozen batteries of field artillery all round it; the Americans were not but big and bold.

I do not intend to present a blow-by-blow account of the conference (this is well documented in many books and has no real relevance here). Suffice to say, its main objective was to decide on Allied strategy for 1943. From the beginning, the Americans had convinced themselves that the quickest way to end the war was to launch an invasion from Britain against the Continent. A plan for this possibility had been drawn up and given the name 'Roundup'. To implement it, for many months past the Americans had been carrying out operation 'Bolero' – the dispatch of large US forces to Britain. In the summer of 1942 Churchill had persuaded them that the German resistance would be too strong for 'Roundup' to have any chance of success for some time to come, and to undertake the occupation of North Africa instead. Then, in the autumn of 1942, the Americans urged that after 'Torch' the next step should be 'Roundup' in the early summer of 1943.

Churchill's conception of 'Roundup' was not a mighty invasion such as eventually took place on the Normandy coast in 1944; but, as the code-word implies, a landing to 'round up' any German units that might still be resisting after the defeat of the German army by other means.

Talks went on, with the outcome that Sicily should be the next Allied objective.

Churchill never wavered in his opinion that the speediest road to victory lay in striking at what he termed 'the soft underbelly of the Axis'. The Italian troops did not have anything like the fighting spirit of the Germans. It was deemed necessary to put Italy out of the war and start a second line of offence against the Germans and so take pressure off the Russians.

Churchill's thoughts caused the Americans to reassess their outlined plans and concede that, after the proposed capture of Sicily (to be known as operation 'Husky'), the project of extending the campaign to the Italian mainland should be given serious consideration. (Churchill had originally taken Wheatley's idea of overcoming Sardinia, but Alan Brooke suggested and stood by the capture of Sicily and CIGS got his way in the end.)

On 10 July General Montgomery launched his successful invasion of Sicily, but because of rough terrain, the first landings in Italy did not take place until early September. Bloody battles ensued, Cassino and Anzio to name but two. It took Alexander nine months to work his way up the leg of Italy and take Rome – the day before the Normandy landings.

XXV

Operation 'Husky' and
The Man Who Never Was

'We were a team. A good team and, by and large, a happy one.'
The Deception Planners

After Casablanca, the workload of the LCS got more intense. They again moved accommodation and took on more staff (see Future Operations Planning Staff and its successor at the start of Part Three for details). Wheatley, as a consequence, suddenly found that he had more time on his hands; at last they had enough people to coherently split up the work load and concentrate on specific issues.

The cover plan for Sicily was Dudley Clarke's responsibility, but the LCS was a tight ship and they pooled their knowledge and thoughts together to form a paper, which was sent up to the Chiefs of Staff.

Its main objective was to conceal from the British forces their true destination (in order to minimise the chance of careless talk being overheard by enemy agents).

This was not easy as three forces were to be dispatched: an Eastern group from Egypt, a central group from Malta and Tunisia, and a western group from Algiers and Britain. All were to sail assault-loaded, so the troops they were carrying would know that they were not just being sent somewhere as reinforcements but were to take part in a landing on enemy-held territory.

It was decided that the Eastern group should be told that they were to seize some of the islands in the Dodecanese; the central group's instruction was to take the little island of Pantellaria, which lies near Malta and was still in the hands of the Italians; and the group from Britain and Algeria were both told that they were part of larger forces which were to attack a French port in the Bay of Biscay and the South of France respectively.

With regard to the force from Britain, the LCS recommended certain measures which could have been taken, such as: brief Force Commanders and secure their co-operation; have models made of the Biscay coast to be put in rooms where a certain number of people would have access to them;

issue English-French phrase books and, to Force paymasters, suitable currency for an occupation; attach French interpreters, carry out mine-sweeping off the Biscay coast, bomb communications with the ports there and indicate an increase in sabotage by dropping dummy parachutists.

But the LCS were debarred by the Chiefs of Staff, who instructed Bevan that he was not to request the service ministries or the Combined Commanders to take any steps in the UK until a Supreme Commander had been appointed, and that all implementation would then be his responsibility. This took two months (Lieutenant-General 'Freddy' Morgan was appointed Chief of Staff to the Supreme Allied Commander) during which 'Husky' was effectively on ice.

The LCS was not totally idle during this time as they put out rumours regarding 'future intentions'. This was done via careless talk. The main ideas they wanted to put in the enemy's mind were the possibility of an invasion of Southern France and an invasion of the continent by way of Holland or Norway.

Among the measures the LCS took during the spring of 1943 for a 'return to the continent' was the printing of a special banknote. This carried an inscription in bold letters 'British Army of Occupation of France'. Wheatley, Bevan and their team carried a few notes each in their wallets and, every time they took a taxi, paid a restaurant bill or bought something in a shop they used one, but snatched it back as soon as their quarry had had a good look at it.

It was apparent – from the early part of the spring – that if 'Husky' was successful, the Prime Minister would succeed in persuading the Americans that they should not be strong enough to launch a cross-channel operation during 1943; so that instead of Allied forces being withdrawn from the Mediterranean, Sicily should be used as a base for going into Italy. But it was hoped that, instead of having to fight up the leg of Italy, her collapse might be brought about by other means. Wheatley was tasked by Vintras to write a long paper reviewing the many ways in which Italy could benefit, both during and after the war, by renouncing her alliance with Germany, and if she was prepared to treat with the British, suggesting means by which proposals for an armistice could be conveyed secretly to the Italian General Staff.

In this paper Wheatley made it clear that unconditional surrender would not be required of Italy. To demand it was the only publicised decision taken at Casablanca; and that had been foolish, it made the way ahead much more difficult. (Wheatley believed that German Generals might have shown more courage and determination in their attempt to rid themselves of Hitler if an armistice had been offered.)

By mid-May, a future strategy had become certain. Sicily conquered, forces were going into Italy. Now the LCS was asked to propose deception measures that might assist in bringing about the Italian surrender.

The LCS, although a larger organisation now, was still working at full stretch; but morale was high and Operation 'Husky' had to be implemented.

On 10 July the landings in Sicily were duly carried out, and a few days later the Chiefs of Staff discussed the operation. Dudley Clarke's cover plan had proved successful, as the element of surprise had been achieved. But the losses were high – from all corners of the Allied forces present.

Apart from supporting Dudley Clarke's cover plan for 'Husky' (by feeding misleading information to the enemy through their own channels), the LCS did make a contribution to its success that later became known throughout the world.

This was 'Mincemeat'. The idea originated with Flight Lieutenant Chumley of MI5. The idea was that the dead body of an officer should be taken in a submarine to the coast of Spain and there floated off at a time when the tide would wash it ashore. In the pocket of his tunic there would be a letter from one of the chiefs to General Alexander, in which indications would be given that the objective of 'Husky' was Dudley's false one. It was hoped that the Spaniards would assume the body was from an aircraft which had been shot down and, as most Spanish authorities were then pro-German, that they would pass on the letter to the German Mission in Madrid.

As deception was the special tool of the LCS, Chumley's idea had to be passed through Bevan and, although the whole team sat on it, the job was handled by MI6. To procure the body of a man who had not obviously died of some disease or as a result of being mashed up in an accident, and who had no close relatives who wished to attend a funeral, was no easy task, but somehow they got hold of a suitable corpse, which had been a Captain in the Royal Marines. He had died of a heart attack, and there was a concern that the Spanish might realise that he had not drowned and smell a rat. But that had to be risked.

The letter he carried was from the VCIGS, Lieutenant-General Nye, to General Alexander. Although on Cabinet Office paper, it appeared to be only a private letter sent from one friend to another, the passage that mattered being just a casual reference to coming events of which two Generals had common knowledge, inserted between passages of gossip about mutual acquaintances.

The body was primed and taken to a northern port, where it was delivered to the Commander of a submarine.

In due course, the Spanish notified the nearest British Consul that the body of a British officer had been washed up, and handed to him all the papers that had been found on it. The Consul saw to the proper burial of the dead man and sent the papers to London. The LCS was disappointed to learn that the important letter had not been opened. But MI6 sent it to their laboratory for special examination, and it transpired that it had been skilfully opened, then re-sealed. Also, as it was discovered sometime afterwards, the letter had been photographed and a copy sent to Berlin.

So the deception had worked, and Chumley succeeded in getting an OBE for his marvellous idea. However, it was Duff Cooper, minister for security, who wrote a book entitled *Operation Heartbreak* (1950), which although well written (according to Wheatley in *The Deception Planners*), was a huge security breach. However, Cooper was not reprimanded for this and the book became a bestseller. Lieutenant-Commander Ewen Montagu (whom Chumley had originally put his paper up to as he was a naval officer) wrote his own version of the story entitled *The Man Who Never Was*. Montagu had won an OBE for his part in the operation and a successful film was made of the book too (modesty must have prevailed on Chumley's part!).

On 3 September the British Eighth Army crossed the Straits of Messina, and at 18:00hrs on 8 September a cease-fire was announced. Four days after the Armistice, a force of ninety parachutists, led by Otto Skorzeny, landed on a plateau high up in the Abruzzi where Mussolini was being held prisoner, rescued him and flew him to Germany. Despite all the wonderful operations the British or Americans took part in during the Second World War, the liberation of Mussolini by the Germans was a breathtaking spectacle – they weren't beaten yet.

XXVI

Bodyguard

'I was undoubtedly highly incompetent in the matter of staff duties. I took long lunches from which, at times, I returned slightly tight. I spent hours coffee-housing with my friends in the mess and the Air Ministry. I was lazy and indifferent about all minor problems to do with deception. But at least I saved dear, brilliantly capable but over-conscientious Johnny [Bevan] ... '
The Deception Planners – My Secret War

It was in early November that Churchill and the Chiefs of Staff proposed to meet with the Russians at the Teheran conference. Wheatley was aware that an Anglo-American force should attempt to liberate Europe in the spring/summer of 1944 and he had spent much time writing a paper on the subject. Wheatley was very conscious that this campaign should be faultless and nothing left undone which might draw enemy forces away from the area of invasion. He headed his paper *Essorbee* – 'shit or bust'.

The Foreign Office didn't sign up to all the proposals, but some did go through, especially in Sweden

When high level conferences were being held abroad, Wheatley and his team received daily reports of the details. Wheatley found that 'Overlord' was to be launched during the first week of May (it was later postponed to the first week in June). Churchill said: 'Our intentions must be surrounded by a bodyguard of lies.' Bevan gave the cover plan the name 'Bodyguard'.

With the date and time of the invasion agreed, planning could begin. Wheatley claimed that the latter part of November and more than half of December proved to be the most interesting weeks during his three years in the Cabinet Offices. He worked extremely hard, submitting paper after paper, only to have them returned for revisions or proofing. 'You can not assume *that*, because we do not know it for a *fact*,' Bevan would say.

The paper grew to twenty pages in length, and more than the odd sleepless night affected the team. They knew that the cover plan was doomed to failure.

Although Wheatley tried to leave at six o'clock every evening, he knew that Bevan would have his dinner and return about ten o'clock. One night, at approximately nine o'clock, Wheatley went back to his office, turned the light on and put the door ajar. He sat at his desk and for the best part of an hour read a novel. Some time close to ten he heard footsteps approaching. Quickly he put the book in a drawer and made out he was working. Bevan stuck his head round the door and said: 'Dennis, what on earth are you doing here at this hour of the night?'

'Trying to rewrite this bloody Bodyguard paper.'

'But why?' Bevan asked.

Throwing down his pencil, Wheatley sat back and said: 'Because if it goes in as it is, you are going to get the sack.'

Bevan frowned, but sat down in the armchair opposite Wheatley. He lit a cigarette and said in his calm, quiet voice: 'I don't understand. Tell me what you mean.'

Wheatley told him that the paper was too long and too pessimistic. The Chiefs of Staff had a lot of confidence in Bevan and his team and didn't expect a paper that failed to deliver a good cover plan. Wheatley proposed to cut out the arguments and pitfalls of 'Overlord' and put them in an annexe at the back of a shorter paper, which simply detailed the best way to deceive the enemy through a list of bullet points. Wheatley told Bevan that the Chiefs probably wouldn't read the annexe, however the potential hazards were covered – and so was Bevan. This made the senior officer smile. He invited Wheatley for a nightcap.

On 21 December a redrafted paper concerning 'Overlord' (at least a third shorter) went to the Chiefs of Staff. It was accepted.

XXVII

Wing Commander Wheatley and the Liberation of Europe

'In all operations in which I had had a share so far, changes in the plan had been necessary and there had been all too little time, e.g. Husky in May 1943, and now Overlord which did not look too good.'
The Memoirs of Field Marshal Montgomery

Churchill wanted to penetrate Hitler's Fortress Europa. Yugoslavia and Greece had far longer coastlines than northern France, Belgium and Holland, and it was impossible for the Germans to garrison all the areas that could be breached by the enemy.

By landing in the Balkans it might have been possible to put Germany's unwilling allies, Bulgaria, Rumania and Hungary, out of the war, then join up with the Russians for a grand offensive from the east against the Third Reich itself. But the Americans – probably with the exception of General Patton – didn't want a 'head-on assault', so Churchill had to accept 'Overlord' (the JPS compromise). However, he still pressed for a minor operation against the Balkans (to reinforce Alexander in Italy, which would enable him to break through the gap in the Karnische Alps and invade Austria and Hungary).

The Americans didn't want to listen. They had other plans: Allied Forces in the Med, then an invasion of Southern France, driving north to merge with the forces of 'Overlord' (this operation became known as 'Anvil').

So Alexander's best forces were taken away from him to support 'Anvil' – consequently he wouldn't be able to defeat the Germans in Italy until the end of the war. (Wheatley was aware of a Chiefs of Staff meeting in London at which both Churchill and Eisenhower were present: 'Leave me my present strength in Italy, and I promise you that I will be in Vienna before Monty is in Berlin.')

By the spring, Bevan's team was deep into the intricacies of the deception plans connected with 'Bodyguard' (to deceive the enemy about the place and date of 'Overlord').

The plan was built around the idea of a new army in Kent making ready for a direct descent on the Pas de Calais. Furthermore, they had to be convinced that the Normandy landings were only a feint in great strength, designed to draw their armour south, so that when a second invasion was launched (Calais-Boulogne), it could establish itself almost unopposed north of the Seine and drive straight down on to Paris.

Knowledge of the 'fake' Army was conveyed to the enemy via the formation of hundreds of dummy aircraft and gliders on specially created airfields along the Thames estuary.

It had been one of the recommendations in plan 'Bodyguard' that no senior officers – other than Alexander and Eisenhower – should be named in connection with high commands, as this might have led to enemy intelligence making certain correct deductions. To this there were two exceptions.

The first was deliberate. It was leaked that General Patton had been given command of the fake First US Army Group (FUSAG) in Kent. It was highly plausible that this forceful American General had been selected by Eisenhower to lead the invasion forces, and so would strengthen the enemy's belief that the real objective was the Pas de Calais.

The second was unforeseen. Wheatley was told that Eisenhower asked Alexander to direct the Normandy landings (codename 'Neptune'); but as the Allied army in Italy was now being so greatly reduced in numbers to carry out 'Anvil', Churchill decided that Alex's brilliant generalship was needed to stop possible disaster there. In any case, Montgomery was appointed to carry out 'Neptune' and brought back to London.

The knowledge that this had been done would be a clear indication to the Germans that the stories Bevan and his team were putting out about an invasion of the Balkans in the summer – to which Montgomery was a natural choice of commander – were probably a bluff. Also, it would clearly show that the 'planned' invasion of France would be led by Montgomery, and his having returned to Britain in the spring indicated that it would take place in the summer instead of not until the autumn, as the JPS wished the enemy to believe.

Montgomery was asked to live quietly outside London, wear civilian clothes and be seen by as few people as possible. Unfortunately, on his first night back in London he took a suite at Claridges, then went on to the Palladium and, before curtain up, received a standing ovation from the audience. Even Monty's greatest fans saw this as sheer egotism on the General's part.

By the end of January, Bevan decided that it would be a good idea to get out a report on the results of strategic deception to date. Wheatley – as the longest serving member of the team – was tasked with drafting the report. The final report was sent to the Chiefs of Staff in February.

There were speculative articles concerning 'Overlord' in the press. It was decided that Wheatley should write a paper that discussed the possibility of taking certain editors into their confidence. This was all a build up to the final execution of 'Overlord'.

'Graffham' was the next step. This was a subsidiary of 'Bodyguard'. Some months earlier, when Wheatley wrote a paper headed *Essorbee*, the Foreign Office had a problem with the threatening of so-called neutral countries, but they backed down, issuing a paper in March, which stimulated Wheatley into writing a follow-up paper.

Montgomery's demand for five divisions in his initial assault meant postponing the invasion by a month, and consequently threw every plan the LCS had for 'Overlord' out of the window.

The LCS had been planning 'Bodyguard' since the beginning of the year, and the longer enemy intelligence was given to investigate and check ruses sent to deceive them, the greater the chance of their discovering the truth.

Throughout April and May preparations continued, building in intensity. The Thames estuary fake force was called 'Third Army Group, C-in-C General George Patton'. A greater deception was the formation of the first mixed USA/British Army troop in East Anglia. Dudley Clarke conveyed to German Intelligence that the Eighth Army was being brought back from Italy to form part of Patton's Third Army Group, which would carry out the invasion via the Pas de Calais. This deception operation had its own codename – plan 'Foynes' – and included a great deal of fake orders of battle.

In July 1944 Wheatley was put up on temporary promotion to Wing Commander. Bevan had sent a memo of recommendation some months earlier, but due to a friend of Wheatley's (in the Air Ministry) mislaying it, the temporary promotion took some time to come through. 'Overlord' by then was reaching fever-pitch, but other games were also afoot.

In order to throw the enemy off the scent as far as the actual day for the 'Neptune' landings was concerned, it was necessary for Montgomery to be seen in Italy the day before. Obviously, German Intelligence would believe that the General would be far too busy the day before the landing to go to Italy. So it was decided that an actor should stand in for Monty.

The LCS went to a firm in Wardour Street and looked through their books. They found a photograph of a man who had a similar countenance to the famous General, a Mr M E Clifton James. Further enquiries revealed that Clifton James had become a Lieutenant in the Pay Corps and was stationed in Scotland. He was ordered down to London and interviewed at the War Office. James was told nothing about the purpose for which he was wanted, but simply asked if he was prepared to go overseas. He said that he was if it was for the greater good of the country. He was then told that he was to become an 'understudy' to General Montgomery.

With little more ado, he was sent up north to where Monty was taking some leave and given quality time to study the General's mannerisms. They then returned to London in great secrecy, where James was fitted with the appropriate clothes and decorations. He was then provided with a plane to take him to Gibraltar.

It was only then asked if this small time actor had ever flown before. It was found that he hadn't. Wheatley was then tasked with getting the man in the air for a dummy flight to see if he would be air-sick. Wheatley booked this for the following day. There was no way the man could be Monty's double if he fell off the plane at Gibraltar unwell, but amidst a great fanfare welcome.

The LCS held their breath whilst the dummy run was made. But their fears were unfounded, James did not suffer from air sickness and was duly sent off to Gibraltar where he performed magnificently. However, at the end of his all-too-brief tour he was room-bound for approximately six weeks with a bottle of whisky before being flown home. Having outgrown his usefulness, he returned to being his old self, a Lieutenant in the Pay Cops. He was not promoted but sworn to secrecy. However, justice was done after the war when he mentioned the story to a group of people, one of whom happened to be a journalist. The story hit the papers but James was never reprimanded for it. His story appeared in book form and then became the classic movie *I Was Monty's Double*, in which Clifton James played himself.

But all of this was far from the reality of war. 6 June was D Day. Six months' planning from the LCS was finally put to the test. And despite poor weather for the preliminary RAF team, success became the watchword of the day.

Most people were aware by the late summer of 1944 the terrible mess the Germans were in. Some believed that the war would be over by the autumn but poor supplies – especially of petrol – slowed down the conclusion of war.

Once Eisenhower established his Supreme Headquarters in France, the LCS became a quiet place to work. All the important decisions were being made elsewhere. They had no battlefront to formulate plans for, so Wheatley soon became quite bored. On 5 August 1944 he sent a letter to the Secretary of State for Air asking, with Bevan's approval, to relinquish his commission in the RAFVR. The cogs turned slowly, but finally, on 20 December 1944, Dennis Wheatley completed his service in the War Cabinet and returned to his day job: one of Britain's best-loved novelists. And it is for this that he is remembered to this day. But let us now remember something more: his astonishing work during the Second World War.

Annexes A to D

The following Annexes are taken from previously unreleased documents written by Dennis Wheatley during the Second World War. They have been selected for publication in this volume as they add extra depth to some of Wheatley's statements written in his war papers.

Dennis Wheatley wrote many articles, speeches and radio broadcasts during the Second World War, which complemented the thoughts and opinions as laid down in his work for the JPS. On reading the following papers, I felt that it was important to include them in this work not simply because of the juxtaposition to be gained (in comparison to the war papers), but because of the extra insight offered concerning the author. I feel that they reveal more of his character, perhaps as a man desperate for the British public to come together and fight their foe as a united front.

I can never get away from the impression that Wheatley felt it was likely that Great Britain would be invaded and that he personally was prepared to lead the motivation in thwarting that evil. It is easy to dismiss such fears with hindsight, but the concerns of these documents were very real at the time they were written.

CC

Annexe A

FIFTH COLUMN

FOOLS OF HITLER

We hear a great deal in these critical times about Fifth Column personnel, hidden in our midst, and of the dangers to national security which this enemy within the gates threatens. It is a very real danger. One traitor, especially if he be in a position of authority, or a position of confidence, can do more damage than a battalion operating from outside. Even the smaller fry can do incalculable damage if effectively organized. Moreover, these Fifth Columnists undoubtedly do exist – and in force – in this country; and we should by this time have learned to respect the enemy's genius for organisation.

Who are these traitors?

They are either enemy nationals, aliens or naturalised British subjects subsidised by the enemy. Or they are of our own people, British born.

What do they hope to gain?

The first are working for their Fatherland, and possibly for money and power. The aliens usually are adventurers working for money. The British-born are traitors working for money or filled with the lust for power. Such men are the fools of Hitler. It is to them that I speak.

What does a man like Oswald Mosley hope to get out of betraying his country? He hopes that, if Hitler conquers Britain, he will make Mosley his deputy, as Dictator of Britain. Those of the small fry, who are not working merely for money, also expect positions of authority under Hitler's regime. I have called them the fools of Hitler, because their trust in Hitler is pathetic.

What would they actually gain if Hitler conquered us? Most definitely, a bullet or a free pass to a concentration-camp; and this despite all promises or assurances they may have received. What man of sense or discrimination today would place any reliance upon the promises of Hitler and his minions?

Mosley, as Dictator of Britain, if he ever got the job, would be Hitler's tool. He would be told exactly what he had to do; if he deviated from instructions by one hair's breadth, he would be eliminated. That is not my idea of power, and I doubt if it is Mosley's either, yet he is presumably so blind that he cannot see it.

There is more excuse for the little men. Yet a study of recent events should have put them wise. Some are cranks, or fanatics, or men with a grievance, who think they see a way, by allying themselves with our enemy, of making their pipe-dreams come true or taking revenge against the existing order of things. Well, I would like to warn them – before it is too late; and my warning should be in these words:

'If you are trusting in Hitler, think again. Think very carefully. First, Hitler is not going to rule Britain. Recent British reverses mean nothing in the long run. There may be further reverses, but the might of the Empire cannot be overcome. If you believe it can – this is your dangerous moment. You will be on the wrong side. England, at long last, is awake to her danger from people like you. The authorities have not been idle, merely slow. You are probably a marked man already. However clever and complete you may think the Fifth Column scheme to be, however infallible, distrust it. We know all about it, and the danger is already met. All except the danger to you – and that is your affair. If you are caught out in treachery and sabotage – as you will be sooner or later – your reward is the firing-squad, or even swifter death at the hands of our defence services. The soft-hearted British public is at last prepared to be ruthless to such as you. My advice to you is to disassociate yourself now from your subversive party, whatever it may be; and if you want to be really safe, make that declaration openly at the nearest police-station. We will protect you from your friends, if you need protection. Tomorrow may be too late. If you have not the courage to declare yourself, then better throw away your orders and your weapons and lie down.

'And to those of you who may still believe that Hitler will triumph and find a nice cushy job for you, I say the same thing. Think again. Get out of it now. Because, even if Hitler did triumph, your fate would be just the same. Are there not hundreds of full-blooded German Gauleiters, or Germans with ambition for power, who would like your job? And who do you imagine would get it – a full-blooded Hun or an English traitor? Do you know what has already happened to the traitors in Poland, Norway, Holland and Belgium? Their fate would quite certainly be yours – the wall or the concentration-camp; and of these two, under German rule, the wall is to be preferred. It is quicker and cleaner.

'No, you traitors, even Hitler would have no use for you after you ceased to be useful to him. He takes all and gives nothing; nothing but death or disgrace and humiliation. But Hitler's days are numbered: soon he will take something he won't like; something that will be crammed down his throat by a force he cannot resist. His already weakened, slaughtered army and air-force; his depleted navy and all his filthy tricks and monkey cunning will not help him then.

Hitler, and the fools of Hitler will perish. See that you are not numbered among the latter. See to it now.'

Annexe B

BRITONS NEVER SHALL BE SLAVES

I hear from various sources that in some of the areas which have been most badly bombed there is now a certain amount of peace talk. This is by no means surprising in view of the fact that in the latter part of the last war, when the bombing of London was nowhere near so severe, there was an occasion when East-Enders marched to Parliament Square in a 'call the war off' demonstration.

Actually, as far as one can gather, the people are standing up to the indiscriminate bombing infinitely better than was to be expected, but it is not unnatural that there should be some defeatism among the poorer classes when their lives are actually threatened. I do not mean by this that the bulk of the poorer classes are one wit less patriotic than our more fortunate citizens – in fact – generally speaking – the British working-man has so far shown up in this war infinitely better than the majority of our Civil Servants and a large portion of the black-coated worker class. I refer to the very poorest people in the community who *think* that they have nothing to lose by the defeat of Britain.

It is to some extent understandable that a man who has been unemployed for a number of years should, if he lives in a badly-bombed area, say to himself at the worst moments: 'What have I to gain by putting up with this hell that they're giving us? If Hitler wins I can't be worse off. I've no money and no property that he can take away from me, and at least if they stopped this filthy war I shouldn't have to face the risk of being killed or crippled for life each night. If Hitler won, things might even be better, as he managed to find work for the 8,000,000 unemployed that there were in Germany before he came to power.'

There is also the very large foreign population of the East End. A considerable section of these people owe no real allegiance to any country; they are small traders or craftsmen who earn a modest living but have no capital assets of which they could be robbed. A certain proportion of these express the view that life must go on whatever form of Government we have or even if Britain fell under the domination of a foreign power. They consider, therefore, that as humble but useful citizens in any state no-one would interfere with them in the event of a Nazi conquest and that their lives would go on very much as before if Britain either made a patched-up peace or was defeated. Therefore, now that their lives and very small properties are threatened they naturally incline towards any suggestion which might lead to a cessation of hostilities.

If we were fighting a purely Imperialistic or Capitalistic war such people might have some grounds for their feelings, and in my view it has not yet been sufficiently brought home to them that this war is not an Imperialistic or Capitalistic war and, in consequence, even the poorest section of the community would suffer should Britain be defeated.

The thing that they do not yet realise is that Hitler would treat Britain just as he has treated Czechoslovakia and Poland or, quite possibly, with even more ferocity. It would not be merely a question of British people losing the right to vote and the right of free speech and a free press; matters which the people to whom I refer do not really give a damn about. It would be a case of every male of Britain between the age of 16 and 50 being rounded up, shipped across to the Continent and made every bit as much a slave as were the Ancient Britons and Gauls when they were marched off in chains to Rome.

These people would *not* be allowed to continue their hard but normal life under a Nazi tyranny; they would find themselves within a few months, torn away from their families and any interests they may have, in a foreign land, tilling the fields, slaving in the mines and rebuilding the continental dockyards for the sole remuneration of enough food to keep the life in their bodies; they would be herded like cattle, beaten and shot at the least sign of disobedience by the armed guards who would supervise their labours.

That is what is happening to hundreds of thousands of poor wretches on the Continent to-day who a year ago were free men, and there is no reason whatever to suppose that Hitler would deal more kindly with us if he proved victorious.

In fact, only by crushing Britain in this way and destroying the race could he possibly hope for permanent world dominion. If he did not enslave our man-power it is quite certain that before many years had passed there would be a great revolt to throw off the Nazi yoke, so, if he wishes for world mastery he has no option but to adopt the course suggested should he conquer these islands.

I feel quite convinced that the fate which lies in store for them is not yet sufficiently realised by the poorest classes, and to them the high talk of Democracy means little.

There is also the question of the women. In China the Japanese are seeking to ensure their mastery of the conquered Chinese territories in years to come by rounding up all young Chinese women and turning them over to the Japanese soldiery, the idea being that with each month that passes there will be thousands of children born with Chinese mothers and Japanese fathers. This is a deliberate policy to sabotage the Chinese race.

We know Hitler's policy for his Black Guards. For years past it has been preached in Germany that it is no dishonour at all for an unmarried German girl to be the mother of the child of a Storm-Trooper. On the contrary, these unmarried mothers are given special allowances, the very best attention in excellent maternity homes and every other inducement to raise children out of wedlock. The idea is that if each Black Guard put one girl per month in the family way, as the Black Guards are picked for their physique in another generation the German race will be greatly strengthened and improved.

This openly immoral policy is only a step from the Japanese policy of breeding from the Chinese to destroy Chinese racial purity. It must therefore be considered as a definite probability that in the event of a Nazi victory, while our virile males were enslaved and deported for reconstruction work in the ruined cities of the Continent, our fertile women would be turned over to Hitler's pagan soldiery, put in the family way and sent back to work in the fields or the factories.

It seems to me that it would be well worth while for the Ministry of Information to make it really clear to the masses what they will be up against should Hitler prove victorious. We have abundant evidence of what is going on on the Continent, so I suggest that a small booklet of about twelve pages might be got out with the assistance of the diplomats who represent Czechoslovakia, Poland, etc., in London. Figures where available of men carted off for labour in Germany, etc., should be given, but the statistical part of it should not be overdone and the more lurid the personal stories included in it the better.

Large numbers of this pamphlet could be printed off and issued to A.R.P. wardens and shelter marshals for free distribution to people in tube stations and air raid shelters who are taking cover while an air raid is actually in progress.

I believe such a pamphlet, if it were written with vigour and imagination, might do an immense amount to check any possible 'call off the war' movement.

(Dennis Wheatley has since put forward the admirable suggestion that Sefton Delmer's articles, which have recently appeared in the *Daily Express* – a specimen is attached – would do excellently for this purpose and has offered to write an introduction for them. It certainly seems that nothing but good could result from educating the public that 'slavery' is a very literal interpretation of German domination, and no mere academic expression. The title would need careful consideration as it should not give the impression that defeatism is widespread.)

Annexe C

THE OPENING OF THE BATTLE OF THE CENTURY
BY
SQUADRON LEADER DENNIS WHEATLEY

8th JUNE 1944

NOTE ON THE ATTACHED ARTICLE

1, <u>OBJECT</u>

The intention of these signed articles by R.A.F. officers, who in peace-time are professional writers, is to get over to the American public the fact that the British have not left the battle almost entirely to U.S. Forces but played an equal, if not greater part in the operation.

In my view, to do this really effectively the whole story should be told, including all the months of careful planning which alone made the operation possible. As an officer who has served on the Joint Planning Staff I am one of the very few people who can do this, but obviously official consent must be obtained before my knowledge gained in this capacity can be published. For this reason I have provisionally marked this document SECRET.

2, <u>SECURITY</u>

As I have worked in the War Cabinet offices for nearly two and a half years, there is no secret about my place of employment. This, inevitably, must have become fairly widely known as I receive requests for autographs and to sign copies of my books from clerks, typists, messengers and home guards with considerable frequency.

About my real work, I have given nothing away. In fact, I have deliberately lied to cover myself by inferring that I am a sort of official historian.

I have also avoided any mention of the part played by the Pathfinders in this operation, and the article will be subject to the usual security scrutiny.

3, HIGH RANKING OFFICERS

It is not, I am aware, customary for generals below the rank of army commander to be named in the press. But I greatly hope that an exception will be made in this case and authority secured to do so; as to delete the name would rob the article of much of its personal touch. Moreover, I submit that the time has come when it would be a very good thing to build up some of our generals.

4, LENGTH

I was asked for an article of about 3,000 words. This is about 5,500 because I could not tell the full story in less. But this should not invalidate it from publication in an American magazine, as such periodicals as Saturday Evening Post and Cosmopolitan often take stories of 5,000 or more.

If publication in neutral countries is also intended, I suggest that the Swedish rights should be offered to the Svenska Bagbladt. I have a very big public in Sweden and this paper has often serialised my novels.

5, PROCEEDS OF THE ARTICLE

I understand that in the normal course of events all royalties for such material go to the treasury. May I, however, point out that I am not paid as an R.A.F. officer working for press relations, but am on the strength of the Department of Plans. In view of the difference, perhaps it could be arranged for the proceeds to go to the Royal Air Force Benevolent Fund.

(Intld.) D.W.

8th June 1944

THE OPENING OF THE BATTLE OF THE CENTURY
BY SQUADRON LEADER DENNIS WHEATLEY

I'm one of the lucky ones in this war, because I'm a square peg in a square hole. Truth is not only stranger but more fascinating than fiction, so you can imagine how thrilling it is for a professional writer of thrillers to have the job of recording much of the inner history of the war. To do that one must know, not only about the great operations as they take place, but all that has led up to them, so I have the privilege of working with the Joint Planning Staff of the War Cabinet.

It is amazing to look back now and realise that even in the darkest days – during the Battle of Britain – during the terrible year that our little island stood alone in Europe to face the might of Hitler – we were already planning the return to the continent, the perhaps distant but, we felt, certain day when we should bring liberty, freedom and justice, lights dancing and laughter back to the stunned, terrified, enslaved millions of Europe.

Never for a moment did the confidence of the prime minister and those around him waver. When the Nazis of the East struck their foul blow at Pearl Harbor and while the sickening telegrams came in telling us of the massacre at Hong Kong, the sinking of Prince of Wales and Repulse, and the fall of Singapore, we were already planning 'Operation Roundup'. There is a lot in a name and that was the codeword the prime minister chose for the job which will bring about the final defeat of the German armies.

But we all knew one thing. Whether the first stage of our return to the continent was an assault on Norway, Denmark, Belgium, France, Italy or Greece we must achieve air superiority before we were in any position to make it. In air power alone lay the key to victory. And then the long up-hill struggle to achieve it, while not neglecting other more immediate priorities, began.

Many big men on the air staff believed that the slaughter of a western front could be averted if only all our resources were directed to the air battle which has now been waged by the R.A.F. for one thousand, seven hundred and thirty-seven days and nights without cessation. First, drive the German air force from the skies then destroy German industry and it will be utterly impossible for the enemy to continue the conflict, was their argument.

But there were other calls which could not possibly be resisted. In 1942 our shipping losses were appalling. The U. Boats were right on top, if they could not be got under, Britain would be starved, not only of food but of all materials of war necessary to keep our own aircraft factories going, and denied the men and weapons that the United States was sending us. Squadron after squadron of long-range aircraft had to be diverted to patrolling the vast spaces of the Atlantic Ocean for the protection of our ever more precious convoys.

Then, even the most rabid 'Through Air Power to Victory' enthusiast had to admit, that, however punch drunk we might make Germany by bombing, sooner or later the army would have to go in to administer the coup de grace. For that parachute troops and airborne forces would be necessary. The training of such highly specialised troops is a long and arduous business. Once more many squadrons of bombers had to be diverted from the air battle to this essential role.

Again, the air war was constant and the resulting wastage greatly hampered our build up until America could give us really powerful help in taking the strain. Aircraft had been built in British factories since 1939, but our pilots, aided by only small contingents of United Nations air force personnel, have had to operate them in Greece, Crete, Egypt, Syria, Madagascar, Malaya, Burma, Algeria, Tunisia, Sicily, Italy, Yugoslavia, Australia, the Atlantic, Indian and Arctic Oceans, as well as waging the main battle in western Europe.

Many of us had hoped to see the launching of 'Roundup' in the summer or autumn of 1943 but it just could not be done. We had broken the back of the U. Boat menace and the airborne forces were hard at their training, but the sailors and soldiers freely admitted that we could not possibly go in until the R.A.F. had done, with the assistance of the now mighty and gallant United States Army Air Force, the job for which it had been originally designed.

Yet the Royal Air Force had as its head a man whom all of us who wear R.A.F. uniforms consider to be, after the Prime Minister, the most brilliant and remarkable that Britain has produced in the present war – Marshal of the Royal Air Force Sir Charles Portal. Calmly, logically, while meeting all the really vital demands of his fellow chiefs of staffs, he so allocated his own forces that he gradually managed to build up the vast British Empire Air Armada which is co-operating with the United States Air Forces over Europe today. Never, during all the months and years of defeats and victories did he lose sight of his long-term aim – to bring about the annihilation of the Luftwaffe and so make possible the invasion of Europe.

The planning for that never ceased. In the quiet rooms of the underground fortress, to enter which one must pass successively, special police, home guards, army sentries and finally royal marines, officers worked day after day and often far into the night, sifting intelligence, noting the movements of army divisions, examining geological data on continental beaches, reading endless reports on the availability of shipping, manpower, progress of secret weapons, morale, state of training, and slowly but surely co-ordinating the intricate machinery which is to bring the spearhead of the nine million six hundred thousand men which the British Empire now has under arms against the enemy.

Thousands of hours were spent in conferences, thousands of tonnes of paper consumed on working out the innumerable aspects of the plan, thousands of telegrams were exchanged with Washington. Every document was marked 'Top Secret' and a high proportion of the secret cipher cables 'Most Immediate'. Then, at last, in January of this year, the news was flashed from Teheran. 'Operation POINTBLANK is to have top priority and it has been agreed with Roosevelt and Stalin that this summer we shall destroy the enemy by a series of hammer blows delivered from East, South and West.'

Operation 'POINTBLANK'! At last, the air forces of the United Nations were to come into their own. Everything else must now take second place to driving the German air force out of the skies to be followed by the destruction of the enemy's aircraft plants and associated industries.

For many months we had known the beaches against which the first assault in the west was to be launched; soon after Teheran, we knew the fateful day. A terrible secret to carry with one during the four long months that were yet to go, with always the awful fear that one might be injured in a street accident, taken to hospital, operated on and, while under an anaesthetic, talk of those vital things which were never absent from one's mind.

General Eisenhower came home from the Mediterranean to take over the supreme command in the west and supervise all the intricate detailed planning which yet had to be done. With him he brought that mighty master of air strategy, Sir Arthur Tedder, to be his deputy.

Tedder, who had saved Egypt in the ghastly retreat of 1942 by keeping his fighter airfields in operation long after the army had withdrawn, so that the ground staffs often only got out by the skin of their teeth as the enemy's tanks raced up. Tedder, who made General Alexander's long victorious advance into Tunisia possible by destroying Rommel's ports and cutting his supply lines. Tedder, who wiped out the headquarters of the German general staff in Sicily the night before the allied landing, and thus, by destroying the centre of their communications system rendered them incapable of directing the operations of their troops during the first week of the battle. Tedder, who laid the groundwork in Italy for his successor, Air Marshal Sir John Slessor, to blast the Italian railway system and prepare the way for General Alexander's brilliant campaign which has culminated in the defeat of Kesselring and the capture of Rome.

The moment he got back to England, Tedder got down to it with those other great airmen General Spaatz, who had shared his Mediterranean triumphs, and Air Marshal Sir Trafford Leigh Mallory, who played as splendid a part in the Battle of Britain. They revised our air strategy for the final phase. Air Chief Marshal 'Bomber' Harris was already hammering the guts out of Berlin by the most terrible night attacks which have ever ravaged a city. General Eaker's boys, with tremendous courage, had been pressing ever deeper into Germany by day. The colossal air offensive now went on with ever mounting intensity. In the great air battle of recent months, thousands of German aircraft have been shot down, hundreds more have been destroyed on the ground but, more importantly still, factory after factory which makes aircraft or the ball-bearings instruments, lenses and other components essential to their manufacture, have been razed to the ground.

In consequence, operation 'POINTBLANK' has achieved its objectives. The enemy still has an air force but there is nothing behind it. He has been compelled to husband the few thousand planes he has left for one final battle when our invasion is launched. This has enabled Tedder in the last few weeks, to use his tactical air forces virtually with impunity. Day after day thousands of sorties have been flown, but to targets nearer home, against the rail centres of Belgium and

France; against many tank depots, ammunition dumps, radar warning stations, coastal batteries, and the vital bridges without the use of which the enemy cannot bring up his tanks, heavy guns and other reinforcements into what was soon to become the battle area.

The air force has in fact done its job for the navy and army. It has made the crossing of the narrow seas, without unacceptable casualties from enemy air attack, possible; and it has made it possible for the army to hold a bridgehead on the continent long enough to build up the hundreds of thousands of tonnes of stores and equipment necessary to the waging of a campaign before the enemy can bring up sufficient forces to throw our assault troops back into the sea.

Yet, during the last phase there has been no let-up for the planning staffs. Enemy dispositions are constantly changing, air reconnaissance, without which we would know practically nothing of what our army will have to face, was constantly finding new defences which must be tackled, and there is the terrific problem of the security of the operation – taking every measure that brains can devise to prevent the enemy learning the date and place of the assault.

All sorts of precautions have had to be discussed and settled. The censorship of mails and telegrams, the stopping of rail travel and telephoning, the clearance of hospitals without arousing suspicion, at what date neutral diplomats should be deprived of the centuries old privilege of sending uncensored cables to their own capitals, the prevention of our newspapers being sent abroad, restricted areas and the ban upon anyone leaving the country by ship or air. In fact the drawing of an invisible but impenetrable ring round the United Kingdom since, upon the planners doing so efficiently, depend the lives of scores of thousands of Britain's and America's bravest men.

And then, at last, D-Day was almost upon us. For the second time only since the end of 1941 I was allowed to leave the quiet room where the temperature and light never varies, in which I perform my normal duties, to go to an airfield – in this case the one from which the key operation for the first act in the liberation of Europe will be directed.

On the sunny morning of June 3rd I left Whitehall in an air ministry car. We sped along the Great West Road now, owing to the impossibility of obtaining petrol except for war purposes, almost empty of traffic, to Maidenhead. In peacetime the river there would have been gay with picnic parties in punts and launches, now it was still and deserted. On we went past the even lovelier upper reaches of the Thames, passing a large meadow near Goring, which brought back to my mind a scene of thirty years ago.

On the night of August 3rd 1914, I slept in a tent in that field with a territorial regiment. At 1 o'clock in the morning we were awakened by the order to break camp and return to London. Next day Great Britain entered the First World War against Germany. After four and a half years we fought Germany to a standstill. Since then, twenty uneasy years have passed, plus another five of even more terrible conflict. Now Britain, America, Russia and the free continents have again fought the Germans until they have been robbed of all power of initiative – and I was on my way to see the launching of the penultimate act in the final destruction of the German armies.

More miles of England's green and pleasant land; the country lanes, the little cottages, inviolate for centuries from the brutal hand of an invader, and inviolate still, thanks to God and the Royal Air Force. Then downlands and, over the horizon, came the widely spaced building of the R.A.F. station which I am to visit.

It is a peacetime aerodrome with well-designed buildings and comfortable, commodious quarters, but they are crowded now as it is also headquarters of the 6th. British Airborne Division. I see the adjutant and am taken to the mess. I do not feel in any way a stranger, for never, since Nelson held the seas against all Europe and termed his captains: 'that band of brothers' has there been such a band of brothers as those who wear the Royal Air Force uniform. Within half an hour I have made a dozen new friends and more drinks are pressed upon me than I can comfortably manage.

Among them is Wing Commander Macnamara who suggests that I should go for a flight that evening in the glider that is to carry Major General Gale, the commander of the 6th. Airborne Division, to France. Then I am introduced to the station commander, Group Captain Surplice. He is a tall, well-built fellow with a quiet manner, very blue eyes and white even teeth which makes his frequent smile particularly attractive. Half a dozen officers have told me already that he is the best C.O. that they have ever served under; a marvellous memory, incredibly efficient and never angry. One only has to talk to him for a few minutes to know that he is the type of man who does not have to drive his people but has at times to restrain their eagerness from fear that they should overwork in their efforts to please him.

Squadron Leader Pound, Principal Administrative Officer, a veteran of the last war with a row of decorations, fixes me up with a room and tells me something of his job – one that has little glamour but is so absolutely vital to the success of operations. Men cannot fight their best unless they are well fed and cared for, and they cannot fight at all if their equipment lets them down.

Pound takes me to the briefing room where I meet Squadron Leader Johnson, another beribboned veteran. Behind a locked door with an armed sentry on guard and blacked out windows, he is already preparing the maps from which the air crews will be briefed when the signal comes through that the 'party' is definitely on. We have a most interesting chat about the forthcoming operation, but I have to let him do most of the talking as I am not certain how much he knows and it is still possible that there may be a postponement.

At six o'clock, I go out onto the great airfield with its broad runways and its scores of parked aircraft and gliders. They are wearing their war-paint; special recognition signs put on only the night before, after the camp had been 'sealed'. No one who enters it may now leave it, or write, or telegram from it until after the job is over.

Major Griffiths, the glider pilot who will take General Gale to France, tells me a bit about gliders, then we go up for a twenty minutes flight. There is a stiff wind so it is a bit bumpy but that does not worry me as I have never been airsick. We can hear the roar of the engines in Macnamara's aircraft which is towing us. Suddenly there is silence and, after a moment, I realise that the towrope has been cast off, yet we are flying smoothly on. A few minutes more, and we come safely down on the airfield.

That evening I attend the preliminary briefing. There is a colour film showing a part of France. It is just as though we were all seated in a huge aircraft flying over the country of the film. Again and again we run in over the German held beaches to the fields in which the paratroops are to be dropped and the gliders come down. As we make our series of chair-borne flights to the different objectives, the commentator points out the principal landmarks of the area by which the pilots can identify their targets.

Back in the mess, I meet scores more officers; there are about equal numbers in khaki and air force blue, they are all talking and laughing together. They all look incredibly fit and their morale is terrific. To my utter amazement, they ask me what I think the prospect [is] of the Germans withdrawing to the Rhine immediately the invasion is launched, apparently bets are being given and taken in the mess at evens that the Germans will not dare to face us on such a long and vulnerable front as the Atlantic wall.

After dinner, Macnamara introduces me to General Gale. He is a huge man with a ready laugh, shrewd eyes and a bulldog chin. He stands out from the crowd, not only on account of his size but also because, instead of the conventional battledress, he is wearing beautifully cut, light-grey jodhpurs. We soon discover that we are the same age – 47 and, as the general says: 'a damned good vintage'. We find too that we have many friends in common, and among them a brigadier now, alas, dead, who was one of the real brains of the army. The general tells me that he worked with our dead friend all through 1938 and 1939 which, without more being said, gives me the fact that the general must have one of the original members of the Joint Planning Staff and is therefore a top-line thinker as well as a born fighter.

An airman asks him what weapon he is personally going to take for the battle. He roars with laughter and replies: 'weapon! What the hell do I want with a weapon? If I have the good luck to get near any of those so and sos, my boots are good enough for me. I'll kick the something something's where it tickles most.'

A little later the station doctor, Squadron Leader Evan Jones, tells me an amazing story. Seven days earlier one of the airborne captains had broken his ankle. They all knew that the job was coming fairly soon and Jones told him: 'I'm sorry, old chap, but if it is within the next three weeks it will be absolutely impossible for you to go.' 'I've been training for this job for two years,' replied the captain seriously. 'If I can't make it, I'll kill myself.' And he meant it.

Jones was so worried that he got a specialist down from London, but the break was a bad one and the specialist verified the verdict – impossible under three weeks. There then occurred what the doctor considers to be one of the most remarkable examples of the triumph of mind over matter that he has ever seen. The captain determined to make it somehow. After six days, he threw away his crutches; on the eighth, he had only a slight limp and went to France. What hope have the tired, dispirited Germans against such men?

Half a dozen of us, including the general, talked on until midnight, then the others went to bed while the general and I stayed up alone for a further half an hour talking about the qualities which make a good leader.

He insisted at first that only one thing mattered – efficiency. If the men knew that you really knew your stuff, they would follow you blindly anywhere. I argued that that was nine-tenths of the game, but the last tenth was personality, the capability of showing oneself to be independent minded and a little out of the ruck of other men. Then to make my point I instanced his wearing of grey jodhpurs instead of battle dress.

'What's that got to do with it?' he wanted to know. 'I wear the damned things because they're comfortable and I hate the feel of that beastly khaki serge.'

'Exactly,' I agreed. 'Most people would feel a little shy of dressing differently because they would be afraid that they would be thought to be doing so just to make an effect. But you don't care a hoot about that. You have the courage of your convictions, and if you have them about clothes, you must have them too about far more important matters.'

'Well, that's very nice of you,' he said, modestly. 'And maybe you're right that in leadership, personality does make up the last tenth. But nine-tenths is knowing your job and sticking to it. Efficiency, that's what really counts.'

When we went to bed we were a bit worried about the weather, but we knew that there could not possibly be a postponement unless it became exceptionally bad. That Saturday night, ships were already moving to their concentration points and the security of the whole operation might be jeopardised if it were put off for even a single day.

But in the morning the weather was worse. Soon after nine o'clock, Wing Commander Bangay took me up for a flight in one of the paratroop dropping aircraft. We did a practice run up to a diagonal road which had certain similarities to a road in the target area and I had the treat of seeing the aircrew go through the exact drill they would follow when they dropped their human cargo in France. Then soon after I got back, the blow fell. At 11-30, the station commander sent for me and told me the operation would not take place that night.

I was utterly appalled. Even an hour earlier, in spite of the poor weather, I would not bet anyone a 100 to 1 in pounds that there would be a postponement. The general was almost certainly the only person on the station besides myself who realised the full implications. There were now over 4,000 ships which had moved up in the night and many thousands of smaller craft all massed round the Isle of Wight. The Bosch had only to send over one recce plane to spot that vast concentration and he would know that the invasion was just about to start. It would give him twenty-four hours to move additional troops up to the beaches and, when our forces arrived they would find every gun manned. Worse, he might send his whole bomber forces over to the Solent that Sunday night, in which case there could be the most appalling massacre among our close berthed, stationary shipping. Again, he knew that we had airborne forces and that they would form the spearhead of the attack. He probably knew too the airfields upon which the hundreds of tugs and gliders were assembled so it was quite a possibility that he might either bomb them that night or launch his own paratroops against them to forestall our attack. In fact, all operational officers on the station had been ordered to wear their revolvers from the time that the camp was sealed as a precaution against just such an emergency.

Fortunately, however, very few people even knew that a postponement had occurred, far less the possible use the enemy might make of it if his recce aircraft were active and alert. In consequence, that night the crowded mess was again the scene of gaiety and mirth. At about nine o'clock an impromptu singsong started and for over three hours we made the rafters ring with all the old choruses. The station commander sent an urgent summons for the doctor, who came expecting to find an accident occasioned by some high-spirited horseplay, but actually it was for the doctor to bring his accordion, and the clever little Welshman entertained us royally with a score of special versions of popular songs.

The general had been singing with the rest of us but gone off to bed at eleven o'clock. Later he told us that, just as the rest of us were breaking up, around a quarter to one, his A.D.C. woke him. The secret codeword had come over the wire from London. Tomorrow, the 'do' was on.

The morning of Monday June 5th. passed quietly. Very few people as yet knew that was now definitely D–1. But at lunchtime, the whispered word ran round among the operational officers: 'final briefing at 3 o'clock!'

There were three briefings each taking an hour, for three separate but co-ordinated operations, and I listened to them all with rapt attention. Major-General Crawford, Director of Air Operations, War Office, had arrived from London to join us and, soon after, Air Vice Marshal Hollinghurst, the A.C.O. of the group came in. Both had played a great part in the preparations of the forthcoming operation and the Air Vice Marshal was responsible for it, since under his command lay all the airfields in the area on which the aircraft and gliders that were to take the 6th Airborne Division to France were assembled.

The station commander, Group Captain Surplice, opened the proceedings in each by reading orders of the day from the supreme commander, General Eisenhower, and the commander-in-chief, Air Marshal Sir Trafford Leigh Mallory. Then, having explained the general layout of the sea borne assault, he asked General Gale to describe the part his division was to play.

The general told us that his task was to protect the left flank of the allied armies. To do this, three separate landings would be made to the east of the river. It was imperative that a large German battery which enfiladed the assault beaches, should be silenced. One of the first groups to land would storm a small chateau and seize a car in its garage. Two paratroopers, both Austrians, would get in the car and drive hell for leather towards the steel gates of the battery shouting in German: 'open the gate! Open the gate, the invasion has started!' The Germans would have heard the aeroplanes overhead, so it was hoped that they would open up, then the paratroopers could hurl bombs through which would render it impossible to close the gates again. It was a suicide job. This fortress battery had a twenty-foot wide and a fifteen feet deep concrete ditch all round it filled with barbed wire and to make certain of the job, the general meant to crash three gliders right across the ditch.

The two other parties were to seize two adjacent bridges crossing the river Orne and the Dive canal about five miles from the coast and to blow up others bridges further inland. He general then meant to establish his battle H.Q. between the two seized bridges, to infest, with his men, all the territory to the west in order to delay a German attack against the British flank and, when the attack came, as come it must, to fight with his back to the double water line.

No thought that the 81st German Panzer Division would be at him pretty soon so he would need every anti-tank gun that he could get in. 'We shall need those guns pretty badly,' he said; and then, as though it had just occurred to him, he added: 'as a matter of fact, we shall want them tomorrow.' At which a great roar of laughter went up from the packed benches of the briefing room.

The station commander then briefed his pilots; giving detailed instructions to each flight as to their course in and out with the navigational aids arranged to get them safely home. This may sound a simple matter, but when great numbers of aircraft are flying from many different airfields to objectives all crowded into one locality, it becomes an extraordinarily complicated business, unless there is to be grave risk of losses by collision. Group Captain Surplice was followed by the signals officer, the meteorological officer, and the secret devices officer. Of these, I understood only the 'met' man who predicted clear skies under 2,000 feet and broken cloud above which would let the moonlight through so that the pilots should be able to pick out their dropping zones without difficulty.

The briefing over, we returned to the mess. After dinner a few of us knocked off a rather special bottle of wine which had been produced for the occasion. General Gale asked his A.D.C., his chief intelligence officer, General Crawford, Air Vice Marshal Hollinghurst, Wing Commander Macnamara and myself to join him, and together we drank success to this great venture.

While we drank the wine we talked of the coming battle. I remarked that I had never had the least doubt about the ability of the navy to put the bulk of our main forces safely ashore, or about our troops being able to overcome the enemy's initial resistance; but the real crisis would be between D + 6 and D + 20 when, moving more swiftly overland than we could across water, the enemy might be able to counter attack our bridgehead with greatly superior forces.

'Yes, a lot of people are afraid of that,' replied the general quietly. 'But they fail to take into account our immense air superiority. Think what the destruction of those bridges over the lower Seine means. Instead of the enemy being able to bring his divisions north of the Seine cracking straight against our flank, he has to take them all the way round by Paris. They'll bottleneck there and General Spatz will be able to knock merry hell out of them. As for their being able to bring a superior force against us from the centre and south of France by D + 6, that's all right in theory. But to do so they must concentrate on a relatively small area. The sky will be all ours. Leigh Mallory will see their every move and his boys will break up their formations wherever they become a serious menace. No, if we can secure our first objectives, I don't think we need worry.'

It was a great tribute to our airmen by a great soldier, and I have no shadow of doubt about his trust being justified.

It was now 10 o'clock, and Group Captain Surplice had very kindly suggested that if I accompanied him, I would see the take off to the best advantage. First we made the complete tour ot the airfield in his car, everything was in order; there was no necessity for any flap or a single last-minute instruction. Then we went to the watchtower, to within a few yards of which each aircraft taxies up before receiving the signal to go.

The weather was still not good but it had improved a little; there were breaks between the clouds and twilight faded almost imperceptibly into moonlight. The first wave consisted of 14 paratroop carrying aircraft followed by 4 aircraft towing gliders containing special material needed as soon as possible after the paratroops had landed.

Wing Commander Bungay, in the aircraft in which he had taken me up the day before was to lead the first wave. With him was going Air Vice Marshal Hollinghurst, or 'Holly' as this plump, dynamic, little man is known affectionately by his subordinates. There had, I think, been a certain amount of discussion as to the wisdom of his going, but he is mad-keen about his highly specialised job of transporting airborne forces, and insisted that the experience of seeing the actual operation would be invaluable to him in the future.

At three minutes past eleven precisely, the first aircraft took off and 'Holly' led the boys he has trained so thoroughly in the assault against Hitler's Fortress Europe. The other aircraft followed at thirty-second intervals except for the four glider tugs which took off at one minute intervals. A wing commander beside me timed them with his watch. Not a single aircraft was either early or late by a split second.

We now had a period of waiting as the second wave was not due off until 1.50 am. In the interval a signal was flashed to us that the air commander in chief, Sir Trafford Leigh Mallory, was about to arrive at the station, and soon after, his plane came in. He talked for a little to the station commander and the two generals, wished them luck and took off into the night to visit other aerodromes where important operations were about to take place.

Midnight came, but somehow we did not think of it as the beginning of the long awaited D–Day. That had already started hours ago for us. A number of us rendezvoused at General Gale's glider, No. 70, in which I had been taken up two days before. There was no awkwardness in that last three quarters of an hour. The general had just returned from a last visit to his men before they left their camp. He had drunk good English beer with them, and they were still cheering him as they came onto the airfield.

We told funny stories and laughed a lot. The general looked a more massive figure than ever, and with reason, as the innumerable pockets of his special kit were now stuffed with maps and scores of other things he would need when he landed in France. Over everything, he had a light coloured mackintosh, but he was still wearing his grey jodhpurs.

'What about your Mae West, Sir?' one of his officers asked.

'Oh, I can put that on later if it's necessary,' he protested.

'Might be a bit tricky then, Sir,' the officer persisted.

The general turned to me and said good-humouredly: 'I'm supposed to be commanding this damned division, yet look how these fellows bully me. All right, I'll put it on if you like.'

About six people endeavoured to help him into it, and one of them said: 'the tapes should go up as high under your arms as possible, Sir.'

He burbled with laughter again. 'I know what you're up to. If we fall in the water you want my head to go under and my bottom to be left sticking up in the air.' Then, a moment later, he slapped his broad chest and exclaimed: 'Good God, look at me! I must look like Henry the Eighth!'

The comparison was not without point and a moment earlier I had noticed that chalked on the side of the glider was the name of another English king – Richard the First. That meant, I knew simply that Richard Gale was to be the first British general to land in France for many hours, but the unintended parallel struck me most forcibly. The great crusader, Richard Coeur-de-Lion, was physically just such another big man as he who towered over our little party now, and this modern lion-hearted Richard was about to lead another great crusade.

The last scene before the general emplaned was one of those simple, kindly jests in which all British-speaking people delight. A few mornings before, Richard the Lion Hearted had exclaimed with joy on finding that there was golden syrup for breakfast. 'By Jove, I love golden syrup and I haven't seen any for years!' Upon which he proceeded to heartily tuck into it. So now, our smiling group captain, who had been his official host, formally presented him with a tin to take with him to France.

A few minutes later the group captain and I were back at the watchtower. He gave the signal and the second wave, this time 25 gliders towed by Albermales, began to move off. Macnamara's aircraft, S for Sugar, led the way with General Crawford in it, as he too was determined to learn every lesson which could be learnt from the operation and, as he had told me with a grin, see that his friend Richard really went. At the end of their towrope was glider 70 carrying the G.O.C. 6th. British Airborne Division, and his personal staff. Once again, at one-minute intervals, as regularly as the ticking of a clock and without a single hitch, the aircraft and their tows took off.

The job took 25 minutes, so having saluted the general's glider as it passed within a few feet of us, there was still plenty of time for me to drive over to the control room and, from its high balcony, see a panorama of the moonlit airfield while the last dozen gliders left it. Up there too I saw another thrilling sight, a great cluster of red and white lights all moving at exactly the same pace. It was a wing of United States aircraft carrying personnel of the American Airborne Division to the Cherbourg peninsula.

Immediately after our second wave had gone, the leading aircraft of the first wave were due to return. We could hear them coming in as we went over to the briefing room, but it takes the best part of a quarter of an hour from the landing of a plane to the crew coming in, after having parked her in her allotted place and walked across. We spent some anxious moments.

At last the first pilot and his crew came in. He seemed a little surprised and very disappointed. They had dropped their parachutists right on the spot in spite of much worse weather than the 'met' report had predicted; time 17½ minutes past midnight, for ever now the date line for opening our second front in Europe. 'But,' they said, 'it might have been just one of the practice night droppings we've carried out over England. It was quite dark, no flak, nothing to see, no excitement. In fact, it's difficult to believe that we've had anything at all to do with opening up the second front.'

This may have been nothing but a rather poor party to them, but to me it was terrific news. It meant that we had achieved an almost unbelievable triumph. Security had been so good that the Germans had known neither the time nor place of assault. We had achieved the dream of all commanders for any operation; complete tactical surprise.

As other pilots came in, this fantastically good news was confirmed. Only the later comers had seen anything. After a bit, some enemy batteries had opened up with light flak and, Air Vice Marshal 'Holly' safely returned, told us that he had seen the synchronised attack by heavy bombers on the German battery – a last attempt to put it out by pin-point bombing. All who had seen the terrific explosions by the light of which the fort had been lit up agreed that, even if it was not totally destroyed, very few of its German garrison of 180 could still be alive and in any state to lay a gun.

Then, to discount this good news, the first bad break occurred. A little group of black-faced paratroopers came in. On being questioned it transpired that the first of their team to jump was the brigade major. He had stuck in the hatch; they could not push him out or pull him back. The pilot had taken the aircraft out to sea and ran it up and down the coast for half an hour but his comrades could not get the major either in or out, and when he lost consciousness, they felt that the only thing to do was to return to England. After they landed, they got him free, and although badly shaken, he was uninjured, but his mishap had prevented any of the rest leaving the aircraft. The pilot pleaded desperately to be allowed to make the second trip, but the group captain would not let him. There was too much going on.

But worse was to come. A pale-faced youngster entered the room and came up to the group captain. 'I'm sorry, Sir, I don't know what to say, but my string broke. We lost the glider about three miles from the French coast.'
Surplice laid his hand on the boy's shoulder. 'I'm sure it wasn't your fault. Tell me what happened.'

'Well, Sir, the 'met' report was wrong. Our orders were to drop the gliders off at 1600. There was cloud down to 800 and no moon coming through. It was black as pitch. I went down as low as I dared, to try to get clear, but in the darkness the glider must have lost our tail-light and became unmanageable. With her trailing wild, the strain snapped the tow-rope and there was nothing we could do about it.'

We reckoned that the glider might have had enough light to make the beach, or at least shallow water, but our hopes were father to our thoughts, and we knew that in any case that load of stores would not reach the leading paratroops in time to be used for their special operations.

A few minutes later a second tug pilot came in. The same sad story. In his case too he had entered low cloud several miles before he reached the coast of France, the glider had become uncontrollable and broken away. Soon after we learned that the third and fourth pilots were back, and they too had lost their gliders.

The big briefing room was now crowded with aircrews drinking tea, munching hot scones and waiting their turn to make their detailed reports to the intelligence officers. No roomful of men could have more representative of the Empire; all the dominions were well represented, there were a number of colonials and the rest spoke with accents ranging from Oxford to Glasgow, Dublin to Devon and Cardiff to Cockney London.

It was now about 2.45 am and the next two hours were grim. If all four of the first flight of gliders had gone into the drink, what chance had the general and his string of 25, and all the other flights now heading for the same area from the other stations in the group with the rest of the airborne division? Some of the young dare-devils we had had drinks with only a few hours before were now almost certainly dead and others, weighed down by their heavy equipment, swimming desperately for their lives in the cold waters of the channel. Hundreds more might be crashing and drowning as we stood there. If the general and a large part of the airborne division were lost, their vital task would remain unaccomplished and the left flank of the British army be left open to attack. There were hours to go yet before the first seaborne troops were due to touch down on the beaches, and the Germans must have known for two hours now that the invasion had at last started. If the airborne operation failed, the enemy might counter-attack the open beaches in the morning and hurl our troops back into the sea, rendering the whole vast plan a complete failure. The strain of waiting to hear how the second wave had fared was appalling.

During that time only one piece of good news came to cheer us. We had been misinformed about the last tug pilot back. He too had entered cloud, but he managed to get well over the coast before his towrope snapped.

At last, about 4.30, we heard the drone of aircraft. The tugs of the second wave were returning. At a quarter to five, the first aircrew came in. The cloud had lifted, they had cast off their glider dead on the mark.

Crew after crew appeared with the same glad tidings. When Macnamara and General Crawford came in we rushed towards them. They were smiling, laughing. They had put General Gale down at half past two exactly in the place he had planned to land. Of the second wave, not a single glider was lost.

Douglas Warth, an official war reporter, had gone over with the first wave of paratroopers and was thus the first reporter to witness the opening of the second front. He had a jeep waiting, and now that he knew the general had got in, offered us a lift back to London.

We were standing beside the telephone at the time and I heard the chief intelligence officer receive a message from the control room: 'All aircraft safely landed and no wounded.'

A moment later I was saying goodbye to Group Captain Surplice, and having thanked him for his kindness to me, I added: 'I would like to congratulate you, Sir, on the wonderful show you've put up and on all your aircraft having arrived back safely.'

'What?' he exclaimed, his face lighting up. 'Are they all back? How splendid.'

'Yes,' I assured him. 'All back and without a single casualty.'

By seven o'clock I was in London. Hurrying to the cabinet war room, I got the broader picture. Of the 286 aircraft despatched on this mission, only eight had failed to return, and the glider losses were far less than had been anticipated. A few hours later, I learned that General Gale had landed without accident and, achieving complete surprise, had secured the two bridges which were his principal objectives.

That night, I heard the King make the marvellous broadcast which I knew that he had prepared personally with much care and fine understanding of his people.

D–Day was over. In champagne we drank a health to George the VI and Richard 'The First' and, last but not least, to the Royal Air Force which had saved his kingdom for the one and carried the other as the first general in the great crusade which is to bring light back to Europe.

Dennis Wheatley

Annexe D

SOME SUGGESTIONS REGARDING PROPAGANDA

BY DENNIS WHEATLEY

Some of the principles enunciated in the following pages are now so generally accepted as to be virtually clichés; others may appear so wild that they may be considered more suited to a thriller novel than for practical application; but it is hoped that some of them, at all events, may prove developments of lines already laid down or may provide the germ of new schemes which, after further consideration, might be adapted to practical ends.

It is, I think, accepted that propaganda falls under four general heads.

THE HOME FRONT. To stiffen the resistance of the nation.

THE ENEMY. To weaken his resistance.

THE DOMINIONS AND COLONIES. To ensure their unity and maximum effort.

NEUTRAL COUNTRIES. To sway their opinion in our favour.

THE HOME FRONT

This is both the easiest to influence and also the most important. In this era, when every man, woman and child must be to some extent involved in a war, the morale of the civilian population will probably prove the decisive factor and be even more important than relatively superior armaments and forces at the outbreak of hostilities.

The first objective should be the destruction of political groups and organisations that might embarrass the government in power.

This can probably be best achieved by dealing separately with the rank and file and the leaders.

a. The leaders of such groups must obviously be men of some ability and therefore valuable to the nation if they can be persuaded to co-operate with the government. Each such leader should be sent for; the necessity of a united front put clearly before him and an offer made to employ him in national work of importance. Should he refuse to undertake the work offered, that fact should be published in the national press and it would inevitably discredit him with a considerable portion of his following. If he accepts the employment offered, he will be (a) under the eye of the authorities and (b) kept too busy to do much harm elsewhere. Such leaders of political factions would naturally only be placed in positions where trustworthy men could report upon their work. If it was found that they had experienced genuine change of heart and were indeed doing their utmost for the nation, well and good. If they abused their position, evidence of their activities would be collected, after which they would be publicly tried and imprisoned.

b. Having dealt with the leaders in this manner, a nation-wide appeal should be issued, directed at the rank and file. It should be pointed out to them that whatever their political opinions may be, they have only been enabled to give public expression to those opinions because this is a democratic country. The government does not ask that they should give up these opinions because it may be that the bulk of the nation will agree with them at some future time and thus, in due course, their leaders may be the government of the country. But what the government does ask is that they should support it fully and loyally throughout the war so that after the war they may still be free to give vent to their views and not be suppressed and terrorised, as is the fate of all minorities in the totalitarian states of the enemies.

THE FIGHTING FORCES

It is very essential that the fighting forces should realise to the fullest extent what they are fighting for. This would, of course, be made manifest in the general press; but the personal touch is important. It might be a good thing to publish a small leaflet setting forth as simply as possible the essential event which had led up to the country being plunged into war. This should be followed by a very carefully worded dissertation upon freedom – what it really means and how the man in the street of a democratic country and his wife and his family are protected by our laws against the ever-present threat which hangs over his opposite number in a totalitarian state, of conscription for either military service or forced labour, interference with his business or trade, restriction upon his marriage to a woman not of his own nationality and many other abuses. It could end, perhaps, with some extracts from some world-famous speeches such as that of Lincoln before Gettysburg. One of these leaflets should be passed to each member of the fighting forces and they might possibly be circulated among the civilian population with good results as well.

BROADCASTING

Broadcasting will obviously play a large part in propaganda but it is probable that there will great interference and jamming owing to the action of enemy states. In the totalitarian countries, I believe that only specially privileged persons are allowed to have high power sets capable of receiving from distant nations and the bulk of the populace is furnished with small sets which are run off hand batteries.

Small hand battery sets have almost disappeared from this country, but they should be re-introduced and, if necessary manufactured by the government in large quantities so that in the event of electric power being sabotaged or destroyed by bombing raids, the people can still listen in to our broadcasts for emergency instructions and propaganda matter, whereas they would not be able to contact the propaganda of the enemy.

CONFIDENCE IN LEADERS

It is very essential that the nation should have confidence in the leaders of the fighting services. Undoubtedly, publishers would bring out books about them as soon as they possibly could, since these would find a ready sale; but such books should be vetted by a competent authority first, and every possible facility given for the authors to present such leaders in a light that will ensure public confidence in them.

BILLETING

It is to be feared that considerable friction may arise between the householders in the counties and the populations of the slums that will be evacuated and billeted on them. Even in the last crisis a regrettable lack of cooperation was observable in the peoples who were informed that they would have children billeted upon them, and this, even before the children arrived.

Some effort should be made to counteract this and a leaflet should be circulated to all householders appealing to their goodwill and co-operation. In such a leaflet, it might be a good thing to reproduce a photograph of a bomb-shattered room with a dead man, woman and baby in it and a child of about four left unharmed and all alone, with the legend underneath: 'This is war. We are at war, but for the grace of God this photograph might show you and your family. It is asking little, therefore, that you should put up with a little inconvenience and do your best to make a happy temporary home for the strangers who are coming to live with you.'

On the other hand, there is the question of the people who are being evacuated. Unless they are rapidly employed in some form of war work they will become discontented and troublesome; therefore local committees in which should be included elected representatives of the people should immediately institute games, concerts and useful occupations until work of national importance can be found for the newcomers.

For the evacuated people, there should also be a pamphlet issued showing the same photograph with the same legend under and the appeal: 'By evacuating you to the country we have greatly lessened your risk of such a fate overcoming you. It is, therefore, very little to ask that you should do everything in your power to make yourselves agreeable to your hosts, regard their home and everything in it as thought it were your own which you would not wish to soil or damage.'

UNITED FRONT

A useful pamphlet might be issued containing the photographs of a couple of dozen famous people such as Sir Malcolm Campbell, Patrick Hastings, Len Harvey, John Gielgud, Lord Nuffield, C.B. Cochran, Robert Donat, G.B. Shaw, Mr. Ogilvie of the B.B.C., Dr. Cronin, A.P. Herbert, Lord Horder etc., with the legend: 'These men differ most widely in their political opinions. Half of them at least could not have risen to their present eminence in any totalitarian state, whether Communist or Fascist. It is to preserve for you the same chance of rising to fame and fortune whatever your political convictions may be, that the democratic countries are fighting.'

COMMERCIAL ADVERTISING

Here is an enormous field for propaganda. A conference of the biggest advertising agents should be called as soon as possible after the outbreak of hostilities and it should be impressed upon them that they can help their country enormously by getting their big clients to draft all future advertisements with an eye to national solidarity. This can be done without any loss of advertising value to the firms concerned. 'Gordon's Gin' and 'Kestos Body Belts' will not cease to be advertised because there is a war, but the highly efficient men who draft such advertisements can help the country enormously if they are properly instructed as to what lines of thought the government wishes to bring home to the population.

NATIONAL ADVERTISING

Up to the moment national advertising such as that used for A.R.P. is far behind that of the leading commercial firms. Doubtless the trouble is that the people responsible pay too much attention to the artists they employ. Artists are rarely practical people and most of them at the present time are dominated by the post-war fashion of presenting ideas in a rather obscured clever-clever form than in straight dramatic telling pictures. They also have a great love of inventing weird, almost unreadable lettering.

Few people bother, actually, to study advertisements and the art of advertising is that it can catch the passing eye and bring the message home almost unconsciously, even to a busy person who is thinking about something else. For this, bold, clear lettering is absolutely essential. I am convinced that the rise of my own book sales is very largely due to the fact that I have insisted that in every advertisement issued by my publishers from the beginning, the name 'Wheatley' should dominate the whole of the advertisement in bold and clear black type. Government employed artists, therefore, must be forced to return to clarity and directness.

MUSIC

Music has an immense influence upon the masses, more so than ever today in view of broadcasting. Patriotic songs are certain to appear soon after hostilities open but if possible these should be directed into certain channels. It may be recalled that an American millionaire purchased the Island of Avalon off the Californian coast in the nineteen twenties. He built a great hotel and did everything in his power to convert the island into a luxury pleasure resort, but no one would go there. In consequence, he hit upon the idea of offering $250,000 for the person who would produce the best song about this island. The winner was a classic which is still played today, 'I met my love in Avalon'. That song went round the world and since that time there is hardly a rich person in the United States who has not visited this now famous pleasure resort.

A similar line should be taken and approved songs should be rapidly popularised by frequent transmission from the B.B.C.

HUMOUR

Humour is another angle and a book should be rapidly published in which stories are collected ridiculing the enemy. Mr. Cecil Hunt, late fiction editor of The Daily Mail, and the author of 'Schoolboy Howlers', would probably be an excellent man to undertake the editing of such a book. It should, of course, be illustrated by numerous well-known artists.

Another book incorporating the Cockney witticisms of the troops would also have a good effect in cheering the population. Such books would probably appear in due course in any case, but the point is that one should avoid the delays incident to individual effort and co-ordinate the work to ensure its rapid production. Possibly, also, financing the publishers if necessary in order to ensure large printings and wide distribution.

ATROCITY BOOKS

These also would assist in developing the horrible but necessary war spirit. The old stories will naturally soon be going the rounds again and we already have ample material in the putsches by which the dictators have eliminated their political opponents and the fate of large numbers of people in concentration-camps. Certain books have been written by survivors already. These should be reprinted in cheap editions in large quantities and, if necessary, the government should finance the publisher to re-advertise them to ensure a wide sale

PUBLIC TRIALS

Few events grip the mind of the public so much as a spectacular trial. In the Great War, numerous German spies were immediately arrested but the public heard nothing about them until years afterwards. This time, the most colourful individuals among enemy spies arrested in this country should be brought to trial publicly, as much capital could be made out of this if properly handled.

It is almost inevitable that in any future war there will be a certain amount of sabotage by fanatics. These should also be brought to public trial. Further, it is certain that profiteers will endeavour to ship goods to the enemy via neutral countries, and here again, if any trickery to evade government restrictions is discovered, such people should be prosecuted with the utmost rigour, both as an example to others and to show that the government is active.

STAKHANOVISM

Co-operation with trade union leaders and observation of trade union ordinances is obviously essential, but even so, by propaganda much can be done to increase the efforts of the workers in the production of war material. Records should be established for a day's or a week's output wherever possible and the photographs of such record-breakers published in the national press with laudable comments upon their patriotic endeavours. This will tend to break down the trade union resistance to low [sic] working hours and thus enable us to increase output.

In the same way, everything should be done to make heroes of the members of the fighting and essential services. In the last war, men on leave were restricted almost as though they were criminals instead of being given every possible facility to enjoy their short respite from the horrors of war. It is a small thing, but I can recall myself that on one occasion I came up against an order by which I found that because I was in uniform I was not allowed to spend more than 4/6, including drinks, on my lunch in the Carlton Grill, whereas I could have spent what I liked had I been in civilian clothes. While I agree that it is necessary to have some regard for the morality of the metropolis, this policy of penalising the fighting man should unquestionably be reversed.

LIAISON BETWEEN THE REGULARS AND VOLUNTEERS (OR CONSCRIPTS)

In the last war there was a most lamentable lack of good feeling shown to the volunteers who joined up and the Territorials suffered particularly in this respect. The majority of the regular officers of higher rank with whom I came into contact behaved with civility and showed a reasonable understanding that civilians could not be expected to be acquainted with all the traditional practices of the army; but the majority of junior officers, and particularly first line Territorials, arrogated to themselves intolerable airs of superiority. In some cases they would not even have the newly joined officers in their messes and treated them rather as if they were scheming interlopers rather than men, many of whom had sacrificed their businesses or professional careers to join up. That such was the case, I am confident, will be borne out by a majority in any group of civilian officers who volunteered in the last war.

Such a situation is obviously detrimental to the service as a whole and a pamphlet should be issued to every serving officer in the regular forces impressing on him the necessity of setting aside class distinctions and treating newcomers purely on their merits as people who are eager to learn and not necessarily fools because it happens that they have had no previous experience in one of the services.

It might also be helpful if a pamphlet was issued to each of the volunteer officers on joining, giving him information regarding the customs of the service, how essential it is to preserve the dignity of his rank and other information which would prevent him from making unfortunate social gaffes.

SAMURAI

It is, unfortunately, a fact that not only are the infantry looked down on by the other arms, but owing to their wholesale slaughter in the last war through misuse against impregnable positions, it will be found most difficult to recruit the ordinary line regiments should the voluntary system continue. It is already noticeable that volunteers show much greater interest in mechanised units, the artillery and other forms of specialisation. Yet infantry remains an essential and, in fact, decisive factor in land warfare, so something must be done to rectify this situation in case it is considered necessary to send an expeditionary force overseas. Propaganda can probably be of considerable use in this through building up the infantry soldier and glorifying him on the lines of the Japanese Samurai, as the man who does the actual fighting and is therefore the bravest of us all.

War office co-operation would be essential here and one way in which they might lift the status of their infantry is by creating a special rank called 'Bayonet Fighter' which would be opened to all non-commissioned ranks after passing certain tests.

The test need not be purely confined to feats of endurance tested by forced marches, actual prowess with bayonet fighting etc., but to be made of much more practical value by combining with these certain efficiency tests in elementary engineering with particular reference to trench construction, as defence is as important as attack. A pass in First Aid might also be required. My point is that besides the rank and a handsome arm badge for it and a small additional pay on receiving the rank which would make it the object of endeavour of the bulk of the troops, and left the status of the infantryman generally in the public estimation, it would have the effect of creating within each infantry unit a body of men on the lines of the old pioneers of the pre-war German army. One out of these, I think, was specially trained as a pioneer and it was largely owing to this that the German trenches were so infinitely superior to our own and they were better able to accommodate their troops than ourselves throughout the whole of the war.

MARAINES

Another manner in which their status could be made more attractive would be some official adaptation of the unofficial custom which arose very large in France during the war, of soldiers having godmothers.

There will inevitably be many women who are unsuited to any but the lightest form of war work but who would be willing enough to godmother fighting troops if they were enabled to contact them easily. A bureau might be opened where such women could register and have lonely soldiers allotted to their care. This would result in the exchange of letters, a more even distribution of comforts sent to the front and companionship for the men when they came on leave.

It may be objected that this would be countenancing immorality as this would be certain to follow to some extent, but I do not think that such an objection could hold water on closer scrutiny; as if men are left to their own devices when on leave, there is no less likelihood of their being immoral, should they wish to be so, and there is much more likelihood of their falling into bad hands. If every infantryman could be provided with a godmother on these lines, it would certainly be an additional inducement for them to join foot-slogging regiments and at the same time lift their status in the eyes of the public by having this privilege which would not be available to other units.

A.R.P. FACTORY DEFENCE

It is, I gather, settled that essential factories are to be provided with anti-aircraft guns which will be manned by the employees in the event of a raid. Those workers who devote their time to passing a gunnery course for this purpose, should obviously also be rewarded by some special recognition. One gathers that they will not be in uniform, but they might be given 'an old school tie' (scarves available with the same colours) as a distinction that, although unfitted for overseas service owing to age or other causes, they are participating to the best of the ability in the country's defence.

FILMS

Films will naturally play a large part in propaganda and a special bureau should be set up to collaborate with the chief executives of the big film producers to this end.

In addition to documentary and news films, fiction should not be neglected or full-length films which could be made to serve a similar purpose. Here are three suggestions of the type of film I mean:

a. Might be somewhat on the lines of 'An Englishman's Home' brought up to date, but in it the principal male character would be a communist and a pacifist. We see his reactions in his home and in the factory to Imperialism and the National Government. When the war breaks out, although he is quite fit, he deliberately shirks his duty and swings the lead with the medical board to evade conscription. His girl is indignant and throws him up, but he persists in the error of his ways. There is then an air-raid in which he is caught and in which he endeavours to rescue his girl but finds her seriously wounded. As a result, he goes off to join up. This, admittedly, is pure slop in such bald phrases, but the multitude loves slop, if the characters are naturally developed and the story well written up so that it can be got over.

b. A good comic film could be made called: 'Grin and Bear it', in which we see a rather simple-minded, clumsy fellow join up and the awful time that he is given by his sergeant major. But he rescues his sergeant major under fire when they go into action, and is duly decorated; demonstrating that it is not only clever people who can win distinction, and that a slow-witted, clumsy fellow does not necessarily lack courage. In this film, the training of troops in camp could be demonstrated, stressing the lighter side, the jolly ragging that young soldiers get up to, the attraction of communal life with men of one's own age, the sing-songs etc., into which one could probably introduce some excellent numbers.

c. A very excellent film could be based on the life of the late Field Marshal Lord Robertson, showing that even in these days, every private had a marshal's baton in his knapsack. I know little of the details of the earlier life of Lord Robertson, but it is quite obvious that there must have been many episodes in such a career which would make excellent film material.

****

Operations and Deceptions

Operations

Sea-Lion: German plan for projected invasion of England, 1940

Ironclad: capture of Madagascar, 1942

Bolero: dispatch of US forces to Britain, 1942

Husky: Allied invasion of Sicily, 1943

Roundup: plan for Allied invasion of Europe, 1943 (superceded by Overlord)

Overlord: Allied invasion of France, 1943

Torch: Allied invasion of North Africa, 1943

Neptune: Normandy landings. Part of Overlord, 1944

Point-Blank: Intensive bombing of German cities, 1944

Anvil (later Dragoon): Allied invasion of South of France, 1944

Deception Plans

Hardboiled: notional invasion of southern Norway, 1942

Passover (later Steppingstone and Overthrow): part of the cover plan for Torch – notional invasion of Pas de Calais, 1943

Solo One: part of the cover plan for Torch – notional invasion of Norway, 1943

Mincemeat: part of the cover plan for Husky 'The Man Who Never Was', 1943

Bodyguard (formerly Jael): overall cover plan for Overload

Fortitude: part of Bodyguard – notional invasion of Pas de Calais, 1944

Foynes: part of Bodyguard – notional transfer of Eighth Army to England

Graffham: part of Bodyguard – notional invasion of Norway, 1944

Dennis Wheatley: Full UK Bibliography

What follows is the most complete bibliography of Dennis Wheatley's UK publications ever published in book form. It does not include his war papers (which are detailed within the text of *Churchill's Storyteller*), or selected articles appertaining to his research into the occult (those can be found detailed at the back of my essay *Dennis Wheatley and the Occult*). However, all other UK publications of note are detailed, clearly showing the depth, diversity and importance of Dennis Wheatley's work outside the War Cabinet.

First Edition Fiction
The Forbidden Territory (Hutchinson, 1933)
Such Power is Dangerous (Hutchinson, 1933)
Black August (Hutchinson, 1934)
The Fabulous Valley (Hutchinson, 1934)
The Devil Rides Out (Hutchinson, 1934)
The Eunuch of Stamboul (Hutchinson, 1935)
They Found Atlantis (Hutchinson, 1936)
Contraband (Hutchinson, 1936)
The Secret War (Hutchinson, 1937)
Uncharted Seas (Hutchinson, 1938)
The Golden Spaniard (Hutchinson, 1938)
The Quest of Julian Day (Hutchinson, 1939)
Sixty Days to Live (Hutchinson, 1939)
The Scarlet Imposter (Hutchinson, 1940)
Three Inquisitive People (Hutchinson, 1940)
Faked Passport (Hutchinson, 1940)
The Black Baroness (Hutchinson, 1940)
Strange Conflict (Hutchinson, 1941)
The Sword of Fate (Hutchinson, 1941)
'V' for Vengeance (Hutchinson, 1942)
The Man Who Missed the War (Hutchinson, 1945)
Codeword – Golden Fleece (Hutchinson, 1946)

Come into my Parlour (Hutchinson, 1946)
The Launching of Roger Brook (Hutchinson, 1947)
The Haunting of Toby Jugg (Hutchinson, 1948)
The Shadow of Tyburn Tree (Hutchinson, 1948)
Faked Passport (Hutchinson, 1949)
The Rising Storm (Hutchinson, 1949)
The Second Seal (Hutchinson, 1950)
The Man Who Killed the King (Hutchinson, 1951)
Star of Ill-Omen (Hutchinson, 1952)
To the Devil – A Daughter (Hutchinson, 1953)
Curtain of Fear (Hutchinson, 1953)
The Island Where Time Stands Still (Hutchinson, 1954)
The Dark Secret of Josephine (Hutchinson, 1955)
The Ka of Gifford Hillary (Hutchinson, 1956)
The Prisoner in the Mask (Hutchinson, 1957)
Traitor's Gate (Hutchinson, 1958)
The Rape of Venice (Hutchinson, 1959)
The Satanist (Hutchinson, 1960)
Vendetta in Spain (Hutchinson, 1961)
Mayhem in Greece (Hutchinson, 1962)
The Sultan's Daughter (Hutchinson, 1963)
The Bill for the Use of a Body (Hutchinson, 1964)
They Used Dark Forces (Hutchinson, 1964)
Dangerous Inheritance (Hutchinson, 1965)
The Wanton Princess (Hutchinson, 1966)
Unholy Crusade (Hutchinson, 1967)
The White Witch of the South Seas (Hutchinson, 1968)
Evil in a Mask (Hutchinson, 1969)
Gateway to Hell (Hutchinson, 1970)
The Ravishing of Lady Mary Ware (Hutchinson, 1971)
The Strange Story of Linda Lee (Hutchinson, 1972)
The Irish Witch (Hutchinson, 1973)
Desperate Measures (Hutchinson, 1974)

Short Story Anthologies
Mediterranean Nights (Hutchinson, 1942)
   Revised paperback (Arrow, 1963)
Gunmen, Gallants and Ghosts (Hutchinson, 1943)
   Revised paperback (Arrow, 1963)

Historical Non-Fiction
Old Rowley. A Private Life of Charles II (Hutchinson 1933)
Red Eagle. A Story of the Russian Revolution (Hutchinson, 1937)
A Private Life of Charles II (Hutchinson, 1938)

Reference

The Devil and All His Works (Hutchinson, 1971)

Crime Dossiers with J G Links

Murder Off Miami (1936)

Who Killed Robert Prentice (1937)

The Malinsay Massacre (1938)

Herewith the Clues (1939)

Autobiographical

Total War (Hutchinson, 1941)

Stranger Than Fiction (Hutchinson, 1959)

Saturday With Bricks and Other Days Under Shell Fire (Hutchinson, 1961)

The Time Has Come ... The Young Man Said 1897–1914 (Hutchinson, 1977)

The Time Has Come ... Officer and Temporary Gentleman 1914–1919 (Hutchinson, 1978)

The Time Has Come ... Drink and Ink 1919–1977 (Hutchinson, 1979)

The Time Has Come: The Memoirs of Dennis Wheatley (includes the three-vol. The Time Has Come... autobiography detailed above) (Arrow paperback, 1981)

The Deception Planners: My Secret War (Hutchinson, 1980)

Wine Publications

Historic Brandies (Wheatley, 1925)

Old Masters: catalogue of Old Brandies etc ((Wheatley & Son, 1930)

At the Sign of the Flagon of Gold (Wheatley & Son, 1930)

Note: the above wine publications are of historical value today in the wine trade, let alone being the earliest Wheatley collectables in print.

Private Printings for Bi-Centenary of Justerini & Brooks, Wine & Spirit Merchants

The Seven Ages of Justerini's (Riddle Books, 1949)

1749–1965 The Eight Ages of Justerini's (Dolphin Publishing, 1965)

Other Private Printings

Of Vice and Virtue (1950) (commissioned by the Foreign Office in foreign langauges only)

Box Sets

Christmas Gift Box (Hutchinson, 1935) (includes *The Forbidden Territory, Such Power is Dangerous, The Fabulous Valley, Black August*)

Note: some copies of this box set had signed labels under the lid depicting a young Wheatley, other more collectable copies Wheatley gave as personal presents to friends and relations. Copies with interesting dedications and dated 'xmas 1935(36?) are amongst Wheatley's most sought after collectables on today's antique book market.

Second Christmas Gift Box (Hutchinson 1937) (includes *The Devil Rides Out, The Eunuch of Stamboul, Contraband, They Found Atlantis*)

Lymington Edition Box Set (Hutchinson, 1961) (*The Forbidden Territory, The Scarlet Imposter, The Launching of Roger Brook, The Haunting of Toby Jugg, They Found Atlantis, The Eunuch of Stamboul*).

Anthologies

Those Modern Musketeers (Hutchinson, 1939) (*Three Inquisitive People, The Forbidden Territory, The Devil Rides Out, The Golden Spaniard*)

Note: a special note is needed for the above mentioned anthology, because although a re-issue of three of Wheatley's early titles, copies of this book are extremely scarce. Nice clean copies are highly desirable today.

Those Modern Musketeers (Hutchinson, 1954) (*Three Inquisitive People, The Forbidden Territory, The Golden Spaniard*)

The Early Adventures of Roger Brook (Hutchinson, 1951) (*The Launching of Roger Brook, The Shadow of Tyburn Tree*)

Worlds Far From Here (Hutchinson, 1952) (*They Found Atlantis, Uncharted Seas, The Man Who Missed the War*)

The Secret Missions of Gregory Sallust (Hutchinson, 1955) (*The Scarlet, Faked Passport, The Black Baroness*)

The Black Magic Omnibus (Hutchinson, 1956) (*The Devil Rides Out, Strange Conflict, To the Devil – A Daughter*)

Roger Brook in the French Revolution (Hutchinson, 1957) (*The Rising Storm, The Man Who Killed the King*)

Death in the Sunshine (Hutchinson, 1958) (*The Fabulous Valley, The Secret War, The Eunuch of Stamboul*)

Plot and Counterplot (Hutchinson, 1959) (*Black August, Contraband, The Island Where Time Stands Still*)

Into the Unknown (Hutchinson, 1960) (*Sixty Days to Live, Star of Ill-Omen, Curtain of Fear*)

Dennis Wheatley (Heinemann / Octopus, 1977) (*The Devil Rides Out, The Haunting of Toby Jugg, Gateway to Hell, To the Devil – A Daughter*)

Lymington Edition

Shortly after the Second World War, the Wheatley's moved to Lymington. At the turn of the 1960s, Hutchinson decided to publish a uniform collector's edition of Wheatleys work entitled the Lymington Edition. Although re-issues of Wheatley's work in contemporary dustwrappers, a complete set of this edition is quite scarce nowadays and, therefore, command respectable prices on the collector's market.

Lymington Ed No. 1 The Forbidden Territory (Hutchinson, 1961)

Lymington Ed No. 2 The Scarlet Imposter (Hutchinson, 1961)

Lymington Ed No. 3 The Launching of Roger Brook (Hutchinson, 1961)

Lymington Ed No. 4 The Haunting of Toby Jugg (Hutchinson, 1961)

Lymington Ed No. 5 They Found Atlantis (Hutchinson, 1961)

Lymington Ed No. 6 The Eunuch of Stamboul (Hutchinson, 1961)

Lymington Ed No. 7 The Fabulous Valley (Hutchinson, 1963)

Lymington Ed No. 8 Faked Passport (Hutchinson, 1963)

Lymington Ed No. 9 Three Inquisitive People (Hutchinson, 1963)

Lymington Ed No. 10 The Ka of Gifford Hillary (Hutchinson, 1962)

Lymington Ed No. 11 The Shadow of Tyburn Tree (Hutchinson, 1963)

Lymington Ed No. 12 Contraband (Hutchinson, 1964)

Lymington Ed No. 13 The Island Where Time Stands Still (Hutchinson, 1963)

Lymington Ed No. 14 The Secret War (Hutchinson, 1963)

Lymington Ed No. 15 Such Power is Dangerous (Hutchinson, 1965)

Lymington Ed No. 16 The Rising Storm (Hutchinson, 1964)

Lymington Ed No. 17 The Second Seal (Hutchinson, 1964)

Lymington Ed No. 18 Black August (Hutchinson, 1966)

Lymington Ed No. 19 Uncharted Seas (Hutchinson, 1964)

Lymington Ed No. 20 The Quest of Julian Day (Hutchinson, 1967)

Lymington Ed No. 21 The Devil Rides Out (Hutchinson, 1963)

Lymington Ed No. 22 Star of Ill-Omen (Hutchinson, 1963)

Lymington Ed No. 23 The Man Who Killed the King (Hutchinson, 1962)

Lymington Ed No. 24 Strange Conflict (Hutchinson, 1966)

Lymington Ed No. 25 The Golden Spaniard (Hutchinson, 1967)

Lymington Ed No. 26 The Black Baroness (Hutchinson, 1966)

Lymington Ed No. 27 Mediterranean Nights (revised) (Hutchinson, 1965)

Lymington Ed No. 28 The Man Who Missed the War (Hutchinson, 1964)

Lymington Ed No. 29 To The Devil – A Daughter (Hutchinson, 1966)

Lymington Ed No. 30 The Dark Secret of Josephine (Hutchinson, 1962)

Lymington Ed No. 31 'V' For Vengeance (Hutchinson, 1966)

Lymington Ed No. 32 Sixty Days To Live (Hutchinson, 1966)

Lymington Ed No. 33 The Sword of Fate (Hutchinson, 1966)

Lymington Ed No. 34 Come into My Parlour (Hutchinson, 1967)

Lymington Ed No. 35 The Rape of Venice (Hutchinson, 1963)

Lymington Ed No. 36 The Prisoner in the Mask (Hutchinson, 1963)

Lymington Ed No. 37 Codeword – Golden Fleece (Hutchinson, 1962)

Lymington Ed No. 38 Curtain of Fear (Hutchinson, 1967)

Lymington Ed No. 39 The Satanist (Hutchinson, 1964)

Lymington Ed No. 40 Vendetta in Spain (Hutchinson, 1964)

Lymington Ed No. 41 Traitor's Gate (Hutchinson, 1966)

Lymington Ed No. 42 Gunmen, Gallants and Ghosts (revised) (Hutchinson, 1965)

Lymington Ed No. 43 Mayhem in Greece (Hutchinson, 1966)

Lymington Ed No. 44 Bill For the Use of a Body (Hutchinson, 1966)

Lymington Ed No. 45 The Sultan's Daughter (Hutchinson, 1968)

Lymington Ed No. 46 They Used Dark Forces (Hutchinson, 1967)

Lymington Ed No. 47 The Wanton Princess (Hutchinson, 1970)

Lymington Ed No. 48 Dangerous Inheritance (Hutchinson, 1970)

Lymington Ed No. 49 Unholy Crusade (Hutchinson, 1971)

Lymington Ed No. 50 Red Eagle. A Story of the Russian Revolution (Hutchinson, 1967)

Lymington Ed No. 51 "Old Rowley". A Private Life of Charles II (Illustrated by Frank C. Papé)
    (Hutchinson, 1967)

Lymington Ed No. 52 Gateway to Hell (Hutchinson, 1971)

Lymington Ed No. 53 The White Witch of the South Seas (Hutchinson, 1971)

Lymington Ed No. 54 Evil in a Mask (Hutchinson, 1971)

Lymington Ed No. 55 The Ravishing of Lady Mary Ware (Hutchinson, 1975)

'Heron' Edition

Between 1972 and 1977 a mock red leatherette edition of selected works of Dennis Wheatley was published (some illustrated by noted artists such as Ian Miller, with approximately half a dozen illustrations). With gold leaf and ribbon the complete collection has proved to be a much desired and relatively easy-to-find acquisition on the collector's market. However, some of the gold leaf titles on the spine do tend to chip or darken with age, and only pristine copies are deemed most collectable.

The Forbidden Territory (1972)

The Scarlet Imposter (1972)

The Launching of Roger Brook (1972)

They Found Atlantis (1972)

The Eunuch of Stamboul (1972)

Faked Passport (1972)

The Ka of Gifford Hillary (1972)

The Shadow of Tyburn Tree (1972)

The Rising Storm (1972)

Uncharted Seas (1972)

The Quest of Julian Day (1972)

The Devil Rides Out (1972)

To The Devil – A Daughter (1972)

The Satanist (1972)

The Man Who Killed the King (1972)

The Black Baroness (1972)

Strange Conflict (1972)

'V' For Vengeance (1972)

The Prisoner in the Mask (1972)

The Haunting of Toby Jugg (1973)

The Golden Spaniard (1973)

Mediterranean Nights (1973)

The Fabulous Valley (1973)

Three Inquisitive People (1973)

The Dark Secret of Josephine (1973)

The Sword of Fate (1973)

Come into My Parlour (1973)

They Used Dark Forces (1973)

Unholy Crusade (Hutchinson, 1973)

Traitor's Gate (1973)

Mayhem in Greece (1973)

The Second Seal (1973)

Black August (1974)

Bill for the Use of a Body (1974)

Contraband (1974)

The Island Where Time Stands Still (1974)

The Rape of Venice (1974)

Codeword – Golden Fleece (1974)

Vendetta in Spain (1974)

Curtain of Fear (1974)

The Sultan's Daughter (1974)

The Wanton Princess (1974)

Gateway to Hell (1974)

The White Witch of the South Seas (1974)

Evil in a Mask (1974)

The Ravishing of Lady Mary Ware (1974)

Dangerous Inheritance (1975)

The Irish Witch (1975)

Desperate Measures (1975)

The Secret War (1977)

Such Power is Dangerous (1977)

The Strange Story of Linda Lee (1977)

Books Edited by Dennis Wheatley

A Century of Horror Stories (Hutchinson, 1935)

A Century of Spy Stories (Hutchinson, 1938)

Dennis Wheatley's First Book of Horror Stories (Hutchinson, 1968)

(previously released as an Arrow paperback in 1964 as Shafts of Fear)

Dennis Wheatley's Second Book of Horror Stories (Hutchinson, 1968)

(previously released as an Arrow paperback in 1964 as Quiver of Horror)

Dennis Wheatley's Library of the Occult

Wheatley had an impressive book collection and indeed had many interesting titles concerning the macabre/occult; both fact and fiction. During the mid-1970s he decided to issue a set of Sphere paperbacks under the title 'Dennis Wheatley's Library of the Occult'. This would furnish his readers with as much diverse material within the horror genre as they would desire (Wheatley planned for over 400 titles to be in the original set, however ill health and his subsequent untimely death halted the series after only forty-five paperbacks). Copies of the following books are extremely scarce nowadays and a lot of money is paid for copies in fine condition on the collector's market.

Vol 1 (1974) *Dracula* by Bram Stoker

Vol 2 (1974) *The Werewolf of Paris* by Guy Endore

Vol 3 (1974) *Moonchild* by Aleister Crowley

Vol 4 (1974) *Studies in Occultism* by Helena Petrovna Blavatsky

Vol 5 (1974) *Carnacki The Ghost-Finder* by William Hope Hodgson

Vol 6 (1974) *The Sorcery Club* by Elliot O'Donnell

Vol 7 (1974) *Harry Price: The Biography of a Ghost Hunter* by Paul Tabori

Vol 8 (1974) *The Witch of Prague* by F Marion Crawford

Vol 9 (1974) *Uncanny Tales 1* selected by Dennis Wheatley

Vol 10 (1974) *The Prisoner in the Opal* by A E W Mason

Vol 11 (1974) *The Devil's Mistress* by John William Brodie-Innes

Vol 12 (1974) *You and Your Hand* by Cheiro (new edition revised by Louise Owen)

Vol 13 (1974) *Black Magic: A Tale of the Rise and Fall of the Antichrist* by Majorie Bowen

Vol 14 (1974) *Real Magic* by Philip Bonewits

Vol 15 (1974) *Faust, Parts 1 and 2* by Jonathan Wolfgang von Goethe, translated by Bayard Taylor

Vol 16 (1974) *Uncanny Tales 2* selected by Dennis Wheatley

Vol 17 (1974) *The Gap in the Curtain* by John Buchan

Vol 18 (1974) *The Interpretation of Dreams* by Zolar

Vol 19 (1974) *Voodoo* by Alfred Metraux, translated from the French by Hugo Charteris. 2nd English edition with new introduction by Sidney W Mintz

Vol 20 (1974) *The Necromancers* by Robert Hugh Benson

Vol 21 (1974) *Satanism and Witches: Essays and Stories selected by Dennis Wheatley* (includes six of Wheatley's articles on Black Magic)

Vol 22 (1974) *The Winged Pharaoh* by Joan Grant

Vol 23 (1974) *Down There* by J K Huysmans translated from the French by Keene Wallace

Vol 24 (1974) *The Monk* by Matthew Lewis

Vol 25 (1975) *Horror at Fontenay* by Alexander Dumas translated and adapted by Alan Hull Walton

Vol 26 (1975) *The Hell-Fire Club: The Story of the Amorous Knights of Wycombe* by Donald McCormick

Vol 27 (1975) *The Mighty Atom* by Marie Corelli

Vol 28 (1975) *The Affair of the Poisons* by Frances Mossiker

Vol 29 (1975) *The Witch and the Priest* by Hilda Lewis

Vol 30 (1975) *Death by Enchantment. An Examination of Ancient and Modern Witchcraft* by Julian Franklyn

Vol 31 (1975) *Fortune Telling* by Cards by Ida B Prangley

Vol 32 (1975) *Dark Ways to Death* by Peter Saxon

Vol 33 (1975) *The Ghost Pirates* by William Hope Hodgson

Vol 34 (1975) *The Phantom of the Opera* by Gaston Leroux

Vol 35 (1975) *The Greater Trumps* by Charles Williams

Vol 36 (1975) *The Return of the Magi* by Maurice Magre, translated from the French by Reginald Merton

Vol 37 (1975) *Uncanny Tales 3* selected by Dennis Wheatley

Vol 38 (1976) *The King is a Witch* by Evelyn Eaton

Vol 39 (1976) *Frankenstein* by Mary Wollstonecraft Shelley

Vol 40 (1976) *The Curse of the Wise Woman* by Baron Edward Plunkett Dunsany

Vol 41 (1976) *Brood of the Witch Queen* by Sax Rohmer

Vol 42 (1976) *Brazilian Magic: Is it the Answer?* by Pedro McGregor in association with T Stratton Smith

Vol 43 (1976) *Darker Than You Think* by Jack Williamson

Vol 44 (1976) *War in Heaven* by Charles Williams

Vol 45 (1977) *Morwyn: The Vengeance of God* by John Cowper Powys

Introductions by Dennis Wheatley

The Black Art by Rollo Ahmed (John Long, 1936)

   The Black Art by Rollo Ahmed (with revised introduction by Dennis Wheatley) (Jarrods, 1968)

You Can't Hit a Woman and other stories by Peter Cheyney (Collins, 1937)

Characters From the Face by Jacques Penry (Hutchinson, 1939)

How to Judge Character From the Face by Jacques Penry (New edition) (Hutchinson, 1952)

The Smell of Evil by Charles Birkin (Library 33, London, 1964)

The Smell of Evil by Charles Birkin (Tandem Books, 1965)

The Kiss of Death by Charles Birkin (Tandem Books, 1964)

Mostly Joy. A Bookman's Story by Thomas Joy (Michael Joseph, 1971)

Malleus Maleficarum translated from the Latin by Montague Summers (Arrow, 1971)

Witchcraft (Boxed set of three paperbacks including The Black Art and Malleus Maleficarum)

A Note on Signed Editions

A great many signed editions of Wheatley's work can be found on the collector's market today. Most of the books found are personally signed to friends and relations. Wheatley would almost always sign in blue, black or mauve fountain pen on the main title page of the book, and many collectors attempt to acquire as many signed editions as possible to complete a full set of hardback editions; not necessarily first editions.

Wheatley was also a prolific letter writer, and some signed books also have the bonus of a neatly folded letter secreted somewhere amongst the pages.

Dennis Wheatley

Born in London on 1 August 1897, Dennis Wheatley's early life was filled with drama. Expelled from Dulwich College, he was forced to join HMS *Worcester* as a naval cadet. In 1914 he left in order to gain a commission in a London Artillery Regiment. He fought at Passchendaele, Cambrai and St. Quentin. Gassed and invalided from the Army, he entered the family's wine business in Mayfair. Among his customers he numbered three kings, twenty-one princes and many of the period's great families.

He sold the business in 1932 and took up writing. He became a bestseller overnight. His first book, *The Forbidden Territory*, was reprinted seven times in seven weeks.

During the Second World War, Wheatley was a member of Winston Churchill's Joint Planning Staff of the War Cabinet, brainstorming ideas and opinions whilst constantly burning the midnight oil writing his 'war papers'.

Wheatley wrote over seventy books, was published in twenty-seven different languages, and sold an estimated 50,000,000 copies worldwide. Along with Agatha Christie, he was one of the most prolific of bestselling writers in the 20th century. Nowadays, he is best known for his occult fiction, titles such as *The Devil Rides Out, The Haunting of Toby Jugg, To the Devil - A Daughter* and *Gateway to Hell*, all are testament to his imaginative strengths. Wheatley died on 10 November 1977.

About the Author

Craig Cabell's writing career started in his early teens writing short stories for local radio. On leaving school he became a freelance reporter, working in the Arts, most notably for *The Independent* newspaper.

He joined the Ministry of Defence at the age of 18, soon working as a contracts officer during the Gulf War and becoming an active member of the Main Building Charities Committee. He eventually spent five years working for *Focus*, the House Journal of the Ministry of Defence, where he wrote news, features, book reviews and a regular wine column. He has also written freelance for *Soldier* and other government departments and magazines; most notably for the military police and Crown Prosecution Service.

His features, book reviews and interviews have appeared in other, more diverse, publications, such as *Wine Magazine, Book and Magazine Collector, Midweek* and *Shivers*.

At the age of 25 he provided editorial service and wrote a special introduction to Simon Clark's and Stephen Laws' short work *Annabelle Says* (Hodder & Stoughton/British Fantasy Society), and recently undertook similar duties for Graham Thomas' military history *Fighting Furies*, a book concerning the Korean War.

Cabell is the author of seven previous books, including the acclaimed *Operation Big Ben – the Anti-V2 Spitfire Missions 1944–45* (with Graham Thomas) and *Frederick Forsyth – A Matter of Protocol*.

Other Books by Craig Cabell

Frederick Forsythe – A Matter of Protocol

The Kray Brothers – The Image Shattered

James Herbert – Devil in the Dark

Operation Big Ben – The Anti-V2 Spitfire Missions 1944–45
(with Graham Thomas)

VE Day – A Day to Remember
(with Alan Richards)

Snipers
(With Richard Brown)

Dennis Wheatley and the Occult

Witchfinder General – The Biography of Matthew Hopkins